W9-BEK-962

Jove Titles by Judie Aitken

A LOVE BEYOND TIME
A PLACE CALLED HOME

A Place Called Home

Judie Aitken

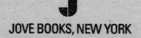

JOVE BOOKS, NEW YORK

This is a work of fiction. Names, characters, places, and incidents either are the product of the author's imagination or are used fictitiously, and any resemblance to actual persons, living or dead, business establishments, events, or locales is entirely coincidental.

A PLACE CALLED HOME

A Jove Book / published by arrangement with
the author

PRINTING HISTORY
Jove edition / November 2001

All rights reserved.
Copyright © 2001 by Judie Aitken.
Cover art by Donald Case.
This book, or parts thereof, may not be reproduced in any form
without permission.
For information address: The Berkley Publishing Group,
a division of Penguin Putnam Inc.,
375 Hudson Street, New York, New York 10014.

Visit our website at
www.penguinputnam.com

ISBN: 0-515-13180-6

A JOVE BOOK®
Jove Books are published by The Berkley Publishing Group,
a division of Penguin Putnam Inc.,
375 Hudson Street, New York, New York 10014.
JOVE and the "J" design
are trademarks belonging to Penguin Putnam Inc.

PRINTED IN THE UNITED STATES OF AMERICA

10   9   8   7   6   5   4   3   2   1

In 1994 I had, if you will pardon the pun, the very good "Fortune" to meet a wonderful lady who would help change my life. To you, Gail, many, many thanks. It is a privilege to be one of your "girls."

To my dearest friend Faith, my *Naah Me*, who has always had, and always will keep . . . the faith; who is always there when I need her, and who always keeps my feather straight.

And, to my beloved Hawk, my beautiful "beaded pony," who gave me so many years of perfect days and championship gold. Every now and then when sunset colors splash across the evening sky, I catch a glimpse of you galloping through the clouds.

Author's Note

Dear Reader:

I am so very pleased to be a part of Berkley's new line, Seduction, and to have the opportunity to tell Cody Butler's story. My heros have always been cowboys or Indians, and writing Cody's story was the best of both worlds. He is a blend of every trait that I love in a man, and I hope he rides, at a full gallop, into your heart and dreams as well.

Once deciding to set my story in the beautiful state of Wyoming, I then couldn't decide on an actual locale. In the end it was a whole lot easier to create the wonderful town of Dorland and put it right in the middle of another fictional location, Cheyenne County. Thank you, Wyoming, for the inspiration.

Many thanks to my long-time friend, Phil Dyer, DVM, Equine Practitioner, for sharing his expertise and forty pounds of text books on bovine and equine diseases. Any errors made about animal diseases and the care of the animals in the telling of this story are mine and mine alone.

Heartfelt thanks also to my mentor and dear friend, Earl C. Fenner. His knowledge and information about the American Indian is a bottomless well that he has always graciously shared with me. *Oodah.*

To a very special Texas friend who plays a "tigerish" game of golf, thank you for the "manly" feedback, Russ.

And to you, dear readers, thank you for the warm and wonderful welcome that you gave my debut book for Berkley's Time Passages line, *A Love Beyond Time*. I hope that you enjoy Cody Butler's story as much.

Happy reading,

Judie Aitken
10535 E. Washington Street, PMB 105
Indianapolis, IN 46229

http://www.judieaitken.com

Chapter One

He was dead.

Lying facedown on his bed in a tangled wad of sheets and blankets, Cody Butler had no one to blame for his condition but himself.

A moan slid from between his lips and his thumb twitched. It seemed that some part of him still worked. Maybe he hadn't died after all.

His arm slid off the mattress and the back of his hand knocked against the drained fifth of Wild Turkey. The bottle toppled, rolled, gave a hollow clank as it struck the leg of the bed, and then stilled. No. Dead only told half of Cody Butler's story. Dead drunk said it all.

The pain in his head hammered like a kick from a green-broke colt, and the colt was merciless as it kept kicking, again and again.

"Whoa." The word slid from Cody's mouth accompanied by a sour belch. But the darned colt didn't pay any attention to either, and kicked again.

Slowly lifting his hand, Cody dragged his palm over the beard stubble on his face. The resulting noise was thunderous, like twenty tons of loose gravel pouring out of a dumptruck and into his head. With another protesting moan, he inched his hand higher until his fingers raked through his hair and curved over the top of his skull. There was no doubt about it, his head could come off any minute, but maybe if he held on tight the explosion wouldn't be too loud.

Performing what felt like a near-impossible feat, he raised his left eyelid and peered out. The morning sun shone in bright shafts through the open slats of the bedroom window blinds.

"Damn," he rasped. The glare hurt his eye. Hell, it hurt his hair. He dropped his eyelid and flinched, positive he'd heard the darned thing slam shut.

Methodically breathing in and out, in and out, Cody lay still for what seemed like an hour or two. With his fingers gripping the side of the mattress to steady its rolling, he waited for the queasy lurching in his belly to go away. As the mattress slowed its pitch and sway and just as his stomach settled, a knock on the bedroom door broke his concentration and set the hell-bound colt in his head off on another kicking tangent.

"Yeah," he murmured, or at least he thought he'd said that. His fuzzy reasoning concluded he must have made some response because the door opened. Getting drunk was certainly not something he did well.

"Cody? You awake?" Maribeth hesitantly stepped into the room.

"No . . . I'm dead." He pulled the sweat-soaked bedsheet up over his head.

"Phew! No kidding," thirteen-year-old Maribeth Butler countered. "From the smell in here, you've been dead for a long time."

"Go away," Cody growled.

"Nope. You told me to wake you at seven so you'd be ready when that lawyer got here. I've already tried to roust you out four times. It's now after nine."

Cody rolled onto his back. His stomach didn't. "Get outta my way . . . quick!"

Naked, except for the loosely draped bedsheet judiciously held around his waist and the well-scuffed boot on his left foot, Cody stumbled toward the bathroom.

"Well, you're off to a great start," Maribeth declared over the sound of Cody's heaving. "If you're too sick to come downstairs, maybe you could have your meeting up here. How about doin' it dressed just like you are now, too? That oughta impress her."

"Her?" Cody felt his stomach flip again. Word around town had mentioned Hubbard had gotten himself a new big-city lawyer, but nobody had said anything about it being a *her.*

"Yup. She called about a half hour ago. She should be here in ten minutes or so."

Maribeth's chatter rattled painfully in Cody's head. He tried to focus on her words but ended up taking another dive toward the porcelain bowl.

"Cody, you never have more'n a beer or two. Why'd you have to go and get drunk last night?"

Maribeth's question was punctuated by the sound of the whiskey bottle rattling against the leg of the bed. Cody grimaced. She'd found the evidence. "Quiet. Quit your nagging," he grumbled, closing the bathroom door. It was a whole lot easier to tell Maribeth to be quiet than to answer her question. How do you tell your kid sister that like a tough piece of meat, sometimes it's best to marinate a tough problem in whiskey to soften it up a little before you try to solve it?

Cody pushed himself upright and, teetering on his right leg, began grappling with his boot. He paused. How in the hell had he managed to get his jeans and undershorts off and end up with the boot still on his foot? "Beats me," he muttered.

With a final tug that sent him stumbling against the

wall, the boot came off. It flew from his hand and the sound it made hitting the floor made him cringe. Still struggling to keep his balance, he tentatively stepped into the shower and gave the faucet a turn.

The water hit him with an icy jolt as it poured over his body, tightening his skin into a field of goose bumps and forcing a gasp from somewhere in his gut. A shiver racked him from head to toe, and for another agonizing moment or two his stomach rebelled and insisted on performing a few more somersaults. Cody pressed his forehead against the cool slick tiles beneath the showerhead, closed his eyes, and prayed that he could get through the meeting with Hubbard's lawyer without making a complete fool of himself. He'd already done that by getting drunk, but he didn't need to make his idiocy public. After a few deep breaths, the queasy feeling began to ease. Maybe he'd live after all.

With hot water added to the mix, Cody rubbed the bar of pine-scented soap over his chest. The fragrance, thankfully, seemed to sooth his condition. Working up a thick lather, he slid the soap across his stomach, over his hip, and down his left leg to the red sock that remained on his foot.

"What the . . ." With an exasperated grunt he leaned against the wall, swayed on one foot, and peeled the sock off. He wrung it out and tossed it over the top of the shower curtain. With a quick glance down his body to make sure there were no more surprises, he grabbed the bottle of shampoo and gave it a shake. There was just a squirt or two left. It would have to do. Wet, his hair reached his shoulders. It was much too long. He should have gone to the barber yesterday while he was in town. Instead, he'd dropped by Casey's Buckin' Bar and Grille.

With his fingers working the shampoo through his hair, Cody's mind wandered through the haze of his hangover. Why had he agreed to talk with Glenn Hubbard's attorney?

The topic of the meeting was no surprise and just thinking about it made him angry. Maybe it was simple curiosity. How high would Hubbard's offer go? It didn't really matter. Cody's mind was made up. He'd rather sit his bare butt down on an angry porcupine than sell any part of Medicine Creek. The ranch meant everything to him. With the exception of the Cheyenne and Shoshone Indians who had once hunted and camped through the area, no one but a Butler had ever lived on the land. From the ridge rocks on the high land to the crystal-clear streams and lush meadows, five generations of Butlers had called the place home. Every square inch was now and always had been Butler land. He was the last of the line, a proud mix of Butler and Cheyenne blood, and now it all came down to him. The weight of the responsibility, the legacy, the honor of the land, the ranch, was his alone. He'd gladly suffer the fires of Hell before he'd let it go.

Glenn Hubbard, with all his money, fancy cars, and big mansion, was a newcomer. He'd only been in the county a little more than eleven months, and the man and his land-grabbing habits stuck out like a giraffe in a herd of rabbits. The man had barely allowed the ink to dry on the purchase agreement for the Davis ranch before he'd torn the old buildings down and put up fancy new ones—a huge classy house, all glass and stone, and barns that looked just as showy. Word in town was that there were six bathrooms in the house.

"Some folks in the county'd be happy to have just one john . . . inside," Cody groused, rinsing the last of the shampoo from his hair.

Next Hubbard had bought the Webster place to the south, then he'd snapped up twelve hundred acres to the northeast from the bank's foreclosure sale of the Jessop ranch. Buildings on both properties that had stood the test of years, and the harsh Wyoming winters fell in minutes under Hubbard's bulldozers. All this for a damn ego-building private wildlife game preserve.

That leaves me and my overdue bank loan on the west. And I'll be damned if I'll go down easy. Cody gave the hot water faucet a hard twist. His head still hurt like hell, but somehow the steady drive of the near scalding water against the back of his head and neck made him feel much better.

Stepping out of the shower, he quick-dried with a thick towel, then wrapped it around his hips. Unable to put off the inevitable, he leaned over the sink and closely examined his reflection in the mirror. He winced. An ashen face with bloodshot eyes stared back at him. "If it looks dead and smells dead . . ." He shook his head, disgusted with himself.

The flavor of his toothpaste clashed unforgivingly with the sour taste in his mouth, but he plied his toothbrush until the peppermint won out. Then, after spreading a layer of shaving cream on his face, he dragged the razor through the two-day growth of beard and tried not to slit his throat. Hubbard would probably want to do that himself when his high-priced lady lawyer told him the bad news.

With only two nicks on his chin and satisfied that he hadn't cut off his right ear the one time the razor had slipped, Cody tried to tame his long hair into some semblance of neatness. He failed. Disgusted, he tossed his comb back on the sink. "Aw, hell, my hat'll cover it."

"You still here?" he asked, returning to his bedroom to find Maribeth perched on the edge of his bed. "You know, a little privacy would be nice."

"I wanted to see how many times you cut yourself shaving," she sauced back. Bouncing off the bed, Maribeth raised the blind and looked out the window. "I think that lawyer's coming up the lane now. Should I send her up?"

"Do that and I'll disown you." Cody stood behind the bathroom door and stepped into his briefs.

"Won't matter none," Maribeth rebutted. "I'm an orphan anyway." She dramatically placed the back of her hand against her forehead and sighed. "I'll wear Ping-Pong balls for eyes, get a dog and name him Sandy, and be a pathetic, homeless waif."

"My heart bleeds," Cody countered, pulling a pair of clean socks from his dresser drawer.

"So do your eyes," Maribeth shot back before turning to look out the window again. "I'd better go heat up a gallon of coffee for you, and from the hoity-toity looks of your lady lawyer, I'll make some tea, too."

"She'll have coffee or go dry," Cody growled, hauling his tight-fitting, work-faded jeans up over his hips.

Maribeth moved away from the window and faced him. "Cody?"

She had spoken in a near whisper, but he heard all the concern her voice held. "What is it, Tater Tot?"

"Have we lost?"

Looking up from where he sat pulling on his boots, he saw the tears that rimmed her eyes. His heart wrenched as a single tear spilled over and trickled down her freckled cheek. "Not yet, we haven't. Not by a long shot." The hard thud his booted feet made as they hit the floor punctuated his words. "Maybe I shouldn't have taken out the loan for the new indoor training arena when I did, but there's still enough time to pay it off. You watch, everything's gonna be okay, Tater, I promise."

He gave Maribeth a quick hug as he headed across the room to his closet for a clean shirt. "Go let the lady in." He buckled his belt, then turning, pointed an admonishing finger at Maribeth. "Be nice to her. Only one of us Butlers needs to make her day hell."

Shaye stepped out of the sleek silver sports car and took in every view the Butler ranch had to offer. The house, a large, beautifully rustic, timber-framed two-story, faced the snowcapped mountains. The broad porch spanning the perimeter would be wonderful for evening dinners or just sitting and gazing up at the Tetons. Everything about the ranch showed the hard work and pride that had gone into the place over the years. From the freshly painted sign at the turnoff from the highway declaring this to be the Medicine Creek Ranch, to the neatly kept lawns and flower beds around the house, it had the wonderful feel of a well-loved home.

What would you know about how a home should feel? She gave a resigned sigh and tucked an errant lock of hair behind her ear. *You haven't had a real home in years. Not since . . .*

Shoving the encroaching memories from her mind, Shaye straightened her gray pin-striped suit skirt with a determined tug. She was getting better at putting the past behind her. Often two or three days went by now without it elbowing its way into her thoughts. And, with each passing day, the solid wall she was building around her feelings grew higher and stronger. Emotional construction had become second nature to her. She was almost safe. Almost.

Tucking the tail of her red blouse under her belt, she took a deep breath and hefted her briefcase off the passenger's seat. Time to get to work. Whether she agreed with Glenn Hubbard's business practices or not didn't matter, she had accepted his retainer. He was her client and she was required to do his bidding. She closed the car door and moved toward the house.

Her meetings with the other ranchers had gone well; they'd all quickly agreed to sell their land to Hubbard, but from what she'd learned about Cody Butler, he wasn't going to be so easy to deal with. She was in for a rough morning.

"Hi."

Turning, Shaye found herself face to face with a pair of the bluest eyes she had ever seen. A young girl, who looked to be about twelve or thirteen, greeted her with an open, friendly smile. "Good morning, I'm Shaye Frazier. I have an appointment with Mr. Butler. Is he in?"

"Yup. He sure is. I'm his sister, Maribeth." The girl smiled and placed her hand on Shaye's arm. "Just wait here a minute, let me make sure it's okay." Turning, she called back toward the house. "Cody, did you put the boys up when you came in last night?"

Maribeth Butler had no sooner posed the question than three huge dogs bounded around the corner of the house. All three made a beeline for Shaye, each apparently determined to be the first to plant a wet lick on her face. At first glance Shaye had thought they were black bears. Completely unnerved as the massive beasts shoved and bumped against her, she clutched her briefcase against her breasts as though it would safely shield her while she timidly backed away. The three-inch heels of her shoes sunk into the ground with each backward step, causing her to teeter precariously, threatening to send her toppling backward.

"Stay."

The pony-sized dogs stopped in their tracks at the sound of the deep-voiced command. So did Shaye.

"Sit."

Immediately dropping to their haunches, each dog looked expectantly toward the house, their pink tongues lolling from their mouths, their bushy tails sweeping back and forth in the grass like wipers on a windshield. Shaye resisted the absurd notion that she should sit as well.

The screen door opened, and glancing up from watching the three beasts, Shaye found herself staring at a Madison Avenue adman's ultimate casting dream for one of those rugged cowboy commercials. Although her taste in men rarely strayed from the well-dressed corporate types, she quickly decided that tight-fitting, well-worn jeans that were faded in the most interesting places did more won-

derful things for this man than any three-piece suit could
ever hope to accomplish.

"Mr. Butler? Cody Butler?" Her voice was little more
than a whispered croak. She tried to step forward and immediately discovered she had to lift first one and then the
other heel out of the ground before she could move.

"Yeah."

She glanced at the dogs and took a nervous step to one
side. Her heels slipped into the dirt once again. She realized the only way to keep her heels from sinking into the
ground again was to balance up on her tiptoes. She tried to
look calm and collected, but teetering on her toes wasn't
easy. "I . . . uh . . . I'm Glenn Hubbard's attorney. . . ."

Cody Butler stepped out onto the porch.

The dogs didn't move, and neither did Shaye.

"If you're gonna ruin my day, come on in and let's get
it over with," he said, holding the door open for her in an
off-handed invitation.

Shaye hesitated and looked down at the dogs once
again, unsure whether she should move or not.

"Don't worry," Maribeth offered with a friendly smile.
"They won't move till Cody tells them to. They're harm-
less." With a tilt of her head, Maribeth motioned toward
Cody and whispered, "So's he."

Shaye looked at the girl, down at the dogs, and then
back up at Cody Butler. From his hard, unfriendly expression, she figured she might be safer outside taking her
chances with the dogs. Unfortunately, Hubbard wasn't
paying her to cower in the front yard with a pack of what
she suspected were Newfoundlands, straight out of the
Canadian wilds. Still struggling to stay up on her toes, she
gingerly sidestepped the huge creatures, successfully kept
her heels from sinking back into the dirt, and climbed the
porch steps.

Cody quickly hustled her through the foyer, down the
hallway, and into the kitchen. Bright, cozy, and filled with

the aroma of freshly brewed coffee, the kitchen offered the warm greeting that Cody Butler had not. A row of pink and purple African violets provided a splash of color along the windowsill over the sink, and someone had buffed the oak cabinets to a warm, golden sheen. Except for a short crockware vase holding spatulas and wooden spoons, a neat row of matching canisters, and a microwave, the countertops were free of clutter. For a bachelor's kitchen, it had a surprisingly well-tended appearance.

Hubbard had told her that only Cody and his sister lived in the house. Their parents had died in an accident on an icy road three winters earlier, and Cody was raising the girl himself. A few cowboys lived in the bunkhouse east of the barns, but the rest of Medicine Creek's hired hands lived off the ranch.

This was the last property that Hubbard wanted her to purchase for him, and "saving the best for last" wasn't exactly the way she'd describe this particular meeting. Just getting an appointment with Cody Butler had been next to impossible to arrange. The man was adamant about keeping his ranch, no matter who wanted it.

"Mr. Butler, my name is Shaye Frazier." She offered her hand and flinched as he seized it a little too hard for a polite handshake. *So, that's how it's going to be.*

"Let's get this over with," Cody said. "Sit down, Miss . . . or is it *Ms.* Frazier?"

"Actually, it's *Mrs.* Frazier," Shaye replied, returning his direct stare before settling herself on one of the high-backed chairs at the broad kitchen table. She thought she'd seen a spark of surprise in his eyes, but it had vanished so quickly she wasn't sure if it had really been there. She had surprised herself, though. Almost two years had passed since she'd last referred to herself as *Mrs.* Frazier.

"Coffee?" Maribeth offered.

Grateful for the distraction, Shaye accepted the mug with a nod and a smile.

Cody Butler slowly eased his tall body into a chair across the table from her and pushed a crockware bowl forward. "Sugar?"

"Uh . . . no . . ." The way he had languidly moved captured her full attention, distracted her, and was to blame for the warm flush that now heated her body. "No . . . thank you." Dropping her gaze to the sugar bowl, she slightly shook her head, then dared to look up. *Get a grip. You're not some silly, impressionable schoolgirl.* "I'd prefer sweetener, if you have any."

"Nope, don't think we do," he answered with a cocky lift of his left brow. "Just sugar. Sorry." Cody Butler dumped four spoonsful of sugar into his own coffee as if declaring a challenge, then lifted the mug and took a sip.

Maribeth placed a few blue packets of sweetener on the table. "I prefer this to sugar, too." With a slight push, she moved the sugar bowl back across the table until it came to rest in front of Cody. "I've heard that too much sugar can make you kinda hyper and *really* hard to live with."

Stifling a smile that threatened to expose itself, Shaye looked up from opening a packet of sweetener and found herself staring into bold, openly appraising, dark-brown eyes. Hubbard had warned her Cody Butler would be difficult to deal with, but she hadn't expected him to be so darned attractive.

Shaye guessed he was about thirty years old, maybe even a little older, and although a navy-blue ballcap shaded his brow, she could clearly see his features. Long dark lashes fringed his eyes, the kind of lashes that sent every woman jealously reaching for her mascara. The faint webbing of squint lines radiating from the outer corners of his eyes and the bronze hue of his skin told of the hours he spent working outside. His nose, straight and finely sculpted, led her gaze to his lips. Though taut and hard at the moment, his mouth showed promise of being very appealing, if he'd only smile. His nearly black hair curled over his collar and was still damp from his morning shower. Did he always wear it so long? The bothersome question had tiptoed quietly into her mind, shoving every other reasonable thought aside, creating more disturbance than she wanted, needed, or expected. Before she could push it aside, another quickly joined it. Would his hair feel as soft as it looked?

Shaye watched him gulp a few mouthfuls of coffee and then stand to hand his mug across the table to Maribeth for a refill. Cody Butler was tall, at least six-feet-three, and athletically lean. She liked the way his faded jeans and chambray shirt fit against his body like a second skin. The large oval trophy buckle on his belt was obviously a favorite and worn daily. Its once shiny surface was now dulled with scratches and a few dents pocked the edges. Well worn, it was still impressive.

She noticed his hands as he held his cup. Though veterans of hard work, they were nicely shaped with long, tapered fingers and clean, manicured nails. Just like Medicine Creek Ranch, Cody Butler was beautiful to look at and well tended.

"Mrs. Frazier?"

Yanked from her musings, Shaye raised her eyes from Cody Butler's hands and found his all too appealing mouth curved in a mocking smile. Embarrassed and feeling very much like a child caught with her hand in the cookie jar, Shaye quickly reached for her briefcase, hoping the warmth she felt on her cheeks wasn't a tomato-red blush. The sooner she got down to business, the sooner she could get this meeting over with. She'd always preferred family law and wasn't the least bit comfortable with this kind of work. But it was the job she'd been hired to do, and like it or not, she'd do the best she could. "I suppose we should get started. I've brought some information that . . ."

The ring of the telephone interrupted.

Maribeth lifted the receiver. "Butler's." After a few moments she handed the telephone to Cody. "It's for you. It's . . . Doc Campbell."

Shaye watched as Cody pressed his fingers against his temple. She caught the slight grimace on his face and suspected he was fighting a bad headache. In fact, she'd bet her next retainer that Cody's headache and the bloodshot tracks she'd noticed in his eyes added up to one thing. Cody Butler had a hangover. She glanced at Maribeth and discovered a worried frown creasing the girl's freckled brow. What was going on? Hubbard hadn't said anything about Cody having a drinking problem. But, if he did, then maybe that could partly explain why he couldn't pay his bank loan. Did one have to do with the other? If it wasn't the reason, what *was* going on that would cause Cody Butler to get drunk and have his sister so worried? Was it something that might benefit Glenn Hubbard's bid for the ranch?

Cody turned his back to the table, obviously trying to keep his conversation with Doc Campbell as private as possible, but she could still overhear what he was saying.

"I've got about twenty head down with it now, and ten or twelve more are looking suspicious." He glanced back over his shoulder, and before he turned away, his eyes met Shaye's and lingered for a moment. "Yeah, I'll be here. Around noon is fine." He handed the phone to Maribeth and sat back down at the table. "Sorry to keep you waiting."

Shaye knew who Doc Campbell was. She'd met him just three days ago at Hubbard's. Harold Campbell was said to be the best cattle and horse veterinarian in the quad-county.

The pained look around Cody's eyes deepened as Shaye watched him swallow the three aspirins Maribeth put on the table in front of him. A hollow ache gripped her. Her suspicions were right. Something was wrong at Medicine Creek. Shaye looked up at Maribeth and then back at

Cody. "If it isn't convenient for you to talk with me now, I could come back some other time."

His glance met hers again with those darned gorgeous eyes. A cynical tilt lifted the corner of his mouth. "Is another time going to make our discussion any different?"

"Well . . . no. I don't suppose it would," she answered, uncomfortably forced to the defensive.

"Then let's get to it."

Giving a slight decisive nod, Shaye opened her briefcase and withdrew a copy of Hubbard's proposal. She placed it on the table in front of Cody. "As you are aware, my client is Glenn Hubbard."

"Yeah, the big land baron."

Ignoring Cody's sarcasm, Shaye opened the cover of the report. "My client is in the process of building what will be one of the largest privately owned wildlife preserves in the country. As you will see from the prospectus, this state-of-the-art facility will not only accommodate the natural wildlife—deer, elk, bears, buffalo, and wild mustangs—but Mr. Hubbard plans to raise some exotic animals such as eland, llamas, and perhaps Watusi cattle as well."

Cody ignored the folder. Shaye reached across the table and flipped from the first to second page. "Aside from the natural environment areas and exotic pens, the park will also be a licensed rehabilitation facility for injured or ill animals and birds—raptors—eagles, hawks, and the like. Mr. Hubbard is building a specially designed infirmary, complete with a surgery area, cages, and holding pens."

She turned the page.

"A relocation program will also be instituted. The park will accept animals that have become management problems in other areas. For example, the Bureau of Land Management is already relocating some mustangs from Nevada to Mr. Hubbard's facility." She turned to another page of the prospectus in front of Cody. "Of course, all phases of the sanctuary will be fully licensed with the proper authorities, federal and state agencies."

"Do you know that in the last two months some of your client's Nevada mustangs have broken through my fences three times? Do you know my men have had to round them up, get them away from my beef cattle, get them back on Hubbard's land, and then repair all the fence these . . . equine immigrants broke down?"

"It's my understanding that Mr. Hubbard paid you very well for the damages."

Cody Butler grunted his disagreement but didn't waste any more time arguing the point.

"Mr. Butler, I believe this also more clearly points out why my client needs more land." She turned to another page. "Mr. Hubbard's plans will require a great deal of land, and as I'm sure you are aware, he has already purchased a few of the local ranches to—"

"He didn't purchase them," Cody interrupted. "*Purchase* is too nice a word, too clean. The truth is your client vultured them. He waited until their owners were in financial trouble, barely hanging on, and then he swooped in for the kill."

Although Cody's charge closely matched some of her own feelings, Shaye didn't have the luxury to voice them. From the moment she'd accepted Hubbard's retainer, she'd had to put her own opinions aside and do the best job she could for her client. She had also expected far worse from Cody than he had just given her, but then, their meeting wasn't over yet.

Taking a deep breath, she continued. "Mr. Hubbard would like to expand to the west of his existing property. As his legal representative, he has authorized me to make what he feels is a fair and generous offer for your ranch—Medicine Creek."

"I bet he has," Cody scoffed, leaning back in his chair and folding his arms over his chest.

"Aside from the grasslands and wooded areas on your ranch, which are ideal for the buffalo and mustangs, the spring-fed lake and creeks make Medicine Creek ideal for all of Mr. Hubbard's purposes."

"My cows and horses like it, too," Cody said, rocking his chair a little. "Tell me, is your client planning on relocating cougars and wolves to 'Hubbardland'?"

"Yes, I suppose, if there's a need," Shaye answered, sidestepping another jab.

"So, aside from buying up all the land he can, he's planning on jeopardizing the livestock that's already here and belongs to the rest of the ranchers in the area." Cody Butler's face moved into a scorn-filled mien. "Why am I not surprised?"

"I confess I don't know very much about animals, wild or domestic. I'm from Boston." She shrugged. "Aren't these animals already natural inhabitants here, Mr. Butler? Why should a few relocated ones endanger local livestock?"

"Because, Mrs. Frazier, there's a thing called the ecosystem," he replied, leaning forward as though he were talking to a child. "The natural food sources that support the wolves and cougars here now might not be large enough to feed the imports." Cody took another sip of coffee and then sat back. "Has Hubbard thought about that? Or has he thought about the possibility of disease being brought into the area by any of these imports? And just what is your Mr. Hubbard's past experience in animal husbandry?"

"Mr. Butler, your questions are all very valid, but I'm not familiar with these matters and am in no position to answer them. I'm an attorney, not a wildlife specialist. I'm sure Mr. Hubbard would be glad to meet with you and the other concerned ranchers to address these matters. My job is to convey his proposal to purchase your ranch and, when all parties agree on the price, prepare the necessary paper-work."

"Okay," Cody said, rubbing his hands together in obvious counterfeit greedy anticipation. "Dazzle me with Hubbard's generosity."

"Glenn Hubbard's offer for the Medicine Creek Ranch, all three thousand, five hundred and forty-two acres, is nine hundred dollars an acre. Added to that would be a sum of two hundred and fifty thousand—good faith money."

"Well, isn't that generous," Cody scoffed. "That's the most generous offer I've ever heard."

Shaye watched the tightening of the muscle along the edge of Cody's jaw. Cody Butler's manner was beginning to get under her skin, but ignoring his sarcastic tone, she pressed her bid further. "I believe my client is being very generous. The real-estate market lists the top price for your prime land around seven to eight hundred an acre. As you see, Mr. Hubbard is not making any distinction between grassland, rocky outcroppings, or uncleared land." She paused, but the hard edge to his jaw remained. "There is one condition to this offer, though."

"And just what might that be?" Cody tipped his chair back against the wall and crossed his arms over his chest again. His body language was clear, but the insolent expression firmly ensconced on his face left no doubt.

Shaye wished she could wipe the sardonic smile from his lips. Her gaze lingered on his mouth longer than she should have allowed, and she knew she'd been caught once more when his lips curved into a crooked smile. She'd been right. Not only was his smile appealing, it was downright devastating. She quickly glanced away and tried to steer her thoughts back to the issue at hand, and after a hearty mental tug, they reluctantly complied.

"Should you accept Mr. Hubbard's offer," she said, "he insists that your outstanding bank loan of two hundred thousand be paid immediately and in full. This would keep your credit clear of any problems that a foreclosure would cause."

Cody abruptly sat forward, setting the front legs of his chair back on the floor with a loud thud. "I see your Mr. Hubbard has been poking around into my private business."

"You have me to blame for that," Shaye replied, squaring her shoulders. "I was asked to glean as much information as I could about your property. Besides, the lien on your ranch *is* a matter of public record."

His glance slid away from hers, and Shaye realized Cody Butler wasn't just angry, he was embarrassed. Knowing she had added to his discomfort, she felt a sharp stab of regret. She couldn't allow it to matter, though; she had to continue to press Hubbard's proposal. "I assure you, it isn't anything personal. Just business, Mr. Butler."

Cody Butler's knuckles whitened as he gripped his coffee mug. "You tell your Mr. Hubbard that the Butlers aren't selling, today . . . or ever."

She pushed further. "If you accept my client's offer, you'll be clearing well over three million dollars. I'd say that's a very generous sum to purchase another piece of land and resettle elsewhere. The Jessops were able to find a wonderful new place north of Jackson with the money they made off their sale."

Unfolding his long, lean frame from the chair, Cody slowly stood. His hard gaze never flickered from her face. Shaye felt the heat of her quickening pulse and in that instant realized that Cody Butler could be a formidable foe. Although it offered little to no protection at all, she instinctively lifted her hand to her throat. Her fingers toyed with the collar of her blouse.

"Mrs. Frazier, our meeting is over."

"Mr. Butler, please, consider . . ."

He held up his hand to silence her. "I'm afraid your client hired you to waste your time . . . and mine. I've already told you in the plainest words I know, but I'll do it again: Medicine Creek is not for sale."

He turned away, moved back to his chair, and just before sitting down, looked across the table at her. "This ranch has belonged to my family for more than a hundred and fifty years. Wyoming wasn't even a state when my great-great-grandfather built the original homesite with his bare hands, with his sweat and blood." Cody's hand tightened into a fist. "He cleared this land with an ax in one hand and a rifle to protect his family against the Indians in the other. There's a hill out back where he buried his Philadelphia bride and their unborn child after she died in labor. Two years later he married a Cheyenne woman and raised a son. They're all out on that hill." He glanced out the window, clearly wrestling to keep his emotions in check. A moment passed before his gaze returned to Shaye. "This land has always been Butler . . . and Cheyenne land. It's never been for sale, and it never will be." He closed Hubbard's portfolio and propelled it back across the table. It slid to a stop in front of Shaye.

"If you wish to negotiate for a higher price—"

"Lady, I didn't realize you were hard of hearing. Perhaps you can hear me better if I stand real close," he said, stepping back around the table.

He stood within inches of her and placing both hands on the table, leaned over her. Shaye could smell the clean, subtle tang of pine-scented soap, and the tempo of her pulse cranked up another notch.

"I said—Medicine Creek's not for sale. Did you get it that time?"

Fighting to ignore the pounding in her chest, unsure if it was caused by the man himself or his attempt to intimidate her, Shaye quickly offered another proposition. "Mr. Hubbard is aware of your family's history with this land and anticipated you might be hesitant to accept his offer." She looked up at Cody and hoped none of the turmoil simmering inside of her cracked the businesslike facade she fought to keep on the outside. "Considering your emotional and historical ties to this ranch and your obligation to the bank, I've been authorized to add another fifty dollars an acre to the offer."

She watched, mesmerized, as Cody's expression turned hard and cold as steel.

"Mrs. Frazier, if you were a man, I'd be throwin' you out the door on your ass for suggesting that it would only take fifty extra bucks for me to sell out."

He turned away, took a few steps from the table, then spun around to face her, his anger so evident that she drew an uneasy breath.

"You tell your . . . damn client," Cody continued, "he can offer a million an acre, and if he'd care to bend over, I'll show him—up close and personal—where he can put it." He paused once more and seemed to study her face as if trying to read her thoughts. He shook his head as if the whole discussion repulsed him. "Let me tell you something, Mrs. Frazier. I'm just like this land, Butler and Cheyenne . . . and I'm not for sale, either. Got it?"

Cody moved away from the table, and Shaye took in a deep gulp of air. When had she stopped breathing?

He refilled his coffee mug from the pot on the stove, returned to the table and settled back into his chair. Without looking at her, he dumped another four spoons of sugar into the dark brew in his mug and then glanced up at Maribeth. "Tater, it looks like I'm going to be very hyper and damned hard to live with today."

"Mr. Butler—"

"Save yourself the trouble," Cody interrupted with a lift of his hand. "Quit wasting your time. You seem like a nice lady, maybe a little naive about the son of a bitch you work for, but nice. So, I'll politely ask you to tell him that my answer is no."

Cody pushed the sugar bowl back to the center of the

table. Without thinking, Shaye reached out and covered his hand with her own. "Mr. Butler, please, think this through. According to the bank, you have little more than one month to repay the entire loan. No one will give you another mortgage, and if you don't repay the note, Glenn Hubbard will buy the mortgage and you won't receive a penny. Then where will you be? He could easily wait out the month, but because he's a fair man he's offering you a way out, a way to stay in the ranching business and keep your livelihood. Doesn't accepting his offer and finding another place make more sense than losing everything?"

"Losing this ranch *is* losing everything," Cody replied, his voice a haunted whisper.

Suddenly realizing where her hand lay, Shaye quickly withdrew it and began fumbling in her purse. "Please, think over your decision. I beg you . . . reconsider. If you do, call me." She withdrew one of her business cards, jotted down the number of her cell phone, and placed the card on the table.

Cody watched the slight sway of Shaye Frazier's hips as she walked toward her car.

"Do you suppose that with a lot of dieting, ten hours of aerobics a day, a hundred thousand dollars of plastic surgery, and a great set of boobs, I could ever be that gorgeous?" Maribeth leaned over and placed her elbows on the porch rail. Resting her chin on the heels of her hands, she watched Shaye leave.

"I don't know, Tater." Cody gave his sister's long auburn ponytail a playful tug. "We'd have to do something about those Ping-Pong ball eyes of yours." He turned his attention back to the Mercedes convertible receding down the lane in a cloud of dust.

Maribeth straightened up and poked her brother in the ribs. "I saw you lookin' at her butt."

"Where'd you get such a smart mouth?" Cody demanded with a laugh.

"Well, let's see—I've got this darned crazy, hungover brother who's just turned down more than three million bucks, who drinks his coffee black but dumped half the sugar in the world in his mug, and who can't stop staring at some married woman's tush. Where do *you* think I got my smart mouth?"

Maribeth turned and disappeared into the house. The screen door slammed shut behind her.

Sitting on the porch stoop, Cody buried his head in his hands. Shaye Frazier's image immediately slid into his mind. He hadn't been immune to her cool green eyes, nor the soft curtain of dark brown hair that fell over her cheek and tempted his fingers to brush it aside. He hadn't been immune to the touch of her hand, either. In fact, when she'd touched him, he'd almost come out of his chair. He knew the well-tailored business suit covered a lush, feminine body, and the long slender curve of leg that showed below the hem of her skirt had been pretty impressive, too. Only three things bothered him about Shaye Frazier: She worked for that bastard, Glenn Hubbard; she was right— he was in deep financial trouble; and damn it, she was married.

Cody lifted his ballcap. Wiping his damp brow with his sleeve, he squinted against the late morning sun. He sniffed his hand. A light hint of Shaye's fragrance lingered on his skin where she'd touched him. "Damn," he muttered. The woman could send a man's libido skyrocketing.

He set the cap back on his head and stood. Leaning against the porch support, he gazed out over the lawn to the barns and pens. Twenty-four hours ago he wasn't the least bit worried about meeting the bank payment, but that was before he'd gotten drunk. And he'd gotten drunk just after Doc Campbell had given him the worst news possible.

Chapter Two

"Well, was I right?" Glenn Hubbard draped his arm around Shaye's shoulder and drew her into his study. "I warned you he'd be a tough nut to crack." Taking her into his arms, he placed a resounding kiss on her cheek. "But I don't want you to give up. Every man has his price, and you'll just have to work a little harder to find Cody Butler's."

"He doesn't want to sell, Hub." Feeling none of Glenn Hubbard's exuberance, Shaye shrugged away from his embrace and sank wearily into the overstuffed leather chair by the window. She tipped her head back, resting against the cushion. "He's determined to hang on."

"Then he'll be left hanging on to nothing," Hubbard said, shaking his head in apparent regret. "You can't say I'm not trying to be fair with the man."

Shaye drew her hand across her brow and looked up at the handsome gray-haired man. "I know you are, but do you have to have *that* land? Can't you buy farther north, or—"

"Butler's ranch has got the water and grass I need—plain and simple." Hubbard settled his tall frame into the chair behind his desk, rested his elbows on the desktop, and propped his chin on his steepled fingers. "What's wrong, sweetheart? Are you having a problem with this? You're not getting soft on me, are you?"

Knowing Hubbard wouldn't be pleased with her answer, she still gave it. "Maybe a little." *Maybe a lot.* A small sigh escaped her lips. "Hub, they're really nice, hardworking people, and I—"

"*I'm* nice people. *You're* nice people. Come on, Shaye, be realistic and stop thinking with your heart. You've got to toughen up. This is business." He leaned back in his chair. "I've got nothing personal against Butler. He *is* a good man, but this is strictly a business proposition. And it's a damn good one, at that. Where else is someone like Cody Butler ever going to come up with the kind of money I've offered?" Glenn Hubbard pointed a well-tanned finger at Shaye. "I don't have to offer him a single dime, you know. I can just sit tight and let him sink. All I have to do is wait for the bank to foreclose, then pick up the phone and buy his note for pennies on the dollar." Hubbard pointed at the large, leather-bound checkbook on his desk. "Hell, I'm offering him a check for more than three million dollars so he won't be embarrassed by a foreclosure, so he'll have money to buy another ranch. He'll be committing financial suicide if he turns me down. He'd be a damned fool."

"He may be a lot of things I don't know about, but I don't think Cody Butler is a fool." The image of dark eyes and near-black hair, a challenging grin, and the deep, velvet-smooth sound of the man's voice filled Shaye's mind. "He loves that ranch, Hub. It's been in his family for generations. He isn't going to give it up without a fight."

"Is that so? Well, I can guarantee there won't be much fight to it by the end of the month. The bank has instructions to notify me the moment he defaults."

"And you're sure he doesn't have the money?"

"You're the one who got the information, you tell me."

He took a sip from the glass of iced tea that had been sitting on the desk in front of him and grimaced. Reaching into one side of the richly carved credenza behind his desk, he retrieved a bottle of vodka. "You know he's already requested three extensions. That means he's scrambling to get a payment together. He's also consigned about forty head of breeding cows and one of his best young Simmental bulls to the Cheyenne Cattleman's auction next week. Does that sound like someone who's got enough money on hand to pay off a loan?"

Hubbard paused long enough to spin the cap off the bottle of Cristall and pour a generous measure of the clear liquor into his iced tea. After stirring the drink with his finger, he raised the frosty glass to his lips and downed a gusty swig. "It's possible he can get enough money for his beef, but his best bet would be to sell some of those high-priced polo ponies he raises and trains."

"Cody Butler raises ponies?" Shaye was astonished. What good were little ponies on a cattle ranch? No wonder the man was in financial trouble.

Hubbard's hearty laughter filled the room. "Shaye, darling, you've spent much too much time in the city. Polo ponies are full-sized horses, it's just the accepted name for horses trained for the game of polo. I wanted you to go to a match with me the last time I was in Boston. You remember, don't you?" He shook his head with obvious amusement. "It's like . . . uh . . . croquet on horseback."

Embarrassed, Shaye offered a slight shrug. "Hub, you know I don't know anything about horses or cows, ranching, or animals of any kind. I didn't even know how to take care of that cross-eyed Chinese apartment cat that you gave me." If she'd known when she'd accepted Hubbard's retainer that she'd have to become personally familiar with horses and cows and big black dogs, she might have told him to find someone else. Anything larger than a gold fish was out of her comfort range. Hopefully she could get her job done in a short time, get out of cow country and back to her cozy, critter-free Boston apartment.

"Siamese," Hub chuckled.

"Excuse me?"

"Siamese," Hub replied, still laughing. "He was a five-hundred dollar, lilac-point Siamese . . . apartment cat."

"A card or a phone call would have been just as nice," Shaye said, wishing she'd never brought up the darned cat.

Trying to distance herself from the topic of cross-eyed birthday presents, she rose from the chair, moved to the window, and watched the activity in front of the large, newly built barn. "When I came up the drive, I noticed that more animals have come in."

"It's the last shipment of mustangs from Nevada. They sure are a wild bunch." Glenn Hubbard chuckled. "They beat the inside of my brand-new stock trailer all to hell."

"So, now what do you do with them?" Shaye watched as Hubbard's men herded the horses into a large, high-railed pen.

"We'll hold them down here for about a week or so before we move them out to join up with the rest of the herd. It'll give us a chance to give them their shots, look them over good, and treat them for things like shipping fever, run some baseline blood tests, and take care of any wounds they've picked up in transport."

Shaye slowly turned away from the window. "Hub, what would cause a bunch of animals to come up sick at the same time?"

Hubbard's teasing was obviously at her expense. "Horses? Cattle? Apartment cats? A bunch of what?"

She chose to ignore his teasing. "I don't know. Let's say . . . cattle."

He shrugged. "It could be any number of things—bad feed, sour water, chemicals of some kind, a virus . . . anything. Why?"

"While I was at the Butlers', Cody got a call from

Harold Campbell, the veterinarian you introduced me to a few days ago. From what I heard of Cody's side of the conversation, I think he's having trouble."

"With what?" Hubbard asked, a little too quickly and a little too eagerly for neighborly manners. "His cattle, ranch horses, polo ponies, what?"

"Like I said, I don't know. Does it really matter?" Shaye sighed, disappointed by Hubbard's excitement. "If the man has got trouble with his animals, it's all the same, isn't it?"

"Not necessarily, my darling girl," Hubbard replied with a sly grin. "If he's got sick ranch horses, we're talking a thousand dollars or so per animal. That's not much of a loss. If he's got sick polo ponies, that's a big cash crop. Those babies sell for thirty, forty thousand each—sometimes more if they're good, and Butler only breeds and trains good ones. But if he's got sick cattle, he's in real trouble. That's his bread and butter, his most convertible stock. And the ranchers around here get damned touchy about diseased herds, especially if it's something like an airborne virus that can jump fences and hit someone else's herd down the road." He took another swallow of his spiked tea. "Besides, if he's got sick cattle, the state and federal agriculture boys will get involved." Hubbard raised his glass in mock salute. "If there's a disease in his herd, he won't be able to run 'em through the auction."

Shaye carefully watched Hubbard for his response to the question she was about to ask. "So, if his horses . . . uh . . . polo ponies are worth that much, then it's possible he could sell some and make the bank payment."

"I don't care how good a trainer Butler is. If it's those horses that Doc Campbell's looking at, Butler won't be able to sell them if they're sick, and there isn't much of a market for dead polo ponies, either."

"And without the money from selling those horses or his cattle, he loses, right?"

For the first time since she had begun working for

Glenn Hubbard and his proposed game preserve, Shaye truly regretted her decision to accept his business. She closed her eyes for a moment as if that simple act would erase the discomfiting feelings she had. It didn't. She was also beginning to question her own principles for accepting his retainer. Granted, she needed the money—the six-month sabbatical she'd taken after leaving her partnership at Calvert, Bennett, and Frazier had gobbled a huge chunk out of her bank account, but she could have taken on another client. There had been the widow in Concord with the wrongful-death suit against her late husband's employer, and she'd been offered the case of a woman who wanted to sue one of the tobacco companies. Either would have padded her bank account very well. She glanced up at Glenn Hubbard once again. No. She couldn't have taken on another client. She'd been discontent too long, and it was time she tried to find a solution.

"Ranching's a business, Shaye, and sometimes it's a harsh business. Butler's a businessman, just like I am." Hubbard put his empty glass on the credenza. "He knows what it takes to keep things going. Unfortunately, he's run into some bad luck. No one ever promised him it would be a bed of roses, but I don't call three million bucks a thorny landing." He rose from his chair and moved to her side. Wrapping his arms around her, he drew her into a hug and placed a kiss on the top of her head. "Maybe you need to stop by Medicine Creek in a couple of days. Pay them a friendly, neighborly visit and see if you can find out what's going on . . . but keep pushing. I want that land."

Shaye moved out of his embrace. "Before I left Butler's this morning, I invited his young sister, Maribeth, over for a swim. I hope you don't mind. She's a nice kid." Why did her friendly invitation to Maribeth now seem so deceitful?

"That's my girl, keep at 'em," Hubbard replied, returning to his desk and pouring himself another tumbler of iced tea from the pitcher on the credenza. "She's adopted, you know."

"Maribeth?"

"Yeah. The Butlers adopted her out of some children's welfare residence in Laramie when she was about three or four years old. From what I hear, she'd been pretty badly abused."

Shaye's conscience took another hard twist.

"I'm sorry, son." Doc Campbell stepped away from the wheezing steer. "I want you to keep these sick ones away from the rest of your cattle. I'll run the blood samples through the lab on a rush and see what we've got. It'll still take a few days though." He wrapped an identification label around each of the blood-filled vials. "I guarantee you've got more sick ones in your herd. As they're spotted, have your boys cut 'em out from the others and bring them in."

Cody's gaze scanned the cattle in the quarantine pen. They'd gotten worse since he'd looked at them a few hours before. Standing with their legs splayed and their heads drooping low, heavy drool hung in strings from their mouths. On many, white pustules coated their tongues, and lesions had spread to their lips and nostrils. Cody drew a ragged breath and cast a speculative look at the veterinarian. "Come on, Doc. Let's stop ballet dancing around the truth. It's what we talked about yesterday, right?"

Doc Campbell dropped the used needles into a red-lidded container in the bed of his pickup, then carefully peeled the latex gloves from his hands and discarded them in the same bin. He rubbed the back of his neck before his hand moved across his chin to stroke his white, short-cropped beard. "Like I told you yesterday, it could be a lot of things. We can inoculate them when they're calves and boost them every year, but there are new strains of viruses hitting us every day. Even some symptoms caused by ingested pesticides can fool us." He paused, his eyes scanning the pen of sick cows. "Without lab confirmation it's difficult to say for sure, and I want to be *real* sure, considering what's been going on in Europe, but it looks like hoof-and-mouth disease."

God, I'll lose the whole herd! "How fast does this stuff spread?" Cody already had a fair idea what the answer was; he just needed to hear it spoken aloud. He felt as though a well-cocked fist had just been jack-hammered into his gut. He could barely breathe.

"Quick," Doc Campbell replied, slipping the blood samples into red shipping tubes. "Four to eight days is usual, but sometimes a little longer—two weeks at the most." Doc jotted an identification number on the address label of each tube. "I'd hate to see it happen, but if this gets out of hand, you might have to put the herd down." He looked up. "Cody, you know I've got to notify the authorities about this. They'll be contacting you for more information and will probably send out their own vet."

Cody felt the jackhammer strike again. "Can't we keep this under wraps for a little while?"

Doc Campbell slowly shook his head. "I'm sorry, son. You know I've gotta call them. It's the law."

Cody lifted his ballcap and finger-raked his hair before setting the cap back in place. "Yeah, you're right." Biting down on his bottom lip to crush the harsh profanities he really wanted to say, he turned away from the sick cows. Looking down at the ground, he idly bounced the heel of his scuffed right boot in the dirt. "Do what you gotta do, Doc."

"Have you any idea where you might have picked this up?" Doc Campbell closed the side bin on his truck.

Cody shook his head.

"You had some new stock come in a little less than a month ago, didn't you?"

Cody looked up. "Yeah, I did, as a matter of fact. There

were thirty head that came in from the Triple D Ranch outside of El Paso—the last on a trade my dad made before he died."

"If they'd mixed up with some cattle from south of the border before they were shipped here, they may have brought the virus in. There have been some hoof-and-mouth outbreaks in Mexico in the last few years." Doc Campbell pulled his truck keys from his pocket. "The Triple D cattle might not have had active disease and would have gotten shipping papers without any problem, but sometimes they can be carriers."

"I'll give Triple D a call and see what I can find out."

The vet gave a slow nod. "I know you've got some cattle consigned to the Cattlemen's auction. You're gonna have to pull 'em out, Cody. As of right now, your entire herd is under quarantine. Tell your men, if this is what I think it is and they're not careful, it can make them sick, too. I also want you to make sure Maribeth stays away from them." He looked back at the cattle in the pen. "It sure is a damned shame." He rattled the keys in his hand. "If you need me . . . well, I'll keep in touch." He placed a consoling hand on Cody's shoulder, then moved away. "I'm real sorry, son."

Cody listened to the sound of Doc Campbell's truck as it pulled away from the pens. Without a backward glance at the ailing cows, he untied the gray gelding that had been standing cant-hipped and patiently waiting at the gate. Swinging up into the saddle, Cody reined Possum toward the oak-shaded hilltop a little over five hundred yards from the end of the lane. Four generations of Butlers lay buried inside the wrought-iron fenced plot beneath the big trees.

Stepping out of the saddle, Cody glanced from one grave marker to the next. Removing his cap, he draped his arm across the saddle and rested his forehead against the swell of the saddle fork. From Jacob Butler, who first settled on the land in 1854, to Jack, Cody's father, no Butler

had ever let the ranch slip through their fingers. No Butler . . . until now.

Cody wrapped the gelding's reins around a low branch.
The ornate gate gave a rusty screech as he pushed it open.
He made a mental note to bring a can of oil with him the
next time he stopped by. He settled down under one of the
large oaks. After placing his ballcap on the ground beside
him, he leaned back against the tree and rested his forearm
on his bent knee. This place was where he did his best
thinking, and today he had to do some of the best thinking
he'd ever done.

Doc Campbell had said the cattle were under quarantine, but horses didn't get foot-and-mouth disease. That
meant he still might be able to sell the six polo ponies he'd
been training since March. He had the number of an interested buyer with one of the elite polo clubs in California.
He'd call Miguel di Prado and a couple of other regular
customers who might be in the market for some new stock.
There was also a broker in Florida he'd touch bases with.
Might as well call everyone he could think of. *That's still
not enough. Even if I get lucky and get thirty grand a piece,
I'd still be twenty short.*

He tipped his head back and could feel the rough bite of
the bark on his scalp. He closed his eyes. The drone of bees
collecting pollen from the nearby blooms and the songs of
nesting birds was a soothing symphony. Despite the chaos
in his life, Cody had to admit, it was a beautiful late June
day . . . the kind of day that it would be fun to pack a picnic lunch and ride up to the lake with a pretty lady. Shaye
Frazier. Green eyes, soft brown hair, and that nice tush he
knew would fit so well into the curve of his hand, immediately slid into his mind. *Damn, Butler, you aren't so hard
up for a woman that you'd fraternize with the enemy, are
you?* His head said no, but his body had another answer.

Cody drew a ragged breath, reluctantly shoved his
thoughts of Glenn Hubbard's beautiful lawyer aside, and

began looking for an answer to his more pressing problem. Yeah, it was a beautiful day, and if the weather held, maybe he could put a good polish on the fifth colt he'd been working with and finish up the sixth. Maybe he could get closer to the full two hundred thousand if he started his price higher than usual and promised to cut it down some if the buyer would consider taking all six in a package deal. If he couldn't get the full amount, at least he'd be a whole lot closer to covering the loan, and every dollar would help. And maybe if he had to make up some extra, he could find a buyer for the stock trailer he'd bought two years ago.

"Thanks," he quietly said, getting to his feet. Answers always came easier to him up here on the hill. Before he left the enclosure, he knelt at Kate's and Jack Butler's graves. He passed his hand over the lush, green blanket of grass in a loving caress, letting the blades slide through his fingers. God, he missed his folks.

Firmly setting his ballcap back on his head, Cody pulled the bill low over his eyes, blaming the bright sun and the nagging hangover headache for the burn of tears in his eyes. He gazed at each headstone, from his great-great-grandfather Jacob's to the small marble angel atop the grave of the stillborn brother he had never known. Family. They signified who he was . . . what he was . . . and what Medicine Creek Ranch was all about.

The muscle along the edge of his jaw tightened. "I promise you all, I'll be damned to hell and back before I let anyone take Butler land."

Stepping up into the saddle, Cody turned the gelding toward the eastern meadows of the ranch. There was no point going back to the house, and he couldn't do anything more for the cattle in the quarantine pen. It made more sense to spread the word to the hands who were working the herd along the northeast sector of the ranch and see if any more cows had begun to show symptoms. Besides, one of the men had mentioned that Glenn Hubbard had moved some buffalo and wild mustangs into the grassland that abutted Medicine Creek. He wanted to have a look at them for himself. It was going to be a problem keeping fences repaired along the east line. Buffalo were notorious for walking right through regular livestock fences, and wild horses didn't fare well with them, either. He'd seen mustangs strangle themselves trying to escape the tightening hold of barbed wire.

The gray gelding settled into an easy, ground-covering jog-trot causing Cody's hips to move with a slight rhythmic back and forth sway. In an instant the thought of a pair of slim, sweetly curved hips entered his mind. Shaye Frazier. Her name even sounded smooth and soft, like expensive silk stockings.

"I've gotta hand it to Hubbard," he muttered with a wry smile. "The man may be a bastard, but he sure knows how to pick lawyers."

The gelding's ears swiveled to pick up the sound of Cody's words.

"What the hell are you listening to?" Cody grumbled, admonishing the horse with a light slap to its neck.

Glenn Hubbard dropped the receiver back onto the cradle. Martha Tinsdale at the Cheyenne Cattlemen Association's office had just given him the news. As a matter of fact, Hubbard was positive she'd make it her duty to give the rest of the folks in the county the same news as well.

"Brucellosis," he whispered. "Brucellosis." The word had the ominous sound of a hissing snake. "Son of a bitch!" He slapped the flat of his hand on the polished top of his desk. Rising, he paced from his desk to the window and back again. "Brucellosis! Son of a bitch!"

Hubbard grabbed the telephone and punched 4 on the intercom line. The receiver was picked up on the third ring. "Shaye, honey, can you come downstairs? Something's come up." Without waiting for a reply, he dropped the receiver and continued to pace.

Moments later Shaye stood at the door and watched him stalk about the room. At fifty-four, Glenn Hubbard was still a very handsome man. He kept himself in top physical shape with vigorous workouts in his private gym and afternoons on the tennis court. He hated jogging but religiously ran at least five miles each morning before breakfast and could probably outdistance many men half his age.

He always drew admiring glances from women and more often than not was pursued by at least half. The problem they soon learned was that since his wife, Susanne, had died, Glenn Hubbard had foregone the art of fidelity. Shaye had watched it happen time and time again. None of the women ever remained in his life for long. No one could ever replace Susanne and for that reason alone, Shaye could forgive him. But, there was one other reason. Glenn Hubbard was her father.

They were compatible companions, but there had always been a distance between them, leaving Shaye to believe she had never quite measured up to his expectations. He had given himself completely to Susanne, leaving very little for his daughter. She was positive few, if any, people in the area were even aware they were related. When he'd introduced her it had always been as his attorney. Perhaps it was best kept that way until she no longer represented him on the land deals.

Had she ever missed having a doting father? She knew growing up that her relationship with him had been very different than what she'd seen her friends have with their fathers. With her mother's illness sapping so much of her strength for years, Shaye had been sent to the Bowers, an upscale boarding school near Boston. That had added even more distance between them. So how could she miss what she'd never had? How could she miss what she'd never known? Was it possible? Maybe. Maybe as a child when she'd fallen and skinned her knees and hungered to climb into his lap and be comforted. Maybe when Davis Procter, III had stood her up on her first dress-up date and she needed her daddy to tell her that Davis didn't know what he was missing. Maybe she hungered for his praise when she'd graduated from law school at the top of her class. Maybe after her husband died in a boating accident with his latest mistress and she needed a strong shoulder to cry on. Even calling him "Dad" had never felt comfortable. He'd always been Hub. He was like a friend, an acquaintance.

All of his love had been for Susanne, and when she died Hub's capacity to love seemed to die as well. Shaye knew her father cared for her, but she had never had the sense of a bond—that special bond that was supposed to exist between a father and his daughter. She had pushed herself, determined to excel at everything she did to gain his love, his fatherly attention. She hungered for it still. Was it this lack of connection with her father that had led her to make so many wrong choices in her adult relationships with men? She shoved the disquieting, but all too familiar, question from her mind. One thought remained. Perhaps helping him complete the land acquisitions for the wildlife preserve would help her win her coveted prize.

"Hub?"

Hubbard swung around to face her, knocking his desk chair into a spin. "I just heard," he said, excitement or something close to it coloring his voice. "Butler's got brucellosis." He paused as if expecting Shaye to understand the dire message of his words. "The son of a bitch has got brucellosis!"

Shaye's stomach lurched. "Cody's sick?" She quickly stepped into the room, not even trying to analyze why she felt so worried about a man she had met only a few days before. She was positive he had been hung over when she'd been at Medicine Creek, but she never would have thought there was more to it than that. "Is it serious? Is he in the hospital?"

Hubbard stopped pacing and looked at her with disbelieving eyes. "We've definitely got to get you out of Boston more often. No, Butler's not sick. Well, maybe he is about this news. It's his cattle." With a gesture that punctuated his bulletin, Hubbard raised his hands, one to either side of his head and waggled his index fingers, emulating cow horns. "That's what Doc Campbell called him about the day you were there. Butler's got a virus in his herd." Hubbard continued to pace, his stride mirroring his agitation. "Do you have any idea what this means?"

No, she didn't have any idea. She shook her head.

"It means that every cow on Medicine Creek has to be quarantined. It means that every bovine in the area is in jeopardy of contracting the disease and damn it, that includes my buffalo and elk. When word spreads about this, and believe me it will spread faster than the plague itself, Cody Butler is going to become the local pariah. And, my sweet, it means that in a little over thirty days I'll own Medicine Creek for a whole lot less than three million dollars."

Shaye ignored Hubbard's boast. "You're saying Cody can lose his whole herd—his ranch—to this?" Her heart felt as though a huge rock had fallen upon it and was pushing it down.

"Some bovine develop antibodies to the disease and survive, but he'll lose most of 'em. Most likely the Department of Agriculture will demand that every animal in the herd that comes up sick be shot. They'll bury the carcasses in lye or burn 'em."

Shaye felt the rock push to the bottom of her stomach. Granted, it was horrible to think of a man losing his livelihood, but why did it bother her so much that the man was Cody Butler? Why should she care whether he lost his herd—or his ranch? As Hub had reminded her, it was business—the breaks of being a rancher; besides, she'd only met Cody once and it hadn't been a friendly meeting at that. She didn't know why, she just knew she cared and it scared her . . . a lot.

Chapter Three

Shaye cut the engine on the Mercedes and sat for a moment, her hands gripping the steering wheel. Damn Hub for badgering her to stop by Medicine Creek. If he wanted to find out what was going on, why didn't he snoop around himself? This certainly fell outside the bounds of legal work. Although she'd called Maribeth and suggested that today would be perfect for an afternoon in Hubbard's pool, she still felt uncomfortable intruding into Cody Butler's home territory. She had presented Hubbard's offer, Cody had turned it down, and that should be the end of it. But, according to Hubbard, that was just the beginning of the game. Apparently her father intended to turn the deal into a tug-of-war for the Butler ranch.

"You gonna sit in that fancy car of yours all day and gawk at the house or are ya comin' in like proper company?"

Startled from her thoughts, Shaye looked up in search of the owner of the twang-filled voice only to have the late morning sun shine in her eyes. Lifting her hand for shade, she found a wry grin and a pair of twinkling blue eyes set in a tanned, craggy face. Years of hot sun, mountain winds, and harsh Wyoming winters had carved deep, weathered paths across the man's cheeks. A battered cowboy hat squatted on his head and he stood with his gnarled hands resting on his scrawny hips. He was small, wizened, and wiry, and had the look of a terrier about him. Shaye sensed he'd be a tenacious scrapper.

"Well?" He opened the car door and stood back.

"Hello, I'm Shaye—"

"I know who you are, Miss Legal. Maribeth's been goin' on 'bout you for days. She's all excited 'bout you comin' for her. Right now she's inside finishin' her kitchen chores. Your timing's just right to save her from the dish-pan." With a gentleman's considerate touch, he helped Shaye from the car and shut the door firmly behind her. "I'm Diggins, Roscoe Diggins. You might say I'm the nanny 'round here." A gleeful laugh rearranged all the crimps and crinkles in his face into a wonderful landscape.

"Sounds like a tough job to me," Shaye teased, surprised to feel so much at ease with this old cowboy.

"Maribeth's the easy one. It's Cody who makes me believe in child abandonment," Roscoe parried, leading her up the walk.

"At his age he can hardly be called a child," Shaye said.

"Don't be too sure, ma'am. I know a passel of women that'd tell ya a man's a child all his life." Roscoe turned and studied her. "He don't think too highly of your boss."

"I know." Shaye gave a slight nod. *There are times I don't think too highly of him myself.*

Roscoe's eyes narrowed. "I'm gonna ask you this out-right and excuse me if you think it's rude, but you ain't just bein' nice to Maribeth so Cody'll take Hubbard's deal, are ya?"

A sharp arrow of guilt poked at Shaye's conscience. Was she so hungry for her father's approval that this was possible? No. She refused to accept that her invitation to Maribeth was anything more than what it was—the offer to take a young girl out for an enjoyable afternoon. "Of course not, Mr. Diggins. I'm sorry you thought you needed to ask."

"I had to ask. She's like a granddaughter to me."

"I understand, sir."

"Roscoe. Call me Roscoe. All my friends do." His face moved into another grin.

A responding smile tugged at Shaye's lips. "Okay, Roscoe it is."

"You're kinda far from home, aint'cha?"

"A little farther west than I'm used to," Shaye replied. "I'm from Boston."

"While you're here doing Hubbard's work, are ya stayin' at that fancy new Ramada hotel place over by the interchange?"

Roscoe's question had come out of the blue and Shaye answered without thought. "No, I'm staying with Hub at the ranch."

Roscoe's woolly brows shot up, but if he had any more questions, he apparently decided not to ask them. Turning, he headed up the porch steps and into the house. "Yup, it's sure a good day for a swim."

Shaye preferred the Butlers' rustic house to Hubbard's angular mansion with its expanse of glass, stone, cold chrome, and splashes of decorator art. The Butler house enveloped its guests in a warm embrace that gave a heart-felt welcome. Colorful Navajo rugs hung on a couple of the living room walls and a few larger ones lay on the polished oak-plank floor. Big, overstuffed chairs and sofas, gleaming wood tables, and bookcases filled the room, and the huge fireplace on the west wall promised cozy winter nights. Although the house was definitely part of a working ranch, it would rival many featured in western decor magazines.

A collection of fine western art added to the ambience. Beautifully rendered bronze sculptures of longhorn steers, horses, and buffalo stood interspersed with the Indian pottery along the mantel and bookshelves. Original paintings of western landscapes and working cowboys decorated the walls and a glassed étagère near one window held a collection of beaded Indian artifacts. There was a sense of warmth and permanency in this home that was sorely lacking in Glenn Hubbard's new house.

Shaye bent to more closely examine an exquisite bronze on the long credenza that separated the living room from the entry hall. It depicted a lanky young boy, his arms around the neck of his horse, his cheek resting against the horse's mane. She glanced up to find Roscoe watching her.

"That was one of Cody's mom's best pieces," he said, his voice soft with memories. "Kate sculpted it when Cody was about twelve. She could've been a famous artist . . . if she'd wanted. A couple of them fancy galleries in Jackson Hole sold out of her work each year, but I guess she liked bein' a rancher's wife and a mom a whole lot better." Roscoe lightly sniffled, then squared his shoulders as if bolstering his emotions. "You're still gonna try to get Cody to sell out, ain'tcha?"

"That's what I've been hired to do," Shaye answered, straightening up and lightly running her fingers over the cold smooth hip of the bronze horse.

"It ain't gonna happen, you know. That boy was born upstairs in this house, as was his daddy, his grandpa, and his great-grandpa. All his life he's sworn he was gonna marry and raise his own kids here. And when his time comes, he plans to be laid up on that hill with all the Butlers who've gone on before him. Then it'll be *his* kids that'll keep the place going. Just like always—one generation stepping into the boot prints of another."

The old man moved across the room to the tall étagère and tapped on the glass front. "See this stuff? All this here Indian stuff, these moccasins and beaded things?" He waited until Shaye stood beside him before he continued. "These little moccasins belonged to Cody's great-great-grandma, *Eve'haoohe'e*. She was the youngest daughter of a Cheyenne war chief, a man named *Haestohena'hane*, Many Kills." He moved his finger and tapped the glass again. "And that pair there belonged to Cody's grandma. Her real name was *Ameohne'e*, Walks Along Woman, but everyone called her Amy. Her pa was Emil Standing Bull." He turned away from the glass case and faced Shaye, eye to eye. "It ain't unusual for folks around here to be part Indian. Ain't no shame to it here like some places." He picked up a framed photograph of a young dark-haired boy sitting on the lap of an old Indian woman and handed it to Shaye. "Cody was about eight when this picture was taken with his grandma."

Shaye could feel Roscoe watching her, waiting for a response, good or bad, as she looked at the photo.

"Cody's three-eighths Cheyenne and five-eighths Butler," he said. "That's a pretty strong mix, Miss Legal. You ain't gonna be able to push him off this land."

"Mr. Diggins, please understand," Shaye replied, looking up from the photo. "I'm only doing a job that Glenn Hubbard has hired me to do. I can't force Cody to sell. The final decision is still his." She gently placed the photograph of Cody and his grandmother back on the table.

"You got that straight, Miss Legal," Roscoe said with a nod and a wink before leading her toward the kitchen. "You're sure all business, ain'tcha? We've gotta teach you how to relax."

The old cowboy paused at the kitchen door. "I heard you callin' me 'Mr. Diggins' again. Like I said, it's Roscoe . . . unless you don't wanna be my friend." His grin returned. "Now, take a deep breath and smell." He paused, then gave a rusty chuckle. "If you insist on callin' me Mr. Diggins, I ain't sharing any of my special cream-cheese brownies with ya, either."

"I bet you wear your hat when you bake them," Shaye

said, pointing to the battered Stetson that still sat on his head.

Roscoe sighed and tugged at the brim. "Gosh darn, you've guessed the secret part of my recipe."

Cody dropped his hand onto the low pommel of the English saddle and loosened the reins, keeping the young bay gelding beneath him working at an easy gait. He preferred to ride western tack, but the type of training he did on the polo ponies demanded a lighter saddle that gave him better leg contact with the horse. He moved the gelding out into the middle of the arena at a relaxed canter. Giving a light squeeze with his left leg, he smiled as the horse immediately responded, changing his lead leg from right to left and turned to the left. The bay completed a full circle as the light pressure from Cody's leg continued. At the apex of the circle, Cody repeated the cue with his right leg, and the colt quickly responded, changing to a right-hand circle and changing the lead leg as smooth as whipped cream. The workout had lasted more than half an hour, enough to keep the colt tuned up but not bored, and Cody was pleased with the intelligence and agility this colt showed. Pulling the gelding down to a walk, he gave him a solid yet enthusiastic pat on the neck.

"Good boy," he praised. "Good boy."

In the past six years Cody had added champion cutting-horse blood to his breeding program, and the result had been some phenomenal colts who were quick to learn and just as quick on their feet. The last couple of foal crops were proving to be the best polo ponies he'd ever raised and trained. Just like this bay, they were quick, savvy, athletic, and pretty to look at. The ideal combination. The swing of the mallet never bothered them, and each had the special knack of chasing after the ball like a cat after a mouse.

Stepping out of the saddle, Cody gave the reins to the

teenage boy who'd sat on the top rail of the arena fence throughout the whole workout. Cody had hired Tim Mallory for the summer. The boy's father, Gene, was one of Medicine Creek's top hands, and the boy had grown up around livestock. Like any young teenager, Tim's heart was set on buying his own pickup truck, a dream he wanted to fulfill before heading back to school for his junior year. Money for extra trucks, even old clunkers, didn't come easy on a cowboy's pay.

Tim was good with the horses, and there didn't appear to be a lazy bone in the boy's body. He worked hard and earned every cent Cody paid him. There was only one problem. Maribeth had a Texas-sized crush on Tim Mallory.

"Hormones," Cody grumbled.

"Excuse me?" Tim asked. "Did you say something?"

Cody turned from loosening the girth on the gelding's saddle. "I . . . uh . . . said I'm going up to the house for a minute." He lifted the flat saddle from the horse's back and set it on the top rail of the fence. "I need to get my gloves." He opened the gate and waited for Tim to lead the gelding out of the training pen. "Cool him down, then tack him up with my western saddle. I'm going to ride up to the east fence line and give him a look at some buffalo."

Cody could smell the tantalizing aroma of Roscoe's brownies as he jogged across the back lawn and up the walkway to the kitchen door. Sometimes when the old cowboy was cooking and the aromas wafted out of the kitchen, if Cody closed his eyes he could imagine his mom working at the stove. His dad would be there, too, sitting at the table with a cup of coffee and watching her, his love and need for the woman plain as the nose on his face. The two of them would be shamelessly flirting with each other as they had for more than thirty years. His father would snag her with his arm as she walked by and pull her down into his lap, and in a few minutes the pot on the stove wouldn't be the only thing heating up in the Butler kitchen.

Nothing less would suit Cody when he married, and so far, none of the women he'd dated had come within a million light-years of making the grade.

Pulling open the screen door, he burst into the kitchen, and joking to rid himself of the lump that memories had put in his throat, he called out a greeting to Roscoe. "Hi, honey, I'm home!"

Cody stopped dead in his tracks. The "honey" he'd expected to find wasn't the one sitting at the kitchen table with Maribeth. But he had to admit, Shaye Frazier filled the bill of a honey a whole lot better than Roscoe ever could. He didn't know whether to stand and gawk as the sunlight streaming through the window put a golden glow on her cheek and fiery highlights in her hair, or be angry because she was obviously here to push Hubbard's proposal at him again.

Damn. What was it about this woman that put him off balance? Doing what he felt was the safest, he offered her one of his best scowls and a growl for a greeting.

"Don't go getting all ornery," Maribeth chimed in. "Shaye isn't here to see you, she's here to see me. We're going swimming."

"I've got cattle up near the pond, you can't go."

"We're not swimming in any muddy, old watering hole. Shaye's taking me someplace real posh."

"Well, isn't that nice," Cody replied, sarcasm dripping from each word. "And why do you suppose she's being so nice to you and taking you anywhere?"

Maribeth's chin moved upward in a defiant tilt as she glared at her brother. "Maybe it's because unlike your old report cards from school, mine always say I have excellent social skills, I'm well liked by everyone and play well with others." She hopped out of her chair and glanced at Shaye with a wide grin on her face. "I'll be right back, gotta get my bathing suit."

In Maribeth's wake, an uncomfortable silence filled the kitchen. Finally, unable to resist any longer, Cody moved to the table, picked up a warm brownie from the plate, and popped it into his mouth. Settling into a chair across the table from Shaye, he lifted the half-full glass of milk sitting in front of her. Ignoring her protest, he took a long draught then handed the glass back to her.

He could have sworn she stared at the spot on the rim of the glass where his lips had been. For a moment he even thought she was going to take a sip from the same place. Just thinking about it made his stomach take a silly hop and jump, but it landed with a hard thud when she wiped the rim with her napkin and put the glass back down on the table.

Definitely hormones.

Roscoe was right, he was a little too edgy these days where women were concerned. Well, this one in particular. It had been a while since he'd last taken care of edges, and he was long overdue. Maybe he needed to take Bunny Gibson up on the offer she made every time he went into Casey's Buckin' Bar and Grille for a beer.

He'd been in high school with Bunny, and even then she'd made it her life's goal to smooth out as many edgy men as she could find. The guys used to joke about doing the "Bunny hop." Maybe that's what he needed, a good, old-fashioned, sweaty, wham-bam-thank-you-ma'am, go-round of bedroom rodeo. Maybe then this green-eyed brunette with the great legs and fabulous tush wouldn't get to him like she did.

Tipping his chair back until it balanced on two legs, Cody looked across the table at Shaye. He forced himself not to look at the tempting swell of her breasts against her T-shirt and he miserably failed to stifle the groan that left his throat as he watched the tip of her tongue slip out from between her lips and lick a brownie crumb from the corner of her mouth. Damn. Double damn. He couldn't ever remember getting hard sitting at the kitchen table before.

Cody dropped the chair back on all four legs and tried a different, safer, tack. "So, how does a busy, big-time, big-city attorney like you get time off to play? I thought all you lawyers believe that time is money."

"Right now I'm working freelance, Mr. Butler. Like you, I'm responsible for my own time. I'm taking the afternoon off."

Her coolly delivered answer left Cody strangely dissatisfied. He wanted to get at her, ruffle her pretty feathers at least half as much as she ruffled his. "I'm surprised you expect me to let my sister go off with you. I don't know you . . . don't know where you're taking her or if you can even swim. What if she gets cramps and goes under?" He pointed to the plate on the table. "She's been eating brownies."

Shaye released a long sigh as she leaned back and folded her arms across her breasts. "Mr. Butler, first let me assure you that my taking Maribeth swimming has absolutely nothing to do with Hubbard's proposal. Second, I am very capable of taking care of her. I'm certified in first responder CPR and advanced lifesaving techniques, and I'm a strong swimmer, as proven by the three gold medals I won in college for the 200-meter breaststroke."

Cody stifled another small groan as his gaze plummeted a little more than eight inches below her chin. The word *breaststroke* stuck like a burr in his mind, and he wasn't thinking about the swimming kind, either. Suddenly aware of the silence in the room, he looked up. The expression on Shaye Frazier's face could have frozen the Amazon River. The tone of her voice proved to be just as chilly.

"Third, we'll be at Glenn Hubbard's ranch. I've already left the phone number with Roscoe. And fourth, if you think Roscoe's brownies are going to make Maribeth sink to the bottom of the pool, you'd best take that complaint up with him."

Cody had just enough time to shoot the old cowboy an astonished gape before Maribeth bounded back into the kitchen.

"I'm ready." Maribeth stopped in the middle of the room and looked nervously from her brother to Shaye Frazier and back again. "We can go now . . . unless Cody has decided to lock me in the castle tower and ruin my life forever . . . again. He's been treating me worse than Rapunzel for weeks."

"You're too young to be thinking about boys and . . . uh . . . stuff. Besides, Tim Mallory's too old for you." Cody certainly didn't want to get into this private family discussion in front of Hubbard's beautiful lawyer, so why had it all just spewed out of his mouth? And on top of everything else going on in his life, he still needed to give Maribeth the birds-and-the-bees lecture, but he'd gladly postpone that for ten or twelve more years . . . if he could get away with it. Hormones. Had his been awake at thirteen?

Cody glanced at Shaye and watched spellbound as she licked the end of her finger, dabbed at a couple of brownie crumbs on the plate and then sucked them from her fingertip. His breath caught in his chest and he felt as though he'd been zapped by a cattle prod. Oh, yeah. His hormones had been awake at thirteen. Wide awake. And they hadn't slept a moment since.

"You girls better get going before I have you help me ride herd on the vacuum cleaner," Roscoe said, pushing Maribeth and Shaye out of the kitchen, while delivering an over-the-shoulder scowl at Cody.

"Have Tater back by five," Cody ordered.

"Six," Maribeth rebutted.

"Five-thirty," Shaye bargained.

"Lawyers," Cody grouched, knowing he'd been bested.

• • •

Lifting his aviator-styled sunglasses from his pocket, Cody put them on as he and Roscoe watched the silver Mercedes head down the long lane. At Maribeth's request, Shaye had put the convertible top down, and Cody could hear his young sister's gay laughter all the way from the highway.

"Your mom would've liked her," Roscoe quietly announced.

"On what basis have you formed *that* opinion?" Cody asked with more edge to his voice than he'd intended.

"For a cowboy who's used to sizing up the foals for the best of the spring crop, I don't think you've taken a good enough look at this filly."

"And just what do you think I should be looking at that I haven't been enjoying already?"

"Well, if you'd been paying attention with your head and not your glands, you'd have realized the pretty lady doesn't quite cotton to the job Glenn Hubbard has her doin'."

"Is that so? Then why doesn't she quit?"

"Poor eyesight again, boy," Roscoe answered, lifting the edge of his beat-up cowboy hat to scratch his head. "She ain't a quitter. She's got a rare commodity in today's world. The lady's got integrity. She'll stick to her contract with Hubbard because she agreed to do the job, but she'll do it her way, not his."

"You forget, old man, she's married," Cody added, putting voice to one of the burrs that had goaded him since he'd first met Mrs. Shaye Frazier. "I don't date married women."

Having opened the screen door, Roscoe paused and gave an indignant snort. "Hell, who said *anything* about you datin' her? All I said was that your mom would've liked her." He shook his head, his disbelief apparent by the expression on his face. "Were you *really* thinkin' about askin' that *nice* lady out?"

Feeling the burn of being rubbed hard the wrong way, Cody growled at Roscoe, "Shut the door, old man; you're letting the flies into the house."

Roscoe, working the wad of chewing tobacco in his left cheek, sent a healthy gob of juice sailing in a high arc over the porch rail and into the flower bed. "That's what you know, Romeo," he harrumphed. "There's too many damn flies inside the house already. I'm just lettin' the pesky buggers out."

Without another word, Roscoe stomped into the house and allowed the screen door to slam shut behind him. It resounded like a gunshot.

"Hormones," Cody hissed, doing his own bit of stomping down the porch stairs and across the lawn to the barns. "Damn hormones."

Throughout the rest of the afternoon Cody tried to stay busy, but his thoughts kept scattering. After taking the young bay gelding out for a ride in the eastern high meadows and not seeing any of Hubbard's buffalo, he reined the colt south along the fence line. As he crested the next rise, the thunder of hooves resounded and Cody pulled the bay to a halt. He could feel the colt bunch up beneath him, getting ready to spook and take off. Speaking calmly, soothing the young horse's fear, Cody watched the herd of wild mustangs explode through the tree line and out onto the grassy plain on Hubbard's property. Excited by the galloping herd, the bay tried to bolt, but Cody's firm hand kept him in check and together they watched as the wild horses settled down and began to graze on the rich grass. Cody estimated thirty-five to forty mares and foals made up this group of range-bred horses. He looked for the stallion but could only find the lead mare. Maybe Hubbard had a little more in mind for these horses than maintaining the same breeding they'd done in the wild. Maybe the absence of a mustang stallion meant he'd be introducing some finer blood into the herd, bringing up the quality of the horses.

It was an interesting concept . . . but from what he'd seen and heard about Glenn Hubbard, Cody wasn't too inclined to find anything good about the man or his proposed game preserve.

Without bidding the image of Glenn Hubbard's lawyer filled his mind . . . again and with thoughts of Shaye Frazier constantly jabbing at him, he rode home.

An hour later, sitting at the desk in his office, he should have been thinking about trying to find enough money in his bank account to pay the next week's salary for his men, but he couldn't get the image of soft lips, a flitting tongue, and brownie crumbs out of his mind.

A half hour later he had a real big mess on his hands. While using the hose to fill a water bucket in one of the broodmare stalls, his mind was filled with other watery thoughts—Shaye Frazier in a swimsuit—a bikini—no swimsuit at all.

It wasn't until the water seeped through the split sole of his boot that he realized the bucket had overflowed and the stall was flooded.

"Shit!" He quickly crimped the hose. "I'd better do the Bunny hop soon, or else I'm gonna wreck the ranch even before the bank tries to get their hands on it."

Around five-fifteen three of his men brought eleven sick steers in from the eastern grazing land, and before an hour had passed, another sixteen had been added to the growing herd in the quarantine pen. Cody stood outside the high-fenced lot. Resting his forearms on the top rail, he settled his chin on his wrist and slowly looked at each and every steer. The rank odor of their disease burned his nostrils.

"What happens if we get too many to put in there?"

He turned and found Gene Mallory, Tim's dad, standing beside him. "Use another pen, I suppose. You told the boys to be careful if they have to handle these steers, even the dead ones, didn't you? Remind them to wash up real well.

Roscoe put some disinfectant soap in the bunkhouse. I don't want anyone picking up this damned virus. Doc Campbell said it could spread to humans faster than the flu."

"Yeah, I told them. Cody, I'm real sorry about all of this."

Gene pulled back from the fence, shuffled his boots in the dirt for a moment, then looked up at Cody. "I feel really bad saying anything." He hesitated, his unease apparent. "But the . . . uh . . . men have been worrying about their paychecks. I thought you ought to know."

Cody drew his gaze from the sick cattle and looked at his foreman. "Tell them not to worry, they'll be paid." He turned and studied the sick steers once again.

"Cody, you've been a real good friend to me. When my wife died and things were bad with me and Tim, you were there for me." Gene paused and cleared his throat. "I want you to know, I've got a few dollars set aside, so if your money's gotta go for vet bills or payroll, I'm okay for a month or two."

Without pulling his attention away from the cattle in the pen, Cody gave a nod. He didn't want to chance looking at Gene, didn't want to chance that his sunglasses wouldn't hide the sudden rush of tears that rimmed his eyes. Few men were lucky enough to have friends like Gene Mallory. Cody knew he was blessed. "Thanks. I really appreciate it."

Gene stepped away from the fence, then poked Cody in the ribs. "Well, speaking of appreciating things." He gave a low wolf whistle. "That's certainly worth appreciating." As he began to move off, he turned and grinned at Cody. "I'll talk to you later."

Cody swung around and found Shaye walking across the barn lot toward him. She was dressed in a lot more than the bikini he'd imagined, but had to admit the tight jeans and turquoise T-shirt looked almost as good.

He leaned back against the fence with the heel of his right boot hooked on the bottom rail. Folding his arms across his chest, he watched her easy, long-legged gait and tried like hell to ignore the heat that flared inside him. *Cool your jets, Butler. This one's already got someone else's brand on her.*

Taking Roscoe's reprimand to heart, Cody took the time to really look at her. He'd seen women who were more flamboyantly beautiful, but Shaye's beauty was different. She was classy like expensive crystal or a piece of fine artwork, exquisite like a fine-boned mare. There was a hot sexiness about her, too, but it was coupled with an unnerving air of naïveté, as if she wasn't even aware she could raise a man's blood pressure, among other things, by just casually walking across a barnyard.

Keep thinking things like that, Butler, and you're either gonna get yourself in a whole lot of trouble for rustling some other guy's filly or you'll have to soak in a cold horse trough for the rest of the week.

A flurry of movement pulled his gaze away from Shaye, and he almost laughed aloud as Larry, Curly, and Moe, his three Newfies, lumbered from the cool shade of the barn and bounded toward her. This time he wouldn't call the dogs to heel. If Mrs. Shaye "Sweet Tush" Frazier, Attorney-at-Law, insisted on poking her pretty nose into his territory, she'd better get used to the livestock—all the livestock.

A moment later he felt an odd mixture of disappointment and pride. Despite a timid back step or two as the dogs jostled and shoved against her, Shaye's tentative touches soon became full-blown pats and scratches behind the dogs' ears. She looked up as if seeking acknowledgment for her great feat of bravery, but Cody's response was directed at the dogs. "Traitors."

"Hi." Shaye laughed and leaned to pat Moe who kept pushing his huge head against her leg. "You're going to have to tell me their names and who is who so I can keep them straight."

He could have told her that she wouldn't need to know his dogs' names if she stayed away. He could have told her how great she looked in tight jeans and a T-shirt that showed the pale lacy shadow of her bra. He could have told her he liked the way her toes peeked out of her sandals. And, he could have told her he'd always been very partial to pink nail polish on pretty toes. He could have told her a lot of things, but sarcasm seemed a whole lot safer.

"Have you come to tell me you've drowned my sister or that you're holding her hostage until I give Hubbard what he wants?"

"Neither. I came to apologize."

Boom! She'd knocked his sarcasm and bluster for a loop and had bested him again. "Apologize?" Damn. He didn't like feeling two feet tall.

"Yes. I'm sorry. I was wrong." She self-consciously looked at her foot as she drew an arc in the dirt with the toe of her sandal. "I should have asked *you* if I could take Maribeth to Hubbard's for a swim. It was pretty presumptuous of me not to. I'm sorry."

Cody's attention was caught by the wiggling of her toes on her left foot as they worked to dislodge a small rock that had slipped into her sandal. He drew a ragged breath. Even her toes nudged his libido.

"I said, I apologize," she repeated, as if he hadn't heard her the first time.

Cody looked up, hoping the expression on his face didn't reflect the thoughts whirring around in his head. "Accepted."

She fidgeted in silence for a moment, then looked over at the steers in the pen, slid her hands in the back pockets of her jeans, and moved closer to the fence.

"Are these the sick ones?"

"What do you know about it?" Cody asked, amazed that the word about his sick cattle was out already. Hell, the Department of Agriculture guys had only phoned that morning. There was only one other possibility. "Did Maribeth say anything about them?"

"No. I was here the other day when Doc Campbell called you. Remember?"

Cody quickly replayed in his mind the conversation that he'd had with Doc Campbell. "You didn't hear me say anything about sick cattle. All you heard was that Doc was coming out to the ranch."

"Yes, and then the woman who works in the Cheyenne Cattlemen Association's office called Hubbard."

Cody winced. Martha Tinsdale, C.C.A.'s secretary, loved to gossip. It hadn't taken her too long to spread the word that he'd canceled his consignments for the sale, and he'd bet a new pair of boots that it hadn't taken her long to tell everyone why.

"So, where's he sitting?" Looking around, he pointed to a line of trees along the lane. "In which tree is the vulture crouched and waiting to swoop in and take over? It looks better and better every day that your client's going to get my ranch. I bet you're both gloating. He gets my land and you get a bonus from a happy client. You both get what you want."

"That's not what I want," Shaye softly replied, looking at the steers in the pen. "Just because I work for Glenn Hubbard doesn't mean I want you to lose your home." Her gaze met his, then slid away with a hint of regret. "I should go. But, again, I apologize for taking Maribeth swimming without asking you first. Next time I'll remember. Goodbye." She turned to leave, paused, and then looked back at him. "I'm real sorry about the brucellosis."

"Brucellosis?" Cody felt a cold chill wash over him. He turned to the steers in the pen. "Who the hell says my cattle have brucellosis?" Had Doc Campbell gotten the results back already? Had he given the report to the C.C.A.? No, Doc wouldn't have done that. Cody didn't doubt Doc's integrity. The vet would have told him the results first, whatever they were.

He quickly swung his gaze back to Shaye, but she had already turned and was walking away. He reached out to grab her arm but missed.

"Look, this isn't brucellosis." He took a few steps, going after her, but stopped. "Is that what Martha Tinsdale said? Is that what Hubbard's saying? It's a damned lie!"

Shaye stopped and looked back at him. "Cody, I'm so sorry."

He watched her walk up the road to her car, the three dogs tagging along.

The icy chill settled into a tight knot in the pit of his stomach and he clenched his hand into a tight fist. Brucellosis. That one word would panic the whole ranching community and turn everyone against him.

Chapter Four

"Is he blind?" Shaye strode across the lawn to her car. Sliding behind the steering wheel, she fumbled with her keys until she finally slipped the key into the ignition. "Any fool, even me, can see those cows are sick." The engine roared to life, and she pulled the gearshift into drive, spraying gravel as she sped down the lane to the highway. She muttered to herself the entire distance. "I don't understand why he's denying the truth."

She admired Cody Butler's determination to hold on to his land, no matter what or who came his way, but his reluctance to accept the hopelessness of his situation puzzled her.

Her breath came out in an exasperated sigh. Other things bothered her, too, things she couldn't control, things that threatened the goals she'd set for herself. Why did she notice everything about him? If she closed her eyes she could easily conjure him up in her mind, every detail in place, from the small crescent-shaped scar that showed white against the tanned skin high on his left cheekbone to the slight cleft in his chin, or the soft breadth of his lips. And why did every shred of her comfort level go haywire whenever she was around him?

She wrapped her fingers around the steering wheel in a strangling grip that rivaled any Jackie Chan hold. "I don't want any of this," she murmured, her words whipped away in the wind. *I don't want this damned job of Hubbard's. I don't want to be the slick city lawyer hired to take advantage of someone's bad fortune, wishing all along that the underdog would win. And I certainly don't want to find the underdog so darned attractive.*

Frustrated, she trembled as a sob shook her, but she choked back the tears. "Oh, stop it," she chided herself. When had she become such a little whiner? No one had held a gun to her head when she'd accepted Hubbard's job offer. She had accepted his proposal for what she believed were very good reasons.

With Hubbard's retainer in her pocket and the rest of the money she'd earn for procuring the land he wanted, she'd be able to go back to Boston and open her new law practice. She'd be able to reestablish the independence and self-respect that she'd lost when she'd married Michael Frazier. But perhaps the most important reason was the one that had driven her most of her life. She needed her father to give her something he'd never given her before, something she'd always craved. Maybe if she got Hubbard the land he wanted, Cody Butler's land, he would finally tell her he loved her, and he would finally tell her he was so very proud of her.

Her plan was perfect, as perfect as a plan could be, considering it had one beastly dilemma. She didn't want Cody Butler to lose his ranch.

Shaye swiped her hand across her cheek, drawing a lock of hair back behind her ear. Tears filled her eyes once again. She shook her head as if this alone would ward off their arrival. Despite her protests, and in the midst of trying to add more mental bricks to her emotional bulwark, the tears spilled from her eyes, and she sniffled the remaining length of the lane.

Instead of heading back to Hubbard's, Shaye turned the Mercedes west, toward town. She needed a change of scenery, something without cows and horses, and she needed to calm down before she did something foolish like marching into Hubbard's office to tell him he could stick his job where the buffalo never roamed.

"Damn it, Hub, why did I agree to do your dirty work?" *Because you thought it would solve all the problems in your world. Because you thought you'd prove to yourself that you could make it on your own. And, you fool, because you thought it would make your father love you.*

She hated it when the voice of reason in her head gave impromptu lectures. Besides, what did the voice know? Where had all its wisdom and good advice been when she'd met and married Michael Frazier?

Determined not to allow herself to go down that bumpy road of memories, she turned on the car radio and pushed the search button, looking for something other than agricultural reports on beef or pork-belly prices. She didn't want any country music stations that insisted on spewing out mournful songs about cheatin' lovers, unrequited love, and broken hearts. She'd lived that woe-filled tune for three years.

As if in answer to an unspoken prayer, the last push of the button gave her a station playing exactly what she wanted. Bach. Johann Sebastian in all of his glory. If the Brandenburg Concerto didn't get her mind off of cowboys, tight blue jeans, dark brown eyes, overgrown dogs, and her guilty conscience, nothing would. Of course, she wasn't counting on the next Bach selection being the one that had played as she'd walked down the aisle to marry Michael— *Jesu, Joy of Man's Desiring.*

It had been man's desiring, all right. She'd been swept off her feet by Michael Frazier and thought she loved him, but Michael's desires had been elsewhere. He'd married her to make partner in the law firm, nothing more, and there had been other women almost from the beginning of the marriage. After a less than meager attempt at discretion, he'd flaunted his affairs. He accused her of being too boring, too prim, and not adventuresome enough for his taste of enjoying more than one lover at a time. To Shaye, multiple choice referred to questionnaires, school exams, and game-show quizzes, certainly not bed partners.

She dried the tears from her cheeks with an angry rub of her hand. Men. Damn the whole blasted lot of them. *And you, too, Cowboy Cody. You, too. You're bullheaded and unreasonable; you . . . you and your . . . overblown pride. You, too.*

Steering the speeding convertible around a long, sweeping bend in the road, Shaye concluded that Cody Butler's only redeeming qualities were Maribeth and Roscoe. "No. That's not true," she whispered a moment later. "When it comes to his family's land, his family's legacy, the man's got marvelous principles."

She pressed the accelerator, and the speedometer leaped to eighty, then eighty-five. *And I've got to ignore all that, put aside what few principles I've got left, and do everything I can to take that all away.*

The sudden wail of a siren clashed with the sweet strains of Bach and jarred her thoughts back to the road. Glancing in the rearview mirror, she saw the brown-and-tan county sheriff's car pull out onto the highway from behind a stand of tall pines. The warning flash of red and blue lights on top of the cruiser was unmistakable.

"Oh, great." Shaye sighed, easing her foot off the gas and steering the Mercedes over to the side of the road. *It must be illegal to have any unkind thoughts about males in this testosterone-filled state. There's even a damned cowboy on the license plate and now some big-bubba cop is going to give me a ticket.* She cut the engine and waited.

"Hi, there."

Shaye quickly looked up from rummaging in her purse for her license. "You're a woman!"

The petite deputy sheriff met Shaye's remark with a wide grin. "Yup, that's what the man I love tells me." She ignored the offered driver's license in Shaye's hand. "Do you know why I stopped you?"

"I know, I was speeding. Sorry, I was kind of distracted and—"

"Hell, no!" The deputy laughed. "I wanted to meet you. You're quite the buzz around town." She lifted the sunglasses from her pert nose. "Hi, Julie Prine." She pointed at Shaye's license. "You can put that away; I don't need it."

"Oh, okay. Thanks." Shaye shaded her eyes from the sun and looked up at Deputy Julie Prine. "What makes me the buzz?"

"Well, let's see. First we heard that Hubbard had fired his Laramie-based attorney and brought in some big eastern-city legal beagle, then we found out it was a woman. And then we heard she was young, and we all know lawyers make a ton of money." Julie counted off each answer on her fingers. "Then when we find out you're above average in the looks department . . . well, do you get the picture? Female, young, pretty—got a good job and money, too."

"That's all it takes to be 'the buzz'?" Shaye wasn't too sure if she should be flattered or uncomfortable with Deputy Prine's itemized list. She also wasn't sure where it was all leading.

"Yup, around here that's about all it takes. Girl, there's a ratio of 5.3 cowboys for every cowgirl. Now I didn't say anything about the age spread of those 5.3, which settles anywhere from three months to a hundred and two years." Julie peered closer at Shaye. "You said you were distracted, so I suppose those red eyes of yours are from havin' the top down on this fancy set of wheels and have absolutely nothing to do with a crying attack." She gave a quick scornful snort. "I won't buy that excuse, but I will buy you a cup of coffee and offer a sympathetic ear. I'm off duty in ten minutes. Follow me into town. Like I said, I'm buying."

Within an hour Shaye felt as comfortable with Julie Prine as if the two had been friends since grade school. She heard all about Julie's boyfriend, Gene Mallory, and his son Tim. Both worked at Medicine Creek for Cody Butler. Small world. Then Julie filled her in on some of the local information.

"There's two movie theaters in town and the nearest McDonald's is fifteen miles away at the Diesel Junction Truck Stop by the Interstate. There are church socials and dances held year 'round in the Cattlemen Association's hall, and Lilly Varnum is the only doctor in town I'll recommend. She wears blue jeans, sweatshirts, and cowboy boots under her white coat, she's an old grump, but she keeps hand-knitted pink cozies on the stirrups on her exam table." Julie paused for a breath, then charged ahead again. "I love my job, think my boss is a jerk, and can't wait to snuggle up every night with my honey."

"How'd you two meet?" Shaye asked, now thoroughly captivated by her new friend.

"I arrested him."

"You didn't."

"Yup, sure did," Julie replied, licking her coffee spoon before putting it on the table. "I'm originally from Davis County and was a deputy over there before moving here. Gene and his pals were in town for the rodeo at our county fair. I took one look at him riding broncs that afternoon and knew I wanted to put a rope on that studmuffin for myself." She grinned. "I waited until they were ready to leave town and pulled them over, right on Main Street." Julie laughed in a low, throaty timbre.

"In my part of the world that's called false arrest, or worse, police harassment."

"Oh, shoot, girl, those boys were beggin' to be harassed." Julie leaned forward and continued to share her story. "I told them to get out of the truck, lean over the fender, and spread 'em." She rolled her eyes. "I've never seen such a gorgeous sight." Putting her hand up beside her mouth, Julie whispered, "Of course Gene was the only one I patted down."

Shaye's sides began to hurt from laughing. "Then what?"

"While I still had my hand on his leg, Gene asked why I'd stopped them. I told him, in my most innocent voice of course, that I was sorry I'd stopped them . . . that I'd mistaken him for someone I'd seen on a wanted poster."

"And?"

"Hell, that sweet hunk just grinned and said, 'No, you didn't darlin'.' He then told me I was gonna have to arrest him for assaulting a police officer. When I asked him why, that gorgeous man leaned over and kissed me right there and then."

"In Boston, you'd both be in big legal trouble—that's a double case of harassment."

"Shaye," Julie said as though she were explaining it to a child. "This is still the Wild West Wyoming . . . out-in-the-sticks Wyoming. Around here harassment is when someone shoots at you more than once. This was just a little old grope and a kiss. Hell, that's pure American."

"Okay, I see the difference." Shaye sighed, dramatically placing her hand over her heart. "*Vive l'amour.* It is so . . . so touching and romantic. I could just cry."

"Oh, no, you don't," Julie quickly countered. "I just got those red eyes back to looking normal. Don't you dare tear up on me again."

Shaye immediately finger-wrote an elaborate *X* over her heart. "Okay, I promise. No more tears."

"Now," Julie charged, "what's your story?"

A cup of coffee turned into three or four while Shaye

told Julie about her mother and father, about Michael, and about why she'd accepted Hub as a client. Then Shaye found herself eating one of the best hamburgers and plate of French fries she'd ever tasted. She couldn't remember the last time she'd enjoyed such a good session of girl-talk. Talking with Julie had been emotionally draining but wonderfully easy. Maybe because it was time to get rid of some of her emotional baggage. Maybe because it was the friendly and sympathetic ear.

"Wow!" Julie exclaimed. "You're so young to be widowed." She reached across the table and gave Shaye's hand a sympathetic pat. "But your age and good looks are on your side. There's another man out there for you somewhere, a good man who'll treat you right and make you happy."

Shaye shook her head. "I'm not interested, and I'm definitely not looking, thank you."

"Okay, I agree. From the sound of it you had a lousy experience, but that doesn't mean it's supposed to be that way or is going to be that way again. You need to open yourself up to the possibility of finding yourself that special someone." She dipped a long French fry into a blob of ketchup and popped it into her mouth. Talking around the potato, she added, "Wouldn't it be great if you found someone here this summer—"

"Stop right there," Shaye interrupted, lifting her hand as if she were a traffic cop. "Although the scenery is breathtaking, the air exhilarating, the people wonderful, the animals . . . I guess they're okay, but there are so many of them . . . I'm a city girl, born and bred." Shaye paused and grimaced. "I don't want to pet the cow in the morning and then eat him on a bun later that afternoon." She shook her head. "Nope. I'm sorry, this place just isn't for me." She looked down at the burger on her plate and shivered.

"His name was Bud," Julie said solemnly pointing to

Shaye's plate. "The Linderman kids are really gonna miss him."

Shaye quickly looked up to find Julie's somber expression explode into laughter. "Fine, make me the brunt of your jokes, that's okay." She picked up the burger and took a bite. "Yummy, yummy. Good Bud."

"Boston, you're a breath of fresh air," Julie said between fits of near hysterics. "So, what do you do for fun when you're not working for Hubbard?"

Shaye put the burger back on her plate. "Nothing too much, read, take walks. I would like to learn how to ride a horse, though."

"Well, it should be pretty easy to find someone to teach you. Provided you don't expect any self-respecting cowboy to teach you how to ride on one of those prissy English saddles you Easterners like to sit on while chasing foxes all over the place."

"Julie, I don't know anything about any of this political stuff—cowboys against the English." Shaye laughed, warming to Julie's teasing. "All I've been able to figure out is that it takes very special people to ranch. Not that I don't admire the life, I'm not cut out for anything like it. I'd just like to learn how to ride a horse."

"Ranching is a hard life for a woman . . . unless she truly loves the land . . . and the man."

The man. Cody Butler's image zapped into Shaye's head and stuck like an irritating burr. She tried to dislodge it, but Julie's next question firmly set its barbs.

"So what do you think of Cody?"

Shaye had been toying with her coffee mug, running her finger around the rim, but with Julie's question, her finger came to a full stop. "What's to think?"

"You tell me."

"He seems nice enough . . . I suppose, not that it makes any difference to me," Shaye replied, not wanting to get caught in Julie Prine's conversational quicksand. "Our relationship is strictly business." From the smirk on Julie's face, Shaye had the distinct impression that her answer was being met with a truckload of skepticism. "I don't approve of mixing business with pleasure."

Julie nodded thoughtfully and then her mouth curved into a grin. "So, you think *mixing* with Cody would be a pleasure, eh?"

Too late. Shaye realized she'd stepped into Julie's snare and was now knee-deep and sinking fast. "This is just like one of those old western movies," she said, trying to joke her way out of the trap.

"How so?"

"I think you've just run me into the box canyon, Sheriff."

Julie chuckled. "For a city slicker, you're pretty quick at picking up on this Wild West cowboy stuff. There's hope for you yet."

A low wolf whistle from a man sitting at a nearby table interrupted their conversation, and Shaye and Julie looked up as a curvaceous redhead approached their table. Although there was a pretty softness to her face, the woman's hair had an impossible flame tint to it. A pouty shape had been drawn over her own lips and then filled in with a glossy fire-engine red lipstick. With each step, the five-inch heels on the woman's clear acrylic, sling-back sandals struck a syncopated beat with the Travis Tritt tune playing on the jukebox.

A red Spandex halter top barely covered the woman's large breasts and Shaye couldn't help but wonder what would happen to everyone in the restaurant if the Spandex would suddenly give way. The image of it breaking and flying about the room like a large, snapped rubber band had Shaye choking on a very impolite chuckle.

"Hello, Julie."

"Hey, Bunny."

"Phew, it sure is a scorcher today, ain't it?" Bunny

breathed, furiously fanning herself with a menu she'd picked up from the table. "I'm fairly dying from this heat. I can't remember a summer this hot so early." She paused, lifted her chin, and briskly fanned her neck for another moment or two as Julie introduced her to Shaye. Bunny glanced at Shaye, twiddled her scarlet enamel-tipped fingers in a ridiculous tiny wave, and looked back at Julie. "Are you and Gene going to the Cowboy Ball this year?"

"Probably, if I don't pull shift that night. Why?"

Bunny placed her hand on her hip, which caused her breasts and the Spandex to expand. Shaye fought the uncontrollable urge to duck.

"Well," Bunny replied. "I thought maybe you guys would like to double with Cody and me."

Shaye choked on the swallow of water she'd just taken.

"Cody's asked you to the dance?" Julie asked, after a quick glance at Shaye.

"Well . . . no, not yet." Bunny sighed, then took a deep breath that caused the Spandex halter top to stretch even more. "I'm workin' on it . . . real hard." She smoothed her hand down over her hip. "I'm sure he will, though, ya'll know he's my sweety."

"Oh, yeah, sure," Julie replied with a nod. "Well, okay, I'll talk with Gene. You just let me know when Cody asks you."

"Super . . . I will." Bunny giggled, causing her Spandexed breasts to jiggle. "Well, gotta go, I've got a hair appointment." She twirled a lock of her hair around her finger. "I sure hope the air-conditioning is working at the Clip 'n Curl. Well, toodles."

Shaye, Julie, and every male in the restaurant watched as Bunny toddled across the room and out the door.

"Trust me," Julie said. "*That* was not the town's mayor." A wicked smile curved her lips. "Her father is."

Not sure how she felt about what she'd just heard Bunny Gibson say, Shaye smiled and tried to sound very casual. "She's . . . uh . . . Bunny is Cody's girlfriend?" The redhead was nothing like the kind of woman she expected Cody Butler would be attracted to . . . but then what did she know about Cody's likes or dislikes? And why should it make any difference to her, one way or the other?

"Bunny?" Julie laughed. "No. She'd like to be, but Bunny's . . . let's just say she's very friendly with a lot of men. Bunny's a sweet, big-hearted gal. Bunny is . . . uh . . . everybody's girlfriend." Julie's scrutiny seemed to intensify. "You're not worried that Bunny and Cody are . . ." She crossed her index over her middle finger and moved her index finger up and down. "Oh, no, hon. Don't worry, she's no competition for an uptown, city girl like you."

Surprised how the idea of Bunny Gibson and Cody going to a dance together bothered her, Shaye tried to push the irritating thought from her mind. It scooted over only to be replaced by the very bothersome image of them in each other's arms . . . not dancing. And she didn't like that one at all. Shaye looked up to find Julie watching her. "What?"

"Oh, nothing, I'm just watching all those thoughts about Cody and Bunny run rampant through your head." Julie grinned. "Hmm, I think I might have stumbled onto something here."

"No, you haven't." Had she answered too quickly? Had she protested too emphatically? Shaye squared her shoulders and summoned up the tone of voice she always used for closing arguments in the courtroom. "Julie, you've stumbled onto absolutely nothing. I'm not interested in finding a man, nor dating . . . and believe me, I'm certainly not interested in Cody Butler."

"Okay, I believe you. Honest, I do." Julie nodded. "Not!"

"I like you a lot, Deputy Prine," Shaye countered, matching Julie's Wyoming twang, tone for tone. "But yer getting me riled up with all this kinda talk. I ain't interested in anything but doin' my duty for Rancher Hubbard. So drop it, or there's gonna be a showdown at high noon."

"See?" Julie chuckled. "You're a born cowgirl. You're gonna love it here!"

"Oh, no, not me." Shaye raised her index finger. "One, I'm a Boston lawyer, who with the proper state licensing, is currently working for a client in Wyoming." She raised her middle finger to join the first. "Two, when my job here is done, I'm going to grab my fee, pack my bags, and go back to Massachusetts as fast as that big jet will take me." Her ring finger joined the first two. "And three, I'm going to set up my own practice and be a full-time, full-fledged Boston lawyer once again." She closed her hand into a fist and pretended to take a punch at Julie. "End of story."

"Oh, don't be too sure, city girl," Julie replied, feinting to the left from Shaye's counterfeit punch. "I think your story is just getting started."

Chapter Five

Cody drove his pickup into the last parking spot in front of the diner. After turning off the motor he sat and stared at the wide plate-glass windows of the restaurant. Every impulse told him to leave—to head back to the ranch—but his conscience firmly held him. He had known since the first steer showed up sick that sooner or later he'd have to face the local ranchers. If Martha Tinsdale had been spreading rumors about brucellosis hitting his herd, then sooner was going to be a whole lot better than later.

Rumors had the bad habit of mutating, and Martha Tinsdale had already given this one a healthy push. It didn't matter that there hadn't been an outbreak of brucellosis in the United States in years or why anyone would believe there was one in his herd now, but the word had come from the Cheyenne Cattlemen's Association's office, and coming from the C.C.A. gave the rumor all the credibility it needed. Cody knew if he didn't talk to his neighbors as soon as possible, things could, and would, get a lot worse for him. He'd lived in Dorland all of his life—he'd known these people all of his life. He hoped he could get the truth told before friendships and the Butler family's reputation suffered too much.

Before heading into town, he had called Doc Campbell to see if the lab results were in. They weren't. Although he'd talked with Doc for only a few minutes, not once had the vet said the word *brucellosis*. Cody didn't believe Doc Campbell had said it to anyone else, either.

Resigned to his unpleasant chore, Cody took a deep breath and quickly scanned the other parked vehicles in front of the Chuckwagon to see who might be inside.

The Chuckwagon—it was a hokey name for a restaurant in cattle country, but the few tourists who still ventured off the Interstate looking for some local color seemed to like the name. The collection of antique spurs, well-worn woolly chaps, branding irons, and old harness pieces and saddles that decorated the diner added authenticity to the cowboy atmosphere. The hamburger on the kiddies' menu even came on a tin chuckwagon plate with a brand, the Bar C, toasted on top of the bun.

The Chuckwagon was also the favorite gathering place for the local ranchers when they were in town. There was nothing better than a cup of coffee or a glass of Maddie Crawford's ice-cold, fresh-squeezed lemonade with a piece of her homemade, county-fair-blue-ribbon-winning rancher's pie—a tart-sized mixture of apples, cinnamon, pecans, raisins, and cream custard, all wrapped in an envelope of flaky, sweet-tasting pastry.

Cody spied Ronny Doyle's truck at the corner and Jeff Granger's Jeep was next to Carl Nesbitt's old Dodge. He recognized Bobby Brindle's blue Chevy pickup. Buck Linderman's mud-covered stock truck, and Jet Linderman's 4x4. He was surprised to see Julie Prine's patrol car at the curb. If she wasn't pulling a late shift, she was usually home by this time cooking supper for Gene and Tim. But it was the next car in line that really sent him for a loop.

The silver Mercedes convertible stuck out like an expensive Arabian mare in a barn full of mules. Cody frowned. Shaye Frazier and the Chuckwagon just didn't go together. She was champagne, caviar, and paté. The Chuckwagon was steak, potatoes, and burgers. In fact, Cody was positive the words *champagne, caviar,* and *paté* had never even been spoken in the Chuckwagon. Mrs. Frazier had *uptown* and *city* written all over her, and the Chuckwagon was down home and country, through and through. So what was a girl like her doing in a place like this?

A slight grin curved his mouth as he remembered the first morning she'd come to the ranch, her expensive, high-heeled shoes sinking in the dirt each time she took a step across the lawn. Maybe some cowboy atmosphere and one of Maddie's rancher's pies was just what Glenn Hubbard's high-priced, Boston lawyer needed . . . and maybe rubbing elbows with a cowboy or two wouldn't hurt, either.

Shoving the discomforting thoughts of long shapely legs aside, Cody yanked his keys out of the ignition. He certainly didn't need the distraction of Shaye Frazier in his life right now. Besides, married women had never been his style.

He stepped out of the truck and shut the door with a decisive slam. The heat and humidity of the late-June day immediately closed in around him. The temperature hadn't begun to cool down for the evening yet, and the heat radiated up from the concrete sidewalk. It was going to be a long, hot summer.

Cody paused in front of the café door and steeled himself against what he knew was waiting for him on the other side. He'd known some of these people all of his life, had gone to high school with a few, rodeoed with one or two, and had dated the daughters of others. This must be what it felt like for a condemned man to face his sentence.

A tempting thought skimmed through his mind. If he took fifteen steps backward, he'd be back at his truck. He shook his head, disgusted with himself for having such a cowardly idea. Lifting his ballcap, he anxiously raked his fingers through his hair, then tugged the cap back in place. *Come on, Butler, quit stalling. Get it over with.*

He firmly pushed the door open and stepped inside, barely mindful of the melodic clang of the old brass bell that had hung over the Chuckwagon's door for years. Maddie insisted the bell had once hung around the neck of her great-great-grandmother's favorite goat so the milking nanny wouldn't be lost on the trek west with the wagon train. Like the Butlers, many residents of Dorland and the quad-county were folks who were descended from the pioneers of the early and mid-1800s. There wasn't a coward among them, and Cody wasn't about to let a Butler be the first.

The cool air of the air-conditioned diner felt like a refreshing balm on his skin after the sweltering temperature outside, but Cody knew it wouldn't take too long for things to begin to heat up inside the Chuckwagon.

Most of the tables were taken by the evening dinner crowd. Ronny Doyle, sitting at a table just to the right of the door, was the first to see him.

"Hey, Cody." He motioned to an empty chair at his table. "Carl and me was just talking 'bout you. What the hell's going on out at your place with your herd?"

Cody pulled the empty chair out from the table, turned it around, and straddling the seat, sat down. Facing the room, he rested his forearms on the back of the chair. There hadn't been any time wasted in pleasantries, not even a friendly "how're you doing." Ronny had gotten right down to business, and it seemed as though everyone in the diner had heard him. The buzz of conversation that had filled the room when he first came in was now replaced by silence. Even the George Strait song on the jukebox ended, and no selection moved up to take its place.

Slowly looking around, Cody took stock of everyone in the diner. Sam Bailey and Jeff Granger were at the next table, and Bo Dillman and Wayne Dustin were in a booth against the far wall with Buck and Jet Linderman. Carl Nesbitt and Tink Baker were sprawled in their chairs at a table in the middle of the room. Bobby Brindle and Pud Martin were having dinner with their wives in the middle booth, and Louie Cobb was treating his kids to a pizza at the counter. There were so many familiar faces that Cody couldn't help thinking that it looked as though someone had called a special meting of the C.C.A. Maybe someone had.

His gaze traveled from table to table, friend to friend. None offered a cheerful greeting except for Louie's kids, who gave him tomato-sauce and pepperoni-filled grins. A second later Cody knew he must have looked like a ridiculous cartoon character doing a classic double take as his gaze slid by the occupants in the corner booth and then snapped back to them again. He'd forgotten about the patrol car and the Mercedes outside. What were Shaye Frazier and Julie Prine doing in here . . . together?

Julie waved. "Hey, Cody."

"Julie, good to see you." His gaze moved to Shaye, and for a shadow of a moment he wondered if she would acknowledge him. She'd walked away from him less than two hours ago when she was at the ranch. Shaye offered a slight smile, then dropped her attention to the nearly empty plate on the table in front of her. Cody didn't know why he'd expected more . . . wanted more. The woman was firmly situated in Hubbard's camp, but damn, why was she always around when he was at his worst . . . not that he'd had the opportunity to be at his best for the last week or so. *Hasn't she seen me lose enough of my pride already?* He wasn't sure if what he was feeling was regret or embarrassment.

"Word is that you pulled your steers outta the sale. Are you gonna tell us what's going on?" Wayne Dillman asked, dragging Cody's attention away from Shaye.

Maddie placed a glass of iced lemonade on the table in

front of him. After looking up and thanking her, Cody took a long drink, his taste buds rebelling for an instant against the tart flavor. He took a second swallow, then answered Wayne Dillman's question. "I've pulled my sale entries because Doc Campbell has my herd under quarantine."

"So what we've heard *is* right. You've got a damn brucellosis outbreak at your place!" Tink Baker charged, his booming voice filling the room.

Cody hoped the mental flinch he made at the sound of the word hadn't outwardly exposed itself to anyone. His gaze strayed once more to the corner booth where Shaye sat. He found her staring back at him. A slight frown creased her forehead, but her eyes gave no clue about what she was thinking. A moment passed until she gave a nearly imperceptible nod. Encouragement? The very idea puzzled him. Warmed him. Worried him. *You're seeing things, Butler. You'd damn well better remember . . . your loss is her gain.*

He turned back to the question. "No, Tink, what you've all heard *isn't* right. My herd's had an outbreak, that's true, but Doc Campbell's pretty sure it's hoof-and-mouth. When the lab results come in, they'll back up his diagnosis." Cody drained the glass of lemonade, allowing the crushed ice to ride against his teeth as he drank. Setting the glass back on the table in a puddle of condensation, he continued. "The federal ag boys are supposed to get here in a couple of days, and they'll do their own tests. Right now we don't know where the virus came from, but we're hoping to figure it out and work out the best plan for cure and containment."

"Well, this is a hell of a deal, Butler. We gotta hear 'bout this from somebody else before you come crawling into town to tell us. It's a damn good thing other folks have our best interests in mind . . . even if you don't." Sam Bailey's cutting words gained agreements from the two Granger brothers who were sitting with him.

Cody was hit by mixed emotions. Anger and hurt seemed an odd combination, and they didn't mix too well in his gut, either. "Nobody's doing any crawling, Sam, and I'm not going to argue with you about when and where you should've heard about this. Let's just say that I've got a pretty good idea *who* you heard it from, and believe me, the source isn't reliable. Your informant didn't have the facts nor the authority to tell anybody anything."

He glanced about the room once more, seeing worried faces, angry faces, and some that even held a touch of pity. Cody easily understood the fear these men were feeling. The anger was expected, too. Any one of them could go home after enjoying Maddie's cooking and discover their herds were sick, their livelihoods in jeopardy. It was the pity he didn't want, the pity that was all over Bobby's and Kitty Brindle's faces. One question kept coming to Cody's mind . . . where were the solid friendships that he and his father before him had forged with these folks? Shouldn't they count for something? Especially trust?

"When the lab tests come in, I'll let you know what they say. I'm not going to keep anything from you," Cody said, making eye contact with every rancher in the room . . . and one Boston lawyer. "Yes, hoof-and-mouth can kill, and depending on how bad things are, sometimes you gotta destroy your herd, that's the worst scenario. We all know what happened in England. But most often an infected herd will just get sick, nothing more; that's why we vaccinate them." His gaze swept the room again. "The downside is that a sick steer can't go to the stockyards for a while, and he won't look like any blue-ribbon winner for a few months."

"Yeah, and in the meantime we're losing money on vet bills and drugs," Jet Linderman stated. "We've got a herd of unsalable steers that are losing pounds and cost a ton of money to feed back again to sale weight."

"The damn stuff spreads like a curse," Buck Linderman, Jet's twin brother, added. "It'll go through a herd like wildfire. They destroyed whole herds in Europe."

"Cody," Pud Martin said, drawing Cody's attention from the Linderman brothers, "I've known your family since I was a boy, your grandpa taught me how to fly-fish. I've respected every Butler I ever met, but you got to understand, son, I raise beef to sell, to make my living, to feed my family and pay my bills, not just to keep the grass mowed. This thing's got me damned worried."

"And what are ya gonna do if that test comes back and says you're wrong? What are *we* supposed to do then? It started in your herd, and dammit, I'd say you're responsible for any losses we have." Carl Nesbitt hit the tabletop with his fist, punctuating his charge.

"I can't afford to lose any more money this year," Ronny Doyle added. "Tess had surgery, and then I had to dig a new well after my pond dried up. If my cattle get sick, I might as well pack everything in and try my hand flipping burgers at McDonald's."

"Ain't gonna be no burgers to flip if this damn thing spreads," Carl Nesbitt countered. "We all might as well start raising chickens."

"It's kinda hard to put a brand on a chicken," Louie Cobb interrupted, turning away from the counter. "You guys ever smell burnin' feathers? They used to burn feathers and use 'em like smellin' salts in the old days. My grandma told me she—"

"Shut up, Louie," Carl Nesbitt broke in. "Ain't nobody gonna brand a chicken, for gawd's sake. Sometimes you're worse'n an old maid with a panty knot in her crotch."

"Hey, listen up, guys," Julie interrupted, her voice rising above all the rest. "Why don't y'all give Cody a break." She shot exasperated glares at both Louie and Carl. "You're acting like he had this outbreak on purpose." She glanced about the room with a disgusted look on her face and slowly shook her head. "You folks really surprise me.

I've seen y'all pull together, stand elbow-to-elbow while stacking sandbags when the river rose up two years ago. I've seen y'all pitch in and take care of Jeff's ranch work for him when he went to his dad's funeral in Tulsa last year. I know how much you all gave to the high school band program so the kids could go to state competition last May. So don't you think you could give Cody a little support here and quit tearing him apart?"

"Don'tcha think you're a little close to the situation yourself to be doin' any bitchin' at us, Julie?" Carl Nesbitt challenged. "It stands to reason that you're gonna stick up for Butler. Without his ranch and herd, Gene doesn't have a job. Right?" He leaned back in his chair, an insolent smirk on his face as he looked from Julie to Shaye and back again. "So are you and Glenn Hubbard's sweet-piece little lady lawyer just enjoyin' some girly talk, or are you makin' sure it ain't gonna cost you too much for Gene to get a top job with Hubbard when Butler goes under?"

"You son of a bitch!" Cody didn't know what angered him more, Nesbitt's attack on Julie or the insinuation that Shaye could be bought off. He quickly rose from his chair, surprised to see Shaye had beat both him and Julie to their feet.

He'd never seen green eyes get so hot and fiery before in his life. It was obvious that Shaye was furious, clear to the bone, but he was amazed to see the check she held on her anger. Her outward appearance seemed coldly composed, only her eyes, her tightly clenched hand, and the swaying strand of hair over her cheek told the truth. Fascinated, he watched her tuck the curl behind her ear and calmly move toward Carl Nesbitt as though she were walking across a court room.

"You have me at a disadvantage, sir," Shaye coolly said, stopping within a few feet of where Carl Nesbitt sat. "You seem to know who I am, but I don't have *any* idea who you are."

Cody watched as a smirk moved into place on Carl's face and the insolent swagger in his posture increased. It was obvious the man had completely missed the condescending edge to Shaye's tone.

"My name's Carl, baby, and you're the girl of my dreams." He guffawed, and glanced around the room as if expecting to receive accolades from the other men.

Shaye clasped her hands behind her back in good lawyerly fashion, paced a few steps away, and then turned and looked down at Carl again. A slight arc tilted her left brow. Cody sat down. The show was getting good, and he wanted a front-row seat.

"Ah, Carl," Shaye replied with a slight nod, offering a "butter wouldn't melt in my mouth" smile. "You're right, Carl, I do work for Glenn Hubbard . . . as his lawyer. And how astute you are—you're also right on point number two, Julie and I are enjoying some girl talk."

Cody watched as Shaye paused and seemed to allow Carl the opportunity to increase his self-satisfied smirk, which he did without delay. Cody nearly laughed out loud. The jerk was hanging himself.

"But let me tell you something you don't know," Shaye continued, the soft timbre of her voice turning to steel as she took a couple of steps toward Carl Nesbitt. "I'm not anybody's 'piece.' My business with Glenn Hubbard is just that, *my* business, Carl. I want you to remember that. I am a lady, but some folks will tell you I'm not so sweet." She took a few more steps toward Carl Nesbitt, her mouth curving in a scornful smile. "You might think I'm the girl of your dreams, but I just might be your worst nightmare."

Shaye turned on her heel and began to march back to the booth where Julie sat with her mouth agape. After five or six steps, Shaye stopped and slowly turned once again and hit every rancher in the room with her I-mean-business gaze. "You know, I've always heard that communities such as Dorland were the backbone of this country, built from

the pioneering spirit of their grandfathers . . . great-grand-
fathers . . . great-great grandfathers; where neighbor stood
up for neighbor and where long-term friendships meant
you helped each other out when things got tough." She
shrugged. "But then, I'm just a big-city girl where muggings happen every day in the city's parks and streets,
where no one will stop and help you if you're in trouble,
so what the hell do I know about you *good* people."

The grin on Carl Nesbitt's face dissolved, and he
straightened up in his chair as if someone had kicked him
in the butt. The whir of the air conditioner and a few self-
conscious coughs were the only sounds in the room until
Maddie stepped out from behind the counter with a pitcher
of lemonade in her hand.

"I'm buyin' the ladies a drink, boys. So if you're done
making asses of yourselves, I'd suggest y'all pay your tabs
and go home. Let Cody take care of his problems. He'll tell
ya what's going on when he can."

Most of the men rose from their chairs. After digging in
their pockets, they left money on the tables for their meals
and moved toward the front door, one or two mumbling a
few words as they passed Cody.

"Hope everything works out for ya with the ag boys,
Cody."

"It's a damn shame, Butler, what with everything hittin'
ya at once."

"Hang in there, son. We're prayin' for ya."

Shaking a few of the ranchers' hands as he stood, Cody
then crossed the room to the booth where Shaye sat with
Julie. The surprised look on her face when he settled in on
the bench beside her was worth the trip. "Thanks," he said.
"I appreciate you sticking up for me." His long legs didn't
fit comfortably in the confines of the booth and his thigh
pressed against her leg. The heat of the contact surprised
him, teased him.

"I didn't stick up just for you," Shaye replied, looking

down where their legs met and touched. For a moment she seemed mesmerized, but in the next tick of time she pulled away and moved as far into the corner of the seat as she could and placed her purse on the seat between them. "I was sticking up for myself. I don't like being talked about as though I were a piece of . . . merchandise. And I definitely didn't like my integrity, and in this case Julie's integrity, being questioned."

"So all that stuff about community and taking care of your friends and neighbors was just all hogwash?"

Shaye looked stunned for a moment, and for that moment Cody was sorry he'd goaded her.

"No," she replied, moving out of the corner of the seat. She placed her hands primly on the tabletop and faced his challenge. "Sometimes good people just need to be reminded of these things." She picked up her purse. "Now, if you'll excuse me, I have to go." She looked at Julie. "Thanks for the burger and conversation." She looked up at Cody and neither spoke as their eyes locked and held. Shaye finally broke the silence. "Move . . . please." She prodded him with her elbow.

Disappointment jabbed harder than Shaye's elbow. Cody looked at Julie for support and received only a noncommittal shrug. He didn't want Shaye to leave, and that in itself was trouble. He wanted to spend some more time with her, get to know her better—not as Hubbard's attorney, but as herself. And that was very big trouble.

He slid out of the booth and reached out to help her stand. She reluctantly gave him her hand, a hand that felt too soft and too comfortable in his own. When she looked up at him, there was a vulnerability in her eyes that took him by surprise. The woman had done it again. She'd made him feel as though any moment he'd lose his balance and fall . . . physically and emotionally. And then, acting like an immature ten-year-old, regretting it the moment he opened his big mouth, he gave one last prod. "So, are you *my* worst nightmare?"

Her guileless expression disappeared, replaced by what Cody didn't want to think was pity. "No," she replied, her voice soft, a near whisper. "You've got nightmares enough without me."

Pressing her body against Gene's hard frame, Julie smiled, enjoying the delicious after-sex glow that saturated her body. She watched his fingers trail lightly around her nipples in a lazy figure eight, then down through the valley between her breasts and farther down to trace circles around her belly button. Her nipples pebbled into hard buds, and goose bumps rose up all over her skin. "If you do that much longer, cowboy, I'm gonna have to arrest you."

"Got your handcuffs handy?"

"Right here, darlin'." She reached up and flipped the chrome-plated police-issue cuffs hanging on the bedpost. The cuffs clinked merrily against the brass headboard.

"You gotta catch me first," Gene murmured against her ear.

"I've already done that." Julie laughed, moving her hand between his legs and taking hold of his ebbing erection. "But I'll do it again," she whispered, slowly pumping her hand up and down, "if you insist."

"Enough, woman! Eight's my limit."

"You wish," Julie countered, playfully nipping his arm.

"Ouch!"

She snuggled closer, cupped her stilled hand around him, and placed her head on his shoulder. "Guess who I met today."

"Hmmm," Gene pondered for a moment. "Tom Cruise?"

"No . . . better."

"Harrison Ford?"

"I wish . . . but no."

"Sean Connery?"

"Wrong sex and a lot more interesting."

"Now you've really got me curious."

"Give up?"

"Yup."

"Shaye Frazier."

"Who?"

"Gene, you know . . . Glenn Hubbard's new lawyer."

"Oh, *that* Shaye Frazier." Gene's tease was met with a slap to the flat of his stomach. He barely flinched. "Yeah, me, too. Well, I didn't meet her, but I did see her today . . . at Medicine Creek."

"So what do you think?"

Gene raised himself up on one elbow and looked down at Julie. "What do I think about what?"

"You know . . . Cody and Shaye." Julie almost laughed aloud at the stunned look that crossed Gene's face. Men were so darned transparent at times. "So?"

"You mean Cody and Shaye . . . together?"

"Bingo!"

"Oh, no . . . no . . . definitely not," Gene argued. "You're kidding, right?" He paused and took another close look at Julie. "No, you're not kidding." He flopped back down on the bed with an exasperated sigh. "Aw, honey, please, no matchmaking, okay? And definitely not between those two. Cody's got enough on his mind right now. Between the bank and his cattle, he doesn't need to add a woman to the mix. Least of all, *that* woman. She's Hubbard's lawyer, for God's sake. Are you crazy?"

Julie allowed a knowing little smile to tweak her lips as she moved her fingers lightly over him and felt him harden beneath her touch, and she finally answered his question. "Maybe yes . . . maybe no."

Chapter Six

Cody settled into the chair at the kitchen table and looked out the window. The rising sun pinked the eastern sky, giving promise to another hot day. Although a little rain would be nice—his grazing lands and retention ponds could use the water—the wet and the mud would make dealing with his sick cattle a miserable chore. Yeah, he'd gladly suffer dry and hot a while longer.

Stifling a yawn, he reached for the yellow box of cereal and finally answered the question Maribeth had greeted him with when he'd first come down stairs. "I'm sorry, Tater, the answer is no. I don't have time to go. There's too much to do around here. Besides, I'm still waiting for a call from California about the polo horses." He opened the box and dumped a pile of cereal into his bowl. "Why don't you ask Roscoe to take you?" He glanced up in time to see a pout puff out Maribeth's bottom lip.

"Roscoe's riding on the pioneer float in the parade and has to go early. I don't want to get there at eight and have to sit around all day. Besides, I want *you* to take me. I want *you* to go. Cody, please." Maribeth clasped her hands in true beggarly form. "It's a holiday." She passed him the carton of milk. "The picnic doesn't start until noon, and the games don't begin until later, and then after supper there's always fireworks." She retrieved a spoon from the cutlery drawer for Cody and, sitting down, held it just out of his reach. "We've never missed the Fourth of July picnic . . . we'd always go when Mom and Dad . . . when all of us were . . ."

Cody leaned forward and grabbed the spoon out of Maribeth's hand, angry with himself because sometimes he forgot that she had lost her parents, too. "Things were a lot different then," he mumbled, driving the spoon into his cereal.

"We're the defending three-legged race champions. We've got to go. You don't want Carl Nesbitt and his ugly kid to win it this year, do you? Tim told me they've been practicing real hard in the parking lot behind the Co-op."

With the spoon raised to his lips, milk dripping over the rim, Cody looked at his young sister. "Do we have to discuss this now? The sun is barely up, and I've got a full day ahead of me." He paused and frowned. "By the way, what are you doing up so darned early?"

"This is the only time of day I can track you down." She slightly tilted her head, and her mouth curved into a mischievous grin. "I suppose I could wait till you're in bed sound asleep, wake you up, and then ask you."

Cody sighed. "Tater . . . it's just not a good time for me to be going off on picnics. Besides, I gave the hands the day off for the Fourth, which leaves me to do all the chores by myself."

"It's just for one afternoon, and I can help you. I'll feed and water the mares and foals. I'll even clean their stalls if you want me to."

Cody slowly chewed on a mouthful of Cheerios, hoping to come up with an idea that would get Maribeth off his back about the Fourth of July picnic. The last place he wanted to be was smack dab in the midst of the whole community with questions flying at him from all over the place about how his cattle were doing, how many were sick or had died, and whether or not he'd sell out to Hubbard.

The unpleasant scene in town at the Chuckwagon two days earlier quickly replayed in his mind. No, he definitely didn't want to go through that again. "Hey, I've got a great idea. How about calling Bonnie Linderman and ask her if she'd mind picking you up when they go? You like the Linderman kids, don't you?"

"No."

Exasperated, he dropped the spoon. It careened off the edge of the bowl and onto the table. "Aw, Tater, please . . . come on, help me out here. I'm trying to hang on to everything we've got, and it's like waltzing with a wet octopus. Be a little understanding, will you?"

"Understanding? You want me to be understanding?" Maribeth jumped to her feet, her chair hitting the wall. "You don't think I understand about the financial trouble we've got? You don't think I understand what might happen if we lose the ranch? You don't think I understand about those sick and dying steers? Yeah, I guess you don't think I'm understanding." She drew a deep breath, leaned back against the wall, and looked as though she was going to cry. "Cody, our problems don't have to gobble up every bit of our lives, do they? One afternoon isn't going to make a difference, except maybe help take our minds off our troubles for a little while. Please say yes, say you'll go."

"No, Tater. Not this year." He felt like a heel.

Pushing away from the wall, she stood over him, her hands on her hips. "Don't you think you're being darned selfish, Cody Butler? I certainly do."

Up to that point Cody was just annoyed with the constant begging and whining, and maybe a little sympathetic to her tears, but Maribeth's last remark scraped a raw nerve. How in the billy blue blazes could she think for one second that he was being selfish? He was working his butt off, day and night, to keep a home for them.

Without tempering his anger, he allowed his words to bite back, knowing that he sounded every bit like the child he accused Maribeth of being. "You could always call your new friend, Shaye. I'm sure she'd like nothing better than to go to an old Fourth of July town picnic with a bunch of cowboys and their families. I bet she's never been to one. It'd give her something to laugh about with all her yuppie friends when she gets back to the big city."

Maribeth threw her hands up. "Fine, just *fine*. If you want to be that way, never mind. I won't go." She plopped into the chair across the table from him. "And Cody, you've really got to get with it. The word *yuppie* went out of style about five years ago." She paused for a moment, just long enough to rearrange her freckled face into a scowl. "You know, thanks to you my summer vacation is sucking big time!"

Maribeth slouched farther down in her chair, crossed her arms over her chest, and pouted again. This time her bottom lip stuck out so far, Cody was positive that with a little Michael Jordan finesse, he could land one of the cereal *O*'s from his bowl on the middle of her lip without any trouble. Instead, he reached for the jar of peanut butter, spun the lid off, and shook his head in wonder. "Since when did you become such a whiner?"

"Oh, gee, let me see," Maribeth replied. "Maybe it was after all the hassle you gave me about Tim Mallory. Maybe it was when you told me I couldn't wear a two-piece bathing suit until I was thirty. Oh, golly, maybe it's just the way you keep treating me like I'm a child!"

"Tater"—Cody sighed—"cut the melodrama. We've been through all this before. And when you act like this, you *are* a child." He shoved the empty cereal bowl away and picking up a piece of cold toast from the plate, began to slather it with peanut butter.

"You might have a really good time if you went, Cody. It might even be good for you. It would take your mind off things around here for a while and show folks that you're not burying yourself in your problems. Please, say yes."

The sound of Maribeth's voice had changed, the whine had disappeared. A softer, more mature tone had taken its place. He looked up and for the first time saw the young woman that was evolving out of who only months before had been a tomboy with pigtails and skinned knees. Just as a butterfly changed from pupa to chrysalis to winged magnificence, Maribeth was changing, growing into her own beauty.

A current of panic surged through him. Did they teach about those puberty things in health class at her school? Did she know about all the changes that were going to be happening to her? Did she know how to deal with them? Another thought quickly followed and slapped him hard. Had any of those changes started yet? And if not, how much longer did he have before he had to give her the "facts of life" lecture? He licked a glob of peanut butter off his thumb. Hell, what *was* the "facts of life" lecture for girls?

He'd only gotten the one for boys, and by the time his dad had taken him out riding in the hills to give him the whole lecture, he'd already figured out most of it on his own. After sneaking a couple of peeks during breeding season, he was familiar with the mechanics; Ronny Doyle had provided even more graphic details after spying on his older sister and her boyfriend in the hayloft; the finesse came later with dedication, some hayloft groping of his own with Connie Granger, and his fair share of practice.

"Damn," Cody mumbled, this was another problem he'd have to deal with . . . and soon.

He lifted his glass of milk and downed the remaining few swallows, watching Maribeth as the milk poured down his throat. The poor kid was dealing with his problems, too. A day didn't go by when she wasn't trying to bolster him up by telling him that somehow the money for the loan would come in, that the steers would get better, that Hubbard wasn't going to get the ranch. Her summer really *was* sucking big time. The poor kid deserved much better.

The federal agriculture office had called yesterday when he was out on the western ridge bringing in five more sick steers. The message the agent had left on his answering machine said that with the holiday weekend, their veterinarian wouldn't be out to examine the herd until Tuesday or Wednesday. Under other circumstances Cody probably would have been mad as a hornet for the delay. As it was, he welcomed the extra days of reprieve. He might as well make good use of them.

"You know, Tater, if you wanted to do an A-1 job of buttering me up, you should've cooked me a big breakfast: bacon, eggs, potatoes, biscuits, gravy . . . the works." Rising from his chair, he headed to the sink with his dirty dishes. After giving them a good rinse and stacking them on the drainboard, he turned around. "Okay, you win. We'll leave about twelve, that'll give me time to get some work done around here, and we'll still get to the picnic in time to defend our three-legged title."

Maribeth jumped up and leaped into his arms, the force pushing him back against the counter. "Yes! Oh, Cody, you're the best, the very best. Thank you! Thank you! You're going to have so much fun, you'll see, I promise."

"Yeah, right," Cody grouched, extricating himself from Maribeth's tangle of arms and wiping the evidence of her wet kisses from his cheek. He headed out the back door, wondering if Shaye was going to be at the picnic, wondering how many friends he had left among the ranchers who usually congregated around the iced keggers, wondering how many more steers he'd find had been added to the quarantine pens this morning.

•   •   •

Shaye slowly woke, stretched, and yawned. Glancing at her bedside clock, she found it was after ten. No wonder the room was so bright. The sun shone through the windows gilting everything it touched, and dust motes danced in the golden beams. In another half hour the sun's rays would have reached her bed, waking her with its heat.

After going to bed last night she had tossed and turned for hours before finally falling asleep. Reading hadn't helped, either. Her concentration kept wandering away from the new romance novel she'd bought; the hero with his dark good looks, his Indian heritage and sardonic manner kept reminding her of Cody Butler. Finally, a little after three, she'd drifted off to sleep, and from the jumbled mess of the bedsheets, the pillow on the floor, and the mangled paperback book, it was easy to see that she'd spent a very restless night.

The ringing of the telephone on the bedside table startled her, and she almost knocked over her clock reaching for the cordless phone. "Hello."

"Hey, Boston, what are you doing on the Fourth?"

"Julie?"

"Yeah, it's me. Did I wake you up?"

"Oh, no, I'm up," Shaye replied, quickly swinging her legs over the edge of the mattress and standing. She finger-combed her tousled hair and padded across the room to look out at the half-gone morning.

"So what's your answer? What are you doing on the Fourth?"

"I don't know," Shaye answered, watching Hub running up the driveway, returning later than usual from his morning jog. "I really haven't given it any thought. I don't suppose Hub has any special plans. Why?"

"I want you to come to the Fourth of July picnic with Gene and Tim and me. It's a big community affair with great food, fun times, and a really nice fireworks display in the evening. How about it?"

Every fiber of Shaye's being told her to say no. She didn't want to get involved in community affairs, or affairs of any kind, for that matter. Even a friendship with Julie would make it difficult to leave and begin her new life when her job for Hub was finished. "Julie, I don't know." Shaye frowned as she turned away from the window and headed for the bathroom. She cradled the telephone between her shoulder and ear while she turned the tub faucets and dumped some lilac-scented bath salts into the water. "I don't know anyone, and it might be a little . . . awkward what with me working for Hubbard. I imagine there are some ranchers who think he's taken advantage of their friends' misfortunes. Thanks anyway for the invitation, but I think I should pass."

"Don't be silly. You'll have a great time. We'll pick you up about ten-thirty. I want to get there early to find a real nice picnic spot. Wear jeans or shorts, something comfortable, and bring a sweater in case it gets chilly in the evening. Don't worry about a lawn chair, we've got plenty."

"Julie, at least let me think about it, and I'll get back with you later?" Shaye really didn't want to go, but she didn't want to hurt Julie's feelings either. If given a day or two, maybe she could fabricate a believable reason for not going.

"Nope. This is Thursday and on Thursdays I don't take any 'no' or 'I'll think about it' answers," Julie countered. "I gotta run, see you on the Fourth."

"Julie . . ." Shaye quickly realized she was talking into a dead line. Julie had hung up.

Resigned to a date for a Fourth of July picnic with Julie and her boyfriend, Shaye slipped out of her Mickey Mouse nightshirt and stepped into the tub, slowly easing her body down into the hot water. Leaning against the back of the tub, she closed her eyes and began to relax. In an instant she bolted upright, splashing water over the lip of the tub and onto the marble floor.

Julie had asked her the afternoon they'd spent together at the diner what she thought about Cody. At the time Shaye remembered not giving much credence to the questions, but now . . . was it possible that inviting her to the picnic was a setup? Was Julie playing matchmaker? It was possible, but no, she didn't want to think her new friend would do something that devious. Shaye figured that Cody would be there, but she hoped Bunny had snagged him for a picnic date as well as the Cowboy Ball.

She settled back in the water, a despairing groan escaping her lips. There was no way she could head back to Boston until after the deal for the Butler ranch had been solidified—one way or the other—and until then she'd just have to face the fact that she could run into Cody Butler anytime, anywhere.

Shaye unconsciously rubbed her hand up and down her right thigh, the soap causing a sensuous glide of skin against skin. When Cody sat down beside her at the Chuckwagon, his leg had pressed against hers. She remembered the unsettling sensations that the simple contact had caused, the total awareness of that contact, and the arousing quickening that raced through her. Her body's betrayal had startled her.

She suddenly realized the track her fingers were taking up and down her soapy leg and immediately dropped her hand into the hot water. If just the touch of his leg against hers could cause so much turmoil, what would a kiss bring? She shook her head. Thinking about these things was ridiculous. Thinking about these things was pointless. Thinking about these things was dangerous. Granted the man was attractive, but she had decided when Michael died that she was through with men. One marriage, one cheating husband, and three unhappy years were enough. There was no room in her life or her future plans for any kind of a relationship with a man other than a professional one, the kind that would further her legal career . . . the safe kind.

With her mental ducks all neatly back in place, Shaye relaxed. Okay, she'd go with Julie and Gene to the picnic, and if Cody Butler showed up, so what. If she could successfully handle the many legal cases she'd dealt with over the past few years, she could surely handle one Wyoming cowboy. Couldn't she?

"Well, did he bite?" Roscoe asked, shoving the last load of dirty clothes into the washing machine.

"Yup," Maribeth smugly replied, retrieving the still-warm, clean laundry from the dryer, "just like a hungry bass going after a juicy, juicy worm. I'm getting pretty good at this. Maybe I should go for bigger stakes, a car, a date with Tim Mallory . . . what do you think?"

"Harrumph," Roscoe grunted. "I think you better slow down and stick to one plan at a time. And speaking of plans, how'd Julie do with her little job?"

Maribeth gave Roscoe a thumbs-up. "We're all set there, too. I don't believe how easy this was."

"Well, don't go getting yourself all worked up. There's still a lot to do. Has anyone told Cody yet that she's not married, that she's a widow?"

"Oops." Maribeth flinched. "I forgot." She placed the folded clean clothes into the laundry basket and turned to leave.

Roscoe breathed an exasperated sigh, and shook a gnarled finger at her. "This whole plan ain't gonna work unless Cody knows. You gotta tell him."

"I know, I know. I'll tell him on the Fourth while we're driving to town, I promise. I'll slip it into our conversation."

"Don't forget, it's very important."

"Don't worry, I'll do it."

"Okay." Roscoe gave a decisive nod. "Has anyone figured out how we're gonna get 'em together at the park?"

"Julie's going to call me later, and we'll figure that out, but I'll keep you posted."

Roscoe dumped some soap into the washer and closed the lid. "I don't know what all to expect, but I bet there's gonna be more'n one kind of fireworks at that Fourth of July picnic."

Chapter Seven

The large oak not only offered shade, but the drape of its branches provided camouflage as well, giving Cody the opportunity to look around the park, to see who all was here without being seen. He felt like a coward, but he certainly didn't want a replay of how things had gone at the Chuckwagon a few days before. Sure, there'd be questions, he expected that. He just didn't want to be grilled as if he was on trial; after all, all the evidence wasn't in yet.

Maribeth had already run off and joined up with her friends from school. By now the kids were heading for the amusement rides that Big Bob's Carnival Company set up each year. Every picnic table was occupied, and the blankets that other picnickers had spread out on the freshly mowed grass made a crazy quilt of bright colors. Some folks tailgating out of the backs of their pickups had even brought their portable barbecues. Families from all over the county had come to town to celebrate the nation's birthday.

Off to his left Emmaline and Cynthia Bradshaw, sisters by blood and spinsterhood, sat chatting with the Presbyterian minister's wife. A little farther across the wide lawn, Jet Linderman's boys were arguing over a fried chicken leg. Cody chuckled as their dog benefitted most, grabbing the drumstick one boy held away from the other, then running off with the prize.

In the large gazebo in the center of the park, a local country band offered their renditions of Reba's and Garth's hits without mutilating them too much, and in front of the gazebo on the portable dance floor, five or six couples were executing the latest two-step maneuvers. To the west side of the park at the edge of the line of traders' stalls, business at the cotton candy booth was booming, and across the way the ladies from the Methodist Church auxiliary were doing quick business at their popular bake sale table.

If Norman Rockwell had ever painted a community Fourth of July picnic, he would have painted today in Dorland, Wyoming.

A burning sensation touched and lodged in Cody's throat. It then spread like wildfire, causing an ache that reached into the depths of his soul. This was just another piece of the whole . . . the whole that made him who he was. He'd lived here all of his life, these people were his people, this community was his community, but like quicksilver, he could feel it all slipping through his fingers.

"Cody, over here."

The canopy of the wide-spread oak obviously wasn't as good a camouflage as he'd thought.

"Over here," Gene Mallory called again. "I was beginning to worry that you'd changed your mind about coming. What took you so long?"

"I gave you guys the day off, remember?" Cody answered, putting a reluctant smile on his face as he moved away from the tree. "Somebody had to feed and water, and staple a loose fence wire or two."

"Yeah, so while Maribeth and Roscoe were doin' that, what were you up to?" Gene gave Cody's shoulder a playful punch. "Come on, the girls'll be back soon. They've gone to buy one of Bonnie Linderman's famous raspberry pies. I got left with the job of cranking the ice-cream maker. Now that you're here, you can take over."

"Girls?" Cody braced himself for the answer to his next question. "Bunny Gibson's not with you guys, is she?" Cody watched a quick secretive smile move over Gene's lips and then disappear.

"Nope, Julie invited Shaye Frazier."

Cody almost jumped out of his boots. He certainly hadn't expected that answer. "Julie did *what?*"

Gene shot him a sheepish look. "Julie met her the other day. She liked her . . . and . . ."

"And?" Cody pressed. "She's Hubbard's front man . . . uh . . . person, for gawd's sake. Hell, I can't say anything without her reporting back to Hubbard." He shook his head. "What am I supposed to do, be Mr. Congenial and pretend she isn't here to get everything I own?"

"Come on, Cody," Gene coaxed. "It's a holiday. Julie thought inviting her was the neighborly thing to do. She seems real nice. I bet she won't talk business if you don't."

"Since when did a lawyer ever back off when a nice paycheck was involved?"

"Okay, we all agree lawyers are barracudas." Gene laughed. "Now, let's put that and your problems away for the rest of the day and have a great time."

Gene laid his hand on Cody's back and propelled him toward one of the picnic tables. A bright blue-and-white checkered cloth covered the tabletop, and a canning jar of wild ferns and brilliant golden yellow black-eyed Susans decorated the center. Two coolers and the ice-cream maker sat on the ground beside the table. Half a dozen lawn chairs were grouped together in a semicircle beside a nearby shade tree. Cozy, Cody thought, just the touch that a woman would give to a picnic. If it were just him and Gene there'd have been little more than a six-pack or two of beer, a sack of burgers from the local drive-through, and an empty pie plate—one of Bonnie Linderman's raspberry pies would have been the only constant.

Gene thrust an ice-cold beer at Cody.

"No, thanks." He shook his head. "Got a Coke? I've decided to go clean for a while." Cody accepted a can of soda and flipped the pop tab. He took a long pull of the cold drink, enjoying the icy burn as it slid down his throat. "By the way, I've got some chips and stuff in the truck. I think Roscoe brought some things, too."

"I told you guys not to bring anything." Gene opened a beer for himself, sat down on one of the coolers, and began turning the crank on the ice-cream machine. "Julie's had this planned for weeks."

"The part about inviting Hubbard's lawyer, too?"

"There's no lawyer here, Cody Butler, so quit your bellyaching. Today she's just my friend."

At the sound of Julie's voice, Cody swung around and bumped into Shaye, almost spilling the rest of his cola down the front of her shirt. Quick fumbling and a lucky catch saved the moment. "Phew, that was close," he muttered, giving her a meager smile. The light scent of her perfume, a sandalwood fragrance, touched his nostrils and zapped him like a velvet blow below the belt. The effect this woman had on him was unfair. Not only unfair, but damn it, she kept ambushing him, and he still hadn't figured out how to handle it. When he spoke again, his voice was little more than a grunt. "Hi."

"Hello," Shaye replied with similar reserve, backing a few steps away.

"Well, that was nice." Julie laughed. "Somewhat painless . . . civilized. It could use a little work, but I'm encouraged." She glanced down at the pie in her hands. "Let's eat this beautiful thing so we can go get another."

As he turned to follow Julie and the pie to the picnic table, Cody felt a light touch. He didn't have to turn around

to know whose hand rested on his arm. The heat, the arousing heat, told him all.

"I told Julie it wasn't a good idea for me to be here
today," Shaye offered.

He liked the husky quality to her voice. The sound went
right to the special trigger that all men have, the one that
when cocked and pulled by a woman's voice, shoots
thoughts of silky underwear and slow afternoon sex
straight to their brains . . . by way of the long way around.

"I want you to know, I did try to decline," Shaye explained. "After all, this is your celebration—yours and
your friends'."

She removed her hand from his arm.

Cody immediately felt the loss. The sensation took him
by surprise and set off his emotional defenses. "It's a free
country, or at least I think that's what the Fourth is all
about."

"I've heard the same rumor." She offered a friendly
smile and dropped her sunglasses from the top of her head,
settling them on the bridge of her nose and covering her
eyes.

"You're saying it's just a rumor?" Cody countered,
wanting to lift her glasses off and have nothing between
his eyes and hers. "Don't all good Boston patriots celebrate the Fourth?"

"Of course we celebrate it," she said, her smile widening. "You might have even heard about our little tea party
that got the whole holiday started."

"Ah, yes, a very *taxing* moment in this country's history." The joke was bad at best, but he wasn't prepared for
her laugh. The darned beautiful, green-eyed woman
laughed at his stupid joke, and the sound ignited a fire-
brand in his chest. He was falling, losing control, his stoic
facade slipping.

"Come on, you two, the ice cream is ready," Julie
called, holding up a couple of plastic spoons. "Gene's al-

ready polished off two pieces of this pie. You'd better hurry if you want your share."

With Gene and Julie smoothing out the occasional rough and stilted edges to the conversation, the next hour passed amiably with everyone consciously avoiding the topic of Hubbard's wildlife preserve, Shaye's job, Cody's sick cattle, or his banknote.

Cody sat back in the lawn chair, sprawled his legs out in front of him, and crossed his ankles, boot over boot, then folded his arms across his chest. He had to admit, relaxing with friends felt good; relaxing and being able to watch the woman who had been on his mind since the day he'd met her felt even better.

He liked the way the sun played tricks with the gold and copper in her hair, he liked watching her hands move gracefully as she helped set things out on the picnic table for their dinner, and he watched her sample the dill dip by sticking the tip of her finger in the bowl, then into her mouth. As if feeling the touch of his scrutiny, she looked at him and offered an embarrassed you-caught-me kind of smile before she winked and dunked her finger again.

Shaye Frazier looked great in jeans, and he couldn't feast his eyes enough on the slender turn of her waist or the curve of her hip. Her T-shirt, a green that almost matched her eyes, fit loosely but did nothing to hide the swell of her breasts before it disappeared—tucked beneath her waistband. The bend of her neck as it sloped into her shoulder also caught his eye, and he wondered how her skin would taste. He wondered if he would be able to feel her pulse against his lips if he pressed his mouth to that delicate spot.

Cody allowed his gaze to chart every inch of her, from brunette head to pretty painted toe. She wore the thin-strapped white sandals again, and he noticed that she'd changed the color of nail polish on her toes. The frosted pink of the other day was now a scarlet red. He knew with an absolute certainty that the Bradshaw sisters had never done anything as scandalous as painting their toenails a sinful, yet patriotic, red.

There was no question. Everything about the woman said sexy and first class, and the way his luck was going, even if Shaye Frazier weren't married, sexy and first class were far beyond his reach.

He really hadn't been surprised to find her here; in fact, he'd hoped she would be. What did surprise him was the easy way she fit in with everyone, from Maribeth to Emmaline Bradshaw, who'd offered to teach her to tat doilies in her spare time.

As conversation ran the gamut of topics, periodically their eyes met and held, they shared a smile or two, and then one or the other would look away—a tango of glances, a dance that parried and accepted, then retreated once again. She fascinated him with her big city style and her country naïveté, a dichotomy that charmed him, enchanted him. A dichotomy that reminded Cody that somewhere in Boston there was a Mr. Frazier.

"It looks like somebody's not doing too good," Gene said, looking across the picnic grounds.

Dragging his gaze away from Shaye, Cody looked up to see Tim Mallory and Roscoe supporting Maribeth between them as she limped toward the picnic table. Cody leaped to his feet. Running to his sister, he swung her up in his arms.

"What happened? What'd you do?" He set Maribeth down in one of the lawn chairs.

"I twisted my stupid ankle playing volleyball." She held up her left foot and winced as Cody's fingers pressed lightly on her ankle. "Ouch! Stop it!"

Shaye quickly knelt beside the chair and lifted Maribeth's pant leg. "Good, there isn't any swelling yet. Gene, please pass me a couple of beers."

"What do you think you're doing?" Cody challenged. "She's underage!"

"Do you happen to have an ice pack in your pocket?"

Shaye looked pointedly at his jeans, then turned her attention back to Maribeth and lightly pressed the ice-cold cans against the girl's ankle. "Here, honey, this will help keep the swelling down." She glanced up at Cody again. "And when we're finished, your brother can put them safely back in the cooler so you won't be tempted to drink them." Her gaze shifted to Cody's friends. "Could someone bring one of the coolers here so she can put her foot up? She needs to keep her ankle elevated."

"Don't bother, I'm going to take her home." Cody moved to scoop Maribeth out of the chair.

"Are you crazy? I twisted my ankle, that's all." Maribeth shoved him away. She crossed her arms over her chest and settled deeper into the chair. "I'm not going anywhere. We've got to defend our three-legged-race title in about fifteen minutes."

"There's not going to be any three-legged race today for you, Tater, and you're crazy if you think you're going to talk me into letting you run. I'd better get Doc Varnum to take a look at you before we go." Cody began to move away.

"No. Don't," Maribeth quickly responded. "I don't need a doctor. I'll be fine in a little while, you'll see. I'll be able to run . . . I hope." She took the cans from Shaye and inspected her ankle. After a few moments she looked up, a worried frown furrowing her brow. "I've just got to be able to run." She pressed the cold cans against her ankle again. "We've got to race, Cody. If I can't pull all my weight on my foot, you could carry me a little, couldn't you? We can still win it. We've gotta win. This is our third year and the rules say that whoever wins the race three times in a row gets to keep the trophy and wins a hundred bucks." Maribeth dropped the cans and clutched at Cody's hand. "But . . . what happens if . . . I can't run? Oh, Cody, we'd have to forfeit wouldn't we?" She held Cody's hand against her cheek for a moment and then looked up, tears rimming her eyes. "We can't forfeit, we just can't." She paused, glanced at Julie and Roscoe, and then suddenly sat up. Her mood brightened. "I've got it . . . you could race with a different partner. Couldn't you?"

Roscoe straightened up after positioning the cooler under Maribeth's foot. "I think the entry just has Cody's name on it. As long as he's running as half the team, it should be okay."

"But he still needs a partner," Maribeth added. "Who can run with him?"

"I guess I could," Gene offered, stepping forward.

"I don't think so, Sweety," Julie said, patting Gene affectionately on the arm. "Don't forget, you've got that bad knee."

"Julie, could you do it? Please say you will," Maribeth pleaded. "You and Cody'd be a super team."

"Oh, honey, I'm real sorry. I can't do it, either." Julie pointed to the bright red ribbon pinned on her shirt. "I'm on the picnic committee. I can't compete in any of the events."

Everyone turned to Shaye . . . everyone but Cody. He could clearly see where this was leading, and he wasn't about to watch his downfall come rushing toward him.

"Well, Miss Legal, it 'pears like you're elected," Roscoe said, tipping his battered Stetson like a gentleman and beaming from ear to ear.

Shaye began to back away, her hands held up in front of her. "Oh, no. It's impossible. No." She shook her head, still backing up. "I can't . . . not with . . . *him* . . . no."

"What's wrong with *him*?" Julie asked, laughing and pushing Shaye back toward Cody.

"He's . . . uh . . . too . . . tall," Shaye stammered, planting her feet firmly against Julie's prodding. "Stop shoving!" She slapped Julie's hands away. "Besides, I . . . uh . . . he'd go too fast. I wouldn't be able to keep up with him."

Cody arched his left brow in a mocking tilt. "Haven't you heard? I'm a gentleman, sweetheart. A gentleman always goes slow and lets a lady catch up. Sometimes we even let them . . . go first." The quick blush that colored her cheeks told him his double entendre had not been missed. Dammit, why did he constantly bait her like that? Besides, what made her think he wanted her for his race partner, either?

Hearing a sniffle, Cody looked down at Maribeth just in time to watch the largest tear he'd ever seen slide down her cheek. In that instant he knew he'd lost the fight. Women had too many kinds of persuasive ammunition, and Maribeth was learning to use them all without shame. He'd always been a sucker for tears. Gritting his teeth and biting back a cuss word that he hadn't used since hitting himself on the thumb with a hammer three months ago, he turned, grabbed Shaye by the wrist, and began hauling her toward the games field. "Come on, city girl, you're about to have the experience of your life."

Shaye couldn't believe what she'd allowed herself to be roped into. And *roped* was the right word. Being tied to Cody Butler, or any man for that matter, was something she hadn't imagined would ever happen to her. She knew she would gladly go through her entire life without the experience, but that wasn't going to happen. Standing on Cody's left, she counted eleven other couples lined up side by side along the starting line. One of the men she'd seen in the diner a few nights earlier moved up and down the line. Carrying strips of bright red cloth, he told each couple how he planned to tie them together, right leg to left. She watched his progress, knowing that in a few minutes she would be tied, calf to calf, thigh to thigh, to Cody Butler.

She turned away, too nervous to watch. Just remembering her body's reaction to the touch of his leg when he'd sat beside her in the booth at the Chuckwagon was enough to send her running . . . not in the race, but in the opposite direction.

A quick glance up the line caused her even more distress. Each runner had their arm around their partner's waist. She supposed it was for balance, but there was no way she was going to get *that* close to Cody . . . no way at all.

The man with the red strips of cloth finished tying the first couple, then the second, the third, and all too soon stood in front of her and Cody. Maybe if she fainted or threw up she could get out of this.

"Hey, Cody. I see ya got a new partner. I had to check the rules to make sure you could switch if ya still wanna try for the trophy and money."

Shaye silently prayed that Dorland's founding fathers had had the vision to include a clause in the town's charter that disqualified anyone from Boston from competing in the games at the Fourth of July picnic. As no one from the mayor's office moved forward to protest her running with Cody, she realized her prayer was in vain. Throwing up was beginning to sound more and more like the best plan of action.

"Louie, have you met Shaye Frazier?" Cody asked.

"Seen ya around, ma'am," Louie replied, with a tip of his cowboy hat. "Nice to meetcha."

Shaye tried to give the man some semblance of a friendly smile, but he had already knelt at her feet and was about to tie her to the tall, gorgeous cowboy beside her. She'd rather be tied to a gorilla with terminal halitosis.

"Miss Shaye, you're gonna have to move a whole lot closer to Cody so I can get you two tied up together all proper."

"Truss 'em up like chickens, Louis!" Carl Nesbitt yelled from the other end of the contestant line. "Hey, Cody, I'll give ya ten bucks to trade partners with me. My boy here won't feel as good rubbin' up against ya, but he runs pretty good."

Carl Nesbitt's suggestion was met with catcalls up and down the line. Even some of the spectators joined in, laughing louder and louder with each comment.

"Hey, Butler, I hope you didn't bet the ranch on winning."

"Louie, you'd better double-tie those knots. I hear Glenn Hubbard wants her to stay right on top of Butler . . . till he sells out!"

Shaye looked up at Cody to find the muscle along the edge of his jaw rigid and his eyes hard with anger. In Boston she was used to disagreements being solved at a negotiation table in a boardroom, or heard by a judge or jury in a courtroom. She wasn't sure what the procedure in cowboy country was, but she knew however it was done, she wanted no part of it.

She tried to step away only to discover that Louie had already tied the first band. Panic slithered through her and twisted her nerves as it went. If she couldn't walk tied to Cody like this . . . how could she be expected to run?

"Closer."

"What?" Shaye jumped at the sound of Cody's voice.

"I said, you've got to stand closer so the ties will be tight. If they come loose during the race, we'll fall."

She reluctantly edged over.

"Closer." Cody put his arm around her waist and pulled her against him until their bodies touched from shoulder to ankle.

"Stop manhandling me, I heard you the first time," Shaye countered, trying to twist away from him again. The strip of cloth tying her to Cody held firm.

"She's a skittish little filly, ain't she?" Louie teased, waiting to tie the second band.

"Hey, Cody, come on, trade partners with me," Carl Nesbit called out again. "I bet she'd run like hell with me."

"More like *from* you," Shaye muttered, making a mental note to up the price on Hubbard's bill and give herself a hefty raise. This type of duty certainly wasn't part of their original agreement. Louie's hand slid up her thigh with the third strap. Startled, she jumped, moving up tight against Cody.

"That's better." Cody laughed. "I was just about to trade you for Nesbitt's ugly kid." Using his finger, he lifted a lock of her hair, moving it aside as he bent close to her ear and whispered, "But, on second thought, I think I'll keep you." He draped his arm over her shoulders.

The weight of his arm was one thing, the heat racing through her body was quite another. She tried to draw a breath but the pounding of her heart left little room in her chest for air. *I'm just excited,* she thought. *About the race, of course,* she felt compelled to add.

"Just relax, Boston, you'll do fine. This isn't anything like that little marathon they have where you're from. This will be over before you know it. Besides, we're going to win this thing," Cody said, still leaning close to her. "I guarantee."

She tendered little more than a nervous gulp and a nod.

"There," Louie said, grunting as he got to his feet. "That ought to hold you both."

Cody tested the tightness of the ties, pulling against them with his leg, then testing them with his fingers. "Wait a minute," he said, looking down at Shaye's feet. "Take them off."

"Excuse me?" she replied, completely baffled.

"I said, take them off . . . your sandals. You can't run in those."

"Yes, I can," she countered.

"Well, you're not going to, not with me. Take them off."

Angry, she placed her hands on her hips. Forgetting they were tied together, she tried to turn and face him, accomplishing two things. She jabbed him in the ribs and lost her balance. Cody tightened his hold around her waist, steadied her, then drew her up against him again.

"I intend to win this race despite you, *Mrs.* Frazier. If I've got to drag you across the finish line, I'll do it, but I'm not going to do it with you wearing those silly shoes. If you fall . . . I fall. I don't plan to get my leg broken because you're making some kind of fashion statement. Take 'em off."

"I'm not used to going barefoot," Shaye argued.

"Then I guess you'll have to get used to it . . . real quick," Cody rebutted.

"Hey, Butler," someone in the crowd called out. "Quit stalling. I wanna see the little lady strut her stuff!"

Louie stepped up in front of them. "Are you two finally ready? We've gotta get this race run before the fireworks start."

"Oh, all right." Shaye sighed, trying to step out of her sandals without losing her balance. She nudged them out of the way then glanced up at Cody. "Are you happy now?"

She watched him look down at her toes and saw a silly, crooked smile curve his mouth. What was the man's problem?

"Oh, yeah, I'm happy . . . real happy," he answered. "But one more thing."

"What now?"

"Put your arm around me."

"Why?"

Before Cody could answer, Louie raised the starter's pistol. "On your mark . . ."

Cody's arm tightened around her waist and her stomach twisted into a knot.

"Get set . . ."

She quickly submitted to Cody's demand and wrapped her arm around him. She grasped at his shirt, got a handful of skin, withdrew, and finally hooked her fingers around his belt. Hard, hot muscle met the back of her hand. *Concentrate,* she chided herself, trying to breathe deeply and psych herself up for the ordeal ahead. *Don't trip. Don't fall. Don't look down. Don't think, and don't make a fool of yourself . . . too late.*

Carl Nesbitt and his son broke from the line.

"False start, false start!" Louie yelled. "Dammit, Carl. What's your problem? I'm getting hungry and want to eat supper sometime tonight." Waiting until Carl and his boy were back in line, Louie raised the pistol above his head and began the count once again. "On your mark . . . get set . . ."

The sound of the pistol shot drowned out the word *go,* but Shaye didn't have time to wonder if it had even been said. She suddenly found herself being launched across the grass, her right foot yanked forward.

"Run, dammit!" Cody shouted at her. "Left foot, right, now left, right, left . . ."

She clutched Cody's belt tighter and tried to keep up with his long-legged stride only to find herself matching every second step and being dragged along for the other. In the back of her mind she could hear the crowd yelling, cheering, or jeering, she wasn't sure which. The finish line seemed so far away, like a tiny thread in the distance.

"Damn!" Cody yelled.

"What's the matter?" she yelled back.

"The ties are coming loose. No, don't look down, you'll lose your balance."

"What should we do?" The competitive imp that lived in her sense of pride told her she didn't want to give up or lose the race. She wanted to win!

"Just hang on."

"Okay." She had no idea what Cody had in mind, but in an instant she felt his hand shift at her waist and grab on to the waistband of her jeans. A second later she was lifted inches above the ground. He was carrying her. Stride for stride, they covered the ground. Her right leg continued to move with his, but her left leg was only along for the ride. She could hear the other contestants around them, then behind them, and as the crowd's cheering got louder, she suddenly found herself facing the strip of white tape that marked the finish line. With Cody's next step they broke the barrier.

"We won!" she cheered. "Oh, my God, I don't believe it. We won!" Forgetting the loose ties, and forgetting everything she'd promised to deny herself, she leaned into him, grabbed him around the neck with both arms, and tried to hug him. Cody's grip around her waist tightened just as she felt her right leg yank against his left. She twisted and fell against him. She felt him lose his balance, trip, and in the next instant they were tumbling. Everything seemed to be happening in slow motion—the fall took minutes, hours, days, but the moment she hit the ground, real time returned. In half a second Cody landed on top of her, she heard him grunt and felt the hot rush of his breath against her cheek. His right arm and leg took much of the impact, but he still crushed her beneath him. With the wind knocked out of her, the roar of the crowd became little more than a drone in her ears. Gasping, she looked up and immediately lost herself in Cody's dark eyes.

Time and place evaporated all around them. Cody couldn't catch his breath and didn't believe for a moment that it had anything to do with being winded from just running a race. He also knew that as much as he was enjoying the position he found himself in, he had to move and take some of his weight off of Shaye. He'd landed hard, and if he stayed on top of her much longer with his body pressed tightly against hers, there'd be another hard problem to contend with. He propped himself up on his elbow and took a moment or two to catch his breath. "I told you we'd win," he whispered, breaking the silence between them.

"So you did," she replied, her voice like a soft, warm caress.

"You owe me a prize."

"I don't remember making any such bargain."

"You didn't, but you've heard the old saying, 'To the winner go the spoils.' I get your piece of raspberry pie."

"That's not fair," Shaye argued with a smile. "I won, too. What's my prize?"

Cody wasn't sure when he'd decided to make his next move, but everything had been rushing out of control for most of the day, so why would this moment be any different? He slowly lowered his head, watching her eyes grow dark, the pupils widening, her lashes lowering. He heard a barely audible catch in her breath, but nothing could stop him now. With his lips just above hers, he whispered. "This."

He covered her mouth, his lips gently moving, his tongue lightly touching and gliding. The first contact, lip to lip, ignited a flame, her soft moan setting him on fire. The heat of her touch stoked the flames higher and higher. Soft and yielding, giving what he was taking, her response surprised him and he hungrily took what she offered. She tasted like summer honey, sweet, forbidden, and warmed by the sun. He reached up and cradled the side of her face with his hand, his fingers plowing into her hair, the silken strands caressing his skin. Her sweet breath filled his mouth as his kiss deepened, and in that instant he knew he was drowning in her and didn't want to be saved. A thought, beautiful and yet so dangerous, slipped into his mind. If he lost everything he ever owned, at least he'd have this moment.

"Congratulations, Butler. Looks like you've retired the three-legged trophy and won the money." Louie bent over, clapped him on the back, and then using his pocketknife, cut off the ties.

The moment was gone.

Reluctantly Cody stood and offering his hand, helped Shaye to her feet. What was she feeling? He searched her eyes for some clue and found none. He reached out and caressed her cheek with the back of his knuckles. He thought he saw a softening in her expression, and then it was gone, masked with what? Indifference? No, he didn't believe that. Misgivings? Perhaps. That was more likely.

Husband or no husband, something rare had just happened between them, but like it or not, there was a husband. Cody longed to take her in his arms again right in front of everyone—from the Bradshaw sisters to the mayor and the ladies' auxiliary. He wanted to kiss her again and again until they were both senseless. It was a good thing he realized that if he did, it *would* be senseless.

"Yahoo! Cody! Shaye! I knew you guys could do it, I knew you could win!" Maribeth ran toward them and catapulted herself into Cody's arms. "I'm so proud of you, I could just . . . croak!" Jumping up and down, she tightly hugged his neck and kissed him over and over. "It was awesome, just awesome!" Still bouncing with excitement, she broke her stranglehold on Cody and ran to Shaye. "You were fabulous, amazing . . . simply wow! I'm so excited, I can't stand it!"

"Speaking of standing," Cody interrupted, stepping up behind Maribeth and tapping her on the shoulder, knowing she could hear the edge to his voice. "It appears that you're having no trouble standing . . . or running. In fact, you're doing pretty well for someone who fifteen minutes ago couldn't even walk. Maybe we should call one of those TV shows . . . you know, the kind that does those shows on miracle cures."

Maribeth's exuberance disappeared like the air out of a broken balloon and she suddenly stood still.

"Which ankle was it that you twisted?" he asked, moving closer, staring down at her.

Maribeth backed away, one step, two, and then a third.

"My right . . . no, my left . . . my . . ." She gave a big sigh. "Drats . . . I'm busted, aren't I," she muttered, unable to hide her guilt.

"You said it was your left ankle, you little faker." He couldn't decide whether he should be angry or laugh. He glanced at Shaye. "We were set up. If you don't kill her, I will."

"I think this is strictly a family matter . . . and after all, the honor of Medicine Creek was at stake." Shaye laughed. "The trophy and check are all yours . . . so is Maribeth."

"Gotta catch me first," Maribeth shot at them both over her shoulder as she tore across the picnic grounds like a deer.

Cody turned to Gene, Tim, Julie, and Roscoe. "I'm positive Shaye didn't know what Maribeth was up to, but were you guys in on this? Did you know she was faking it?"

All four solemnly shook their heads with counterfeit innocence. Disgusted with the lot of them, Cody strode off, snatching the trophy and the hundred-dollar check out of Louie's hand.

All he had to do now was win two thousand more three-legged races, and he'd be able to pay off his bank note.

Chapter Eight

"Those were some fireworks yesterday," Roscoe said, setting the platter of scrambled eggs on the table in front of Cody.

"You say that every year, and every year they're the same," Cody mumbled.

"I was talkin' 'bout the fireworks between you and Miss Legal." Roscoe chuckled. "Everyone at the picnic was buzzin' 'bout the great big kiss you planted on her."

Chafed by Roscoe's approval, Cody offered little more than a grunt while spooning a helping of eggs onto his plate.

"Yes, sir," Roscoe persisted. "I'll bet that kiss'll be the hot topic in town for at least the next three weeks."

The old man's laughter rankled Cody and prodded him to answer. "I got carried away in the excitement of the moment, nothing more." He bent to the task of peppering his eggs, knowing the kiss was a pretty hot topic for himself, too. "It wasn't the smartest thing I've ever done."

"Well, I think it was kinda sweet—even romantic— what with her working for Hubbard, you two running the race together, winning it, and all." Roscoe fished a few pieces of bacon out of the skillet and dropped them on

Cody's plate next to the eggs. "From where I was standing, it sure looked like *you* enjoyed it."

"Don't go getting all excited, old man. It's not going to happen again. I'm sure if her husband knew, he wouldn't appreciate her being kissed in public . . . especially when it's not him doing the kissing." He took a mouthful of eggs and tried to savor their buttery flavor.

Silence permeated the kitchen, tainted only by the sound of the coffeemaker performing its morning chore.

Roscoe retreated to the counter, filled two mugs, then carefully carried them back to the table. He placed one in front of Cody, took the other for himself, and sat down. "I don't know why you're worried about *that* anymore. Dead men don't get upset."

Cody's fork stopped halfway between the plate and his mouth. The helping of eggs he'd just scooped up tumbled onto his plate. "What are you talking about?"

A look of surprise rearranged Roscoe's face, and he quickly ducked away, avoiding Cody's scrutiny by lifting a couple of pieces of toast out of the toaster. Finally he glanced up, surprise replaced by a worried frown that added a few more furrows to his brow. "Maribeth didn't tell you, did she?" He dropped the toast onto Cody's plate.

"Didn't tell me what?"

Roscoe shook his head. "Doggone it, she promised." Obviously unsure how to get out of this predicament, he began to thoughtfully rub his grizzled chin.

"Tell me what?" Cody failed to keep the sharp, impatient edge from his voice.

"Dammit," Roscoe replied, his exasperation punctuated by the slap of the heel of his hand on the table. "She was supposed to tell you that Shaye Frazier ain't—"

Maribeth bounded into the kitchen, interrupting Roscoe. "Well, are we all bright and chipper this morning?" After stealing a piece of toast from Cody's plate, she looked first at Cody and then Roscoe. "Nope, guess not."

As she began to turn away, Cody quickly reached out and took hold of her wrist.

"What?" Maribeth glanced down at the piece of toast in her hand. "Oh, good grief, Cody, you are such a grouch. It's just a piece of toast. Here, take it back." She tossed it back on his plate and gave a nonchalant shrug. "It's burnt anyway."

When Cody didn't loosen his grip, she offered a loud sigh. "Is this about me faking that I hurt my ankle? 'Cause if it is, I've already apologized."

"This isn't about toast or your ankle." Cody let her go and didn't stop her when she scooped the piece of toast off his plate again. "Roscoe says you were supposed to tell me something important yesterday."

"Like what?" She reached for the jar of grape jelly on the table, then shrugged. "I don't know what you're talking about."

"Something about Shaye," Cody prodded, his patience reaching the short end of the rope.

"Oh, yeah. That." She shot a look at Roscoe. "Oops, I guess I forgot. Sorry." She took her time to add more butter and a thick layer of jelly onto her toast.

"I'm waiting," Cody said, rocking his fork between his fingers like a miniature seesaw.

"Okay, okay." She licked some jelly off her knife, then looked up, an impish gleam shining in her eyes. "I bet you can't guess what I found out the other day when Shaye took me swimming at Mr. Hubbard's."

Roscoe leaned close to Maribeth and hoarsely whispered in her ear, "I really don't think it's a good time to play guessing games with your brother." He jerked his thumb in Cody's direction. "In case you haven't noticed, good humor ain't on his agenda this morning."

"Phew, thanks for the warning," Maribeth replied, rolling her eyes. "It's getting kinda hard to tell the good moods from the bad these days."

She turned and met Cody's glare head on, and instead of shrinking away, she screwed up her face and stuck her tongue out at him.

"Oh, that's nice . . . and so ladylike," Cody sliced at her, wondering what the hell got into his sister sometimes. Was this all about her becoming a teenager or was he failing at this job, too—not that being parent and brother could be called a job, but it sure was a chore at times. With a disgusted grunt he steadied his fork and began to load it with eggs. And that's when Maribeth dropped the bomb.

"Shaye's not married."

His head snapped up and the eggs went flying. He watched with total disbelief as Maribeth calmly turned away as though she'd said nothing more unusual than a comment on the weather. She shot a gamine-like grin at him over her shoulder, retrieved a glass from the cupboard, then filled it with milk.

"Say it again." Cody wanted to make sure he'd heard what he thought he'd heard.

Maribeth answered, enunciating her words with enough exaggeration to rile him further. "She . . . is . . . not . . . married."

He leveled his best scowl at her. "That's it? You've got no more information than that?" He plucked a clump of eggs off his knee and tossed it on his plate.

"What do you want, blood type? Her S.A.T. scores? Dental records? What?" Maribeth sassed around a mouthful of toast. "I don't know much more. Honest. I know that her husband died in a boating accident a little over a year ago and that they hadn't been married very long." Another bite of toast disappeared into her mouth. "Oh, yeah, he was a lawyer, too."

A tangled jumble of feelings hit him hard and somewhere in the mix Cody was able to detect more than a dash of elation and a dab or two of irritation. "You mean I spent the whole night feeling guilty for nothing?"

"Kinda humbling, ain't it?" Roscoe leaned back in his chair, folded his arms across his chest, and cackled like a sitting hen.

Cody scowled at the old ranch hand. "I've got enough humble pie on my plate right now, I don't need any more."

Maribeth drained her glass of milk and set it in the sink with a loud clink. "Well, I gotta get going."

"Go where?" Cody demanded, using his napkin to pick a few more pieces of egg off his jeans.

"The other day when I was swimming at Mr. Hubbard's, he asked if I wanted to come back and see some of his animals. Today's the day. Cody, I told you about it last night. I've never seen anything like a llama up close." She glanced eagerly from Cody to Roscoe and back again. "I can go . . . can't I?"

"You've got chores to do."

"I did the laundry and changed the bed linens yesterday, and I'll get the rest done when I get back." Maribeth leaned against the back door and fiddled with the door-knob.

Nobody needed to know that he couldn't evict Shaye Frazier from his thoughts, and because of this Cody didn't know whether he should ask his next question. What the hell . . . why not? "Is Shaye going to be there?"

"Of course she is. She lives there." As though realizing she'd dropped another bomb, Maribeth's fidgeting increased, and she shifted uneasily from one foot to the other. "I thought you knew."

Cody felt as though he'd been zapped by a cattle prod. Shaye wasn't married . . . she lived at Hubbard's ranch. Dammit, what other little gems of information was Maribeth going to drop like hand grenades? One question shoved its way into his head and persistently dug in. He reluctantly gave it his full attention but didn't like the possibilities it presented. Was there more to Shaye Frazier's relationship with Glenn Hubbard than business? *No.*

Ridiculous. With mulish resolve, he bulldozed the question aside and turned his attention back to Maribeth. "After your little trick yesterday, I'm surprised she'd still want you to go over there."

"She wasn't upset with me, not like you were. I think she thought it was funny." Maribeth finally stood still, cant-hipped and with her thumb hooked into her pocket. "So, can I go? Please."

Cody looked at his sister, allowing his gaze to linger. What a scamp, a scamp who was growing up much too fast. He felt a tightening in his chest. When Jack and Kate Butler had been killed, they'd left him with more than a ranch to care for. What did he know about raising a teenager? To make his task more difficult, what did he know about raising a teenage girl?

He couldn't blame Maribeth for being curious about Hubbard's animals or even enjoying the luxury of the man's pool when it was offered; after all, she was an impressionable kid. And besides, his differences with Hubbard weren't hers to wrestle with. No matter how much he tried to justify it, he realized that his attempt to be fairminded didn't help at all—he still felt as though she was defecting to the enemy's camp.

"How do you plan to get there?"

"Well, when you get through shoving those eggs all over your pants, I was hoping *you* could drive me over," Maribeth answered, impatiently rattling the doorknob again.

He supposed he could drop Maribeth off in the driveway at Hubbard's and make a coward's quick retreat. His foolish stunt yesterday had really wrecked the day for everyone, and he wasn't sure if he wanted to face Shaye Frazier so soon and have to come up with an apology. He had tried to make amends last evening after Julie's fabulous fried chicken and potato salad dinner, but the necessary words wouldn't settle in his head long enough to form any kind of reasonable apology, and if he'd said the words that had stuck in his mind, he'd just have to apologize all over again.

He'd let moment after moment slide by and all too soon evening fell and the Dorland High School Marching Devils began their annual concert from the grandstand. The program was the same as it had been for the last twenty years—every Sousa tune that could be crammed into a twenty-minute performance. An apology couldn't have been heard over the din, even if he'd shouted it in counter rhythm. And he was certainly off the hook once the fireworks began—there wasn't any room for apologies between the oohs and aahs of the crowd.

Throughout the rest of the evening he'd acted no better than a schoolkid with his first crush, sneaking looks at Shaye. He'd even thought about moving next to her and trying to break the ice, but it just felt a whole lot more comfortable to let another one of his mistakes ride itself out of wind.

At nine-thirty, when he declared it was time to leave, he swore he'd heard an audible sigh of relief from everyone. His one stupid act, that one wonderful kiss, had ruined everyone's day.

"Well?" Maribeth interrupted.

Dragged from his thoughts, Cody noticed the bag in his sister's hand. "What's that?"

Giving an exasperated grunt, she reached inside and held up the contents. "My bathing suit, just in case I happen to get invited to fall in the pool." After jamming her suit back into the bag, she then folded her hands, prayer-like, and begged like a pitiful Cockney waif. "Will you take me, sir? Please, sir?"

A knock on the back door resounded a moment before Cody could answer.

"Hi, Doc. Come on in," Maribeth said, holding the door open as Doc Campbell stepped into the kitchen.

"G'morning, Doc. How about some coffee?" Roscoe got up and retrieved another mug from the cupboard.

Half rising from his chair, Cody shook the man's hand, then settled back down. "Are you here with good news or bad?"

"Well, it could be a bit of both," the vet said, making himself comfortable on an offered chair. "It depends on your perspective, I guess." He nodded his thanks as Roscoe put the mug of steaming brew in front of him.

"Cody, I'll drive Maribeth over to . . . the . . . uh . . . the neighbors' so you and Doc can talk," Roscoe offered, taking the keys to the truck off the peg on the wall and hustling Maribeth out the door.

After the door closed, Cody turned to Doc Campbell. "You're out early on a Sunday morning. What should I ask for first, the good news—if there is any—or the bad?"

"Well, for starters," the veterinarian began, "I stopped by your quarantine pens before I came up to the house. It might be hard for you to see right now, but I think things are getting better. That new vaccine does a good job, and I'm pretty sure we've kept the virus contained just to your herd. With everyone afraid they're gonna get hit with it, I'd have heard something by now if it'd spread."

"That's great, Doc. I'm glad everyone else is okay." Cody knew it wasn't fair to wish bad luck on anybody, but he sure would have liked to have some company in his misery. "The number of sick steers that are coming in has dropped off a bit."

"How many do you figure you've lost?" Doc Campbell took out a pad and began jotting down a few notes.

"Ten, maybe twelve. They were out of the first bunch that got sick and were the worst off before we knew what we might be dealing with." Cody paused and took a sip of coffee. "Make that about sixteen. I've lost some calves, too. I guess they were just too young to fight it. I expect there'll be more before I'm done. Right?"

Harold Campbell nodded. "If they weren't weaned and their mamas were sick, that's to be expected. Have you been taking care of the dead ones like I told you?"

"Yeah," Cody replied. "Gene and the boys have been doing a good job."

"I can guarantee you've also had some of your breeding cows that just fevered up without getting full-blown disease abort their spring calves. It'll be hard to tell unless your hands find anything when they check the herd," Doc Campbell continued. "You'll probably have some sterility problems come breeding season, too. It's just the nature of this thing. But, overall, and considering how this situation could have gone, I think you're in good shape." Doc Campbell leaned forward and placed both elbows on the table. "The crazy thing is, there hasn't been an outbreak of hoof-and-mouth in the U.S. since about 1929. I'd just like to know where it came from."

Cody shrugged. "Me, too." He paused, almost afraid to ask Doc his next question. "So, what's the bad news?" He braced himself, thinking that what they'd already been talking about was pretty bad.

"It's nothing like that—just aggravating, that's all." Doc Campbell closed his notebook and slipped it into his breast pocket. His pen followed. He looked up at Cody. "The lab lost the samples I sent last week, so I've got to send another batch. I already pulled 'em when I was down at the pens."

"And in the meantime, I don't have a confirmed diagnosis." Cody grimaced. "I need to have something concrete. There's too much gossip going 'round about this being brucellosis."

"I can tell you flat out—it's not."

"That's great to hear, but you've got to admit, it doesn't look good when word comes out of the C.C.A.'s office that it is. I'm surprised that the federal boys haven't shown up, either," Cody added, offering Doc a coffee refill.

"If I'd thought for a minute that it was brucellosis and said the word to the ag boys, they'd have been here before I could've hung up the phone. Don't get me wrong, this is bad stuff, too." He took a sip from his mug. "As a matter of fact, I spoke with Keith Grant with the ag office last evening. He'll be here Wednesday. They've been busy with a rabies outbreak in Yellowstone. With tourist season in full swing, they had to put extra men on the job." He reached for the sugar bowl and doctored his coffee. "Apparently there was an incident in one of the campgrounds between a family from Indiana and a rabbit."

"I did hear you say 'rabbit,' right?" Cody shook his head in disbelief, then fell quiet, the clink of his spoon as it circled around and around in his coffee mug the only noise in the room. He looked up at Doc Campbell. "I'd trade five rabid Thumpers for what I'm dealing with, any day." His laugh was hollow, humorless, and regret colored his words. "This came at a rough time for me, Doc. I wish you had a magic pill or shot out in your truck that would make it all disappear."

"So, how do you think it went?" Maribeth asked, nervously chewing on her thumbnail as Roscoe drove the truck down the lane. "Personally, I think it was great—of course I played my part beautifully."

"It was the worst case of overacting I've ever seen," Roscoe replied, turning the truck out onto the highway. He shot her a quick glance. "You're sure no Maureen O'Hara, hammin' it up like you did. I thought for sure that Shaye was gonna see right through all that bad acting."

"Bad acting? I suppose you think you could have done better—not that the plan involved you." Maribeth snorted. "Remember, I was his race partner. My getting hurt, that's what our plan was all about." A frown creased her brow. "Who's Maureen O'Hara?"

"You kids today," Roscoe chided. "You have no idea

about great actresses like Miss O'Hara or Betty Grable. Ain't nobody in the movies today who can hold a candle to either of 'em."

"I don't care what you say, I think I played my part every bit as good as that Maureen O'Grable person."

"Well, we'd better just cool it for a while. Ain't no use in spookin' 'em. Maybe they'll even get a few romantic ideas on their own."

Maribeth's second snort was louder than her first. "Cody's idea of romance is spring breeding season for the cows, wrestling a steer in less than ten seconds in a dirty arena, and groping with Bunny Gibson for a quick—"

"Watch your mouth, young lady," Roscoe admonished.

"Well, it's true and you know it. I don't think he'd know how to treat a lady if she walked up and bit him on the butt."

It was Roscoe's turn to snort. "If she were a lady, she wouldn't be biting anybody's butt."

"Well, you've got to admit, that if . . ." Maribeth turned in her seat and looked at Roscoe. "You noticed I did say 'if.'"

"Yeah?"

"*If* anything is going to happen between the two of them, Shaye's got to learn a few things and Cody's gotta, too."

"Such as?" Roscoe waved at the pickup carrying Jet Linderman as it sped by in the other direction.

"She needs to learn more about ranching, about cows and horses, not to wear open-toed sandals around the livestock, and she needs to know how to ride. I've talked it up a bit, and she seems really interested, so now all I've gotta do is talk Cody into teaching her."

Roscoe nodded. "That last one could be a toughie, but it's worth a go. Okay, what shortcomings does Cody have to work on?"

Maribeth offered the loudest snort of the whole morning. "Believe me, this drive is too short for me to answer that question. We'd have to be driving to Nome, Alaska, by way of Argentina."

"Too late, we're here." Roscoe braked the truck in front of Glenn Hubbard's mansion. "Kinda showy, ain't it?" In fact, he thought it looked damned ugly, all that glass and stone.

"Isn't it gorgeous!" Maribeth breathed. "It's like a palace, inside and out. You ought to see the bathrooms . . . huge tubs and showers big enough for two people."

"I prefer 'em when there's just room enough for one . . . me," Roscoe countered.

Maribeth shrugged, gathered up her bathing suit, and opened the truck door.

"Not so fast," Roscoe said. "How're you gonna get home?"

She turned and winked. "I'm sure Shaye will drive me home."

"Why am I not surprised . . . not surprised at all?"

"This is wonderful," Gene said, turning to the sports section of the Sunday morning paper. "I can't remember the last time we both had two days off in a row and got to sleep in, too. Trouble is, thanks to your lousy attempt at matchmaking, and considering Cody's mood when he left the picnic last night, I'm not sure if I've even got a job to go back to."

"Don't be ridiculous," Julie rebutted. "Cody wasn't all that upset. Besides, I wasn't the only one involved in that little scheme."

Gene put the paper down. "Have you and your . . . gang learned your lessons now? Not only was it poor timing, but Cody and Shaye just aren't . . . uh . . . well, they've got nothing in common with each other."

"Nothing except the hots for each other." Julie snuggled up behind Gene, put her arms around his neck, and nibbled on his ear. "You remember what the hots are all about, don't you?" She slid her hand down inside his shirt and sucked on his earlobe.

"Hey, that tickles." He tried to duck away from her.

Julie gave him a kiss on the cheek, then sat on his knee. "Cody is so turned on by the 'up tight' Ms. Frazier, he doesn't know what to do about it without losing what he thinks is his self-respect. And Shaye . . . she's never been in the same room with a man like Cody, let alone think about a man like him in a very improper and unladylike way while she's alone in her own bed."

"Julie, honey, he's runnin' on a thin thread right now." Gene wrapped his arms around her. "You haven't seen him like I have, standing at the pens and staring at those drooling cows. You haven't seen him work and rework his accounts so he can pay the men, or put groceries on the table."

Julie kissed him again, letting her tongue slide along the rim of his ear. "See, maybe he does need a little diversion to—"

"No. Please. Leave him alone, but, baby . . . oh, yes . . . ahhh . . . please, don't stop what you're doing to me."

Chapter Nine

Cody bent over the account books spread out on his desk. Using the computer that sat in front of him and some up-to-date accounting software probably made more sense, but he preferred keeping his balances and debits in the same thick leather-bound journal that his father and grandfather had used before him. Each page held part of the history of Medicine Creek, and Cody liked to look at the strong-inked characters of his grandfather's entries and the more modern script of his father's hand.

He checked the figures on the page one more time. He'd already salted the ranch account with a couple of thousand from his own personal funds, but the ranch's operating resources were still nearly tapped out. Exasperated, Cody drove his fingers through his hair. He still had three thousand tucked away for electricity, a couple of truck payments, fuel, and daily living expenses, but when that was gone there'd be no more. He'd made himself a promise, and no matter how bad things got, he'd use up every cent of his own money and sell every piece of ranch equipment he could, rather than dip into any of Maribeth's college fund.

He laughed, the sound completely void of humor. He

might not have a home left to offer his sister, they might be living out of the back his truck, but at least she'd be well educated.

Cody glanced at the buff-colored envelope that had arrived in yesterday's mail. The Timberline Gallery in Jackson Hole used to represent his mother's work, and now they wanted to buy up all the Kate Butler bronzes and paintings they could find. The letter said they'd pay top dollar. Cody reached for the envelope and methodically ripped it into small pieces and tossed it in the wastebasket. He didn't care if top dollar was enough to pay off the entire loan with money left over to buy an oil field in Qatar, he wouldn't part with a single piece of his mother's artwork.

The ranch account had enough money left to make the next three payrolls. If he couldn't sell the polo ponies and pay the banknote, that would still give his men two week's pay and a separation paycheck before the bank took over. Or Hubbard. He closed the ledger and tossed his pen on the desk.

No question about it, Hubbard still wanted his ranch, but Cody had to give Shaye Frazier credit. Although they'd been together or seen each other a couple of times since her initial visit, she'd never pressed Hubbard's deal at him again. Granted, he couldn't see her without remembering why she was in Dorland, but she hadn't pushed. Maybe Roscoe had her pegged right. Maybe she didn't like her job with Hubbard, after all.

"So, the lady's not married." He liked the sound of those words, liked it a lot. His voice had been little more than a whisper, but it brought the three Newfies lumbering to his side, their bushy tails wagging in unison. Doling out pats and scratches to the huge dogs, Cody couldn't hold back a pleased chuckle. "It's really you guys who are eating me out of house and home."

"Speakin' of eatin', you planning on comin' in for supper or are ya spendin' the night out here?"

Cody turned to find Roscoe lounging against the door frame. The wizened cowboy was beginning to show his age, his legs more bowed, his back more bent. Time was slipping away too quickly. "I'm finished here," Cody said, closing the ledger book with a clear-cut slam. "Maribeth home yet?"

"Nope. She's eatin' high on the hog at Hubbard's tonight."

Cody pushed away from the desk, stood and stretched. His body hated sitting at a desk about as much as it hated an eight-second ride on a Brahma bull. "Safe bet the menu's a little more posh at Hubbardland than what we've had in a long time."

"Oh, I don't know 'bout that," Roscoe countered, clearly offended. "I think my meat loaf and mashed 'tatoes are pretty darned good."

"There'd better be some green beans and buttermilk biscuits with them."

"There's only one way for you to find out." Roscoe stepped away from the office door. "You might even find some spiced peaches for dessert—some of the last that your mama put up."

"So, what are we waiting for?" Cody asked, feeling the touch of melancholy as the image of his mom doing her fall canning slipped into his mind. It would be two years this winter since he'd lost his folks. Funny how so many little things still kept them close to him—his father's handwriting in the ledgers or the hand-braided reins hanging in the tack room; his mother's bronze sculptures or her spiced peaches—all the special threads of family.

Cody scooted the chair back against the desk, turned off the lights, and followed Roscoe out of the horse barn. He liked having the office next to the tack room. He liked to work with the scent of horses, cedar bedding, and leather in his nostrils.

A cool breeze stirred the evening air, and he left the sliding doors open, letting the current drift through the barn. He didn't like to run the stall fans at night when no one was around. The three barn cats did a good job, but like it or not, mice were almost as plentiful as the horses and their sharp teeth liked to chew on everything from the high-priced horse feed to electric wiring.

Night enfolded the two men and the three dogs as they slowly walked up to the house, passing the new indoor arena. Cody stopped, his gaze sweeping the building from foundation to the peak of the roof. Having a heated indoor arena where he could train his colts year-round had once been his dream, but the dream had turned into a nightmare.

There'd been no gamble when he'd taken out the loan to build the arena. Cattle prices were good, his herd was healthy and almost ready for market, and the breeding stock consigned to the Cheyenne Cattlemen's Association's auction would have more than paid off the bank, leaving him with a better-than-average profit for the year. The polo ponies always brought in good money, too, money that paid for the extras: his new truck, the new bedroom furniture for Maribeth, the new stove for Roscoe, and the upkeep on the horses themselves.

From the moment the contractor began work on the arena, the project seemed to go sour. Four days of torrential rain ruined the freshly poured concrete footings, making it necessary to break up the concrete and repour every square inch of it. Lumber prices shot up, four more of the custom free-span trusses were needed than originally planned, the grader had struck solid rock when they'd tried to level the arena floor, the overhead heating system had come in higher than the builder's estimate, and then wiring for the lights and heaters shorted out twice, causing a cou-

ple of fires. Cody didn't believe in jinxes, but the arena
project sorely tested his conviction.

Looking up at the building, he only felt an emptiness
where there should have been pride and a sense of accomplishment. No other ranch in the area had a facility that
came close to this one. He'd already had a number of calls
from folks who wanted to "borrow" the building for roping practice or riding events. But most of all, he'd wanted
to start turning out some of the best saddle horses in the
state. "Little good it'll do me in a few weeks," he said, before turning away.

"You're a good rancher, son," Roscoe said as he laid his
hand on Cody's shoulder. "Don't let anyone ever tell ya
different."

"Yeah, right." Cody shook his head, gave a contemptu-
ous grunt, and moved on toward the house. "That's why
the wolves are skulking at the door."

"You'll pull through this. You're just like your daddy
and granddad . . . they never gave up when things got
tough. Your grandpa made it through the Depression, and
your daddy fought through wildfires one year and drought
another. They stuck in there and made it through, just like
you will. You'll see, it'll all work out."

"It'd better hurry up," Cody answered, opening the door
on the back porch of the house. "I'm just about out of time
and money."

"A lot can happen in four weeks. Just don't stop
fightin'."

The two men settled themselves at the kitchen table and
began filling their plates. Roscoe's meat loaf was one of
Cody's favorites, maybe because the recipe had originally
been one of his mother's, and maybe because it reminded
him of happier times when all the Butlers were crowded
around the dinner table sharing food, sharing the events of
their day, sharing a family's love.

The sound of cutlery clinking on the plates and ice

cubes tinkling against the sides of raised glasses instead of conversation splintered the silence. Roscoe passed the platter of meat to Cody, and in return Cody passed the potatoes and green beans across the table to Roscoe, and still the silence persisted. Only when the last bite of meat loaf disappeared did Cody speak.

"Jeff Granger is coming out in the morning to take a look at the stock trailer."

"What for?"

Cody glanced up from his bowl of spiced peaches. "I'm selling it."

"You'd sell it to that pissant Granger without even lettin' me know it's for sale?" Roscoe harrumphed before slurping peach juice off his spoon.

"What difference does it make?" Cody couldn't figure out where Roscoe was heading.

"Well, I guess it didn't occur to you that maybe I'd be interested in buying it."

"No," Cody replied. "No, it didn't. It's also not occurring to me what you'd want with a stock trailer."

"Maybe I wanna go into the stock-haulin' business. Or maybe I'll rent it out to folks that don't have their own and need to do some hauling. Maybe I'm looking for a little side-line business to bring in a little money . . . for my old age."

"Really?" Cody immediately saw through Roscoe's scheme. For weeks the old man had been trying to figure out a way to help pay off the bank. "Just how much money do you think you're gonna make for your . . . old age?"

Roscoe ignored Cody's sarcasm and pushed his own question. "How much did you tell Granger you wanted for the trailer?"

Cody shrugged. "It's only two years old. I'll take a loss, but I told him ten grand."

"You ain't gonna get it," Roscoe responded. "You'll be lucky if he offers eight."

"Every little bit helps."

Roscoe chewed on another mouthful of peaches. "Well, there's no damn point givin' it away. You ain't running a charity here. I'll give you eleven."

"You'll *what?* Now who's running a charity?"

"That trailer's worth at least fifteen and you know it. I'd be getting a helluva bargain at eleven."

"You know, old man, every time I get to thinking there's no such thing as senile dementia, you start me wondering all over again."

"I don't care if you think I'm nuts, do I get the trailer or not?"

"Not." Cody downed the last of the iced tea in his glass, finding it difficult to swallow with the large emotional lump in his throat. He studied the old cowboy sitting across the table from him. Roscoe Diggins had known nothing but ranching and rodeos all his life. He'd been born in northern Oklahoma on the 101 Ranch, the result of a summer fling between a migrant horse wrangler and one of the ranch cooks.

He'd once told Cody that his formal education ended after only four years of schooling when his mama died and he had to start earning his own keep. At ten he was cleaning stalls for fifty cents a day, meals, and a bunkhouse bed. At fourteen he'd worked his way up to bronc buster, and at twenty-five he'd been married, divorced, busted up riding a wild bull, and fired. Roscoe Diggins had shown up at Medicine Creek over forty years ago and settled in. Arthritis now kept him from wrangling, but he was still the best hand when it came to calving and foaling time. Roscoe Diggins was a friend. But best of all, Roscoe Diggins was family.

"I can't take your money, old man," Cody said, the lump still stuck in his throat. "I appreciate you wanting to help, but you're gonna need every cent you've got."

"Well, I got more'n eleven thousand, so you don't need

to worry none 'bout what I got. What you need to do is sign that trailer over to me so I can put your name on my check."

Cody shook his head. "This is ridiculous. You've got absolutely no use for a stock trailer."

"Like I told ya, I'm gonna rent it out. Heck, I suppose I'll even rent it to you when you need it. Oh, now don't give me any skeptical looks like that. Don't worry, it won't cost you as much as I charge everyone else." He spooned the last peach into his mouth, wiping a rivulet of juice off his whiskery chin. "I think I'm gonna call my business 'Roscoe's Rents.' How's that sound?"

"How about we see what Granger has to offer before we set you up in any kind of business other than meat loaf and brownies? Come on, I'll help you with the dishes."

Roscoe shook a gnarled finger at Cody. "Don't think you can put me off that easy. I'm gonna help you out whether you like it or not. You and Maribeth are the only family I got, and I believe in takin' care of those you love." With a sniffle betraying the old man's emotions, Roscoe began clearing the dirty dishes off the table, clattering dish against dish a little more than usual. "You need to learn how to accept help when it's freely given." He turned and met Cody's gaze head on. "Ain't no strings attached to this, and it don't mean you're weak or less a man 'cause you take it. What it means is that you're a good man and that folks care enough and respect you enough to want to help. And that's what families do . . . help each other."

Cody stood and put his hand on the old ranch hand's arm. "I don't know what to say."

"Well," Roscoe replied, squaring his shoulders, lifting his chin, and trying to hide another sniffle, "you can say you'll accept my offer."

"I just don't think—"

"Ain't no thinking to do. Just say we gotta deal."

Cody shook his head. "The last thing you need is a stock—"

"Deal?"

"Roscoe, this isn't your fight."

"Deal?" The old man's voice had a rusty hard edge to it.

Cody reluctantly nodded. "Okay, okay. Deal."

"Well, I'm glad that's settled. Now, don'tcha feel a whole lot better?"

Ignoring the dishwasher, Cody filled the sink with hot water and a liberal squirt of soap. "I'll wash, you dry."

Roscoe grabbed a towel from the drawer and cackled. "Now, what do you s'pose is wrong with this picture? Here we are, two handsome bachelors home alone and washin' dishes. Ain't we just like that old TV show, you know, *The Odd Couple*?" He shot Cody a sidelong glance, waited a moment or two, then added, "So . . . now that you know Miss Legal ain't married, you gonna ask her out?"

Cody pitched the dishcloth into the soapy water, sending bubbles and water splashing up the wall. He turned and gave Roscoe a flinty stare. "Who are you supposed to be, Miss Lonely Hearts? I don't remember signing up for your dating service, so back off." He fished the cloth out of the dishwater and began scrubbing their dinner plates. "Besides," he mumbled, "any date money I have and the hundred dollars from the three-legged race winnings are one and the same." He thought for a moment. "Make that about fifty—I paid the phone bill."

"A drive on a summer evening is as nice a date as a dinner in a fancy greasy spoon somewhere in the city," Roscoe suggested. "Why, I bet a city gal like her ain't never seen the mule deer or the elk come down outta the hills in the evening for a cool drink. You could show her the bighorn sheep along the north range, or how about the pronghorn dashing across the plains. And it'd be real nice to take her up to the falls on Miner's Creek, too."

"Who the hell are you? The Department of Travel and

Tourism?" Cody put the last dish in the rack and drained the sink. He'd never admit it to Roscoe, but the thought of spending an evening or two or three with Shaye Frazier had niggled its way into his head at least sixty times an hour since the day she first set foot in his life. He mentally shrugged. The idea was hopeless on so many counts. "I'll take care of my own social life, thank you very much. I don't need any help, especially from someone whose last girlfriend dropped her teeth in the salad bar at the Chuck-wagon on all-you-can-eat night."

An hour later Cody relaxed alone on the wicker settee on the porch. He loved the peace that settled over the ranch in the evening as Mother Nature tucked the day shift in for the night and sent her night crew off to work. The bullfrog chorus down by the creek had begun their nightly concert with big brown June bugs bouncing off the screen door filling in as the rhythm section. In the trees, boy crickets chirped love songs to girl crickets, and the soft murmur of night birds in their nests completed the choir. Fireflies flitted through the tall stalks of hollyhocks by the side porch and chased each other out through the high grass at the edge of the lawn. Off in the distance, high on a ridge to the west, the plaintive howl of a wolf triggered an uneasy nicker or two from the horses in the paddocks.

"Howl all you want, you old *ho'nehe,* you're not inside my door yet."

Grandma Amy's Cheyenne word rolling easily off his tongue had surprised him. He hadn't spoken any of the Cheyenne that his grandmother had taught him in a long, long time. Funny that it would come to him tonight. He felt a poignant tug at his heart.

She had died when he was fifteen, but Cody remembered her as well as if she were just as far away as the next room. He could close his eyes on an evening such as this, when the mist hung low in the valleys, when dew drenched the sweetgrass and released its fragrance—the same fragrance of Grandma Amy. She had taught him many things about her Cheyenne people, taught him words, told him stories, sang songs to him, and showed him many skills and crafts of her people. He could still make a three-foot-long leather thong from a two-inch diameter piece of buckskin. They had picked wild strawberries together in early summer and wild blackberries when the summer waned. She showed him the beds of Indian perfume, their yellow blooms fragrant enough to freshen a room, and she taught him about the pride and dignity of his heritage—white and red.

Amy Standing Bull had married a white man, Jesse Butler, a soldier boy fresh home from World War II. They'd worked side by side building one of the finest ranches in the state. She'd raised his children in the white way and left her Cheyenne mark on the Butler generations to come.

Cody thought of the other Cheyenne woman who lay buried up on the knoll, his great-great-grandmother, *Eve'haoohe'e,* Jacob's second wife. He'd read old Jacob's journals and knew that Jacob Butler had called her Eva Rose and had paid her father two horses, a ten-pound sack of flour, and a bolt of red calico for her. To the day he died, he'd laugh, give her a hug, and say it was the best trade he'd ever made.

Cody leaned forward on the settee, rested his forearms on his thighs, and allowed the memories to wash over him.

Closing his eyes, he could easily imagine how it was when his great-great-grandfather, Jacob, sat quietly in the evening when the day's work was done. He supposed the view of the mountains had changed very little over the hundred and fifty years that separated them. The blanket of stars overhead was the same as was the cream-colored moon. Only the change wrought by the hands of the men and women who worked this ranch throughout the years had made the differences—building bigger barns, adding on to the original one-room cabin, clearing more and more land, stretching more and more fence, breeding bigger and better herds. And although generations separated Cody from Jacob, he felt the old man standing beside him—the youngest in the shadow of the oldest. But in that hundred and fifty years, nothing truly important had changed; it was still all about family.

But they were all gone, all those whose blood now surged through his veins—all gone. Each and every one, but him, rested on the knoll.

Cody fought the tightening in his chest. All those years of hard work to make Medicine Creek a success, the sweat and blood and tears—floods of tears—brought about by sweet babies lost to cholera or croup, buildings and stock washed away by floods, grain stunted and water rationing caused by draught, and winters of thirty below with ice storms and waist-high snows, all for nothing. In less than two years his recklessness had brought it all to an end.

He'd never imagined shame could hurt so deeply.

He buried his head in his hands, battling against the burn of threatening tears. *Cowboys don't cry*, his mother's gentle admonition when he was a child and hurt himself at play, spoke to him from his fondest memories. She'd been wrong.

He stood and paced the span of the porch. Why hadn't his California customer called back yet? He'd called Miguel Santos di Prado more than a week ago about the six polo ponies, and di Prado had sounded very interested when they'd talked, but Cody was beginning to worry there wasn't going to be a deal. In the ten years he'd done business with di Prado, it had never taken the international polo star so long to make up his mind. What was the holdup?

He needed an answer soon . . . now . . . tonight . . . to-morrow. He'd give di Prado another twenty-four hours and then he'd call again. He couldn't let it ride any longer. If di

Prado didn't want the six horses, he'd have to find another buyer . . . fast.

Cody sat on the porch rail, leaned against the roof support, and closed his eyes. He breathed the clean, sweet air deep into his lungs, tasting it as it rode over his tongue. He remembered one of his father's favorite expressions . . . "Blindfold me and take me all around the world, and I'll tell you with one whiff when I'm home again in Wyoming." Everyone had teased him, saying it was nothing more than the cow pen he was smelling, but tonight Cody knew exactly what his father meant.

The headlights of a vehicle coming up the lane caught his attention. Cody watched the gray Mercedes come around the last curve, and as though a switch had been flipped, every nerve in his body was suddenly on alert.

The convertible stopped in the yard, and Shaye, her hair beautifully tousled from the wind, turned and waved. He lifted his hand in response, not knowing what to call the amalgam of feelings that surged through him each time he looked at her. None of it made any sense. He'd seen beautiful women before, had even dated his fair share, but none of them turned his ignition on and got his motor running like Glenn Hubbard's high-priced Boston lawyer.

Maribeth jumped out of the car almost before it came to a full stop. "Guess what!" She dashed across the lawn and up the porch steps. "Cody, guess what! No, you're never going to guess." She grabbed him by the arms. "I have a llama! Mr. Hubbard gave me a llama, a baby llama!"

Cody felt a burning twist in his gut. He hated to call it jealousy, but considering llamas were expensive, much more expensive than he could afford to pay for a pet for Maribeth, there was no other name for it. "That's a pretty extravagant gift, don't you think? And just what are you going to do with it? Where are you going to keep this . . . llama?"

"See," Maribeth called over her shoulder to Shaye. "I

told you he'd be a toad about this." Maribeth stomped her foot.

"Tater, there's a damned virus on this ranch that's destroying our herd and quite possibly our chance to hang on to this place. I think its great that Mr. Hubbard gave you a llama, he must like you a lot, but I don't know if llamas can get this damned curse or not. I'd hate for you to lose her."

Maribeth continued to protest, but he didn't hear a word she said—how could he when he was completely, totally, undeniably wrapped up in watching Shaye slide out of the Mercedes.

He felt a sharp jab in his ribs.

"Cody, you're doing it again," Maribeth charged.

"Doing what?" he asked, deflecting her second jab just in time.

"Leering at Mr. Hubbard's lawyer."

Chapter Ten

The dew on the grass felt cool and refreshing on her toes as Shaye walked toward the house. She could see Cody and Maribeth on the porch facing off against each other. A touch of melancholy filled her. She'd never known the bond of family, and now, at twenty-nine, even an argument with a brother or sister was something she craved. Afraid to intrude in Cody's exchange with Maribeth, Shaye slowed her steps.

She didn't know what she based her reasoning upon, maybe it was little more than the way Cody's eyes always softened when he looked at his sister. Maybe it was the gentle hand that always reached out to touch the girl. Whatever the reason, somehow, Shaye knew that he'd give in to Maribeth's excitement over her new pet. Somehow he'd make it okay for Maribeth to keep the llama.

Shaye marveled at Cody's steadfastness. How was he able to hold himself together when everything he'd worked for was crumbling all around him? The bank would seize his ranch in a little more than three weeks, his cattle were under quarantine, with some dying from the virus, and yet he still held the world together for Maribeth.

Someday he'll make a wonderful father . . . someday.

The thought had rushed into her mind, but the image of Bunny Gibson quickly joined it. Shaye's breath left her in an exasperated sigh. She'd only seen Bunny a couple of times, but the woman certainly didn't strike her as someone who would enjoy being a mother. But maybe Bunny was the kind of woman Cody preferred . . . or needed right now. No strings, no pressures, no long-term expectations. At the moment he had more than his share of strings and pressures in his life, and his expectations, at best, were rather short-ranged. Shaye tried to steel herself against any more thoughts about Cody and children and long-range plans. Her own long-range plans had no room for any of that, either.

Stopping at the bottom of the steps, she looked up to find Cody leaning on his forearms against the porch rail, watching her, his dark eyes black in the evening light. She felt oddly vulnerable under his scrutiny. Steadfast, she stood her ground.

Now that she knew to look for it, she could see his American Indian heritage in his features—the angular sculpting of his face, the broad fullness to his mouth, the touch of bronze to his skin, and the pride that often gave his expression the illusion of arrogance.

He still hadn't cut his hair. In front, the shorter strands fell over his forehead, softening his appearance, but the rest was tied back at the nape of his neck. The style defied every clean-cut, courtroom, and *GQ* trend she'd always appreciated and reminded her of the wild and reckless kind of men she'd always steered away from. The truth surprised her. She liked it . . . a lot.

Cody offered no smile, no welcome . . . and then he grinned, slow and easy, his eyes warming on hers. Shaye felt another vulnerable crack break open in her emotional barricade.

"Hi." Cody raised his hand in a slight wave. "Thanks for driving Tater home."

A quickening—warm, unfamiliar, and totally unnerving—teased every secret nook of her body. She fought to collect her scattered fragments of courage and looked straight into his eyes. "I enjoy her company. She's a super kid."

"Yeah." Cody chuckled, tousling his sister's hair. "When she's not being a loudmouthed brat." He touched the tip of Maribeth's nose with his finger. "But you're right, she is a super kid." He drew Maribeth against his side and gave her a one-armed hug. "That damned llama of yours better not spit at me."

Maribeth threw her arms around her brother's neck. "Oh, Cody, do you mean I can keep her? Do you?"

"Yeah, you can. We'll talk to Doc Campbell and find a safe place to put her until the cattle are clear of the virus." He looked down at Shaye and gave a quick wink. "Did I give in too easy? I could have lasted another fifteen or twenty minutes." He ducked another one of Maribeth's elbow jabs.

Shaye rested her hand on the newel post. She'd been right. Once again with what appeared to be an effortless act, Cody had held Maribeth's world together. Now Shaye hoped he'd agree to her request. "May I talk with you for a moment?"

"Sure. Come on up." Cody gestured toward one of the wicker chairs on the porch, then turned to Maribeth. "Hey, super kid, how about seeing if there's any lemonade or iced tea."

Maribeth finally succeeded in landing a jab in Cody's ribs, then jumped out of his reach. "He really doesn't want me to get any drinks, he just doesn't want me listening to your conversation." Avoiding a playful swat from her brother, Maribeth opened the screen door and disappeared into the house.

Accepting Cody's invitation, Shaye sat on one of the wicker chairs. Too nervous to relax, she perched on the edge of the seat. She wanted to talk to Cody, but she wasn't sure how to begin. How ironic, after all the court cases she'd tried, after all the judges and jurors she'd spoken to, all the presentations she'd made at meetings of the Boston Bar Association, that one Wyoming cowboy could completely rattle her.

Relax, she ordered herself. *Just relax.*

Silence, for what seemed like an eternity, lay heavy between them before she found any words to say. "It's a beautiful night," she offered, annoyed with her lame remark. Did her voice sound as tense as she felt? She tried again. "I'm amazed how everything here seems so fresh, so green, so new. I've seen more shooting stars since I've been here than in my whole life." That was better, less uptight, less asinine. She took a deep breath, but now that she'd started talking, she couldn't let the silence take control again. "It's funny, but sometimes I find myself listening for car horns or the rumble of city traffic. I guess it takes a while to get used to the quiet." She took another deep breath, then forged ahead. "Something else I never noticed in Boston is that sweet fragrance every evening and the clean earthy smell after it rains. You can almost taste it. I love it."

She suddenly became aware that she'd been talking much too much and twisting the hem of her T-shirt with her fingers. She closed her mouth, purposefully straightened her shirt, then stilled her hands by folding them in her lap.

"I guess it is a different experience for you." Cody shifted against the porch rail and folded his arms across his chest. "That fragrance you smell is sweetgrass. It grows in areas that hold a lot of moisture in the soil, and when the evening dew hits it, it releases the perfume. In the old days the Indians collected it and stored bunches of it with their clothes to make them smell good, and they stuffed their bedding with it. They also burned it to sweeten the air . . .

like an incense." He shifted again, this time crossing his legs at the ankles.

Body language, Shaye mused. *Closed. Guarded.* "I'd love to find some to take home with me."

"That's no problem," he said. "You can buy braids of sweetgrass at powwows or Indian goods stores."

"Powwows?" Shaye asked. "What's that? A meeting of some kind?"

Cody shook his head. "Not quite. They are get-togethers, but they're social times for the Indians. The people dance, sing, have a good time. Maybe there'll be a powwow while you're still around and you can see what it's all about."

"I think I'd like that." Shaye was beginning to relax, finding the conversation easy, enjoyable, until Cody spoke again.

"Okay," he said, pushing away from the rail. He moved to the chair across from Shaye and sat down. "Now that we've had our polite little chitchat, what do you really want to talk to me about?"

Shaye's stomach tightened with a lurch, but she straightened her back and tried to look calm. Despite the twist of nerves and the butterflies bouncing around in her belly, she hoped she could sound coherent. "Cody, I'm sorry to bring this up, but I have to ask." She paused for a moment, trying to read the expression on his face. She failed. "Have you given any more consideration to Glenn Hubbard's offer? The dollar amount still stands and will up to the time the bank forecloses." She braced herself for an explosion. It didn't happen.

"I wondered how long it would take you to get around to that again." He looked off toward the barns for a moment and then back at Shaye. "Don't think that I don't wonder what a three-million-dollar check would look like with my name on it, because I do. I think about it at least once every hour. I bet it'd look damned nice, too." He stood and paced the length of the porch and back again, stopping in front of her. He looked down into her eyes. "Shaye, I really appreciate you not pushing Hubbard's deal at me every time we've seen each other. I know it's your job, and I bet you're usually real good at doing your job, even the parts you don't enjoy . . . but I'm glad you're not very good at this part of it."

She frowned, unsure if she'd been complimented or insulted. He'd hit so close to how she felt about what Hubbard wanted her to do, she wondered if he could read her mind.

"I know I'm running out of time," Cody continued, forcing a meager smile. "But don't count me out yet. I've got another plan or two in the works."

Maribeth opened the screen door. Pushing against it with her hip, she stepped out onto the porch. "Roscoe made some fresh-squeezed lemonade . . . okay, so he put a little of that powdered stuff in it, too." She passed the tray first to Shaye and then to Cody. "I wanted pink lemonade, so I added the food coloring."

"It looks like a bloody Mary," Cody croaked, suspiciously peering at the glass.

"I think it's very . . . uh . . . festive," Shaye said, holding up her glass to get a better look at the brilliant color. "I'm sure it's . . . delicious."

"So are you two finished talking, or are you going to send me back into the house again?"

"House," Cody said with a jerk of his thumb toward the door.

"Tyrant," Maribeth shot at him over her shoulder as she went back inside and closed the door.

"I envy the closeness you have with her." A hint of sadness touched Shaye's voice. "You're very lucky to have each other."

Cody sat down on the settee. "I take it you're an only child."

"Yup . . . the one and only." Shaye wiped some of the condensation off her glass. "I suppose it did have its good side. . . . I didn't have to share my toys with anyone else or deal with hand-me-down clothes."

Cody's laugh was quick. "Well, I don't think Tater was ever interested in any of my . . . toys. I was nineteen when we got her, and I don't think she'd fit into any hand-me-downs of mine, even now." He raised the glass of lemonade to his lips, grimaced at the color, but took a sip anyway. "I don't know if she told you or not . . . she's adopted."

"I'd heard," Shaye replied. "But that makes the relationship you two have even more special." She placed her glass on the table beside her. "Why do you call her Tater?"

"Tater Tot?" A warm smile lit up Cody's face. "She was a little more than two years old when Mom and Dad brought her home from the orphanage in Cheyenne. She was a tiny little thing . . . malnourished. The first time I saw her, I told my folks she was no bigger than a Tater Tot. The name stuck." Cody sobered and shook his head, his regret unmistakable. "She's growing up too quickly. I can't keep up with her."

"You sound like a father." The words were spoken before she could pull them back.

"Since our folks died, I guess that's kind of what I've become." He rubbed his hand wearily against the back of his neck, then sat up, offering a slight shrug. "I'm doing the best I can. I just hope it's okay."

"I think you're doing much better than okay. Like I said, she's a super young lady."

"Thanks, I appreciate that."

Silence wedged its way into their conversation for another awkward moment or two.

Shaye set her glass aside. If she didn't ask him now, she'd lose her nerve. "Cody, I'm sorry if this isn't the best time to ask, but—"

"I thought we'd already hit that topic." He looked up, a skeptical arc to his left eyebrow.

"No, this isn't about Hubbard. I know you don't want to sell out and that you intend to fight it through. I also know it's useless for me to keep pushing the issue. I guess you cowboys would say there's no point in beating a dead horse." She saw his immediate and disdainful reaction to her poor joke and didn't know if he didn't believe her or just didn't like her humor. "Okay, to put it simply, I'm done asking."

"So? What do you want?"

She struggled for the words, wondering if he might find her request ridiculous and laugh at her. She rushed ahead. "I want to learn how to ride."

Cody sat up. "What?"

"A horse. I want to learn how to ride."

"Why?"

Shaye shrugged. "It looks like fun and I've heard it's good exercise. . . . I think I might really like it. I'd like to see more of the countryside." She swept her hand in a broad arc toward the western slopes and mountains. "Maribeth said that the only way to get to some places is on horseback. And, after all, this is the Wild, Wild West." Damn, she'd said something stupid again.

Cody groaned. "So you've come out to cowboy country looking for the total dude ranch experience, ma'am." His exaggerated drawl rang with a touch of scorn. "Have you ever even been on a horse before?"

"No," Shaye replied, bristling against his attitude.

"Have you ever been near a horse?"

"No. Okay, once. Well, it wasn't really a horse, it was a . . . burro."

In the midst of a sip of lemonade, Cody almost choked. "A burro?"

"A burro named Pablito. He was in a petting pen outside of a Mexican restaurant near Boston—Taco Tico Tommy's."

"Well, why didn't you say so. Wow. That just about makes you a professional rider."

She ignored his teasing and pressed her plea. "I know you have a lot on your mind right now and you're probably too busy, but Maribeth said you were the best." Shaye waited for some indication that he might be a little willing to teach her. There wasn't a clue. "I'd be glad to pay you for your time . . . and the rental of a horse."

Cody's laugh sounded bitter and cold. "What is this, some kind of charity?" The friendly banter had suddenly stopped, and his accusation had a sharp edge. "Believe me, even what lessons in Boston would cost wouldn't pay the interest on my bank loan for one week." He stood and tossed the remaining red lemonade in his glass over the porch rail and into the flower bed below.

"No. Of course I'm not offering charity," Shaye replied. How dare he think such a thing? "Charity would be me giving you twenty thousand dollars without expecting anything in return."

"Okay." Cody suddenly grinned. "If that's the case, I'll take your charity." He raised his hand as if warding off a blow. "I'm just kidding." He appeared to quietly think things through for a few moments and then replied, "I tell you what . . . how about we make a trade?"

"A trade?" Shaye began to get nervous all over again. The last time she'd given in to any of the Butlers, she'd found herself in a three-legged spectacle in front of the whole county.

"You want something from me, and . . . and I need something from you, so we make a fair trade."

Shaye's breath quickened. "What do *you* want?"

Cody's grin flashed wider. He hunkered down in front of her. "Oh, lady, I want a lot . . . but for now, how about I teach you how to ride a horse so well that you could be a member of the Olympic team?" He hesitated, the grin fading to a more pensive mien. "In trade, you'll give Maribeth the girl's version of the 'birds and the bees' lecture."

"What?" Disbelief washed over her. "You can't be serious. I wouldn't know what to say. I can't—"

"Of course you can. Whatever your mother told you will be just fine."

"My mother never told me," Shaye said, suddenly finding it difficult to speak above a shallow whisper. She met Cody's surprised look. "My mother died when I was eleven." She took a fortifying breath. "When she got ill, my father sent me away to boarding school. Sister Maria Theresa Concepcion did the honors. I was thirteen when . . ." She trailed off, feeling the heat of a blush touch her cheeks. "When nature . . . uh . . . forced the issue."

"I'm sorry. I didn't know . . . about your mother." Cody clearly didn't know what else to say.

Shaye shrugged. "You'd be surprised how many of life's lessons I learned from Sister Maria Theresa."

Cody stood, stepped to the edge of the porch, and leaned back against the railing. "I don't have a clue how to talk to Maribeth about this, or even where to start." He dragged his hand wearily over his face. "This summer she's got puppy eyes for Gene's son, Tim. Hell, she's too young to be thinking about boys, and besides, I don't have any idea what she already does or doesn't know."

"Cody, kids today are pretty smart. She probably knows a lot more about . . . things than you think she does . . . more than I ever did at her age." Shaye saw the dubious look on Cody's face. "She's thirteen. If she *wasn't* thinking about boys I'd be worried."

"She's a baby."

"Cody, she's a young woman. There are girls having babies at thirteen." His dubious expression turned to panic. "Of course, that's in the city," she rushed to say. "I'm sure that isn't happening around here." Shaye realized she'd better stop now because there wasn't room for one more foot in her mouth.

She felt sorry for him; this was one problem he didn't need right now. But it was one problem she could help him solve. "Okay, okay. I'll give her the Sister Maria Theresa Concepcion tour through puberty and beyond."

Relief flooded Cody's face, but something still seemed to bother him.

"Shaye, tell her all you can, but do you suppose you could keep the . . . uh . . . 'Concepcion' part out of it?" A crooked grin split his face.

Before Shaye could reply, Maribeth opened the door. "Phone call." She handed the cordless to Cody. "It's Señor Miguel Santos di Prado." She raised her hands over her head, snapped her fingers, and clicked her heels like a flamboyant flamenco dancer. "He's the mucho macho rich guy in California, some kind of Argentinean prince or something, who buys a lot of Cody's polo ponies," she informed Shaye in a loud whisper.

"I think you've got some serious geography problems going on there, Tater." With the phone held against his ear, Cody sat down on the wicker settee, his left knee bouncing with nervous energy. "Miguel? It's good to hear from you, *amigo*. You had me a little worried. I thought maybe you'd changed your mind." He looked up at Maribeth and Shaye. "I'm going to be a little while here, how about you two go see what Roscoe's got in the cookie jar."

"One thing about my dear brother," Maribeth said. "You always know when he thinks something's none of your business." Maribeth harrumphed. "Come on, Shaye, how do you like butterscotch squares or sugar cookies?" She took Shaye's arm and led her to the door. "Just give me a couple of years so I can fill a bra that's five sizes larger, and I'm going to marry that Señor Miguel Santos di Prado."

• • •

Cody pressed the End button on the phone, set it down on the seat beside him, leaned back, and closed his eyes. "Thank you," he whispered into the night breeze. "Thank you."

Di Prado had just finalized the deal for all six horses. The closing price wasn't all he'd hoped for—the deal left him twenty-three grand short of the total he needed for the bank—but adding in Roscoe's check for the stock trailer put him only twelve away. Twelve thousand was a whole lot easier to find than the full two hundred. He was going to be able to save the ranch.

His heart soared. He hadn't felt true joy in so long he wasn't sure how to handle the overwhelming rush.

He'd call the bank in the morning and tell them to let him know the moment di Prado's bank draft arrived— Miguel said it would be about a week to ten days. Cody figured the news would give Roger Warner, the bank's loan officer, a greedy little buzz.

Cody wanted to celebrate. Sure his cattle were still sick. Yes, he'd lost almost forty head. But the number of new sick ones being brought in to the quarantine pens had dropped over the last couple of days. The virus was dying out, he hadn't had to destroy his herd, and the virus hadn't hit any of the other ranches. Things were definitely looking up. Yup, a good celebration was definitely in order.

He pulled the envelope from his back pocket and ripped it open. The invitation was on expensive card stock with an equally expensive deckled edge. He could feel the raised lettering with his finger, and as though it were written in Braille, could almost make out each word.

The Cheyenne Cattlemen's Association
cordially invites you to attend
the 52nd Annual Cowboy Ball.

Cody began a solitaire dance across the porch, putting his own words to the tune of "Buffalo Gals." "I'm gonna go to the Cowboy Ball, Cowboy Ball, Cowboy Ball; with the purtyiest gal in the county, y'all . . . in the state, y'all." He stopped and quickly glanced around, praying that no one had seen him acting like a blathering idiot. "Hey, I'm allowed," he countered, and took off again down the length of the porch, in a brisk country two-step.

The sound of the screen door opening behind him brought him to a dead stop, and he quickly tried to assume a nonchalant pose, leaning against one of the porch posts.

"You're going to have to increase the number of riding lessons I get so I won't tell anyone that you've gone *el loco grande* and are singing and dancing alone in the moonlight."

"That's blackmail," Cody countered, enjoying the cute, smug expression on Shaye's face.

"Hmm, I suppose it is."

"Miss Shaye, I'm appalled that you, a respected woman of the bar, would stoop so low. Being a poker player, I'll call your bluff and raise you." He watched the smug expression change first to surprise, then a show of definite wariness. "I won't tell Hubbard you're not doing your best job trying to get Medicine Creek, and in return you go with me to the Cowboy Ball next Saturday night." He folded his arms over his chest, placed a self-satisfied grin on his own face, and waited to see how she'd wiggle out of this one.

Silent for a moment, obviously thinking over her new predicament, Shaye dug her hands into the back pockets of her jeans. This caused her breasts to jut forward, and Cody not only enjoyed the view but found himself sorely tempted to reach out and lightly touch their tempting peaks. And then she laughed that marvelous deep, full-bodied, and honest laugh that he loved, and he found himself bound tighter by his fascination with this unique woman. "I'm crushed," he responded. "I've never had anyone laugh at me before when I asked them out on a date."

"Is that what you were doing? Asking me for a date?"

"Sort of, I suppose." *Coward, make a damn stand.* "Yes, I'm asking if you'd be my date for the Cowboy Ball." *That was pretty limp, try again.* "Miss Shaye, I'd be right proud if you'd kindly allow me to escort you to the Cowboy Ball this coming Saturday evening." *There, a bit of hokey, humble cowpoke jabber ought to win her over.*

"Thank you for asking," Shaye replied, failing to stop another bout of laughter. "I'm very flattered, but I have to decline. I don't date. Not just you—I don't date . . . anyone."

"I've got some celebrating to do and just thought it would be great if . . ." He shrugged and turned away, disappointment hurting more than he'd expected. "Never mind." He felt as though a big chunk of his excitement over di Prado's phone call had been sucked out of him. The idea of inviting her to the ball had just popped into his mind, but once it was there, he'd really liked it. Now it seemed stupid. He should have known better than to expect her to say yes. Whether she pushed for him to sell Medicine Creek or not, she still worked for Hubbard.

Shaye picked up her glass of lemonade from the table, took a sip, and looked up at the night sky. "I thought you would be going to the dance with Bunny Gibson."

"With Bunny?" Where in the hell had that come from? He swung around and faced her. "What do you know about Bunny?"

"Relax, cowboy. I met her the day I was in the Chuckwagon with Julie. Apparently she's planning on being your date for the ball."

"What?"

She shrugged. "That's what she was saying."

"Bunny's just a friend . . . I've known her for years . . .

but we've never . . . uh, dated. . . ." His miserable explanation trickled off.

Shaye stared into her half-empty glass for a moment and then looked up. "If you aren't going to ask Bunny, instead of a date, how about we have an . . . arrangement."

"A what?"

"An arrangement."

"What kind of arrangement?"

"Hubbard thought it would be a good idea for us to go, but he's going to be tied up with business in Lander. Julie and Gene have already asked me to join them, so I'll drive myself and meet you there. It won't be a date. It'll be more like a few . . . friends sharing an evening—the Fourth of July gang all over again." She gave him another present of her laughter. "I'll dance with you—I know you can dance because I saw you . . . unless you prefer to dance alone. Just don't expect me to let myself get tied to you again."

"Don't make any promises you might not be able to keep," Cody replied, skimming the tip of his finger down the curve of her cheek.

Shaye's eyes locked on his as he held the point of her chin between his index finger and thumb. A warm, exciting rush teased him, tempted every pleasure-seeking nerve throughout his body. He wanted to kiss her, and it was obvious by the tiny flick of her tongue across her lips that she thought he was going to. He heard the sharp intake of her breath, then felt her step away from his touch. Disappointment hit hard when she moved toward the porch steps.

She stopped, turned toward him, and rested her hand on the banister. "I have to . . . I'd better go."

Her voice held a husky quality that aroused every male impulse in him. It took all the grit he had to keep from pulling her into his arms.

"I've got . . . a busy day tomorrow," she said, beginning to turn away.

"How about ten in the morning?" Cody laid his hand over hers, stopping her.

"For?" She looked up at him, her green eyes registering her confusion.

"Your first lesson . . ." He looked down at her feet, at the scarlet- tipped toes that peeked out of her sandals. A groan moved up from the bottom of his libido. He hated to do it, but he had to. "Those have to go."

"You want me to ride barefoot?"

"No, city girl, I want you to go shopping . . . for boots. Go see Bonnie Linderman at the saddle shop in town." He shook his head. "Better still, I've got to pick up some antibiotics at Doc Campbell's office in the morning. I'll meet you at Bonnie's store at ten. I don't want you picking out anything but good riding boots—no high-heeled, sparkly dancing boots with silver toes, fringe, and chains."

He was going to miss those pretty pink toes . . . a lot.

Chapter Eleven

"Here, try these." Cody handed Shaye a pair of plain brown boots. "They're well made, no frills or gewgaws, and will give you the right kind of support and protection."

Shaye frowned. "I really don't care for brown."

"Those come in other colors, too," Bonnie Linderman offered, holding up an identical boot in gray and another in navy. "There's also a dark maroon."

"I didn't realize there'd be so many different colors and styles to choose from." Shaye frowned as she looked at the stack of boxes and boots that surrounded her chair. "I don't know which pair to pick."

"This pair." Cody pointed again to the brown boots.

"Cody," Bonnie said with an exasperated sigh. "Why don't you go grab a cup of coffee at the Chuckwagon and let me take care of Shaye." She shoved him toward the door. "I'll make sure she gets the right kind of boots." She opened the door, and when he hesitated, she smiled at him as though she was reassuring a child going off to school for the first time in his life. "Trust me. I've done this before." The pat she gave him on the back turned into a push. She closed the door on his heels and turned to Shaye, a mischievous grin curving her lips. "I'm tempted to lock it so he won't come back in." She set the brown pair of boots aside. "Now, let's get back to finding you the right pair of boots in the right color."

Fifteen minutes later Shaye found herself wearing a wonderfully comfortable pair of plain, yet handsome dark gray boots. She walked up and down the aisle, trying to get used to the weight, the stiff soles, and the high vamps.

"I gotta tell ya," Bonnie said, beginning to put the rejected boots back into stock, "I was really surprised to see you come in with Cody—you workin' for Glenn Hubbard, and all. But then again maybe I shouldn't be surprised, especially after that kiss at the picnic on the Fourth." She turned and handed Shaye a tin of boot polish. "So, are you and Cody a couple now?"

"No," Shaye quickly countered, holding up her hand to ward off the notion. "Just acquaintances, that's all."

"Really? Hmm, I've never had an acquaintance kiss me like that . . . and then take me shopping."

Shaye realized that the friendly inquisition was going to continue until she gave Bonnie the full reason for the shopping trip. "I'm going to be taking riding lessons from Cody. He wanted to make sure I bought the right boots and clothes."

Bonnie nodded, her smile becoming a little smug. "Uh-huh, okay, whatever you say." She paused and watched Shaye for a moment as if expecting more details. When none were given, she continued. "So what else do you need?"

"What do you think? This is all new to me," Shaye replied, delighted to change the topic of conversation. "Jeans, I suppose, and a pair of gloves. What else . . . a hat maybe?"

Another fifteen minutes slid by, and the stack of items on the counter rose higher and higher.

Shaye fingered the wide brim of a silver-gray cowboy

hat that sat on a display rack. She checked the price tag and almost choked. "Is this right? Five hundred and eighty dollars for a cowboy hat?"

"Yup. That's a genuine 6X beaver Stetson. Believe me, you don't need one of those and neither do 99.9 percent of the folks in the county. I suppose your boss is the only one around here who could afford it. I think a ballcap would suit your needs a whole lot better. Here, try it on." Bonnie handed Shaye a navy blue cap with a galloping horse embroidered on the front. "No, don't plop it on the back of your head, here, let me show you." Bonnie took the hat back from Shaye, rolled the bill, and set it square on Shaye's head. "Now, when you wear it, ponytail your hair and pull the ponytail through the opening in the back." She fussed with Shaye's hair and in moments had it neatly pulled through the back of the cap. "Perfect." She led Shaye to a mirror. "Take a look. What do you think? Nice, eh?" Bonnie nodded. "Now you look like a real cowgirl."

"I'm overwhelmed by all this. I never realized there was so much to just climbing on a horse." Shaye pulled the bill of the ballcap a little lower on her forehead, then, moving to the left, then the right, checked out all angles of her reflection in the mirror. "I like it."

"So do I."

Both women quickly turned at the sound of Cody's voice.

Shaye snatched the cap from her head, feeling flustered under his scrutiny. She followed his gaze to her feet and the gray boots.

"Good choice, ladies. I approve." He moved to the counter and glanced at the clothes Shaye had selected. "Make sure you wash these jeans at least half a dozen times before you use them . . . and use fabric softener. You don't want the denim rubbing the inside of your legs."

Shaye felt a rush of heat to her face and knew without another glance in the mirror that her cheeks were a bright red. The last thing she needed to know was that Cody Butler was thinking about anything rubbing the inside of her legs.

"That was a quick cup of coffee," Bonnie shot at Cody, taking the ballcap from Shaye and dropping it on the counter.

"Yeah, well, I get real nervous about leaving two women alone to shop, especially when one doesn't know what she needs and the other owns the store." He pointed at Shaye's tall stack of items. "See, that's what I mean."

Shaye breathed an exasperated sigh. Cody Butler had some nerve. This shopping trip may have been his idea, but she'd darn well choose what she wanted. He wasn't paying for it, she was. "Have we just been insulted?"

"Probably." Bonnie gave a nonchalant shrug. "Something you should learn right away . . . cowboys have few social graces. It's all that quality time they spend with cows."

Ignoring Bonnie's comment, Cody rifled through Shaye's selections on the countertop. "You need a belt."

"I have a belt."

Cody glanced at her waist, grimaced, looked up, and shook his head. "That little wispy thing isn't a belt." He scooped a measuring tape off the counter and quickly wrapped it around Shaye's waist. "Hmm . . . very nice."

"Stop it!" She pushed his hands away and ducked his second attempt to use the tape.

"Yup, I can see . . . just a couple of acquaintances out doing some friendly shopping," Bonnie Linderman whispered as she began to ring up Shaye's purchases.

"Here." Cody dropped a belt and an oval silver buckle on top of the counter. "Now you're set . . . except for a couple of tubes of Ben-Gay from the drugstore."

The grin on his face wouldn't go away. It had settled there the minute he'd walked back into Bonnie Linderman's

store and found Shaye wearing the ballcap with her ponytail pulled through the hole in the back. The look was
cute . . . trendy. Trendy? Hell . . . it was darned sexy. His
grin had grown wider as he watched her dump the shopping bags with her new riding clothes onto the passenger
seat of her car. He'd gladly tell Shaye Frazier to keep her
Liz Claiborne suits and Versace gowns to herself. *This
cowboy's dream is a woman in tight jeans, a T-shirt, and a
ballcap.* There was no doubt about it—he'd gotten the better half of this trade.

And those toes. She'd worn her sandals again, and he
couldn't help but notice that the scarlet polish was still the
color of the day. He was beginning to really worry about
this new fascination he had with toes. Was it just Shaye
Frazier's toes or anyone's? He gave a mental shrug. Maybe
when most of the women you knew wore cowboy boots, a
glimpse of feminine toes now and then, especially those
with pretty polish on them, was like a peek of an ankle to
a Victorian gentleman. Come to think of it, he mused, he
wouldn't mind seeing a little ankle, either.

"Damn," he groaned. He'd just helped Shaye buy her
first pair of boots. He'd never see those pink toes again.

He checked his watch. Lunchtime. Maybe he should
have taken Shaye to Maddie Crawford's Chuckwagon for
lunch instead of saying goodbye and driving off. It would
have been nice—just the two of them. Cozy. No. He'd
done the right thing. Bonnie'd have it all over town in less
than an hour that they'd been shopping together. Shopping
and eating lunch together would be more than the gossips
could handle in one day.

Shaye's first riding lesson was set up for six that
evening. Most of the hands would be gone for the day, it
would be much cooler, and besides, he could spend more
time with her. He couldn't wait to see her all decked out in
her tight, new jeans.

For the rest of the drive home he sang along with every

top-forty tune that WODG, "Whoa Doggy" Country Radio, played. He crooned the ballads and wailed with the fast tunes. He harmonized with Garth and agreed that some of the best friends a cowboy could have were those in low places.

Cody turned into the lane, drove under the Medicine Creek sign, over the cattle guard, and slowed down. His gaze scanned the land. As far as he could see—Butler land. From the fenced horse pastures that rimmed the road, to the rolling grasslands that fed and fattened his cattle, to the vertebral peaks of the mountains that rose up and met the cloud-fleeced blue sky—Butler land. "And it's gonna stay that way."

As the lane curved around the stand of large oaks, he could see down to the barns and the holding pens. His grin vanished and his singing dwindled. Doc Campbell's truck and a green pickup with the Wyoming state seal on the driver's door were parked beside the quarantine lot. The federal ag guys had finally arrived.

Doc Campbell waved as Cody pulled up to the pen. The other two men, dressed in matching pale blue jumpsuits and rubber boots, never turned away from the sick cattle.

"How ya doing, Doc." Cody extended his hand and met Doc Campbell's grip in a friendly greeting. "Sorry I wasn't here when you arrived."

"Cody, this is Ray Harding and J. R. Scott from the federal ag office."

"Gentlemen, I'm glad you could finally make it." Struggling to look calm, Cody offered to shake hands with each only to be rebuffed by a show of rubber-glove-clad hands and a barely perceptible nod of acknowledgment from either state veterinarian.

"Do you know that you've got yourself some very sick cows, Mr. Butler?" J. R. Scott said, his tone annoyingly patronizing. "I'd like to know why we weren't called in sooner to inspect this herd. This is a serious situation."

Cody shot Doc Campbell a puzzled look.

"Keith Grant in your office was notified the day I first examined these cattle," Doc Campbell answered. "We were told you two were off on vacation and couldn't make it out here until after the Fourth and that the other vets in your office were working a case in Yellowstone."

Ray Harding searched through the papers on his clipboard as if looking for a specific page. "I don't seem to have a memo to that effect, Dr. Campbell." Apparently giving up, he flipped the papers back to the first page. "Well, whatever." After a quick glance at his partner, he slid the clipboard back into his briefcase, then turned to Cody. His manner hadn't improved. "Mr. Butler, these cows are a damned mess."

"Yeah," Cody replied, turned off by Grant's attitude. "Well, I haven't seen a tidy, drooling cow yet."

Grant shot him a piercing look. "Do you think this is a humorous situation, Mr. Butler? I certainly don't."

"Believe me, I find nothing funny about dying cattle, lost income, or danger to my family. So suppose you stop treating me like I gave this virus to my cattle on purpose, or ruined your day because you had to drive out here. Let's get down to figuring out where it came from and how to get rid of it."

"Getting *rid of it* might not be the answer. It's possible you're going to have to destroy the whole herd."

"Now wait a minute," Doc Campbell broke in. "I think that remark is a little hasty. We should wait for the lab results before any decision is made."

An hour later, after putting up with the persistent condescending attitude of the two federal veterinarians, and after filling out a stack of their paperwork, Cody was glad to see them leave. He'd lost count of the number of blood samples they'd drawn, the tongue swabs they'd taken, or the questions they'd asked. By the time they left, Cody couldn't wait to get up to the house for a long, hot shower to erase the stink of disease from his skin and clothes. Only one thing made the whole afternoon ordeal worthwhile—the form he held in his hand that gave a preliminary diagnosis of hoof-and-mouth disease pending the results from the state laboratory. At least this would put a halt to any talk about brucellosis.

He wolfed down his supper, barely tasting the leftover meat loaf and cottage-fried potatoes. After forcing promises out of Roscoe and Maribeth that they wouldn't come down to the barns to watch Shaye's lesson, he left. The walk to the barn was punctuated by him whistling a jaunty tune and wondering if he needed to have his head examined for making the trade with her in the first place.

He nervously paced up and down the aisle of the saddle horse barn, wiped his sweaty palms on his jeans, and jumped when he heard the slam of a car door.

"Hi."

Shaye stood in the middle of the barn doorway, new boots, new jeans, new shirt, and new ballcap all in place. He approved of every square inch of her . . . and the round inches, too.

"Are you ready for this?"

She took a hesitant step into the barn. "I suppose so."

"Don't worry, we'll take it real slow. Come on, I'll show you around."

He led her up the aisle, introducing her to every horse in the barn. Stopping at the last stall, he took a halter and lead rope off the peg and opened the door. "Come on in. Relax and just move quietly. Don't make any sudden moves. Horses are fright-and-flight animals." He waited until she was in the stall, then he closed the door. "Always close the door until you've got the halter and lead on the horse. Sometimes they like to take off on their own." He waited for her to acknowledge that she understood. Taking her nod as a yes, he continued. "This is My Nugget Delight, better known to those who love her as Sophie. She's quiet, well-trained, and loves to be petted."

"Hey, Sophie," Shaye crooned, hesitantly stepping closer to the mare.

"Hold your hand out flat and let her get your scent."

Shaye breathed a soft giggle as the mare lipped her hand. "She is so sweet." Plainly comfortable with her first contact, Shaye stroked the mare's nose and cheek.

"Sophie, as her name implies, is a girl horse . . . a mare," Cody offered. "She's also a palomino—that's her color. And, she's a registered Quarter Horse—that's her breed. Get acquainted, because you two are going to become the best of friends."

Over the next half hour he showed Shaye how to halter the mare, how to lead her out of the stall, and how to put her in the cross ties in the aisle of the barn.

"Aren't I going to ride?"

"Maybe for a little while, later, if there's time. You have to learn how to take care of a horse first," Cody replied, drawing her closer to the mare. "I'm going to name the main parts of a horse's anatomy and show you where they are." He smiled, watching a frown crease Shaye's forehead as she concentrated on what he was saying. Her determination to learn made him feel good.

She quickly grasped all he showed her, beaming from ear to ear after earning a thumbs-up for a perfect score when he quizzed her at the end of the lesson.

"Now, let's go on to something else." He reached into the tack box and withdrew a few items. "These are your grooming tools—a rubber curry, a stiff dandy brush, a soft dandy brush, a comb, and a hoof pick." He held up each one so she could see. "To start, stand on the left side of the horse and use the rubber curry in a circular motion to loosen dirt and old hair." He handed the curry to her. "Begin up behind her ear and work all over her body."

Shaye tentatively began.

"Harder," Cody directed. "You're not going to hurt her, but you need to work in bigger circles and use more elbow grease . . . harder."

She tried again. "Like this?"

"Harder. You're barely moving the hair."

Shaye turned and held the curry out to him. "Show me, please."

"Turn around." He stepped up behind her until their bodies were less than a hair's breadth apart. Light and fresh, the essence of Shaye alone and not the cloying smell of manufactured perfume enveloped him. *Oh, this could be dangerous.*

Shaye glanced at him over her shoulder, the long, dark strands of her ponytail brushing his cheek and throat when she moved her head. His body's response was immediate, and a needy moan slipped through his lips. He battled to get his mind back on track—back to the job of teaching Glenn Hubbard's lady lawyer all about horses. *That was good,* he thought. *If I keep thinking of her as Glenn Hubbard's lawyer, it might take away some of the appeal. Yeah, right.*

His head thought it was a reasonable plan, but his body was determined to ignore anything reasonable. He glanced heavenward and mouthed a silent plea. A little self-control would be nice . . . better still, a lot would be more fitting. Setting a tenacious edge to his resolve, he forged ahead with Shaye's lesson.

"Hold the curry on her neck," Cody said, gritting the words through his teeth. He covered Shaye's hand with his own. The words *soft* and *feminine* flew into his head. With a mental shake to dislodge the thoughts those words roused, he showed her the pressure and the circular motion she should use. *Oh, damn.* He immediately recognized his blunder.

With every circular movement Shaye's hand made, her bottom followed suit, rubbing against him. Around,

around, around. Oh gawd . . . sweet agony. Stunned, Cody couldn't move away. Jolted by the reality of his predicament, he knew he had to . . . but he didn't . . . he couldn't . . . he didn't want to.

"How am I doing?" she brightly asked.

"Uh . . . oh, great." Breathing was nearly impossible.

"Do you want me to keep going?"

"Uh . . . yeah."

"Doesn't this hurt?"

"Oh . . . uh . . . not the horse."

It took every ounce of self-control and more than a dollop or two of integrity, but Cody lifted his hand from hers and stepped away. In this case, retreat meant valor. "Do both sides," he said. Swallowing hard, he headed for his office. "I'm going to get us a couple of Cokes."

At the office door he turned and watched her work, her ponytail swinging with each stroke of the curry, her face set in an appealing look of determination. He liked what he saw. He liked it a lot. He had felt hot, needful lust before with other women, but this was different. Very different. An element existed that was new and unfamiliar to him. It heightened his need, his wanting. It made him feel unbalanced, unsure of himself, yet it electrified him, excited him. A name for this emotional ingredient eluded him, but the thought of exploring every aspect of this new feeling with Shaye Frazier both enticed and spooked him. "Steady, cowboy . . . take it slow and easy . . . break her gently."

Roscoe and Maribeth furtively moved along the uneven ground and through the tall grass on the far side of the horse pen until they found a spot directly across from the horse barn.

"This ought to do fine," Maribeth whispered, raising the binoculars to her eyes. It took a few moments to adjust the lenses and find her target.

"Well?" Roscoe asked, his voice loud enough to startle the horses in the pen. "Can you see anything?"

"Yes," she hissed. "I just got 'em in my sights. And will you try to be a little more quiet?"

"What's going on?" He jostled against her, vying for his own spot along the fence.

"Oops, I've lost them again. Quit pushing me."

"Here, give me them blasted binoculars."

Maribeth pulled away from his grasp. "Hey! Wait your turn."

"Have you found 'em again?"

"Yes. There, I can see them."

"What are they doing?" He began pacing back and forth, looking over Maribeth's shoulder from time to time.

"They're just talking." She gave a low whistle. "Oooh . . . uh-oh . . ."

"What?" Roscoe quickly reached for the glasses again. "What?"

"Oh, never mind. They're still just talking." Maribeth paused and shooed a fly off the end of her nose. "No . . . wait . . . oh, yes."

"Damn it, girl. Will you let me have a look?"

"Now he's showing her how to brush Sophie."

"Yeah, and what's so good about that? Lemme see."

"Here, quit your grumbling." She thrust the binoculars at him and stepped aside.

Roscoe put the glasses to his eyes, fumbled with the lens adjustment, and propped his elbows on the fence rail. "Hot diggity, that sure is an interesting way to show somebody how to brush a horse." He cackled, lost his balance, and teetered precariously for a moment before grabbing on to the fence rail to steady himself. He raised the binoculars to his eyes again. "Well, now, ain't that interestin'?"

"What?" Maribeth demanded, pushing Roscoe aside and taking the glasses from him and putting them up to her eyes. "Doggone it, are you blind or something?" Her fingers quickly adjusted the lens until she could clearly see Cody and Shaye in the barn. "He's going to . . . yes . . . oh, yes, oh, damn!"

"What?"

"The horses in the pen just moved in the way. I can't see a blasted thing." She stood on tiptoe. It didn't help. She moved to her left and then her right. The whole herd was strung out along the fence and completely blocked her view. She clambered up on the second rail of the fence. It didn't help, either. "Go chase the horses out of the way."

"I can't do that."

"Yes, you can. Hurry up. I don't want to miss anything."

"I can't. Cody'll see 'em runnin' and come see what's going on."

"He'll just think it's the dogs messing with them again."

"The dogs are lying down right in front of the barn. He'll know it's not them."

"Well, what are we supposed to do in the meantime? There's no place else we can stand and see them."

"Okay, damn it, but if I get caught, you're gonna have to come up with a believable story." Bending over, Roscoe sprinted along the fence, his bandy legs kicking up grasshoppers and ladybugs as he went. Reaching the far end of the fence, he cupped his hands around his mouth. "Eeeya! Git, you wooden-brained old nags. . . ." He pulled up a couple of handfuls of tall grass and tossed them into the pen. His ploy worked—the whole herd moved to investigate the clumps of fresh grass.

"Good. Great. Thanks, Roscoe." Maribeth sent him a thumbs-up. "The horses have moved . . . oh, butt pimples . . . so's Cody."

Chapter Twelve

Cody dunked his head into the water trough. Compared to the heat stocked up in his body, the temperature of the water felt arctic. He hoped it would help clear his head and cool down some of the thoughts that being near Shaye Frazier had ignited. He counted to twenty before pulling his head out of the trough. He sucked in another gulp of air and dunked his head again. This time he tried for a forty count but only reached thirty-seven before he pulled out. He didn't know if he could deal with another evening like the one he'd just suffered through. The grooming lesson had just about done him in. He hadn't even gotten around to saddling Sophie. He hoped things would calm down a lot more once he got Shaye up on the horse . . . and out of reach.

Mimicking his dogs, Cody shook the water out of his hair, sending droplets flying all around him. He shivered as the spray drenched his bare shoulders and chest. He finger-combed his hair back from his face and, with a swipe of his hand, wiped the remaining water from his face. His head might have cooled down, but the rest of his body still needed a long icy soak.

"So, how'd it go?" Roscoe shuffled into the horse barn,

his tall-heeled boots kicking up dirt and wood-chip bedding.

"You tell me," Cody grumbled his reply over his shoulder as he slid his arms into his shirt and fastened the buttons down the front. "You and Maribeth made enough noise to spook a herd of deaf elephants."

"Did not."

"Did too." He stuffed his shirttails into his jeans, grabbed his ballcap off the hay bale, settled it firmly on his wet head, and began to walk away. "I'm too tired to stand here and argue with you." He looked back. "There'd better be some chocolate cake left over from supper. You owe me."

Roscoe hobbled to keep up with Cody, harrumphing with each step. "Well, if I'd known you were gonna be so darned upset, I'd have brought the whole damn cake down to the barn with me."

Cody stopped and Roscoe almost bumped into him. "I asked you and Maribeth to stay up at the house. But, no. You had to sneak down and spy on us like a couple of little nosy brats."

Roscoe propped his hands up on his skinny hips and, like an angry little hornet, met Cody's glare. "That's what you know." He swallowed and his Adam's apple bobbed down and then back up in his scrawny neck. "We was just out looking for . . . uh . . . at . . . at . . . the . . . uh . . . yearlings." He gave a quick decisive nod. "That's it. We was lookin' at the yearlings."

Cody cynically cocked his left brow. "Yeah, they're a real hard bunch to find in the paddock—all twenty-eight of 'em. I suppose that's why you needed a pair of binoculars."

"Who said we had binocs?" Roscoe rose up on his toes like a bantam rooster ready to meet a challenge.

"The sun kept hitting the lens and I saw you. I saw you both."

Roscoe glared at Cody. "And it was a darned good thing

that you saw us. I was gettin' pretty shocked at what was going on in here. I ain't never seen nobody brush a horse like that." An indignant thrust of his shoulders punctuated Roscoe's censure. "Maybe knowing you was being watched kept ya from taking advantage of that sweet girl."

Cody couldn't believe his ears. He leaned over the short old man. "Taking advantage? You thought *I* was taking advantage of *her*? Well, let me tell you something, you old coot." He raised his hand, pointing a finger in Roscoe's face. "I'm the one who . . . aw, hell, never mind." Exasperated, he threw his hand down and stalked away.

"Hehehe," Roscoe cackled. "Just like I thought." His laughter rolled out of him, shaking his thin frame. "You've got it bad, boy. I knew it. You've got it real bad."

Cody stopped once again, turned, and mirrored Roscoe's previous stance with his hands on his hips. Were his feelings that transparent? God, he hoped not. They couldn't be. He wasn't even sure what his feelings were. "You don't know . . . anything. Why would I be interested in Glenn Hubbard's 'go get' girl?"

"Okay, if that's what you want me to believe, I'll play along and keep ya happy." Roscoe shrugged, but his grin widened. "So, did ya ask her to go with ya to the Cowboy Ball?"

"Were you eavesdropping on us last night, too?"

"So you did ask her, didn't ya?" He cackled with glee again and slapped his knee. "What'd she say?" The old man's face was alight with eagerness. "Come on, tell me. What'd she say?"

Cody looked down and shuffled the heel of his boot back and forth in the dirt. "Not that it's any of your business . . . she turned me down." He raised his eyes and met Roscoe with a challenging glower.

Roscoe's mouth took a regret-filled downward slant, and he shook his head. "You're jest pitiful. Damned pitiful." He continued to shake his head. "Now you'll have to go to the dance with Bunny Gibson."

"Not hardly," Cody quickly countered. "I'd take one of those sick steers first."

"She's been calling here a couple of times a day, and I'm getting tired of bein' your social secretary and making excuses for ya." Roscoe jabbed his gnarled index finger against Cody's chest. "Next time Miss Bunny calls, you're gonna talk to her yourself. She's an old friend and ya owe her that much." He continued to mumble as he walked away. "Pitiful. You're plain pitiful. You're the most pitiful, sorry-assed excuse for a man I've ever seen. Rotten pitiful, through and through."

"Hey," Cody called after him. "If I'm so blasted pitiful, why is Shaye going to meet me at the dance . . . with Julie and Gene?"

Roscoe looked over his shoulder. "So you *are* datin' her." He stopped and waited for Cody's answer.

"No, it's not a date . . . it's like an . . . arrangement."

The old cowboy turned and silently studied Cody for a moment, his face rearranging itself into a frown. "An arrangement? What the hell is an 'arrangement'? You're either datin' her or you ain't."

"I already told you. I'm meeting her there . . . we're going to be with Gene and Julie . . . just like the picnic on the Fourth."

"Oh, yeah?" Roscoe snorted. "Well, we all know what a winner that afternoon was." He shook his head. "An arrangement . . . bah. Strangest damn thing I've ever heard." He shrugged his narrow shoulders, then paused as if thinking things through. He raised his old cowboy hat and scratched the side of his head. "It's not perfect, but I suppose it's better than nothin'." He paused and began to nod. "Yup, a lot more promising." Once more he headed for the house, waving goodbye to Cody without turning around again. "Yup, there's hope for your sorry pitiful butt yet."

"Wow, this is quite a spread," Julie breathed, her voice filled with awe as she looked around the huge living room. "I'd heard some of the construction guys talking when they were building this place for Hubbard, but wow . . . I never imagined."

Shaye led Julie through Hubbard's house to the pool. "It seems a little ostentatious to me for just one person, but Hub's always liked first class."

"I don't understand why you don't just move in permanently and open your legal practice in Dorland. We can use a young, family-practice attorney in town. Mr. Calhoun is getting old and only works half days for three days a week now. If you need anything done, you have to go to the city." She lightly placed her hand on Shaye's arm. "You'd have a great practice here. Why don't ya stay?"

"You know what my plans are."

"Yeah, I know what you *said* they were, but sometimes plans change . . . people change. . . ."

"Stop right there, and save your breath."

"Just don't shut yourself to the possibility. You never know what might come along and change your mind." Julie grinned. "Or who."

"Don't start in on that again."

They tossed their towels on a chaise near the pool.

"Hot tub or a swim?" Shaye pointed from one to the other and then waited for Julie's answer.

"Hmm, you do know how to create a dilemma for a poor, deprived country girl." She looked at the hot tub and then over at the pool. "Never been in a hot tub . . . let's do that first."

As they settled into the water, Shaye turned the jets on high. "How's that?"

"Oh, girl," Julie moaned. "This contraption was built

for one thing and one thing only." She leaned back and closed her eyes. "If you ever hear it crank up in the middle of the night, don't peek . . . it'll just be me and Gene. We'll have hopped the fence and will be hoppin' each other." She glanced up at Shaye. "Of course, I'll have my badge on so it will be classified as an official police . . . investigation." She grinned a wicked, mischievous grin. "That might be all I'm wearing, though . . . just my badge."

"Of course." Shaye laughed. "A dedicated deputy sheriff should never be out of uniform."

"Damn straight." Julie closed her eyes again. "So how'd your riding lesson go last night?"

Julie's question had come out of the blue and caught her off guard. "Uh . . . good, I suppose." Shaye shrugged, trying to appear calm on the outside while inside she could still feel the heat of Cody's body as he'd stood behind her, could still feel the warm brush of his breath on her cheek. Just the memory made her pulse gallop. "Since I've never taken riding lessons before, I really don't have anything to compare it to."

"How did you like riding? I told ya it would be great fun."

"Well, I didn't exactly get to ride."

"What?" Julie's eyes popped open. "You were there for two hours and you didn't even ride? What the hell were you doing?"

I was trying to stay immune to one of the most attractive men I've ever met. Shaye frowned. "How do you know I was there for two hours?"

Julie jumped up. "Hey, I'm ready for the pool now, how about you?"

Determined not to be put off track, Shaye pushed her question again. "Julie, how do you know how long I was there?"

With a sheepish grin and a sigh, Julie sat back down in

the swirling water. "Okay. Maribeth told me when I called this morning . . . looking for Gene."

Shaye laughed. "Your answer stinks like six-day-old fish." She stood and stepped out of the hot tub, then headed for the pool. "Last one in is a monkey's butt!"

After swimming for a half hour they toweled off and raided the kitchen for lunch.

"I'm kinda disappointed. I thought Hubbard would have a full staff . . . maids, cook, the works," Julie said, pulling a handful of potato chips out of the bag. "I thought we'd just sit out by the pool and all sorts of servants, especially one of those cute and buffed Latin houseboys, would be bringing us champagne, caviar, peeled grapes . . . truffles, themselves. . . ."

"I'm so sorry to burst your bubble, but there's only Tess, the cook and housekeeper. She's a sweet lady whose been with Hub for years." Shaye placed some cold fried chicken on a platter. "It's her day off." She pried the lid off a bowl and peered inside. "Do you want any cole slaw? Italian kind?" Without waiting for Julie's reply, she dropped a serving spoon in the bowl and added it to the growing number of dishes on the glass-topped table, then opened the refrigerator again. "There's some chocolate mousse in here for dessert." She removed the pitcher of iced tea and pushed Julie toward the table. "Let's eat."

For the next few minutes neither spoke, both too busy filling their plates and taking their first bites of lunch.

"From what Gene tells me," Julie said through a mouthful of chicken, "it looks like Hubbard's not going to be getting Cody's ranch after all. Did you know his California buyer came through?"

Shaye nodded. "I was there when he got the call."

Julie looked up. "You're over there a lot, aren't you?" She laughed at Shaye's indignant expression and reached across the table to pat her hand. "Just relax, Boston . . . nobody's keeping score." She took another bite of chicken and followed it with a mouthful of salad. "So, how do you feel about him being able to make his banknote?"

Shaye put her fork down and looked pensively out the window. "He doesn't have all the money he needs yet." She turned to Julie. "From what I understand he's still quite a bit short . . . but it's a start . . . a good start."

"And?" Julie persisted. "How do you feel about it?"

"You know how I feel. I want him to keep the ranch. I'm happy for him that he's been able to sell his polo ponies. But, like I said, he's got a way to go and he's running out of time." She spooned some slaw on her plate. "He's pretty sure he's going to make up the difference, though." She looked at Julie. "I don't have any idea what he has in mind. Do you?"

Julie shrugged. "I just hope he's not thinking about trying to pick up the rest of the money by doing some rodeoing." She dunked a few carrot sticks in the dill dip. "He got hurt pretty bad the last time he competed a couple of years ago. Doc Varnum told him another bad spill might cripple him."

Shaye quickly looked up from her plate, a cold chill bolting through her. "I didn't know that." She searched Julie's face for some hint of assurance that Cody had promised never to rodeo again. She didn't find what she was looking for. "You don't think that's what he's planning, do you?"

"No . . . I doubt it." Julie crunched her carrot. "There's only one rodeo in the state that pays off the kind of money he needs—the Cheyenne Frontier Days Rodeo at the end of the month. It's a big one, and usually it's only the big guys who make their living by following the circuit who show up." She looked up at Shaye. "Don't worry, he's not foolish enough to enter. He'd have to go for the 'All-Around Cowboy' title to even come close, and I don't think Cody Butler is fool enough to climb on the back of any rough stock again—bulls or broncs."

Some of the uneasy chill began to disappear from Shaye's bones, but enough remained to keep her on edge. "He could sell some of the ranch machines . . . equipment . . . stuff . . . whatever you call tractors and things. Couldn't he?"

Julie nodded. "Whatever Cody's got planned, he must be feeling good about it. Otherwise I don't think he'd be going to the Cowboy Ball."

"He asked me to be his . . . date," Shaye offered hesitantly, feeling self-conscious about the soft catch in her voice. She didn't want to admit, even to Julie, how much she'd wanted to go with Cody. She didn't want to admit a lot of things about Cody Butler, even to herself. Each day she spent in Dorland, each time she saw Cody, the cracks in her emotional citadel were widening. If she wasn't careful, everything she'd promised herself, everything she planned, would be lost . . . *she* would be lost.

Julie's eyes popped wide with surprise. "Why didn't you tell me he'd asked you! When? What did you say? You said yes, didn't you?"

Shaye shook her head. "I told him no."

"What!" Julie dropped her fork. "Are you crazy? We could have doubled and had a great time." Her eyes narrowed. "You didn't say no just because I asked you to join Gene and me, did you?" She picked up her fork and pointed it at Shaye. "And please don't tell me that you told him no because you knew Bunny Gibson wanted to go with him."

"No, that's not it," Shaye replied. "I've told you, I'm not interested in . . . dating." The lie felt as large as a moose in her throat. Cody Butler had made it a lie. "Cody and I decided that we'd have an . . . arrangement on Saturday night."

"Okay, I'll bite. What in the hell is an . . . arrangement?"

It took only fifteen minutes for Shaye to convince Julie

that an arrangement was almost as good as an actual date. But the more Shaye explained it to her, the less sure she was that an arrangement was the right decision. No matter how she tried to rationalize, despite the fact that she would drive her own car and meet Cody at the dance . . . it still felt like a date.

"What are you going to wear?" Julie rose from the table and took her dishes to the sink.

"I'm not sure. You did say it was formal, right?" Shaye cleared the rest of the dirty dishes and began putting leftovers back in the refrigerator.

"Don't go getting all citified on me, Boston. Formal, out here, sometimes means little more than a bath, clean jeans, fresh underwear, and polished boots."

"Good, I'm all set then . . . I'll even have the optional bath."

"Very funny, Boston. Very funny." Through a mouthful of coleslaw, Julie continued. "The reality is that most of the guys will wear western-styled tuxes, some will wear just the tux jackets with a dress shirt, a good pair of jeans, and their biggest and flashiest trophy buckle. Of course the cowboy hats will be formal . . . black. The women wear everything from country classics—broomstick skirts and Indian jewelry, to Bunny Gibson's attempt to look like she's going to the Oscars. In between are the tasteful and gorgeous gowns . . . that's us."

"That's a big help," Shaye said. "I only have the one gown with me. I never imagined I'd be wearing it, though."

Julie put her arm around Shaye's shoulder and gave her a hug. "I'm sure that whatever you decide to wear will not only be elegant, tasteful, and expensive, but it will leave every one of those 5.8 males in the county drooling for weeks."

• • •

Chewing nervously on her gum, Maribeth checked the clock on the kitchen wall then out the window. She could still see Cody exercising one of the polo ponies in the training pen. Roscoe had gone to town for groceries and wouldn't be back for a while. If she hurried, she could tie up a few loose ends for the night of the Cowboy Ball.

Grabbing the cordless phone off the charger, she quickly punched in the phone number and sat down at the kitchen table. Tapping her finger on the tabletop, she anxiously waited through four rings until the phone was answered.

"Hello."

"Boy, am I ever glad you're home. I tried earlier, but there was no answer." Maribeth craned her neck for another peek down at the training pen. Cody was still working with the young gelding.

"I don't have much time to talk, I've got to get to work. Have you thought of anything?"

"No. I was kind of hoping that you would have come up with an idea or two." Maribeth sucked on her cherry-flavored gum. "The dance is this weekend . . . we've got to hurry and work something out." Maribeth blew a bubble, then popped it with a loud crack.

"It can't be obvious . . . like the infamous twisted ankle scam."

"Okay, okay." Maribeth heaved an exasperated sigh. "I learned my lesson . . . but it worked just the same. Didn't it?"

"Yes, it did, but now they're both suspicious."

"Roscoe said he'd help again."

"Good. That'll be good. Listen, I gotta go. I'll be in touch."

Maribeth hung up the phone and sat back, her hand still resting on the receiver. She could feel her heart running a mile a minute. They would have to come up with a fool-proof, undetectable, whammo plan, and they were running out of time. The phone gave off a shrill ring and she jumped. "Holy crappin' goose," she choked out, picking up the phone. "Hello."

"Hi, Maribeth, how're ya doin', sweety."

"Hi, Bunny." Maribeth screwed her face up in a goblin-like grimace.

"Is your handsome brother home?"

"He's out riding," Maribeth replied, sticking her finger in her mouth, pretending to gag herself. "He'll be gone for another . . . oh . . . two or three hours." *As long as I get the phone when you call, he'll be gone forever.*

"Well, I've just been having a horrible time trying to get a hold of him. He's always gone or workin' or unable to come to the phone for one reason or another. I've left at least five messages with old Mr. Diggins."

"Well, hey, that's part of your problem right there," Maribeth answered, pulling the wad of chewing gum out between her teeth in a long string. She filled her voice with counterfeit concern. "Poor Roscoe, he's getting so darned forgetful in his old age. Just the other night," she continued, fabricating a tall tale, "he fixed us breakfast instead of supper. He had his whole day all mixed up."

"Oh, that poor old man. It's so good of you all to let him live with you. I was just telling my daddy that I thought there weren't finer folks in the county than you Butlers."

The string of gum continued to stretch from Maribeth's mouth to the full length of her arm. "So, are you going to the Cowboy Ball?" She sucked the gum back into her mouth while waiting for Bunny's answer.

"Well, hon, that's what I want to talk to Cody about."

Maribeth could hear the pout in Bunny Gibson's voice. "Why do you need to talk to him about the dance?" *Sometimes I'm so heartless . . . bad me, bad me.* She stifled a giggle.

"I was hoping . . . well, I know it sounds presumptuous

of me . . . but we've been such close friends for so long . . . and—"

"Cody wasn't gonna go to the dance at first," Maribeth interrupted. "He must've changed his mind." She paused and mentally counted to ten before she spoke again. She could almost see Bunny Gibson leaning into the phone and holding her breath, anticipating what was coming next. "He's doing a foursome with Julie and Gene and that lady lawyer of Mr. Hubbard's." *Slam-dunk!*

Silence permeated the line until Bunny breathed one word. "Oh."

"Do you want me to tell him that you called?" The bubble gum cracked in her mouth. "Let me get a pencil and write down your message." Maribeth didn't move from her chair.

"No, that's okay, sweety." Bunny sighed. "I guess I'll be seeing him Saturday night . . . at the dance."

"Okay . . . well, it was nice talking with you, Bunny . . . bye."

The sound as Bunny Gibson hung up the phone at her end of the line was a dejected click.

"You should be ashamed of yourself."

Startled, Maribeth spun around to find Roscoe standing in the doorway, a sack of groceries in his arms. Her tongue quickly moved around her mouth. "Doggone it, Roscoe, you made me swallow my gum." She fished in her pocket for another piece. "How long have you been standing there?"

"Long enough to remind myself to keep on your good side. You're an evil, scheming little girl." He placed the sack on the countertop. "If you ever get caught, I'll swear I don't know you." He twisted an imaginary Simon Legree handlebar mustache, then rubbed his hands together in an excellent imitation of wicked glee. "So, my Sweet Polly Purebread, what kind of a plan have you got cooked up for this weekend?"

Chapter Thirteen

"I don't believe you could do that to me." Hubbard hit the top of his desk with his fist. "Damn it, Shaye, what were you thinking?" He stepped in front of her, his gray eyes dark with anger. "I'm disappointed that you'd do anything so incompetent . . . so unprofessional." He returned to pacing back and forth, from one side of his office to the other, his booted steps silent in the deep carpet.

Shaye stood in the doorway. He hadn't even waited until she was in the room before he'd lit into her. A sigh slipped through her lips. Hubbard's response to her news that she was taking riding lessons from Cody was no surprise, but it still hurt.

After years of trying to meet her father's expectations, to gain his approval, to gain his love . . . it all came down to another failure. The ache in her heart was all too familiar.

She moved to the large couch and perched on the overstuffed arm. "I wanted to tell you myself. I didn't want you to find out from someone else."

"You can tell me about this, but you couldn't tell me about the spectacle at the Fourth of July picnic?" He gave a regret-filled shake of his head.

"What are you talking about?"

"Is this the way you always do business? Is it so commonplace that you've forgotten already?"

"What . . . spectacle?"

Hubbard came to a stop and stood over her, his height forcing her to tip her head back to look up. "I had to hear from Roger Warner, the loan officer at the bank, that my attorney—my land-acquisitions agent, my representative, was rolling around on the ground in front of God and everyone, kissing the man whose ranch she'd been hired to purchase." He threw his hands up, his disgust obvious. "I won't tolerate this kind of behavior by anyone who works for me, not to mention represents me in multimillion-dollar deals." He returned to his pacing.

Shaye dropped her gaze as cold rolled over her like an arctic wave and seeped through her bones. He'd called her his attorney, his agent. He'd called her his representative. But he hadn't called her his daughter. None of the other hurtful things he'd said mattered. With the lack of that one special word, her father had cut her heart to pieces . . . again. "If you'd like to terminate our agreement, Hub, that's your prerogative."

"Are you telling me you want out?" Hubbard's steps halted. He stood by the large bay window, his tall form silhouetted by the sunlight. "When did you become a quitter?"

"I am not a quitter." Although her words held a sharp edge, she swallowed hard, trying to ignore the ache in her pride. *If he only knew how long and hard I've fought for him.* Reaching deep into her reserves of inner strength, a path she'd taken many times before, she straightened her back and took on her professional mien. "Part of my job as your . . . attorney, is to give you counsel." She waited for him to provide some indication of agreement, no matter how slight. He gave a nearly undetectable shrug, but enough to make her continue. "Well, my best . . . lawyerly advice for you is to back away from trying to get Medicine Creek." Her father's face remained impassive. Without his urging, she continued. "Cody Butler is not going to sell his ranch to you whether it's me pushing the deal or anyone else you hire. He will struggle to the very last second." She looked away for a moment, then returned her gaze to her father's, her resolve stronger, some of the chinks in her emotional armor temporarily patched. "Cody Butler might not win—in fact, he'll likely lose everything. And yes, you'll probably end up with the deed to Medicine Creek, but you can bet a bundle that the ranch will never be yours."

"What do you mean, it'll never be mine? I'll own it and every stick of wood, every rusted bolt, and every blade of grass on the property."

She watched Hub settle himself behind his desk. Beyond the yearning she'd lived with all of her life for this man to truly be her father, for the times she'd loved him with the desperation of a starving child, there were those other times—times when she didn't like her father at all. This was one of those times.

She wanted to hurt him for the pain he'd caused her, strike back in some way, but she'd inherited her mother's gentle spirit. All she could do was needle him, goad him like a pesky gnat. "I guarantee that no matter how long you hold the deed to Medicine Creek, how many fancy signs you put up, how many reporters come out and write glowing articles about your hard work to save wildlife and the environment . . . everyone in town will always call it 'the Butler place.'"

"And that's supposed to bother me?" Hubbard's lips curved upward in an indulgent smile. "They can call it the North Pole for all I care. It'll still be my land with my animals grazing on it and my men working it." Never taking his eyes from her, he sat back in his chair, relaxed, appearing to be mildly amused. "So you're all fired up about

learning to ride." His booming laugh filled the room. "I
never thought I'd see the day. Aren't you the one who
didn't even want a pet cat?" He sat forward. "I'd gladly
teach you myself, but"—he gestured at the pile of papers
in disarray on his desk—"I'm working on a deal with
Acumen Technologies and just don't have the time right
now. I'll get one of my men to teach you. I pay them too
much to just ride around as it is." He reached for the telephone. "Herb Dwyer, my chief wrangler, will do it."

Nothing ever changed. It had always been that easy for
Hub. He'd never had the time to teach her to ride her first
two-wheel bicycle, how to play tennis, how to swim, play
golf, how to figure out her math homework, or how to be
the daughter he could love. Someone else on his payroll
was always assigned to the task.

She knew if she surrendered and settled for his edict,
she'd be no further ahead than when she'd first arrived in
Dorland. She'd be little more than another of his posses-
sions that he manipulated to his own will . . . his lawyer,
his representative, his agent . . . not his daughter. Shaye
pushed away from the couch and stood. "No, Hub. I'll
keep the arrangements I've made, thank you."

"You don't care that it makes me look . . . like a
damned fool?"

She cast a skeptical glance at her father, then raised her
chin a notch. "And you don't care that this is something I
want . . . something that has absolutely nothing to do with
you or the job you hired me to do." She moved toward the
door.

Hubbard's blunt words followed her, hurt her, and
brought her to a halt. "Then, damn it, Shaye, *do* the job I
hired you to do."

Turning slowly, deliberately waiting until she fully
faced her father, Shaye bit back the words she really
wanted to throw at him and struggled to keep her temper
under a tight rein. "Maybe you'll feel you're getting your

money's worth if I tell you I met with Jeff Granger this morning." She paused, enjoying the moment as she kept her father anticipating her next words. "There's a three-hundred-acre portion of his ranch that borders the north-east corner of your land." She watched as her father, now completely interested in what she had to say, leaned forward with anticipation. *The game was back on.*

"There's a sizable spring-fed stream that runs through that acreage," she continued. "Over half the land is prime grass with the rest under a good cover of trees. The soil is solid, and there's no erosion around the water." She took a few moments to lean against the door frame, seducing Hub's interest a little longer.

"You say there's good water?"

"Mr. Granger said that the runoff of melting snow also feeds the stream."

"So what are you proposing?"

He's hooked. "If your offer per acre to Jeff Granger is about the same as the one you authorized for Medicine Creek, I think I can make a deal for you."

Hubbard thoughtfully rubbed his chin. "You've seen this land?"

Shaye nodded. "Mr. Granger drove me out there in his Jeep. It would give you the water supply and extra grass you want."

"And Granger's ready to sell?"

"Yes."

"There's no lien on the land?"

"No."

Hubbard gave a slow, thoughtful nod. "Okay. Make the deal."

Elated, Shaye felt as though she'd been freed of the biggest burden in her life. With Hub settling for Granger's land, he'd released her from pursuing the deal for Medicine Creek. She stifled the joy she felt, fighting hard to appear calm. She'd celebrate later. "I'll call Granger and get things rolling."

Hub nodded and bent his attention to the papers on his desk. He'd offered no thanks for her hard work, nor had he even acknowledged her for taking the initiative to talk to Jeff Granger. So this is what it felt like to be dismissed as though she were a mere hireling. A cynical smile moved upon her lips. But that's exactly what she was.

She moved toward the door. The sooner she closed the deal for the Granger property, the sooner she could leave Dorland and her father behind.

"Shaye." Hubbard thoughtfully tapped his pen on the top of his desk. "Keep after Cody Butler. I still want Medicine Creek."

Her steps faltered. Every smidgen of elation died. The burden had been dropped back on her shoulders.

"We moved another twelve head out of the eastern quarantine pen this afternoon," Gene Mallory said as he followed Cody through the herd of cattle in the corral. "I told the boys to still keep 'em separated from the healthy ones, but at least they're back out on grass."

Cody nodded. "That's good to hear. There was a time I thought we were going to lose them all." Cody's gaze swept the corral. "Check the ear-tag number on that red critter next to the fence. I think we missed him." He reached in his back pocket for another bottle of medication.

"You're right, he's not on the list," Gene said, looking up from the notebook in his hand.

"Let's get him," Cody said, filling the syringe.

Gene whistled and two of the cowhands moved their horses out into the middle of the pen. They both uncoiled their ropes, and as the steer ran from the edge of the pen, one cowboy dropped his loop over the steer's head. The other ride moved in behind and, with a flick of his wrist, sent his loop skittering low to the ground and caught both hind legs. The steer went down on his side in the dirt.

"Pull him tight," Cody told the two riders as he knelt over, stuck the needle into the animal's neck, and pushed the plunger. He quickly examined its mouth and tongue. "He's looking a lot better, boys." Stepping back, he glanced around the pen, making sure they'd medicated every steer. Satisfied, he capped the syringe and dropped it in his breast pocket as Gene slipped the ropes off the red steer. "Okay, we're done." He lifted his ballcap and wiped his sweaty brow with his forearm. "I'm glad this day's over. It's been a scorcher." He waved at the men who'd worked with him all day. "Thanks, fellas, see ya'll in the morning." He headed for the gate, then turned back. "Hey, don't forget to use that disinfectant in the bunkhouse before you go. I'd hate to have any of you begin to drool."

Gene fell into step beside him. "This is one day I'm not sorry to see end. I'm gonna head home to my woman, pop the top on a cold beer, and sit back and watch the Cubs get beat again."

"You've been handling those steers, too, don't forget. . . ."

"Yeah, yeah, I know. I'll scrub up." Gene kept pace with Cody as he walked across the corral. "You heard anything yet from the federal vets?"

"Not yet," Cody replied. "I can't figure out all the delays." He closed the gate behind them. "I guess no news is good news." He peeled the latex gloves from his hands and stuck them in his back pocket. "Doc Campbell's pleased with the way this thing seems to be slowing down. We haven't had a new case show up in four days, and none of the other ranches have been hit. I guess my luck isn't all bad. A lot of times the whole herd gets destroyed."

Gene glanced at Cody. "Hey, pal, it's gotta turn good for you soon. This damn streak's gotta stop."

"Yeah." Cody shrugged. "But until it does, I'm kinda stuck with the hand I've been dealt."

"It's not all bad. When does di Prado want delivery of those ponies?" Gene jerked his thumb toward the horse barn. "I'll be glad to go with you . . . help with the driving and all."

Cody nodded. "I'll probably take you up on that." He tossed the soiled latex gloves in a trash barrel just outside the corral. "Di Prado's bank draft hasn't arrived yet. Apparently he's buying three of the horses for his brother-in-law in Argentina. He's got to wait for that money before he forwards it all on to me."

"Is it going to make it here on time?"

"Yeah, no problem." He trusted Miguel. He'd done too much business with di Prado in the past to start worrying about the man's integrity now. "It'll get here in time."

"And then what? Where'll you stand?"

"There'll still be a few thousand I need to pull in, but it's looking good." He grinned. "Yeah, it's looking real good."

Gene slapped him on the back. "That's great, 'cause I've kinda gotten used to your snarls and bad disposition—I'd hate to have to break in a brand-new boss."

Cody laughed. "I don't know anyone else who'd hire you." He ducked Gene's playful punch. His mood sobered and he cast a sidelong glance at his foreman. He wasn't sure if he should tell Gene his plan to get the rest of the money he needed. He didn't doubt for a second there'd be hell to pay when not only Gene found out, but when everyone else found out, too. If he was going to say anything, now was as good a time as any. Cody drew a deep breath and tried to look as though the topic of conversation was just idle talk, nothing more. "Have you given any thought to going to Cheyenne for Frontier Days?"

"Naw," Gene replied. "Those guys are pros. They work the rodeo circuit all year long. A hardworking cowboy like me doesn't stand a chance." He kicked a clod of dirt out of his way. "I'm good at a little po-dunk or a county-fair rodeo, but not in that company. You know how it is, you've ridden the big time."

"There's good money this year, over six hundred thousand." Cody glanced up the lane to the indoor riding arena. "Some of that would sure help."

Gene suddenly looked at Cody, his eyes narrowing. "You're not thinking about riding again, are you?"

"I've given it some thought." Cody tried to keep a light and casual sound to his voice. "The purses are pretty decent. They're paying good money for first and second go-rounds. Even some third-place money would get me a lot closer to paying off the loan."

Gene grabbed Cody's arm and stopped him midstep. "Are you insane?" His eyes grew wide and his grip tightened. "Don't do it, Cody. There's got to be another way." When Cody tried to walk away, Gene stopped him again. "I'm not kidding. You almost got killed the last time. You're too tall. Six-three is too tall to ride rough stock. The shorter boys don't suffer the whiplash like you do." He kicked at a rock. "Man, you haven't been on a bull or bronc since that Indian rodeo out on the Wind River Reservation."

"I'm pretty sure I can leave the rough stock alone and make my points on timed events. If I can hit some good times in calf and steer roping, I'll be in good shape. I can also hold my own in steer wrestling."

"No way." Gene shook his head. "Joe Beavers in ninety-five was the last to win All-Around in timed events, and before that, the last time was eighty-seven. The competition's getting too young and too tough. It's all about money now." He rubbed his index finger and thumb against each other. "And it's all done on rough stock." Gene laid his hand on Cody's shoulder. "You know if a cowboy can afford a Learjet . . . he's a top rider. That's what you'll be going up against. You'd be whistlin' in the wind and getting busted up doin' it."

Cody looked back at the pen of sick steers. "I'm not stupid enough to think I'd have a shot at the All-Around title, but if I have to compete in a rough-stock event, I'll play it safe—bareback."

"Oh, yeah," Gene agreed, sarcasm dripping from his words. "That's real safe. Like I said, you're insane." He pulled a bright red handkerchief from his hip pocket and, lifting his hat, wiped his brow. "You realize just saying that you're thinking about rodeoing is going to scare Maribeth to death."

"I know," Cody replied, already regretting his decision to tell his plan to Gene. "I'm hoping she won't find out. I probably shouldn't have told you."

"Don't worry, I won't say anything to anyone . . . not even Julie." Gene made a broad sweeping gesture with his arm. "Look at this place. You've got responsibilities . . . Maribeth, the ranch . . . the men who work for you, your breeding program. Are you willing to jeopardize everything?" He shrugged. "There's gotta be another way for you to get the money."

"Yeah, sure." Cody gave a cynical laugh. "I could wait for those folks with the magazine contest to show up at the door with their balloons and six-foot check for a million bucks."

"I don't get it," Gene added, "but if you're fool enough to go, I'm fool enough to go with you. Hell, somebody's gotta bring your body back home."

"It's not going to be like that," Cody mumbled, heading for the horse barn.

"The hell it ain't. You're as rusty as last year's nails."

"I've been working out some," Cody rebutted. He even had the sore muscles to prove it.

"You call roping a few sick cows working out?" Gene snorted. "Fine, go ahead, kill yourself. Just do it neat, 'cause I don't wanna spend a lot of time picking up itty-bitty pieces."

"I didn't say that I'd made up my mind," Cody said, trying to defuse the issue. "I'm just thinking about it and have been practicing . . . a little . . . just in case, that's all." He draped his arm around Gene's shoulder. "From the way you worked that rope today, you could use a little practice yourself."

"I never said I was handy with a rope. Well, in the bedroom, maybe." Gene wriggled his eyebrows up and down, and his mouth curved up in a mischievous grin. "But you'd better take it easy and not practice too much. We don't want you coming up sore for Saturday night so you can't dance up a storm." Gene's playful punch connected this time. "Julie told me about your . . . whatchamacallit with Shaye for Saturday night."

Cody was beginning to loathe the word, but uttered it anyway. "Arrangement."

"Yeah." Gene nodded. "That's it. I don't have a clue what an arrangement is, but whatever it is, it sounds like a pretty smooth way to avoid taking Bunny."

Cody shot a quick glance at Gene as he opened his office door. "That's not why I asked Shaye. . . ." He quickly caught himself before he confessed too much. Since Shaye Frazier had walked into his life with Glenn Hubbard's proposal on her lips, he'd had nothing but dreams of putting his own mouth on those lips. The kiss at the Fourth of July picnic had only caused him more frustration. He didn't want a kiss that lasted only a couple of seconds in front of the whole town; he wanted a slow, blazing-hot kiss that left them both gasping for air. He wanted to kiss Shaye Frazier until she couldn't even say the word *Boston*. Hell, he'd admit it—he wanted a whole lot more than a kiss from Shaye Frazier, but he'd be a fool to let anyone know.

He gave Gene a sheepish grin. "Yeah, I had to come up with some way to avoid 'Bunny the Bountiful.'"

"Sure, oh, yeah, right." Gene laughed. "Man . . . you're so transparent I can see your little lovesick heart just beating away like crazy. You've got it bad."

Gene was the second person who'd said those words to him. Damn, was he that easy to read? "Careful, I can arrange for about four weeks of riding the fence line for you." He took off his ballcap and tossed it on the desk.

"Don't pull that stuff on me, Butler. You know you'd miss me so much, you'd come out—even in the pouring rain—and beg me to come home."

Cody glanced at his watch. "Speaking of home, your lady's waiting and I'd better hustle. Shaye's got a lesson this evening."

Gene leaned close to Cody and took a whiff. "Phew . . . first things first. I'd suggest you be a little late for that lesson. You need a shower." He screwed his face up and grimaced. "You're past ripe. Hell, you're past rank." He stepped back and pretended to gasp for air. "You don't want your . . . arrangement for Saturday night to change her mind, do you?"

"What are you, my keeper? I know I need a shower. That's what I'm going to do right now if you'll get out of here." Cody pushed Gene aside, took a clean set of clothes from the desk drawer, and headed to the bathroom. "Go home."

"You want me to close the door?" Gene offered.

"No, I'm expecting a call from Doc Campbell. Just leave it open so I can hear the phone if it rings."

"See ya tomorrow."

After quickly stripping out of his clothes, Cody stepped into the shower stall. One of the smartest things his father had done when they'd drawn up the plans for the horse barn was the addition of two hot-water heaters and a shower stall in the office john.

With a few turns of the faucets Cody adjusted the hot water against the cold, and another adjustment to the showerhead set the stream to a hard pulse. Pressing his hands against the wall, he closed his eyes and leaned under the pounding hot water, lost in the cadence of the watery massage on his work-tired muscles. He didn't move for almost five minutes, letting the water cascade over him.

Worried he might doze off while standing up, he finally reached for the soap. He slid the bar across his chest, under his arms, and down over his body. The pungent pine fragrance soon replaced the sour smell of sick cow, and the lather erased the day's worth of dust and sweat. Gawd, it felt good. He grinned. If he had to put into words how good a shower felt after a long, hot, hard day's work, he wouldn't need a sentence or a paragraph. It would all fit into one word. Sex. It felt almost as great as sex.

Closing his eyes again, he leaned back against the shower-stall wall. Ah, yeah. Sex. That one word conjured up all sorts of wonderful images of a woman with wind-blown hair, a hesitant smile that grew into a throaty laugh . . . a woman with long smooth legs, a slender waist, a great tush, the inviting swell of breasts against her blouse, pretty pink toes . . . a woman soft and lush and tempting. Yeah, definitely. Sex.

He allowed the hot water to pulse against his skin, caressing him with its flow, cajoling him, tantalizing him. Lost in its touch, Cody sighed, growing hungry. Growing hard.

Shaye stepped out of the Mercedes and settled her new ballcap on her head. Following Bonnie Linderman's advice, she pulled her ponytail through the opening in the back of the cap. It was not only a great way to wear her hair around the horses, but it worked wonderfully when the convertible top was down on her car, too.

She looked around for Cody. Two of his cowboys were unsaddling their horses down by the paddock, but Cody wasn't with them, nor was he in sight.

"He's in the barn, Ms. Shaye," one of the men called to her and pointed to the horse barn.

Shaye waved her thanks and headed for the barn. Standing just inside the door, she breathed in the piquant fragrance of horse, hay, manure, liniment, and cedar shavings, surprised to discover she liked the smell.

Somewhere a radio played softly, but the sound of horses crunching their feed and moving about in their stalls masked most of the music.

"Cody?" She waited but didn't receive a response. Walking the length of the aisle, she called again. "Cody. It's Shaye." Still no answer. She looked out the back of the barn, searching across the horse paddocks and runs for him. He wasn't there, either.

Walking back through the barn, she checked each horse's stall, petting every velvet nose that was offered. Coming to Sophie's stall, it pleased her to find the mare waiting for her. She laughed, delighted when Sophie gave a low whicker of greeting. Shaye caressed the mare's sleek golden cheek. "Are you going to be a good girl for me? I'm nervous about this, you know." The palomino pushed her head against Shaye. "Hang on, Sophie, let me see if I can find the boss." With a final pat on the mare's nose, Shaye walked back to the front of the barn. She thought she heard Cody's voice as she moved near his office. The door stood wide open and she stepped inside.

Cody wasn't in the room. A news report on the clock radio sitting on a table was the source of the voice she'd heard. Another sound caught her attention—running water.

She quickly glanced about the room, then shrugged. Cody had mentioned the first time he'd shown her through the barn that each of the stalls had automatic water bowls that filled back up when the horses took a drink. That was probably what she was hearing.

Perhaps she should have stopped at the house to see if Cody was there. She checked her watch. *I'm early.* She'd wait here a few minutes longer and then check at the house. She leisurely looked around Cody's large office, taking in its warm western ambience. Little doubt existed . . . a man had designed and decorated the room, and its masculinity wrapped around her like a lover's embrace.

Two chocolate-brown overstuffed leather chairs faced the large desk. A matching sofa, draped with a colorful Pendleton blanket and flanked by two tables with western-styled lamps, stood against the back wall. A magnificent oil painting—horses running wild across the open plain—hung over the sofa. She moved closer for a look at the signature and silently nodded, finding Kate Butler's distinctive script in the lower right-hand corner. Two more of Kate's bronzes stood on the desk and another on the table by the sofa.

Shaye continued touring the room. A glassed case along one wall held an impressive array of trophies, silver buckles, photos from horse shows and rodeos, and a collection of blue and tricolored ribbons. A bookcase on the opposite wall held well-worn volumes of books and magazines. She traced along the exposed spines with the tip of her finger, glancing at titles as she stepped along . . . *American Quarter Horse Journal, Polo International, The Appaloosa Journal, The History of Beef Cattle in America, Care and Management of* . . . Suddenly Shaye caught a slight movement out of the corner of her eye and quickly glanced away from the row of books. Through the open bathroom door, half-hidden by the large trophy case, she saw Cody Butler.

Stunned, she couldn't move. Mesmerized, she couldn't look away. Cody was totally naked, totally wet, and totally unaware she stood less than twenty feet away from him. All good sense told her she should quietly leave and come back later . . . later when he'd be out of the shower and fully dressed. That's what she should do . . . but that wasn't what she was going to do.

She tried to pull a deep breath into her lungs, but could only summon shallow little gasps.

What do you think you're doing? Her conscience prodded and tried to shame her.

Shaye argued back. *I'm looking at the most gorgeous man I've ever seen. Leave me alone.*

Once more her conscience made a feeble effort to negotiate. *If you leave now, no one will know.*

Go away.

The contest ended with only one winner. Shaye's hormones—1, Shaye's conscience—0.

Heat, all-consuming and intoxicating, began a slow journey throughout her body. Picking up speed with each ragged breath, it soon raced like wildfire, igniting her pulse until it exploded in a wild crescendo. She cried out, then quickly covered her mouth, stifling any other exclamations that threatened to expose her. With the hammering of her heart ringing in her ears like the tympany section of a symphony orchestra, she stepped closer, feasting her eyes.

Although the pebbled glass of the shower-stall door slightly diffused the image of his body, she could make out every exquisite detail. She trembled, her knees nearly buckling beneath her, forcing her to grasp the edge of the desk to brace herself.

You should leave.

Why?

Because it's the proper thing to do.

Be quiet!

She sighed, the sound coming from deep within her woman's soul as she watched Cody tip his head back against the wall and raise his left arm. He rested his forearm across the top of his head. She watched him stretch, pushing himself against the pounding water. Spellbound by the beauty of his body, without conscious thought, she stepped even closer.

Her fingers ached to touch him—beginning at his neck—to trace every curve, every edge, every ridge, to smooth themselves over the flat firm plains, to glide over every inch of him.

Riveted, Shaye watched as he raised his right hand to his throat and flattened the palm over his neck. Had he somehow read her mind? His every movement echoed her thoughts and seemed to happen in delicious slow motion, each gesture drawn out until she almost cried aloud with anticipation.

He slid his hand down his neck to his collarbone, and there his fingers splayed across his skin. She followed every move. His hand circled his chest, riding across each dark nipple, then down to the flat washboard plane of his abs. He stretched again, tightening his chest and stomach, meeting the pulsing water and riding its energy. Shaye held her breath as his hand seemed to wait for a tantalizing moment before it moved again, retracing the pathway back up over his chest. Then slowly, slowly, it turned and backtracked downward, downward, downward.

Shaye couldn't hold back the soft, hungry moan that fled her lips. She crossed her arms over her chest, hugging herself, protecting herself. Perhaps she could close herself up, create a barrier against the pandemonium surging through her veins. She failed. She couldn't deter its delicious progress as it touched, inflamed, and enticed every secret niche and nerve in her body.

Cody's hand moved once more, and once more Shaye's hand flew to her mouth, her fingers lightly resting, then softly stroking her lips, the tip of her finger dipping inside her mouth. His hand, fingers pointing upward, wandered across his belly. Then slowly, ever so slowly turned and moved down, his fingers pointing the way. Another sigh, another shallow gasp fled her throat as she followed their direction.

His penis, long and full and hard, jutted out from his

body. She couldn't breathe. Her body felt engulfed in a whirlpool, and wild horses couldn't coax her gaze away.

A whispered moan put voice to the maelstrom that overpowered her as Cody's hand moved lower. She followed its journey across the dark tract of hair at his groin, then lower still, until he touched his erection and enclosed it in his fist. Her mouth was dry and she licked her lips as he stroked across the head of his penis with his thumb, and pulled it back, pressing it against his belly.

The voice, her nagging conscience, berated her again for staying, for watching, demanding she look away, leave the room, run like hell. But the commanding, needful ache low in her stomach responded to the splendor of the man before her, and she stayed.

In the midst of a deep, steadying breath, a subtle pin-drop of a noise at the door bored into her consciousness like a cannon's blast. Startled, her heart trip-hammered. Yanked back to her senses, she trembled as an addict in the throes of withdrawal. She'd been caught. Humiliation washed over her.

Slowly Shaye turned to find Cody's Newfoundlands sitting side by side just inside the office.

As still as the rocks of Stonehenge, the three dogs sat quietly . . . staring at her. Each dark-eyed gaze seemed to hold a damning accusation.

Shaye's conscience returned, puffed up with self-righteous indignation. *I told you to leave . . . but you didn't. Now look what's happened. Now you've been caught. Look at them. They know. They know what you've been doing.*

And she fled.

Chapter Fourteen

Cody buttoned his shirt, then tucked it into his clean jeans. He'd taken longer in the shower than he'd planned, but the time had been well spent. He felt revitalized.

The blinking light on the answering machine caught his eye. He'd never even heard the phone ring. Pushing the button, he listened to Doc Campbell's message. Disappointed that he'd missed the vet's call, Cody picked up his watch and checked the time before slipping the band on his wrist. Doc's office would be closed by now, he'd call him back in the morning. Besides, Shaye would be arriving any minute. He'd better get moving.

Stepping back in front of the mirror in the bathroom, he combed his hair back from his face. Gathering it at the nape of his neck he wrapped a band around it.

He didn't know what had made him decide to let his hair grow . . . maybe forgetfulness at first, or laziness, maybe defiance against everything else that was going on . . . or maybe the remembering of who he was and where he'd come from. He'd always lived the white side of his heritage, but in the past few weeks he'd given more and more thought to the Cheyenne side. Not that letting his hair grow would suddenly make him more Cheyenne. It just felt right.

He didn't doubt for a moment that he'd take some razzing from Gene or some of the other guys about his long hair. He'd dealt with worse. He'd survive this, too.

He stopped by his desk in the office, reached for his ballcap, then changed his mind. Sweat, still damp and dark, stained it. He looked around for a clean cap and couldn't find one. He'd go without.

Stepping out of his office, he glanced down the barn aisle, expecting to find Shaye at Sophie's stall. The palomino mare stood alone, dozing with her head drooped over the half door. He checked his watch again and headed for the barn door. Maybe Shaye was waiting up at the house. The three Newfoundlands moved into step beside him, and he ruffled the top of Moe's and then Larry's head. Curly nudged in for his attention as well. "Da boys." Cody chuckled. It had been Maribeth's suggestion to name the trio in honor of Cody's penchant for the Three Stooges.

"What've you guys been up to? Been scaring any pretty ladies lately?" The three huge dogs looked up at him as if they'd understood each and every word, their pink tongues lolling out of their mouths, their tails sweeping back and forth like flags in the breeze.

"Hey, cowgirl," he called, spying Shaye sitting in her Mercedes. "Are you going to ride tonight or just sit in that pile of expensive bolts like a sissy city slicker?"

Shaye looked as if he'd startled her. He'd seen people before who were scared about a new experience, but Shaye Frazier was almost catatonic. *Poor kid*, he commiserated. He understood how climbing on a horse for the first time could be nerve-racking for her, especially if the closest she'd ever been to a horse before was a moment or two with a broken-down burro in a petting zoo. Even a passing glance at police mounts or carriage horses in Boston and the forty-five-minute grooming lesson with Sophie the night before weren't enough to make a new rider feel comfortable.

"After how well you worked with Sophie last evening, I think you're ready to saddle up tonight."

Shaye barely looked at him, ducking her head. "Okay . . . good." She didn't move.

"You've got to get out of the car first," Cody cajoled. "Some fun things can be done in a car, but I don't think this is one of them." He grinned. "Come on."

She shot him another dismayed look, and he watched, totally captivated as her cheeks flushed to a bright red right before his eyes. What had he said that embarrassed her? He frowned, then mentally shrugged. She'd driven over with the convertible top down on her car, maybe she'd picked up some windburn on the way. The explanation satisfied for only a moment as he watched her fumble with the door handle and become more and more flustered as she tried to open the latch.

She finally succeeded in opening the car door and then almost tripped getting out. She steadied herself on the fender.

"Are you okay?" He stepped toward her, but she raised her hand to stop him.

"Yes, of course. I'm . . . very well, thank you." She looked at him and offered what he figured was supposed to be a smile. It succeeded in being little more than a slight twitch of her lips.

"Nervous?"

"No . . . not at all."

Why didn't he believe her? Her steps faltered as she walked toward him, and Cody wondered if maybe her boots were too tight or if they hurt her feet because they were still new and stiff.

"Have you been here long?" He tried another tack to put her at ease.

"No. I just got here . . . well, not right this second,

but . . . about ten minutes ago," she quickly replied, her eyes wide and dark with disquiet. Then she quickly added, "But I didn't think I should go in the barn without you." She dropped her gaze to her fidgeting hands. "I've been waiting here . . . in my car for you . . . all the time."

"Sorry I took so long." *Just keep the conversation light and easy until she begins to relax.* "We spent most of the day dosing cattle." He pointed to four quarantine pens. "I had to take a shower . . . actually, I had to take a very long shower."

"I know." Her blush deepened a shade or two. "I saw . . . uh . . . I mean . . . I can see." She immediately pointed at his head. "Wet. Your hair's wet."

"Are you sure you're okay?" He couldn't get a handle on what was bothering her.

"Yes, of course . . . I told you, I'm fine." The odd little smile returned. "So shower me . . . uh, I mean, show me what to do."

Why was she acting like a kid caught with her hand in the cookie jar? She wouldn't even look at him. He shrugged. Whether she admitted it or not, it was probably nothing more than nerves. "Okay, you're going to ride, but you've got to relax. You're beginning to make *me* nervous, and I sure don't want you spooking Sophie." A stunned look struck her face. He stepped beside her and patted her shoulder. "It's a joke . . . ease up, I'm teasing you. Sophie will be fine and so will you. Come on."

Shaye tagged along behind him, and he decided to let her work at her own pace. Being around horses was brand-new to her. He could understand her being scared. Hell, he'd be tense if he found himself in a courtroom facing a jury. Fair was fair. He'd cut her all the slack she needed. Besides, she still had to uphold her part of the bargain and have that pesky little sex talk with Maribeth.

Shaye stayed a pace or two behind Cody, wishing she'd gone home when she'd had the opportunity. How could she spend the next couple of hours with him? How could she look at him and not remember what she'd seen, what he looked like completely naked? Her gaze skimmed down his body from his shoulder to his butt, then down the long length of his legs. Nice. Even with his clothes on . . . very nice.

Stop it. Behave!

Oh, yes. This was going to be a very difficult evening. Another question immediately crowded into her mind. Would she ever be able to look at Cody Butler again without having every stitch of his clothing melt away in her mind's eye?

Only time would tell.

Twenty minutes later, after she'd groomed Sophie and Cody had showed her how to saddle and bridle the mare, he handed her the reins and walked beside her to the outdoor riding arena. She'd been so engrossed in Cody's lesson that she'd only thought about his wet, bare chest, his long naked legs, and everything else in between about ten or fifteen times. She'd definitely failed the "I'll-put-it-out-of-my-mind" test.

"You're okay," Cody reassured her. "Just keep your mind on what you're doing."

"Excuse me?" How did he know about the thoughts that kept racing through her head?

"It's just like walking a dog . . . a big dog."

She glanced up at him, puzzled by his remark. "A dog?"

"I said, walking a horse is like walking a big dog."

"Oh," Shaye replied, relieved that he didn't know her thoughts after all. "I've never walked a dog," she confessed, moving in front of the mare.

"Such a sheltered life," he teased, then touched her arm and pulled her back. "No, stay beside Sophie . . . on the left side. Remember, horses are fright-and-flight animals. If something spooks her while you're in front of her, she may run into you . . . not intentionally . . . but just because her instinct tells her to run."

Shaye swallowed hard, stepped back, and pressed in closer to the mare's side.

Twenty minutes later she was in the saddle, the yellow mare being kind enough to treat her as though she knew what she was doing. She thought she'd be afraid being so high up off the ground, sitting on a beast that had a mind of its own, but instead she was enjoying every moment. The gentle rock and sway of the mare's slow gait felt soothing, and she liked the way Sophie's ears swiveled to catch every word she said.

"How do you like it?" Cody stood in the middle of the arena turning slowly, his gaze following Shaye as the mare circled the perimeter of the arena, close to the fence.

"This is fabulous," Shaye answered, her reply touched by her excited laughter. "What's next?"

Cody laughed. "You think you're ready for the accelerated course, do you?"

Shaye shot a sheepish smile in his direction and lost her breath as she watched him jog to the side of the arena. In a single lithe move he pulled himself up and perched on the top rail of the fence. Clothes or no clothes, he looked yummy. She purposefully looked away. If she kept allowing these kind of thoughts about Cody Butler to take up permanent residence in her head, she'd be in a lot of trouble. The image of him in the shower zapped back into her mind, only this time he wasn't alone. This time she found herself in the image, too . . . their bodies wet and slick, pressed together, arms around each other, their mouths hungrily tasting skin and lips, her leg raised and wrapped around his thigh.

"Okay, cowgirl, tighten your knees a little."

"What?" The burn of a bright blush scalded her cheeks.

"Cluck to her and tighten your knees a little."

"Oh," she breathed, "my knees on Sophie." Trying to

ignore the puzzled frown on Cody's face, she forcefully shoved the watery thoughts from her head and tried to follow Cody's instructions. Sophie decided not to cooperate. Shaye clucked again. Nothing. She squeezed with her knees. Nothing.

"What are you doing?" Cody's laugh came quick.

"I'm doing what you told me to do. What do you think I'm doing?"

Cody tried to talk, his words competing with his laughter. "When you cluck to a horse, you're supposed to make a sound like a kiss." Puckering his lips, he showed her how. "Some folks get the same kind of sound out of the corner of their mouth." He demonstrated that sound, too.

"What was wrong with the way I did it?" Shaye hated herself for pouting.

"You didn't cluck right. Sophie doesn't know what you want."

"You said to cluck, so I clucked."

"Like a chicken."

She harrumphed. "Then why didn't you tell me to kiss at her?"

"What, and have you break your neck trying to kiss poor Sophie on the lips?"

She found his grin so appealing, she almost forgot to be annoyed by his teasing and couldn't stop the smile that moved her lips. She made a kissing sound, imitating the one Cody had made, then shrieked and grabbed the saddle horn as the palomino mare took off at a jog-trot. "Oh . . . what do I do now . . . help!"

"Relax . . . just relax. Let go of the horn. Good. Now drop your left hand closer to her neck. No . . . don't pull back. That's good. Very good. Put a little more weight on the ball of your foot in the stirrup. Sophie's got a nice smooth jog-trot. Sit in the saddle and get the feel of her . . . feel the rhythm. Just let your hips move with her. Yeah, that's it . . . good."

Once she found the two-beat cadence of the palomino's gait, Shaye easily settled herself in the saddle, concentrating on the subtle side-to-side sway of her own hips. The hypnotic rhythm sent her thoughts racing back to Cody Butler, a shower, and a body she couldn't forget.

"Careful."

Cody's voice snapped her out of her daydreams.

"Keep her working close to the fence . . . it's called 'working on the rail.' Don't let her go where she wants. She's testing you. You've got to control her . . . make her work for you."

Shaye touched the reins to Sophie's neck exactly as Cody had shown her, and the mare obeyed, moving back beside the fence.

Fence posts seemed a blur as the mare sped by them, and the wind felt strong against Shaye's face. "How . . . fast . . . am I going?" she asked Cody as she passed where he sat on the top rail of the fence.

"Oh, like a rocket."

She glanced back at him as the mare turned the corner. Damn, he was laughing at her again. "Come on, tell me. How fast?"

"You're going about three miles an hour . . . four tops."

"Then why does it feel wild and crazy, like we're going at least fifty?"

"Because you're loving it."

"Yes." Shaye's laughter joined his. "You're right. I am."

Shaye's progress amazed him. From the first moment she'd sat in the saddle, Cody knew she would ride well. Her posture was natural. Her legs seemed to automatically fall into the right position with her heels dropped lower than the ball of her foot. She held her arms still and close to her body and her hands were easy on the reins—soft on the horse's mouth.

He liked her style. He liked the way she responded to

the mare. Better still, he liked the way Sophie responded to her.

Just watching Shaye created a pleasant warmth that uncoiled from deep within his belly. He allowed the sensation to spread without censure throughout his body, knowing he had never experienced anything like it before. He couldn't deny that he wanted her. That hunger had been there from the moment he'd first seen her on his front lawn. It had been basic lust then, no emotion, just pure hormones. But it had changed, subtly, quickly, until there was more than just male and female . . . now there were feelings involved. Affection? Love? He couldn't put a tag on what he felt, he only knew that when Shaye was around, he couldn't take his eyes off her. He couldn't stand the loss when she left, and he couldn't wait to see her again.

He watched her riding the palomino around the arena, the strength of those feelings taking ownership. He loved the intensity he saw on her face, the quick glances she made in his direction looking for approval, and he liked the way her ponytail swung and bounced with each step the mare took. Roscoe was right. This woman was someone his mother would have really liked, not just as a friend for herself, but as someone special for him. Could she ever be that? Would she ever be that? The thought of Shaye Frazier being in his life, being his friend, being his lover had crossed his mind more than once or twice. He fell to sleep each night with thoughts of her on his mind. He woke in the morning, hard and hungry, wondering what it would be like to find her next to him, warm and willing.

Reality said none of it could happen. What did a Wyoming cowboy about to lose his ranch and the fence he sat on have to give a woman who was obviously used to all the finer things that money and prestige had to offer. Regretfully he tucked his thoughts away and, easing himself off the fence, moved back to the center of the arena.

"Okay," he said, catching Shaye's attention. "Bring her

to a stop. Just say 'whoa,' and give a gentle pull back on the reins. Good." He walked over to where the mare had stopped and, without conscious thought, rested his hand on Shaye's knee. The moment he realized where his hand lay, he looked up at her. The excited flush on her face made him forget about his hand, about his bank loan, about the sick cattle in the quarantine pens. He almost forgot about breathing.

"Oh, Cody," she sighed. "I never knew it would be so . . . wonderful. Thank you."

He'd expected the excitement. The tears in her eyes were something special. "I'm glad you like it. You're doing great."

"Really? You really think so?"

The breathless uncertainty in her voice baffled him. She sounded like a child desperately seeking validation, a puzzling dichotomy to the professional woman he knew her to be.

"Really." He lightly patted her knee reassuringly. "Really." He lifted his hand away. "Turn her around like I showed you, and walk and trot in this direction. Then we're going to call it quits. I don't want you getting too sore."

"I feel okay; I can ride longer."

"Trust me, you're going to have sore muscles in the morning, and I don't want you too sore to dance with me tomorrow night." He swore he saw her blush again.

He let her ride another fifteen minutes, his admiration for her growing with each round of the arena. She'd be ready to canter the mare in her next lesson, and maybe he'd saddle up Possum, take Shaye out on the trails, and show her the land Glenn Hubbard was so determined to own.

"Okay, cowgirl, let's give Sophie the rest of the night off." He waited at the gate until Shaye brought the mare up beside him. He told her how to dismount and glowed with pride as she followed his instructions to the letter. In all the years he'd spent around horses with working cowboys, rodeo riders, and show riders, he'd never seen someone with the natural talent that Shaye Frazier had. With some solid training, she could compete with the best.

Giving Sophie a final pat on the neck, Shaye closed the stall door. "Thank you, sweet girl. Good night."

Cody waited for her at the barn door. "You did a super job. I've got to be honest, you surprised the hell out of me."

"Thanks," she replied shyly. "Thank you for teaching me."

"Have you had supper?"

She shook her head.

"Well, you're invited."

"I really can't."

"Yes, you can." He flipped the switch, turning out the barn lights. "Come on." He draped his arm around her shoulders, enjoying the nice cozy feel of her next to his body. "Roscoe makes some of the best fried chicken, mashed potatoes, and corn you've ever dreamed of eating."

"That sounds wonderful," Shaye said. "I love fried chicken."

"Me, too," Cody agreed. "Too bad he's cooking pork chops, wild rice, and broccoli tonight." He didn't move fast enough, and Shaye's elbow connected with his ribs.

Cody stretched, easing the kinks out of his long legs, and stared up at the ceiling. Kicking the blanket aside, he exposed his naked body to the night air. He didn't remember July being this hot before. But then he'd never had a July with Shaye Frazier in it before, either.

Sleep eluded him, teased him with yawn or two, and then hid from him again. The three Newfs had found sleep, curled up and fitting together like a furry jigsaw puzzle on the rug beside his bed, their deep breathing taunting him.

He raised his arm and rested his forearm on the pillow

over his head. The position reminded him of something. The thought niggled at his brain, and then he remembered. He remembered he'd stood with his arm over his head like this earlier, in the shower.

From the shower and his stance, his thoughts easily slid to Shaye. She'd settled into her lesson, but she'd seemed skittish as a new foal all evening long. Even as they all sat around the kitchen table enjoying Roscoe's breaded pork chops and friendly conversation, there still seemed to be a jittery edge to her. She'd really come unglued when he'd reminded Maribeth to replace the towels in the office shower with clean ones.

He stretched again, his body pressing against the mattress, the cool breeze blowing through the window lifting the curtains and touching his skin. He felt the heat of need and want settle in the pit of his stomach, and with it came a very interesting thought. Crazy yet plausible, it elbowed its way into his mind.

Shaye had seen him. She hadn't waited in her car until he'd come out of the barn like she'd said. She'd arrived early and had come into the barn looking for him. And with the open door she'd seen him in the shower. That was why she was so jittery each time he got near her or spoke to her. Of course, it all made perfect sense.

Another idea began to form. As it built and took shape, Cody found he liked it very much. Liked it—hell, he loved it. He loved it because it made perfect sense, too. Shaye wouldn't have been so bothered by what she'd seen if she wasn't attracted to him. Sure it was possible but not likely. He slightly shrugged, the action more mental than physical. Not likely at all. What was likely was that she'd liked what she'd seen . . . a lot.

From deep within his chest his laughter erupted, full and filled with pleasure. The sound woke the dogs, filled the room, and filled his heart.

Things were definitely looking up.

Chapter Fifteen

The parking lot at the Cheyenne Cattleman's Association hall held an odd collection of vehicles. Everything from fresh-washed pickup trucks, SUVs, and a '55 Chevy convertible to a huge Kenworth semitractor waited in the lot while their owners elegantly kicked up their heels inside. The eclectic assortment brought a smile to Shaye's lips as she parked the silver Mercedes. In the Old West it would have been horses tied to the hitchin' post, buggies, and buckboards.

The clock on the dash revealed the unpleasant truth. Being fashionably late was one thing, being unforgivably late was another. Hubbard's telephone call from Laramie and the paperwork he'd had her prepare and fax to him at his hotel had put her almost two hours behind. Julie had called twice just to make sure she was still coming. She'd tried to beg off, arguing that it was too late, saying she had more work to do for Hub, and then she said she had a headache, but Julie wouldn't accept any of her excuses. So here she was.

She quickly glanced at her reflection in the rearview mirror and adjusted a few wispy curls about her face. Retrieving her lipstick from her purse, she freshened the soft shade she wore and decided she'd delayed her entrance long enough.

Stepping through the foyer of the hall, Shaye couldn't believe her eyes. The room had been transformed into a beautiful wonderland. The rotating mirror ball hanging from the center of the ceiling sent shards of glittering light across the festoons of gauze strung overhead like clouds. Lovely pedestaled arrangements of gladioluses, carnations, phlox, and trailing greenery added a brilliant touch of elegance. At one end of the room a stage lit by strategically placed spotlights showcased the band. Julie had told her who the famous country group and their star singer were, but the word *famous* was purely relative . . . Shaye had never heard of George Strait nor the Ace in the Hole band.

The dance floor stretched from the stage to three-quarters the length of the room with rows of white-draped tables all around. In the middle of each table centerpieces of green garlands, bright blossoms, and old lanterns with flickering candles provided soft, festive lighting. Cash bars in each corner of the large room were doing business at a feverish pace, and the tables with the punch bowls were crowded as well.

Shaye watched couples swirling about the dance floor, the men handsome in their evening finest, their ladies beautiful in sweeping skirts, glittering jewelry, and graceful steps. She had to admit, the finest formal event in Boston would find tough competition with this affair.

"It's about time you showed up." Julie tapped her on the shoulder. "Wow!" As Shaye turned around, Julie inspected her from head to toe. "You look gorgeous. Where did you find that gown in Dorland?"

"This old thing?" Shaye teased with a counterfeit Southern drawl. "I just whipped it up this afternoon from the living room drapes."

"Okay, Scarlett, whatever you say." Julie took her arm.

"Come on. Poor Cody's been running like a scared rabbit all night trying to keep out of Bunny's clutches."

Julie led her through the crowd, winding their way around the tables. Shaye was well aware of the stares she drew as she followed Julie. She'd been unsure whether the navy floor-length strapless sheath would be appropriate. In Boston it had been her safe bet for formal functions and could be dressed up or down with accessories. She'd decided on very simple this evening with her hair upswept in a French twist, a fringe of soft tendrils around her face and nape. She wore a pair of Swiss blue topaz dangle earrings and a matching bracelet as her only jewelry. A modest slit in the skirt provided easy movement, and she'd chosen a pair of navy faille high-heeled sandals for her feet.

"I don't know if it's safe to walk beside you or not. Look at Carl Nesbitt." Julie glanced at a table to her left.

"Do I have to?" Shaye grimaced, remembering the man's boorish attitude and remarks from the few times they'd met before. A few steps later someone took hold of her arm, and she turned to find herself face-to-face with the boorish man himself. His hand began a slow upward stroke on her arm, and she pulled away, quickly looking around for Julie. Julie was no where in sight; she'd disappeared into the crowd.

"Well, well," Nesbitt cooed. "If it isn't Little Miss Righteous." His eyes strayed to her breasts, and he licked his lips. "Very, very nice."

She could smell the alcohol on his breath and the acrid stench of sweat. Carl Nesbitt looked as if he'd like to devour her whole. Shaye shuddered.

"I think it's time for you to be real neighborly." Nesbitt grinned, leaning closer. Swaying a little on unsteady feet, he took hold of her arm again and tried to pull her close as he wiggled his hips. "You're gonna dance with me . . . real close and sexy like."

"Keep your hands off my date, Carl."

Shaye heard Cody's voice behind her, then felt his hand rest possessively at her waist.

"I'm pretty sure you don't want any trouble, Carl, so why don't you just back off and behave."

The hard edge to Cody's voice seemed to get his point across. Carl Nesbitt stepped back, and without conscious thought Shaye leaned against Cody, finding sanctuary in his presence.

"I just asked her to dance, that's all. But I guess she thinks she's too damned good for a hardworking cowboy," Carl sneered. "Ain't nothin' wrong in askin' her to dance, is there? Hell, I'll even share with ya. You can dance with my old lady."

Shaye caught sight of a sad-faced, tired-looking woman sitting at the table behind Carl Nesbitt. The woman looked away, but not before Shaye recognized the hurt in her eyes.

"Well, Carl, I don't know how to tell you this, but I don't share."

Cody appeared to be calm and relaxed, but Shaye could feel the taut muscles in his arm. She glanced up at him, and he tightened his arm around her waist.

"Carl, I'd suggest you spend the rest of the evening showing your wife a good time." He smiled at Lettie Nesbitt. "She sure looks pretty tonight, Carl. You're a lucky man."

Without waiting for Carl Nesbitt's response, Cody led Shaye to the table where Gene and Julie waited for them.

"What happened to you?" Julie shot a worried look from Shaye to Cody, then back again. "I thought you were right behind me."

Cody almost growled his words. "If Nesbitt doesn't start keeping his hands to himself, trouble's going to reach back and put a hand on him."

"Just don't do anything to Carl when I'm on duty," Julie cautioned, a grin flirting at the corners of her mouth. "I

wouldn't be able to help you beat the crap out of him. . . .
I'd have to arrest you instead."

The band started a slow tune, and Gene stood, holding
out his hand for Julie. "Come on, beautiful, we came to
dance. Let's show this crowd how to make love on the
floor."

Julie moved into Gene's arms. "Just don't try to flip me
over your head like you did the last time, honey. I think I
forgot to put my underpanties on tonight."

Left alone at the table, Shaye looked up at Cody as he
helped her to her chair. "I'm sorry. I didn't want to cause
any trouble with Mr. Nesbitt."

Cody sat next to her. "It wasn't your fault, Shaye, and I
can fully understand poor Carl's problem." He lightly
touched one of her dangling earrings. When he spoke his
voice had softened and now sounded almost reverent.
"You're absolutely beautiful."

She ducked her head, embarrassed by his blatant compliment, wishing she could find the words to return the
tribute. She'd never imagined that a man could exude such
magnificence. She smiled at the word. *Magnificence*
seemed best suited for kings or heads of state, great pieces
of artwork, or spectacular scenery. But tonight *magnificence* suited Cody Butler to a *T.*

He still hadn't cut his hair. Her preference had always
been for short-cropped, salon-styled hair on men, but that
was before she'd met Cody. She wondered how it would
feel to untie the black band that held it at the nape of his
neck and delve her fingers into its long, black strands. She
wondered if she would ever get the chance to find out.

Against the stark white of his dress shirt, Cody's skin
looked wonderfully bronzed, and the black, crisp-cut, western-styled tuxedo jacket heightened the whole effect. He'd
foregone the usual formal black bow tie for a classic western string tie. Knotted in a loose bow, the long tails fell
about six inches from his collar. Instead of dress pants and

a cumberbund, Cody wore a pair of neatly pressed jeans and one of the largest, most impressive trophy buckles she had ever seen. When he'd moved to his chair, she'd noticed what appeared to be diamonds and rubies encrusting the design and the words *National Champion* spelled out in gold letters. Yes, magnificence was clearly appropriate.

"Are you two going to sit and stare at each other all night long? I'd suggest you take advantage of the great and expensive music and go out there and step on each other's toes," Gene teased, placing a glass of white wine on the table in front of Shaye. "Julie told me this is what you'd like." He placed a glass in front of Cody. "Branch and bourbon, right?"

Cody nodded. "Thanks." He glanced around. "Where's your lady?"

Gene pulled out his chair and sat. "She had to call in, her pager went off."

Cody grinned. "I want to know where she's got room for a pager in the dress she's wearing. There isn't room for anything but Julie."

"I heard that," Julie said, laughing, as she sat down beside Gene.

"Come on," Cody said, standing and holding his hand out to Shaye. "Please dance with me before I get myself in trouble with the law."

He led her to the dance floor as the Ace in the Hole band struck up another slow tune. They stood facing each other for a moment until Cody slowly reached out. "Come here."

Shaye's heart began to pound in counter rhythm to the music, and she found herself willingly moving into Cody's embrace. His tall, hard body felt wonderful against her . . . no, more than wonderful—divine. Being in his arms felt . . . right. The edge of his jaw rested against her temple, and the delicious warmth of his breath stirred her hair and touched her cheek. His crisp pine fragrance surrounded her and filled her head. She felt completely absorbed by him, and closing her eyes, she allowed him to lead her across the floor.

Together they moved to the music. Step by step the world around them seemed to disappear, and Shaye knew she wanted the song to go on for hours, for days . . . for years.

Cody's arm tightened around her, and he whispered in her ear. "I don't believe how lucky I am to have you in my life."

Had she really heard him say that? She prayed her ears hadn't played tricks. She hoped he hadn't just been repeating the lyrics to the unfamiliar song the band was playing. And she hoped what she'd heard wasn't just wishful thinking, because in that moment Shaye felt the wall she'd carefully built to safeguard all of her emotions crumble and fall. Every brick and piece of mortar fell away, leaving her vulnerable.

When Michael Frazier's casket was lowered into the ground, she had made a solid promise never to open herself up to love again. She had vowed never to allow herself to be susceptible to the humiliating pain that Michael Frazier had inflicted in the name of love, and she had committed herself to following her carefully defined goals. But with the tall Wyoming cowboy in her arms who was fighting tooth and nail for his home and his honor, she'd broken every promise she made to herself and jeopardized every goal. She knew she wasn't supposed to fall in love with him, but intellect had absolutely nothing to do with it.

Laying her head on Cody's shoulder, she carefully wrapped her secret in wishful thinking and hid it deep within her heart.

His hand pressed against her back, taking possession of her, and together they danced.

"Shh, will you be quiet?"

"I'm trying to, but it ain't easy with all this stuff. Keep

your eyes peeled. If we get caught, we're gonna be in more trouble than we've ever imagined possible."

"How much are you gonna take?"

"I brought three ten-gallon cans. If there's any more than that, I don't know what I'm gonna do."

"I've got his extra set of keys, so we can check how much he's got."

Maribeth quickly unlocked the driver's door on Cody's truck and jumped inside. She slipped the key into the ignition and turned it, activating the gauges on the dashboard. Then she flipped another switch, illuminating the dash lights. The last switch she moved controlled the two gas tanks. "We're in luck. The front tank's only about a quarter full." She flicked the button again and waited a moment or two for the gauge to register. "There's about half in the back."

"Get down here and give me a hand," Roscoe hoarsely whispered. "And hurry up. I'm gettin' too damn old for this kinda stuff." He grabbed the piece of rubber hose out of his back pocket and twisted the gas cap off the front tank of the truck. "I don't know why I let you talk me into this . . . any of this. We should just leave him alone and let him find his own woman."

"What, and have him bring Bunny Gibson or another one of his buckle bunnies or rodeo Rosies home? I don't think so. Do you think I want to spend the rest of my life with someone like that as my sister-in-law?" Maribeth grimaced and shuddered. "Yuck . . . the whole idea scares me silly." She jumped out of the truck and squatted down beside Roscoe. Reaching for one of the empty gas cans they'd brought with them, she unscrewed the cap. "Did you know that Bunny Gibson's real name is Elizabeth Ann?" She paused for a moment, a light frown creasing her brow. "I wonder where she got the nickname Bunny."

Roscoe snorted and gave her a disgusted look. "Maybe when you're older, I'll tell ya." He shook his head. "In the meantime, do you suppose we could keep the chitchat to a minimum? We've got work to do." One gas can clinked against another as he moved it into place under the hose that dangled from the blue Ford's back gas tank.

"Quiet," Maribeth warned. "Someone's coming."

Stooped over, Maribeth and Roscoe crept to the back of Cody's truck and watched Lettie Nesbitt help her drunk husband find their truck and leave.

"Phew," Maribeth breathed. "That was close. Old Carl was really skunked, wasn't he?"

"I think that remark's kinda redundant." Roscoe chuckled at his own joke, then wiped his hand across his chin. "Come on, we've got to hurry." He dropped the hose farther into the truck's gas tank, then, putting his mouth on the end of the hose, sucked for a moment to start the flow of fuel out of Cody's truck and into the gas can.

"Damn," Roscoe hissed, spitting on the ground. "I hate it when I get a mouthful of gas." He spit again and again, trying to rid himself of the foul taste.

"Here," Maribeth whispered, reaching in her pocket and offering him some gun.

"If that's bubble gum, you can keep it." Roscoe spit again. "I don't want nothin' in my mouth that's made from horses' hooves."

"It is not," Maribeth argued. "Is it?"

In less than fifteen minutes Roscoe had siphoned all but a gallon or two out of Cody's truck. "Come on, Mata Hari, help me carry these." He lifted the first can with a grunt.

"There you go again," Maribeth grumbled, lifting the can with both hands and struggling to carry it to Roscoe's truck. As she turned back to get the third gas can, she glanced at Roscoe. "Don't you know any actresses who're still alive?"

She yelped as the heavy can knocked painfully against her shins. "Did you talk to Julie about Shaye's car? Did you guys come up with an idea?"

"Got it covered. Julie's gonna take care of it."

After the third can was safe and secure in the back of Roscoe's old pickup, the two conspirators hopped in. Stepping on the clutch, Roscoe started the motor, put the gearshift in neutral, and let the truck coast out of the parking lot. He didn't turn his headlights on until they were well out onto the street and about a block away from the 52nd Annual Cheyenne Cattleman's Association's Cowboy Ball.

Maribeth folded her arms across her chest and sat back against the dingy upholstery. "I don't know why we had to sneak off so soon. I'd have liked to at least peek in the door and see what everybody looked like." Her lip stuck out in a pout. "I've never seen anybody except Cody all dressed up for a ball."

"They ain't no different than when you've seen 'em all before," Roscoe declared. "It's just clothes . . . and that don't make any difference in who they are."

Maribeth nervously chewed on a fingernail and glanced at Roscoe across the dim cab of the truck. "If Cody figures out we did this, he's gonna kill us dead, isn't he?"

"It's a little late to begin worrying about that, ain't it?"

"Yeah . . . I guess, but I'd kinda like to make it to my sixteenth birthday."

"Yeah, well I'd just like to have sixteen more birthdays," Roscoe added.

"Cody wouldn't kill an old man like you. No challenge to it." Maribeth laughed.

Roscoe wheeled his old truck into the local Dairy Delight. "Despite your disrespect for your elders, come on . . . the treat's on me."

Chapter Sixteen

"I guess the party's over," Cody murmured in Shaye's ear as the band played the last dance of the evening. "Thanks for the arrangement; it felt almost as good as a date."

She could feel his smile where his cheek pressed against her temple. "You're very welcome."

He placed her right hand on his shoulder, then put both of his arms around her and pressed her close. She lifted her arms, clasping her hands behind his neck, and they stood in one place, swaying to the music. She heard a heartbeat. His? Hers? Did it really matter? Not anymore.

Cody's lips touched her hair, her forehead, her cheek, and too impatient to wait, Shaye raised her head, sacrificing her mouth to his kiss.

He hesitated for a moment, and she looked up into his eyes and saw their silent question. If she had any doubts, now was the time to stop this craziness before she got hurt again. But her reply to Cody was just as silent as his question—a barely perceptible nod. And then he kissed her, his mouth claiming hers as if it were his own possession.

The comparison came without warning, leaving her stunned. This wasn't at all like the kiss he'd given her at the picnic. That kiss had been about the competition, about the heat of the moment, and about the winning. There had even been anger in that kiss. But this kiss was different. Very different. This kiss grew from tenderness, from hunger, from wanting, and it triggered a yearning in her. It petitioned her response. This kiss was like nothing she'd ever dreamed of. This kiss was like nothing she'd ever known before. This kiss gave her something she'd never felt before, not even when Michael had kissed her. This kiss was hot . . . glorious. And damned addictive.

Cody eased away first, his dark eyes searching her face for what . . . rejection? Disapproval? Protest? She knew he'd find none of those things. What he would find if he looked deep enough was the wariness that still lingered within her.

He lightly touched her lips with the tip of his finger. "I'm glad you came tonight."

How could she respond with the delightful caress of his fingers on her mouth? Reaching up, Shaye took his hand and drew it down to her side, leaving her fingers entwined with his. "I'm glad, too. Thank you for asking me."

"You turned me down, remember?" His lazy grin teased her. "You were Julie and Gene's date, not mine."

She nodded, her mouth curving in a smile. "I still had a wonderful time."

"Me, too." Cody looked as though he'd just received a precious gift. "Could I talk you into having another arrangement with me soon?" His fingers tightened around her hand. "We could talk it over at the Chuckwagon with a cup of coffee before you head home?"

Temptation gave a hard push, but Shaye shook her head. "Thanks, but I've really got to go. Hub will be back in the morning, and I've got some work that needs to be done for him."

They walked back to the table, and Shaye picked up her wrap and purse.

Cody took the shawl from her. Standing behind her, he settled it over her shoulders, and she felt the warm touch of his breath on the back of her neck when he spoke.

"You must know Glenn Hubbard pretty well."

Shaye's heart bounced. He'd caught her off guard. Had he found out? No . . . impossible. As far as she knew, the only one in Dorland who knew Glenn Hubbard was her father was Julie, and Shaye was positive Julie hadn't told anyone. "Yes, I've known him for a long time," she cautiously replied. "Why do you ask?"

Cody moved beside her and answered her question with a slight shrug. "Around here it's unusual for lawyers to live with their clients."

"It made more sense than me driving back and forth from a motel somewhere. Besides, Hub has a full office set up at home—computers, Internet access, a fax machine—so it makes my job easier."

"Yeah, I suppose." He cast a sidelong glance at her.

Cody picked up his black cowboy hat from one of the chairs and squared it on his head. She'd never seen him wear one before. He'd always worn a ballcap or no hat at all. Seeing him in his elegant evening attire with the black hat made her heart rush. Cody Butler was . . . the word came to her again . . . magnificent.

They left the building and walked across the half-empty parking lot to Shaye's car.

"I heard you've made a deal with Jeff Granger for a piece of his ranch."

Surprised that news had traveled so quickly, Shaye wondered who had told him. Then she remembered. She'd seen Jeff Granger and his wife at the ball. He'd probably told Cody himself. "It's a nice tract of land with some of the water Hub needed."

"Now that he's got what he wanted, I'm glad he'll be leaving me alone." He paused and lightly touched her arm, bringing her to a halt. "Does that mean you'll be leaving Dorland now?"

Shaye looked up, memorizing every feature in Cody's face, knowing her next words would start his worries all over again. "No, I'm staying for a little while longer." She didn't want to tell him, but she had to. "Hubbard still wants Medicine Creek."

Cody looked away, and nodded. "I'm not surprised. He's the kind of man that once he gets to wanting something, doesn't stop until he gets it . . . whether he needs it or not."

She could have argued with him, told him some of her father's finer points, but to do that she would have to confess everything. She wasn't ready for the betrayal she knew he'd feel. He would find out eventually, but not yet . . . please, not yet.

"Where did Gene and Julie go?" she asked, quickly changing the subject.

Cody took her hand and walked her to her car. "Julie got paged again and had to go back on duty."

"I didn't get to say good night."

"Don't worry, I bet she calls you first thing in the morning to make sure you survived my dancing."

"You're a great dancer," Shaye said, "for a bow-legged cowboy."

"Ouch," Cody replied, taking a quick look down at his legs. "I think you've got me confused with Carl Nesbitt or Roscoe."

"Oh, no." Shaye laughed. "It was you. I didn't dance with anyone else." She gave him a coy glance. "You don't share, remember?"

He traced a trail with his index finger down the bridge of her nose, to her upper lip. "I remember. I just hope you remember."

Shaye's pulse rocketed skyward. They had kissed, nothing more. Cody Butler had no claim on her. They were nothing more than business acquaintances or riding instructor and pupil . . . at best, friends. But how could she ignore what she'd felt when he'd kissed her?

A pickup truck pulled up behind Cody. "Hey, Butler, why don't you just kiss the lady and get out of the way? You're causin' a traffic jam," Jet Linderman heckled, then drove off, waving good night.

One by one the other vehicles pulled out of the parking lot, horns honked goodbye, and a few folks stopped to say how glad they were Shaye had joined them for the evening.

"This is a nice place," she said, unlocking the door to her car. "Everyone's so friendly . . . not like the city, where you get nervous if a stranger speaks to you."

Cody chuckled. "Could be because the words you hear in the city are something like . . . 'gimme your money . . . this is a mugging.' "

"Oh, and I suppose muggings never happen in Dorland?"

"Not since Carl Nesbitt mugged me in grade school for my *Star Wars* lunch box."

"That's serious stuff. I hope you got a lawyer."

"I'm working on it," he murmured.

A little flustered, Shaye opened the car door. She'd better leave now.

Cody touched her shoulder. "Do you kiss on your first . . . arrangement?"

She slowly turned to face him, unable to stop the quickening beat of her heart. "Aside from the dance floor kind, I only give kisses of gratitude for lovely evenings," she teased, embarrassed by the breathy sound of her voice.

"I'd certainly like to show you again how grateful I am."

He cupped her face between his two hands, gently tipping her head back. He slowly lowered his mouth until she could feel his warm breath touching her skin. When his lips lightly brushed hers, she opened herself to his kiss and fell into his arms. She closed her eyes and fell in love.

Somewhere on the edge of her awareness, Shaye heard a truck pull up behind them, and she heard the honk of the horn. Reluctantly she pulled away from Cody's kiss.

"Hey, Cody, I knew if we drove around the block, by the time we came back around you'd be kissing her." Jet Linderman reached out of the cab of his truck and clapped Cody on the back. "Smooth player."

The tires on Linderman's truck squealed as Jet hit the gas pedal and sped out onto the street.

Cody started to laugh, that wonderful baritone laugh that Shaye loved to hear.

"In Dorland our juvenile delinquents are at least thirty years old." He sobered. "Now, where were we?"

She put the palm of her hand against his chest, holding him at a safe distance. "I was about to thank you for a lovely evening and say good night." She quickly slid behind the steering wheel of her car and shut the door before Cody could touch her again. She lowered the window, then turned the key in the ignition. The motor caught, then died. She tried again. Again the motor caught only for a moment before it wheezed to a stop. She turned the key again, and the sound returned, but this time she could hear the battery had lost some power. By the fifth try the battery had almost died as well.

Cody knocked on the roof. "Let me have a look. Pop the hood."

Shaye searched around with her hand under the dash and on the floor. "I don't know where the hood release is."

"Let me see if I can find it."

She stepped out of the car and Cody took her place.

"It's here on the side, under the dash. Haven't you ever had to pop the hood before?" he asked, walking around to the front of the car.

"No."

He shrugged his shoulders and chuckled. "Women. If it was a new pair of shoes, you'd know exactly where to find them." He took off his cowboy hat. "Here, hold this."

"I don't know what could be wrong," Shaye said, taking his hat and watching him lift up the hood of the Mercedes. "It worked fine on the way over tonight. I've never had any trouble before."

Cody leaned over the motor but couldn't see much of anything in the dim light of the parking lot. He knew that in a few minutes old Charlie the caretaker would be turning out the lights and going home.

"Have you got a flashlight?"

"I don't think so . . . I don't know."

"You don't know?"

"I can't remember."

He peered at her across the open throat of the engine compartment, wondering why she wouldn't look at him. "Do you think you could take a few minutes to look?"

She scowled, he grinned, and then she ducked out from under the hood of the car and slid into the front seat of the Mercedes. He could hear her searching through the side pockets, glove compartment, console, and under the seats.

"There's no flashlight."

"You're sure. There isn't one in the trunk?"

She poked her head out of the open window. "Yes, I'm sure. There's no flashlight."

She turned away again.

"Never mind, I've got one in my truck. I'll go get it. Give me my hat and wait here."

Shaye got out of the Mercedes, handed him his hat, then shut the door and leaned against the front fender. "Where else am I going to go?"

He shot her a quick look, appreciating what he saw. Dressed the way she was, she could go anywhere she wanted. The problem was he wanted to go anywhere with her. But just like Christmas, he reminded himself, you don't always get what you want.

Returning with his flashlight, Cody flipped the switch and caught her in the beam. She quickly raised her hand to shade her eyes. "Here, hold this for me while I take another look." He held the flashlight out to her.

Twenty minutes later the lights in the parking lot had been turned off, his flashlight batteries were dying, and he still wasn't sure what was wrong with the car. He'd checked the battery cables, the wiring seemed to be okay, and he'd checked the air filter. The only thing that seemed out of place was the strong smell of gasoline that permeated the motor. The problem seemed clear. She'd flooded the engine, trying to get it started.

He dropped the hood and gave it a final push to make sure the latch caught. "This car isn't going anywhere tonight."

"I have a motor club card; maybe if I call they'll send someone out to help me . . . even if you can't."

Well, that remark stung a little. He snatched his flashlight out of her hand and swung the failing beam around the parking lot. "Look around. It's after two in the morning. Everyone's gone home." He sent the feeble beam on another sweep. "Carl Nesbitt is Dorland's one-and-only motor club, and at this hour he's in bed—now he's not necessarily at home in his own bed—but he's in bed and I can guarantee that he's not going to get up and try to start anybody's car until morning . . . especially yours after the little go-round earlier."

"So what do you suggest?" She frowned, then glanced around the empty parking lot, empty except for her silver-gray Mercedes and Cody's midnight blue pickup truck.

"Lock up your overpriced ego ride. I'll give you a lift home."

He watched her hesitate.

"I don't know if I should. . . ."

"I don't bite."

"I can't leave my car here. Someone might strip it or something."

"In Dorland?" His exasperation mounted. "Trust me, Midnight Auto doesn't get too many calls for Mercedes parts around here."

She shrugged and ran her hand across the fender of the Mercedes but didn't move.

"Fine. Suit yourself." He turned and walked toward his truck. "Good night." He began a silent countdown in his head. One, two, three . . . betting with himself that before he got to five, she'd change her mind. Four, five, six, seven, eight, nine . . .

"Cody, please . . . wait."

He'd lost the bet, but won the moment.

Shaye ran after him, her fancy high-heeled dancing shoes wobbling on the gravel. "Do you suppose you could slow down and wait for me?"

He stopped and watched her move toward him. He wondered if in another time, another place, he could ever wait for her just like this, watch her move eagerly toward him just like this, and have her run into his arms . . . just as he dreamed. "Reality sucks," he groused.

They walked silently, side by side, across the parking lot to his truck. After unlocking the door, he held it open for her. "Hop in."

Shaye looked up at the truck and then up at him, and then down at her shoes and dress. "You've got to be kidding."

"Yeah," he replied, allowing his words to drip with country humble. "You're right. I guess this old piece of farm junk just ain't up to your Mercedes taste." Hell, his truck was only a year old and was the top model in the line, luxury inside for the comfort of the hardworking rancher, and gleaming paint and chrome outside to show every one how successful he was. The former was nice, the latter was a lie.

"No, no. That's not it. It's a beautiful truck," Shaye said. "But I . . . uh . . ." She tugged the tight skirt of her gown up to midcalf. "I don't think I'm going to be able to climb up in it . . . and keep my dignity."

Cody glanced heavenward into the dark, starry sky. Oh, yes, there were such things as guardian angels, and his had just blessed him mightily.

"I'll help you."

"How?" She stepped back from him.

"Just relax." He couldn't resist teasing her. "Back up about twenty feet, hike your skirt up to your thighs, and take a run at the truck. I'll stand here, and just when you put your foot on the running board, I'll give you a big boost."

"Cody, stop it. Please, just help me get in the truck, and take me home."

He watched her lift the skirt of her gown to an inch or two above her knees and grinned. At least part of his dream had come true. "Take hold of the door frame and step up on the running board. I'll stand behind you—you won't fall."

She followed his instructions, teetering precariously before finding solid footing. "Now what?"

He laughed. "Just hop up into the seat." He placed his hand on the small of her back to steady her.

"Why is this truck so damned tall? Why does everything out here have to be so big?"

Remembering she'd probably seen him in the shower, he struggled against a devilish urge, deciding it best to ignore her remark. "Come on, give it a try; I'm not going to let you fall."

Shaye bounced a couple of times, made a lunge, and Cody suddenly found both of his hands cupping her bottom. The fit was nice. Very nice.

"Hey, watch it," Shaye protested.

"If I let go, you'll end up on the ground on this nice round butt. Now, hush up, hang on, and you'll be in."

All it took was one last shove and Cody made good on his promise. Shaye landed in the passenger's seat, looking very proud of her accomplishment.

"Thank you," she said, pulling her skirt down over her legs like a prim old maid.

"You're very welcome," Cody replied, rubbing his hands together, still feeling the warmth of her body. Oh, yes. Very welcome. "Buckle up." He shut the passenger door, jogged around to the driver's door, and in one graceful maneuver pulled himself up behind the steering wheel.

For the next ten miles they drove in silence with only the sound of the CD player offering instrumental selections from Puccini.

Finally Shaye broke the silence. "I like your choice of music. Puccini's work is wonderful. 'Nessun Dorma' from *Turandot* is one of my favorite melodies."

"Mine, too," Cody replied, glad he still had the CD from Maribeth's music-appreciation class in the player. She'd been playing it the last time he'd driven her to town for her piano lesson. He'd never even heard of this guy Puccinini, or whatever his name was.

Shaye ran her hand over the plush upholstery on the passenger seat. "I never imagined this is what pickup trucks were like inside." She touched the woodgrain trim on the dashboard. "This is very nice. I've never been in one before." She peered out the window. "And we're up so high."

Cody felt like a schoolkid impressing his date with his first old clunker. "So does riding in a pickup turn you on?"

She laughed. "Is it supposed to?"

"Well, yeah, it's the essence of maleness—all testosterone, from bumper to bumper."

Shaye glanced at him out of the corner of her eye. "So tell me, would riding in my Mercedes turn you on?"

Cody laughed. "Hell, yes."

"Why?"

He was trying to figure out how to tell her it would be like making love to a woman, fast and hot and sleek, but never got the chance before Shaye's next words interrupted his thoughts.

"Oh, look." She pointed at the flashing lights on a couple of police cars up ahead. "Have they just pulled someone over or is it an accident?"

"Julie did say something about an accident before she left. We're going to be stuck until they clean it up if we stay on this road, and you need to get home." He slowed down and turned off on the side road that cut away at a sharp angle from the Interstate.

They traveled for another four or five miles, Puccini still playing. The music isn't too bad, Cody thought, listening to Shaye humming along with one of the melodies.

As the truck began to climb a hill, the engine coughed and spluttered. "What the hell . . ." Cody pumped the gas pedal a couple of times, and for a second or two the motor caught and ran smoothly. He quickly scanned the gauges in the dashboard as the truck lurched, burped, and almost died again. Quickly flipping the switch on the dashboard, he changed from the front gas tank to the back. The pickup ran smoothly for another thirty feet or so, but as it crested the hill, the engine died.

Easing the 4x4 onto the side of the road, he allowed it to coast for another fifty feet before he stepped on the brake and brought it to a stop. He turned the key in the ignition. Nothing. He flipped back to the front gas tank and tried again. Nothing.

"What's wrong?" Shaye reached out and touched Cody's arm. Her hand trembled. "What's happening?"

"We're outta gas." In the dark truck cab he could see

her posture stiffen. "I don't understand. I put ten dollars in it this morning."

"Stop fooling around. This is ridiculous."

Cody glanced at her, and then back at the illuminated dials and gauges in front of him. "No fooling . . . we're out of gas."

"Really, Cody, that is the oldest, lamest excuse ever. It's not even funny. Please, take me home."

"Wish I could, Boston, but it's not an excuse. See for yourself." He pointed to the gas gauge. "This truck has dual tanks, and there was gas in both tanks when I was in town this morning."

"Maybe you meant to get gas but forgot," Shaye offered.

"No, I didn't forget." He flipped the gas tank switch again. The needle on the gauge didn't move. "I bought a Coke, a Snickers bar, and ten bucks' worth of gas at the Gas-n-Go in town this morning."

"Are you positive it's not something else? An electrical problem or something?"

He tapped the gauge with the end of his index finger. "I don't know what *E* on a gas gauge means in Boston, but out here, when your needle's on *E* . . . it means you're outta gas."

"I don't believe this," Shaye muttered, turning away from him. "First my car and now your truck. What are we going to do?"

"You take out that cute little cell phone you always carry with you and call someone who'll bring us some gas. The truck stop at the Interstate is open all night, or we can wake up Roscoe. Then we can get out of here."

Shaye groaned and, not looking at him, held up something in the dark.

"What's that?"

"My purse."

"Maybe when it grows up. Right now it's the size of a . . . flea."

"It's an evening bag, it's not made to carry a lot."

"Well, it's living up to its promise," Cody scoffed. "Let me guess, you don't have your cell phone, right?"

Shaye shot Cody a hot glare. "Here," she said, handing him her petite purse. "If you can find my phone, I promise I'll get Hubbard off your back."

"Low blow," Cody admonished. He switched on the interior lights and lifted the tiny clasp on the bag. "I'm not taking any chances. Just in case you figured a way to squeeze that phone in here, you know, like you women squeeze your size nine feet in size seven shoes, I'm gonna take a look."

Opening the purse, he turned it upside down over the console between the seats. A small comb, a couple of tissues, a lipstick, a ten-dollar bill, and her driver's license tumbled out. "Aw, gee, no phone," he said, feigning disappointment. He reached for her license, but she grabbed it off the console and dropped it down the front of her dress before he could take a look.

"I just wanted to check your ID to make sure you are who you say you are."

"Trust me, I am."

He leaned over the console and pretended to look down her dress. "I wouldn't really know, would I, unless I got a good look at your photo on the license?"

"That's not going to happen."

"I should've gone into law enforcement." He withdrew to his side of the truck.

Shaye raised the hem of her skirt and lifted her left foot. "And for your information, this is not a size nine. It is a *perfect* size seven."

Toes . . . pink and painted with scarlet nail polish appeared before his eyes. "And a very nice size seven at that."

She wriggled her toes. He groaned.

"Thank you." She settled back into the seat and pointed at his feet. "And yours?"

"Twelves," Cody replied, warming to the game.

"I'm impressed."

"I'm pretty proud of them." He crossed his left leg over his right knee and buffed the toe of his boot with the heel of his hand. "I've had 'em all my life, wash 'em once in a while to keep 'em . . . sociable, and I've got to admit I'm kinda attached to them."

Shaye groaned. "Well, if I've got the choice of sitting here and listening to your bad jokes until help comes or getting out and walking to find help . . . I'm going to use these size sevens and start walking."

"Take my word for it, you don't want to." Cody stuffed Shaye's belongings back into her purse.

"I certainly don't want to stay here all night long." She unbuckled her seat belt. "Tell me again why you took this back road instead of sticking to the highway."

"You saw the cop car . . . and because Julie told me there'd been an accident on the eastbound lane of the Interstate, an overturned livestock truck. She said the state troopers had closed the road."

Shaye suddenly looked over at Cody, and he met her gaze. "Julie," they said in unison.

"No. Not another setup?" Shaye moaned. "How could you let yourself fall for this again?"

"Hey, wait a minute," Cody countered, feeling that the blame wasn't all his. "You're the one who needed a ride home. You're the one who flooded the motor in her fancy little car, not me."

"I did not flood it. That car is fuel injected . . . you don't pump the gas to start it. I wouldn't be surprised if Julie or one of her partners in crime did something to it. If they've ruined it, I don't know what I'm going to do." She looked away and murmured, "It's not mine."

"What?"

She quickly rounded on him. "I said the Mercedes isn't mine." She sighed, falling back in the seat. "It's a . . . rental."

Cody laughed. "Feel better now? I hear confession is good for the soul."

"Getting home would be better for my soul." She reached in her little purse, pulled out the tissue, and blew her nose.

"Aw, geez, you're not crying are you?" He peered at her through the dark.

"No . . . not much. I'm just so darned frustrated." Her reply wavered as she pushed the crumpled tissue back into the small bag. "Doesn't being stranded like this bother you? How can you be so calm?" Shaye threw open the truck door. The interior light illuminated her face. "Why aren't you angry or upset, or as you macho cowboys say, why aintcha pissed? I certainly am."

"What's the point of getting all worked up? If we sit tight, sooner or later someone will come along and help us."

"The sooner would be nice. The later is what worries me."

"Look, if Julie and the . . . the Lonely Hearts Club did set us up . . . again, they won't leave us out here to rot."

"The what?"

"Well, what would you call them?" Cody stripped off his tie and opened the top buttons of his shirt. "In the morning one of them will come ambling down the road acting all worried because we didn't make it home last night and isn't it miraculous that they found us. Then something more miraculous will happen, they'll take out the full gas can they just happen to have with them, and we're out of here."

"Morning? I've got to sit out here all night with you until morning?" Shaye shook her head.

"You've wounded me." He placed his hand over his heart and moaned. "You make it sound as though I'm some sort of social mutant or something. I'm a really nice guy."

"I've heard that's what Jack the Ripper said just before he sliced and diced."

"You, Miss Shaye, are a cold, cold woman."

"If you think insulting me is going to hurt me, you're wrong. I'm a lawyer. I've been called worse." She checked the contents of her purse.

"Everything's there. I didn't take your money or your lipstick."

"You are exasperating. Scarlet Sin, extra glossy, isn't your shade." Shaye sighed, closed her eyes, and leaned back, resting her head against the seat. "So, if we do lie down and take it like a couple of dogs, what do we do with each other for the whole night?"

Cody grinned and allowed the pause between her question and his answer to stretch out long enough to make her uncomfortable. It didn't take long.

Her eyes popped open, and she immediately sat up. "That wasn't exactly what I meant to say. I . . . uh . . . meant—"

"Oh, I know what you meant," he replied with counterfeit innocence. "Just keep your distance. There's no way I'm going to let a smooth-talking city slicker take advantage of a clean-cut, all-American country boy like me." Keeping his laughter under control was almost impossible. "We need to devise ways to keep our minds occupied and off anything of a lascivious nature. I suppose we could play some games. How about 'I spy with my little eye'?" He peered out the window into the pitch dark. "Oh, never mind, I can't see a darned thing." He shifted in his seat, turning to face her. "There's that game where you call out the states of all the license plates on the cars that go by, and the person who calls out the most states is—"

"Cody Butler, although I'm impressed that your coun-

try vocabulary includes the word *lascivious,* just shut up."
Shaye held on to the door frame and cautiously slid out of
the truck, the skirt of her gown riding up over her thighs.
"I want to go home . . . even if I have to walk." Tugging
her skirt down over her knees, she peered around, then
tipped her head up and gazed at the night sky. "Oh, look, a
shooting star!"

"Quick," Cody said, leaning over the console and looking out the open door. "Make a wish."

"I just did. I said I want to go home."

"Oops, sorry. It won't come true. You're not supposed
to tell what you wished for." Cody leaned back in his seat
and closed his eyes. "You might as well climb back in here
and relax. It's gonna be a long night." He made another bet
with himself. Before he counted to five, she'd ask him to
help her get back in the truck. One . . . two . . .

"Cody, could you please . . . help me?"

We've got a winner! He grinned. It's going to be a long,
wonderful night.

Chapter Seventeen

A cramp in his right leg, a crick in his neck, and the unfamiliar weight against his chest began to pull him up from the depths of sleep. The cool breeze blowing through the partially open window ruffled his hair and brought with it the fragrance of sweetgrass and the pungent scent of dew-wet soil.

He resisted the tug, preferring to linger in the halfway world between sleep and wakefulness, but the cramp and the curious weight remained to nag at him. He straightened his leg, running out of room much too soon, his booted feet hitting the gas and brake pedals. With a sleepy protest, he tried again. The results were the same except for the sound of a soft sigh next to his ear. In an instant he was wide awake.

Cody figured it must be close to five or five-thirty, but even in the pale early morning light, he could make out every detail of the woman snuggled up against him. She lay across his lap, her legs—slightly bent at the knees—stretched across the console with her feet resting on the passenger seat. Her head lay against his left shoulder.

Last night, after finally talking Shaye out of trying to find the nearest telephone in the dark, he'd helped her climb back into the truck. Suddenly aware they would be alone together for the rest of the night, their friendly banter disappeared into awkward silence.

Looking at her across the truck cab, he'd tried to forget how her slender body had felt in his arms when they'd danced or how her lips had felt so good beneath his. He had tried to push away thoughts of how her breath quickened in the moment, matching the cadence of his own. Yeah, sure, trying to forget sounded excellent in theory, but it wasn't working worth a darn. He wanted to remember every detail, and he wanted it all again . . . and more.

His resolve weakening, he had reached out to touch her, whispering her name. She had turned to him, her lashes lowered, her lips moist and parted, her cheeks flushed . . . and then, quickly covering her mouth, she had yawned. An outright rejection would have been a whole lot easier to deal with.

He supposed timing was everything, and obviously this wasn't the time.

Reluctantly he'd pulled back, suggesting they get some sleep. He'd offered the backseat to her so she could stretch out, but she'd chosen to stay up front with him. He'd found some consolation in that.

Using the couple of blankets that he kept in the truck—something most folks who lived in ranch country or near the mountains did—he'd spread them across the console, softening the corners and angles to make a makeshift bed for her. To keep the cool night air from her, he'd draped her shawl and his jacket over her shoulders.

Unable to relax, Cody had watched her fall asleep, her face softening, her breathing deepening. A lock of her hair tumbled across her cheek, and with the tip of his finger, he gently tucked it behind her ear, clearing her face for his hungry gaze.

An hour or so later she had come to him in her sleep like a child seeking comfort and warmth. Eagerly he'd taken her in his arms, settling her on his lap. He'd held her against him, her head resting on his shoulder and the soft touch of her hair against his cheek. Kittenlike, she'd snuggled against him, her breath warm and sweet against his neck. Only then did he finally find sleep.

Now, as morning approached, Cody slowly wriggled his foot back and forth, trying to ease the charley horse in his leg without waking Shaye. Mercifully the cramp eased. The crick in his neck remained, but he enjoyed her weight against his shoulder too much to try to rid himself of the ache just yet.

Smoothing her hair back, he placed a row of light kisses on her forehead, breathing in the delicious sandalwood scent of her. In that instant he regretted every cursed penny he owed the bank. More than that, he detested his own irresponsibility for putting Medicine Creek . . . his home and Maribeth's home . . . in jeopardy. He couldn't believe for one moment that Shaye Frazier would consider him worthy—a man who had foolishly endangered his family's welfare, his family's legacy . . . his own honor. Unless something miraculous happened, in little more than two weeks he'd own no more than the clothes on his back.

Cody fought against the burn in his throat and the shamefilled tears welling up in his eyes. Quicksilver, sand, whatever life's successes were composed of, all were slipping through his fingers. He pressed another kiss to Shaye's forehead, knowing that the overall amount of his expected losses now included the woman he was falling in love with.

Shaye stirred, he head nestling into the crook between his neck and shoulder. "What time is it?" She made a sleepy little moan deep in her throat as she stretched, her body pressing against Cody's.

"I thought you were still asleep." Sorry he'd wakened her, Cody glanced over the top of her head at the clock on the dashboard and tried to ignore the rush of heat that blitzed through his body. "Five-forty."

"Is the morning gas delivery here yet?"

"Not yet. I don't think we'll see Roscoe for another hour or so."

"Why do you think it's going to be Roscoe?" Shaye pushed away from him, moved her sleep-tousled hair away from her face, and sat up in her seat. She pulled the skirt of her gown down over her knees and wrapped one of the blankets around her shoulders.

"He's got my gas, that's why." Cody rubbed the back of his neck, working out the stiffness as he itemized his reasons. "Gene and Julie were with us, Maribeth doesn't have a driver's license, Tim wants his own pickup truck too much to blow his summer job by pissing off his boss, so that leaves the old man."

"You don't think he did it alone, do you?" She busied her fingers, pulling out the remaining pins and trying to tidy her hair.

"Oh, no . . . not by a long shot. The whole Lonely Hearts Club gang was in on this one." He glanced across the truck cab at Shaye. The sun was just beginning to edge up over the eastern horizon, creating a crimson margin along the rim of the hills. The pink glow touched her cheeks and set the highlights of her sleep-tousled hair aflame. In that moment Cody knew he'd willingly wake up next to this woman for the rest of his life, just to see her as he was now.

She gave him a shy sideways glance accompanied by a slight smile. "I'm sorry about . . . draping myself all over you." She fidgeted with the blanket. "You didn't get much sleep, did you?"

"I've had less. You make quite a blanket, though, Boston." He wished she'd move back into his arms.

She quickly looked up at him as if she'd heard his thoughts. They gazed at each other in silence. Cody felt anticipation, solid and compelling, take hold. No doubt existed—he wanted her. He wanted to pull her back into his arms. He wanted to make love to her, taste every bit of her, possess her. He knew he shouldn't even think about it. Thinking led to too much wanting. Devil be damned. He reached his hand out to her, felt her fingers tentatively touch, then wrap around his. "You know, we could stop their crazy matchmaking games." He caressed her fingers with his thumb.

"How would we do that?" she asked, her voice nothing more than a husky whisper.

"By showing them we don't need them anymore . . . that we're doing just fine on our own."

She stared at his mouth as he moved closer. It was clear she understood he was about to kiss her. "Are we?"

"I think so. Don't you?" He touched the side of her face, tracing the arc of her eyebrow, and then drove his fingers into her rich, thick hair. He felt her breath on his lips as he drew her to him and watched her slowly close her eyes, expecting . . . wanting.

Out of the corner of his eye a flash of light caught his attention. Reluctantly Cody turned and watched as Roscoe's old red pickup crested the hill, the headlights casting uneven beams on the road. A jumble of feelings bombarded him. Disappointment, relief, anger. He looked back at Shaye and felt something akin to physical pain get added to the mix. He'd seen disappointment in her eyes, too. "It looks like the gas man cometh." His wry joke tasted bitter on his tongue as he looked back at the oncoming vehicle.

The old pickup wheezed to a halt behind Cody's truck, and he took a deep breath. How should he deal with the old man? The weight of his anger with the Lonely Hearts Club gang had dwindled overnight. In fact, he found their resourcefulness to be impressive . . . even amusing . . . but he'd be damned if he'd let them know that. "Wait here," he suggested to Shaye as he opened the door and swung out of the truck and onto the berm of the road.

Roscoe trundled down the center of the road, his boots thumping on the pavement. "Phew . . . I'm darned glad I found you. Doggone it . . . Maribeth and me was getting awful worried 'bout you when we got up this mornin' and you weren't home." He pulled a red-checkered handkerchief from his pocket and, lifting his battered hat, wiped his brow. "I keep telling ya, son, you need to get yerself one of them little cellular phone things. If you'd called, I could've come ta gitcha last night." He made a big show of peering at Cody's truck. "Oh, my golly . . . is that Miss Shaye in there with ya? Well, well, ain't that a surprise? We didn't know . . . no, sir . . . but I'm sure glad to see you're both okay." With an expression of wide-eyed innocence, Roscoe looked up at Cody. "What's the problem, son? Truck die on ya?"

"Save your breath and quit jacking your jaws, old man. You can cut the bad act and just get the damn gas can out of the back of your truck." Cody flipped open the small gas tank door and unscrewed the cap. "You'd better put back every drop you sucked out of this thing."

He watched Roscoe hobble to the old truck, hoist a red gas can out of the truck bed, then struggle with the weight as he carried it back. "Here, give me that." Cody took the can from the old cowboy. "The last thing I need is for you to drop it and spill all the gas out on the road."

"There's another can," Roscoe mumbled, not meeting Cody's glare.

Cody tipped the gas can, filling his truck. "Uh-huh, there'd better be." He glanced up. "What did you guys do to Shaye's car?" He watched Roscoe give a slight shrug.

"I don't know what Miss Julie—"

"If it costs anything to get it fixed . . . you're all chipping in to pay for it," Cody interrupted. "Your story's full of crap, too. When the hell did you or Maribeth start getting up before eight on a Sunday morning?" He thumped the empty can down on the road and screwed his gas cap back in place. "You two aren't off the hook yet . . . I'll talk to you both when I get home."

Roscoe gave a jittery nod and picked up the empty can. "Can I talk to Miss Shaye for a minute?"

"No, you can't. You're not getting close to her until you and Julie and Maribeth are all ready to apologize to her for putting her through the worst night of her life."

Roscoe pulled himself up to his full height, squared his shoulders, and thrust his whiskered chin out like a pugnacious rooster. "Well, damn it all, boy . . . that'd be your fault, not ours." He gave Cody a hard glare. "You're the one that was supposed to make it a memorable night." He stomped off, shaking his head, and sent a parting shot over his shoulder. "The team sets the kid up, gives him every opportunity to score, and just like a rookie . . . he can't deliver."

"Would you like to come in for some coffee?" Shaye offered as Cody stopped his truck in Hubbard's turnaround driveway. "I'm sure Tess has a fresh pot brewing, and I bet there's some hot buttered scones, too."

"I have no idea what a scone is, and the coffee sounds tempting, but I'd better get on home. Thanks anyway." He hopped out of the truck, went around and opened the passenger door.

Shaye placed her hands on his shoulders and allowed him to lift her out of the truck. "In New York it's bagels, in New England it's scones or English muffins, and out here it's beef—with everything." With both feet on the ground, her hands still resting on his forearms, she glanced up at him. "I guarantee that you'll never forget the first time you have one."

"Scones or muffins, it's a good thing you're out here

and not back in Boston this morning," he said, smiling down at her.

"Why?"

"Just think how the neighbors would talk, seeing the nice, young lady lawyer coming home in the morning all dolled up in the gown she went out in the night before." He affected a falsetto voice. "Gladys, did you see that nice young lawyer lady . . . out all night, not coming home until morning. Why, I've never been so shocked in all my life . . . and with a . . . ugh . . . cowboy, no less."

"They're just jealous," Shaye replied, her laughter filling his heart. "Gladys hasn't been out dancing in years . . . and never with a cowboy." She stepped away from him. "Thank you for driving me home . . . and for dancing with me."

"My pleasure, ma'am." He swept his hat off his head with a grand flourish and executed a gallant bow. Rising, he held out his hand. "Give me your keys. I'll make sure you get your car back this morning."

She fumbled in the little evening bag and withdrew her car keys. "Here." She held them out to Cody.

"Thanks." He took the keys, his fingers first grazing hers, then holding her hand.

"Do you think you'll feel up to riding this afternoon?"

Shaye's face lit up with a smile. "Yes . . . if you do."

"Yeah, sure. Great." He walked her to the door. "I tell you what . . . how about I have Roscoe pack a picnic dinner, and I'll show you some of the ranch. I think you're ready to get out of the arena. Is five okay?"

"I'll be there."

"I'll see you"—he raised her hand to his lips and lightly kissed her knuckles—"later."

All the way home Cody tried to decide what he'd say to Roscoe and Maribeth. Their wild schemes were getting out of hand. He hated to think what they'd try next. Gene could handle Julie, but he needed to do something about Maribeth and Roscoe.

By the time he got to the end of the lane at Medicine Creek, Roscoe's parting words had replayed at least a dozen times in his head. *The team sets the kid up, gives him every opportunity to score, and just like a rookie . . . he can't deliver.* Maybe the old man was right. Maybe he'd let the best opportunity slide by. Then again, maybe the best opportunity to court a Boston lady lawyer would be under a Wyoming star-filled sky later tonight.

Cody parked the truck next to the house and got out. On the drive down the lane, he'd come to a decision. He'd say nothing to Maribeth and Roscoe. Let them stew. Let them wonder how angry he really was or when he was going to chew them out. Yes, sir, a little guilty sweating might be the best punishment of all.

They were sitting at the kitchen table when he came in, and both looked up at him as though they were condemned felons waiting for the executioner.

"Good morning," he said, making sure his voice sounded warm and congenial. He busied himself at the stove, pouring a cup of coffee, then filling a plate with scrambled eggs and sausage patties from the skillet. Sitting at the table with Maribeth and Roscoe, he began to eat his breakfast, ignoring their puzzled looks.

Cody glanced at Maribeth, gave her a wink, then reached for the salt and pepper. "I've asked Doc Campbell to check into whether llamas can get hoof-and-mouth or not. Honey, until he finds out, I think it would be safer to keep your new pet at Hubbard's for a while longer . . . if he doesn't mind. We don't want to expose her to anything that would harm her, do we?" He shook some pepper on his eggs. "You got a name for this critter yet?" He looked up at his young sister as he took a mouthful of eggs.

"Poppy," Maribeth said quietly.

"Poppy?" He nodded his agreement. "I like that. I bet

she's a cutie pie, right?" He picked up his mug and took a few swallows of coffee. "Oh, Roscoe, I need a favor?" He waited for the old cowboy to look up. "A picnic dinner this evening . . . for two." Cody put his mug down and reached for a piece of toast. This was more fun than he'd thought it would be. He looked up just in time to see Maribeth elbow Roscoe, mouth the words "picnic dinner for two," then give a knowing little nod. He caught Roscoe's thumbs-up gesture and then, as if they'd practiced the movement for days, both turned toward him and smiled in perfect synchronization.

"Sure, okay, I can do that. How . . . how about some fried chicken, some nice sliced cucumbers and dip, and maybe some grapes, wine, and—"

"Whatever," Cody interrupted with a shrug, forcing himself to act nonchalant. "I got to get out of these fancy duds and get to work. I'll pick the food up when I come up for a shower a little before five." Rising, he carried his dirty dishes to the sink, then turned to Maribeth. "Hey, Tater, I need a favor from you, too."

"Sure, okay," Maribeth warily replied. "What?"

"Pick a pretty bouquet of flowers from the side garden for me. Would you, please?"

"From Momma's garden?"

"Yeah, thanks."

"Sure. Do you want 'em the same time as you pick up the picnic?"

"That'd be great." After leaving the kitchen, he paused on the other side of the door, allowing a wide grin to spread on his face. From where he stood in the dim hallway he could see into the kitchen and hear the two conspirators.

"I don't get it," Maribeth said, peeling and biting into a banana. "I figured he'd be yelling his fool head off at us and grounding me till I'm eligible to join AARP."

"I'm already there," Roscoe grouched, rubbing his

nose. "He's makin' me twice as nervous acting like he weren't bothered at all by spending the night out there." He shook his head. "Come to think of it, he wasn't really mad when I took the gas out to 'em, either . . . just a little touchy, but then he usually is first thing in the morning." He scratched the side of his head, then dragged his hand over his two-day-old growth of whiskers. "I jest don't get it."

Maribeth leaned forward, pointing the last few inches of the banana at Roscoe. "What do you think happened out there last night? Do you think they . . . uh . . . you know?" She wriggled her eyebrows up and down. "What do you think? Did they?"

Roscoe held up his hand and leaned back in his chair. "I ain't thinking 'bout nothing that did or didn't happen, 'cause it ain't none of our business."

Maribeth snorted and popped the rest of the banana in her mouth. "Yeah, and I'm Porky Pig."

Gene hung up the phone.

"Who was that, sweetie?" Julie stepped out of the bathroom, fresh from her morning shower wearing nothing but a towel wrapped around her head and water droplets on her skin.

"Well, I suppose you could say that was my soon-to-be-ex-boss." Gene turned and saw Julie. "Aw, geez, how do you expect me to read you the riot act when you're naked? Do you know how distracting that is?"

"Okay, if it'll make it any easier for you." Julie took the towel from her head and wrapped it around her body. "Better?" She finger-combed her wet hair.

"No, not better . . . but easier," Gene replied.

"Let me guess." She moved closer to the bed. "That was Cody and he's pissed about last night."

"Damn, I knew it." He slapped his hand on his knee. "I was hoping it wasn't true, but I figured you were up to something with all those phony pages, telephone calls, and asking Buck Linderman to get his patrol car and meet you out on the Interstate." With a deep exasperated sigh Gene fell back on the bed. "Okay, tell me everything."

Julie sat next to him, her head bowed, her hands folded primly in her lap. By the time she'd finished her tale, Gene didn't know whether to laugh or cry. He sat up, propping himself on his elbow. "Cody told me he wasn't going to say anything to you about this . . . that he was counting on me to . . . take care of . . . uh . . . disciplining you myself."

"Yeah?" Julie looked at Gene, offering him her most innocent expression. "So . . . what do you have in mind?"

"How do you feel about a spanking?"

Julie stood and dropped the towel. "Excited."

Cody unlocked the top desk drawer and withdrew the envelope. The entry forms had come in the mail two days ago. He'd thought about waiting until he got to Cheyenne to post his entries, but by mailing them in he'd be able to reserve a box stall in the show barn for Possum rather than take potluck when he got there. He'd take his sleeping bag and share the ten-by-ten space with his gray gelding and save the motel bill.

He pulled his PRCA card from his wallet and ran his finger over the bucking horse emblem of the Professional Rodeo Cowboys Association. Thank God he'd kept his membership paid up. Placing the card back in his wallet, he began to fill out the entry form, putting an x beside each event he intended to enter. He totaled up the fees and wrote the check. That took another nasty chunk out of his bank account, but even if he just won go-round money, he could make up what he needed.

If Gene still wanted to go, that was fine, too, but Cody refused to think he was coming home any other way than as a winner.

He sealed the envelope, put a stamp on it, and slid it

into his hip pocket. He'd drop it into a mailbox in town away from prying eyes when he went to check on Shaye's car.

Cody swiveled in the chair and gazed thoughtfully at the glass case that held photos, trophies, and silver buckles—proof that at one time he could ride out the full eight seconds on most of the rough stock he'd ever drawn. His father had ridden for years before him, and his grandfather before that . . . another tie to the past, another Butler legacy.

Two saddles sat on racks in the corner of the room, both with hand-tooled lettering on the fenders. Cody knew the wording by heart. The first read "All-Around Champion Cowboy, Wyoming State Fair, 1979." He'd been eleven years old when his father had won the title and brought the saddle home with a check for fifteen hundred dollars. Seventeen years later Cody won his own saddle. There were three other trophy saddles in the tack room, but these two were special. No father and a son had ever won the state fair title before.

Nowadays the saddles were flashier, the trophy buckles gaudier, the checks much bigger. He had saddles and buckles, he'd even won a two-horse trailer in Denver one year. They could keep all the hardware . . . it was the bigger check he was counting on.

Cody nervously fingered the envelope in his pocket. Maybe he would draw some good smooth stock, the kind that could make a cowboy look good and help him earn some high scores. All he needed was a lot of luck and a few good rides in Cheyenne to make up the rest of the money he needed for the bank. Di Prado's and Roscoe's checks weren't enough, and unfortunately, he'd been a little short on luck lately. *Keep thinking like that and all you get to do at Cheyenne is eat dirt.*

His eyes strayed to the trophy case once again, settling on a photograph of a cowboy crumpled in the dirt, a ton and a half of black Brahma-crossed bull tap dancing on top of him. That was the last time he'd rodeoed—out near Lander. He'd drawn one of the Skoal Company's bad bulls, Snuff 'Em Out, and that black monster had nearly lived up to its name, had nearly killed him. But losing Medicine Creek would certainly finish the job.

Chapter Eighteen

Cody tied a blanket and the bundle holding the picnic dinner to the back of his saddle. Finding a way to carry the flowers Maribeth had picked for him posed another problem. For the time being, he stuck the stems in the gullet of his saddle, then led Possum and Sophie out of the barn. After looping the reins over the fence rail, he checked his watch: 5:05. He checked the late afternoon sky: gorgeous. He checked himself: nervous. Nervous, hell . . . he was more jittery than a pimple-faced fifteen-year-old waiting for his date for the junior prom. Gawd, he was starting to think in hokey hickisms . . . at least he hadn't told anyone that Shaye Frazier was as purty as a brown speckled pup . . . yet.

He wanted this evening to be perfect . . . for both of them. He wanted her to see what he'd be giving up if he lost Medicine Creek to the bank or to Hubbard. And he wanted her to see the beauty that God's hand had created for the generations of Butlers. It wouldn't get dark for another three hours or so—more than enough time for a nice ride, a leisurely dinner, and then . . .

The throaty sound of the Mercedes interrupted his thoughts and kicked his pulse into high gear. He hadn't felt this nervous since his first date, an afternoon movie with Jeff Granger's sister when he was thirteen. He rubbed his damp palms down his jean-clad thighs, turned, and watched Shaye park next to the barn.

"Hi." She slid from the low-slung sports car. "Thanks for getting the Mercedes back to me."

"Sounds like it's running okay." Cody leaned back against the fence, hooked the heel of his left boot on the bottom rail, and watched her walk toward him. The car wasn't the only thing running okay . . . his hormones were speeding right along, too, until his conscience firmly stepped on the brake. . . . *Remember, this is going to be nothing more than a leisurely ride, a nice picnic dinner, some conversation, and then good night.* "It started up fine this morning, but I had the guys at the garage check it out anyway before they took it back to you."

"So what was wrong with it? Why wouldn't it start last night?"

"I think someone flooded the motor, that's all."

"But how? They'd have to get inside the car to get to the gas pedal and I'm sure I locked it before I went in to the dance."

"I suspect Julie did it. Cops sometimes carry a gadget they call a Slim Jim. It slides down inside the door and pops the lock. I bet Deputy Julie's got a pretty shiny Slim Jim in her patrol car."

Dropping her gaze, Shaye nervously fidgeted with the pair of gloves in her hand. "Cody," she began. "All of their attempts to get us together are making me uncomfortable. I hope you understand . . . it's not you, I don't have anything against you personally, it's just that I'm . . . not interested in a relationship with anybody." She moved on to shuffling the dirt with the toe of her boot. "My career is my priority; it's all I want. When I get back to Boston, I'm going to open my own practice and . . ." She paused for a moment and angled a sheepish glance at him. "Well, as I said, I'm not interested."

Cody lifted his sunglasses out of his pocket and put them on. His Cheyenne grandma had once told him that a woman could see lies in a man's eyes; he didn't want to take any chances that it might be true. "I know they mean well and think we'd be good for each other, but I agree. It's not a good time for me, either." He gave a slight shrug. "I've already talked to Maribeth and Roscoe. I told them neither of us is . . . interested. I don't think there'll be any more surprises."

She quickly glanced up at him as if contesting his opinion. "I hope not." She straightened up, put her gloves in her pocket, and stilled her foot. "I'll be leaving Dorland as soon as I'm finished with Hubbard's business, so you see, their efforts are pointless."

"Yeah, I agree." *Like hell, I agree.* "What you mean is, as soon as you're finished with *my* business."

Shaye casually slid her hands into her back pockets, causing her pale yellow T-shirt to stretch across her breasts. He could see the lacy outline of her bra, the dusky shadows of her nipples. Cody knew just by the look on her face, just by getting to know her, that she didn't have a clue what she was doing to him. With Bunny Gibson it was always deliberate, a blatant tease that had never tempted him because it was so calculated; but with Shaye the innocence of her pose turned on everything inside him. *Just a leisurely ride, a nice picnic dinner, conversation, and good night.* It was a good thing he'd put his sunglasses on, because no matter what he'd told her, he wanted more.

"I thought we agreed not to talk about Hubbard anymore."

"You're right." Cody pushed away from the fence and stepped beside Possum. Hooking the left stirrup on the saddle horn, he tightened the girth on his saddle with a jerk, causing the gelding to give a protesting grunt. He then moved to Sophie, checked her cinch, and tightened the ties holding the small soft-sided cooler on the back of the saddle. He glanced over his shoulder at Shaye. "Are you ready to ride, Boston?"

He stood beside the palomino mare as Shaye swung up into the saddle, disappointed there was no need for him to touch her, to help her. "You're getting pretty good at this." The smile she gave him was more than worth the simple compliment. "Let's go."

He settled himself on Possum and glanced over at Shaye. She looked as if she belonged nowhere else in the world. How could he make her see that? With a mental shrug he negated the possibility. *Just a leisurely ride, a nice picnic dinner, conversation, and good night.* He'd brand the damn litany on his brain if he had to.

He led Shaye down the lane between the horse paddocks, across the grassy meadow, through a picturesque stand of cottonwood trees, and up to the small cemetery on the knoll. "I hope you don't mind, I've got a stop to make before we head out." He stepped out of the saddle. "I'll just be a minute."

"Please, take your time."

He watched her look from headstone to headstone. "That's all of us Butlers . . . except for me and Maribeth . . . and Roscoe, whose every bit family." He pointed to three very old stones in the center of the plot. "There is where it all began . . . Jacob, his first wife, Ruth, and his second wife, *Eve'haoohe'e.*"

He pointed to another pair of matching stones, and then another, and another, sharing the stories of each generation, each member of the family. He paused for a moment when only two markers remained. "My mother and father." He spoke quietly, and Shaye leaned forward in the saddle to hear his words. He looked up at her. "Now do you understand why I'm fighting so hard?"

She hesitantly reached out to touch his shoulder, pulling

her hand back at the last moment and offering a slight nod instead. "I've always understood."

Cody searched her eyes for evidence of a lie; there was none. Did his grandma's little test work both ways? He sure hoped it did.

With the bouquet of flowers tucked under his arm, he handed Possum's reins to Shaye. "He'll probably try to eat. Just keep his head up so he doesn't step on the reins. The same goes for Sophie, too. Okay? You'll do fine." His fingers grazed Shaye's as she grasped Possum's reins. He'd take the warmth of her touch with him.

The gate delivered a rusty squeak when he pushed it open, and Cody upbraided himself for forgetting to bring the oil once again. The grass was also getting too long and a little weedy in places. Now that things had started to settle down—the quarantine pens were slowly emptying out, di Prado had bought the horses—maybe he'd have the time to bring Maribeth up in a day or so. Together they could get the grass cut and take care of the weeds. He had never sent any of the ranch hands to tend the small cemetery, and he never would. Family took care of family.

Cody stood just inside the fence. The passage of time since the accident hadn't made it any easier to come up to the knoll and visit his parents in their graves. Now the shame of his failure made it even more difficult.

Moving to the two most recent graves, he knelt on one knee by the russet granite headstone and traced the lettering with his finger: *Katherine Elizabeth Butler, cherished wife and beloved mother.*

He gently laid the bouquet against the foot of the stone, straightening a bloom or two, arranging the greenery, fixing the pink ribbon Maribeth had tied around stems. "Happy birthday, Mom. Tater picked them for you; they're your favorites . . . out of your garden." He coughed, clearing the emotional lump from his throat. "We're doing okay, but it's hard, Mom." He struggled to hold his emo-

tions together. He stood. His gaze swept from one headstone to the next and then back to his mother's and father's. "I miss you, Mom. God, how I miss you both. I'm
so sorry I've let you down, but I promise, I'll fight this
damn thing . . . to the end." With a nearly imperceptible
nod, he turned and left the enclosure, closing the gate behind him.

He tried to shake off the weight of melancholy, swallowing the grief that still lingered. He looked up at Shaye,
gave a lighthearted smile. "Hungry?" He took Possum's
reins from her. "You'd better be, because I'm absolutely
starved." He swung up into the saddle and reined the gray
gelding around until he was next to her. "I could eat a side
of beef and belch out a hoof. But all we've got is some of
Roscoe's fried chicken."

"I've heard that before." Her eyes warmed on his.

"Well, this time it's true—a special order just for you."

They headed northwest from the knoll. Leaving the single rut of the cattle trail, they rode across the open country
resplendent with brilliant splashes of red Indian paintbrush
blooms. The mountains with their snowcapped peaks lay
ahead. Summer sun and rain had provided a carpet of rich
grass this year, and in places the tall blades grew higher
than the horses' knees.

A small herd of Semmintal cows and their babies raised
their heads from their dinner as they passed, and Cody
couldn't help but wonder how many of the cows had lost
their next spring calves to his plague. He'd find out soon
enough when spring came.

The cattle weren't the only ones enjoying the bounty. A
half mile farther he silently pointed out a small cluster of
mamma elk and their calves dozing in the shadows of a
stand of aspens. Not wanting to spook them, Cody led
Shaye in a wide circle around the herd.

"I've never seen anything so wonderful," she breathed.

"The Crow people call them *wapiti*," he whispered.

"Look, there's another small group over there." He pointed to the far edge of the line of trees. "There's the bull. Look at the antlers on him."

"Where? I don't see them." Shaye stopped Sophie and raised her hand to shade her eyes from the sun.

Cody circled Possum around and stopped beside Shaye. Leaning closer to her from his saddle, he pointed to the elk. "Look down my finger . . . there . . . can you see now?" He watched her eagerly search the area, enjoying her enthusiasm when she spied the lumber-headed elk.

"Yes . . . yes." Excited, she turned to glance at him and never looked away.

A slight breeze touched her hair, lifting and blowing strands across her cheek, and he reached out to gently brush them away. He watched her part her lips and lightly sweep the tip of her tongue across their surface. He tried to muffle the telltale moan that rose up in his throat and knew he'd lose his mind if he didn't kiss her.

His hand cupped her cheek and he drew her closer.

His lips were a hair's breadth away from hers when the explosion took place beneath him. With a loud squeal, Possum humped his back, ducked his head, and jumped sideways, nearly dumping Cody on the ground. "Dammit, Possum! Whoa!" Quickly bringing the gelding under control, Cody saw what caused the gray's tantrum as Sophie reached out to nip the gelding on the flank a second time.

"Oh, my God! Help me . . . oh . . . please hurry, hurry!" Shaye screamed. "Help me!"

Shooting a glance at Shaye as he tightened the bundle on the back of his saddle, Cody couldn't believe his eyes. She sat hunched over in the saddle, gripping the saddle horn in a two-handed stranglehold. Her eyes were squeezed shut, and she'd dropped Sophie's reins. The mare stood with her head down, calmly grazing on the lush grass. Choking down his laugh was almost impossible. "Shaye, calm down. Everything's fine. You're okay."

"No, I'm not. I'm terrified."

"You're fine. Nothing's wrong."

"Are you sure?"

"I'm positive." He leaned out of his saddle and picked up the mare's reins. "Come on, open your eyes. See?" He watched her fearfully open first one eye and then the next. "See? You let go of the reins, and she took advantage of you. She's just eating. Something we should be doing."

Cody handed Shaye the reins, and they moved away from the elks and the cottonwoods. "I don't think Sophie liked Possum being so close." He chuckled. "Or maybe it was me she didn't like getting too close." He couldn't help teasing Shaye. "How about you?" He led her across a crystal-clear stream, watching her swallow her fear as Sophie lunged up the embankment. "Have you noticed that every time I'm going to kiss you . . . and I was . . . that something always stops me?"

Her laughter filled the meadow like music. "No . . . I think you succeeded at the dance."

"Okay, but I failed miserably two out of three times." He tugged on Possum's reins, slowing the horse down. "You've got to admit, that's damn lousy odds."

"Then I guess you shouldn't place any bets on future tries."

"Is that a challenge?" He saw a flicker of apprehension in her eyes. *Just a leisurely ride, a nice picnic dinner, conversation, and good night.* Changing the subject was the best plan for now. They rode side by side in silence for another fifteen or twenty minutes until Cody finally pulled Possum to a halt. "How's this spot for our picnic?"

The northern elbow of the stream they'd crossed earlier tumbled down a wooded hillside and cut through the grasslands on the north, a line of trees stood to the east, and to the west they had a clear view of the mountains and the early evening sky.

"Oh, Cody, this is so beautiful."

After hobbling the horses, he led Shaye to a large rock by the stream. "Sit here and enjoy the view while I set out dinner."

"But I should help." She tried to rise.

"Nope. Tonight you're my guest. How about some wine?"

"You're kidding, right? You brought wine?"

Cody retrieved two canteens from his saddle. Returning to the stream, he chuckled as he watched Shaye ease herself from one side of the rock to the other, obviously looking for a comfortable groove that wouldn't aggravate her saddle-weary bottom. He knew she'd soon discover no such groove existed.

"I may be on the tight end of a foreclosure, and this isn't heirloom crystal, but I thought you should know even cowboys know how to be classy." Cody passed one of the canteens to her. "The best Chablis five bucks can buy."

Shaye lightly shook the container and heard the slosh of liquid inside. "And after all the western movies I've seen, I thought there was nothing but foul, warm pond water in these things." Twisting off the cap, she took a sip. "Hmm, very nice. I must admit, my opinion of the American cowboy has just taken an impressive upswing." She raised the canteen in a salute. "My compliments to the wine steward . . . at Mel's Liquor Shack."

After spreading the blanket on the ground, Cody arranged the dishes Roscoe had packed, laughing aloud when he found the three votive candles and the small tape recorder, the cassettes of romantic music, and an extra set of batteries. The Lonely Hearts Club gang was still at it.

Shaye took another sip of white wine. Cool and crisp, the Chablis slid down her throat as she drank in the magnificent scenery around her. She couldn't remember ever being in such a beautiful place in her life. Everything was pristine, from the crystal-clear water in the stream to the sweet-smelling air. She tipped her head back and looked up at the sun riding the ridge of the mountains, getting ready to send up its evening palette of reds and mauves and golds. *Memorize every thing you can about this place and this evening. . . . You will never find anything like it in Boston.*

She glanced at Cody. What would happen when this was all over? Simple. She had already decided her course. She would go back to Boston, back to her tidy, cat-free apartment . . . just as she had planned. She'd have dinners alone going over briefs and planning court strategies. There'd be an occasional business luncheon, walks by herself in the park, Sunday visits to the Commons, an hour every second day at the health club, where she could mull over her cases as she worked out, and there were always her monthly meetings of the Bar Association. Her life would be full, she'd be respected by her peers, hard work would make her successful. Hub would be so proud of her. And through it all her heart would be safe. That was what she'd planned.

Her gaze swept across the meadow to the stream, to the cottonwood trees, and to the pines and to the peaks of the Teton Mountains beyond. She could imagine Jacob Butler looking at this majestic land and deciding this was where he'd leave his mark.

She couldn't deny that she'd found special things here. She'd found good friends—people who accepted her for herself. She'd discovered that she loved the mountains, the rocky ridges, and the rustling leaves of the aspens. She loved the horses, cowboy boots, and her ponytail sticking out of the back of her ballcap . . . and huge black dogs.

And Cody Butler. She turned her gaze back to study Cody—tall, strong, self-assured. It would be dishonest, even foolish, to say he didn't fascinate her. His moods, withdrawn and quiet one minute, brash as a bull elk the next, then tender, caring, and unexpectedly sentimental. He was funny, making her laugh out loud, something that had rarely happened before. He was serious and prideful without conceit; and sad, sometimes taking her to the brink of tears. Cody Butler moved her in so many ways. The love he had for an adopted child and an old cowboy, and the passion he had for Medicine Creek. The way he'd stood by his mother's grave, the bouquet of birthday flowers held behind his back as if he intended to surprise her with his gift.

He could be so darned hardheaded, determined to gamble with his fate to the ninth hour, and he could be soft hearted, giving in to Maribeth's whim when it only added to his own problems.

And then there was that . . . indescribable attraction, the kind she'd never imagined existed, the kind she'd never felt before for any man. Not even for her husband.

Shaye looked away, watching as the setting sun swept a halo of brilliant color along the peaks of the mountains. Despite the beauty of the sunset, her thoughts of what her future would be held fast. When she left, what would happen to all these feelings that she'd allowed inside her? Simple. She'd rebuild her emotional bulwark, only this time it would be higher, thicker, stronger . . . much stronger. Raising the canteen to her lips, she took another sip of wine to seal her vow, then twisted the cap back in place.

She knew he was standing behind her before he spoke, his nearness as tangible as if he had put his hand on her. Then he did touch her, and all of her resolutions imploded.

With everything from the picnic bundles set out on the blanket, Cody turned to call to Shaye, but his words never left his throat. He watched her sitting atop the large rock, her arms around her drawn-up knees, her chin resting against them. He wanted two things in life more than anything else—Shaye Frazier and Medicine Creek, and it frightened him to wonder which he wanted more. He slowly walked toward her, wondering why he couldn't have both.

Without thought he rested his hand on her shoulder. "Magnificent, isn't it?" He barely heard her whispered response.

"Yes."

"I never get tired of this place. Once in a while when things on the ranch get to me, I'll ride up here. It's like you're closer to God . . . there's such an enormity to the place."

She glanced up at him and gave a solemn nod. "I suppose that's why they call it Big Sky Country."

He grinned. "No. That's why they call it Wyoming." He watched her frown. "Montana is Big Sky Country." He couldn't tell if it was the reflection from the sunset or if she was blushing—whatever the cause, it heightened her beauty beyond belief. He held his hand out to her. "Come on, let's eat." She took his hand, and he wrapped his fingers around hers, feeling the heat of their skin meld together.

He gently pulled her to her feet and into his arms, surprised how willingly she came. Burying his hands in her hair, he tilted her face upward and gazed into her eyes. Deep pools of green, wide with anticipation, met him. "I'm about to change the odds," he murmured, lowering his mouth to hers. God, he was starved, but definitely not for Roscoe's chicken.

Chapter Nineteen

No! Don't let this happen! The voice of caution screamed in her head. *Yes, yes. Don't let this stop.* The yearning voice of her heart countered. She denied the first and submitted to the second.

Raising her hand, Shaye touched Cody's face, at first tentatively and then boldly. Her fingers traced the arch of his eyebrow and across the ridge of his cheekbone to the small crescent-shaped scar on its edge. "How?" She wanted to learn all about him.

"A very upset bull."

Traveling lower, she tracked the bridge of his nose to the fullness of his lips beneath and then to the slight cleft in his chin. Discovering the ridge of another scar under his chin, she looked up for an answer.

"Same bull."

She retraced the path of her caress, her eyes following the journey her fingers took, moving back up his chin, his cheek, his forehead, memorizing the texture of his skin, the composition of his face.

"Do you approve?"

Startled from her reverie, she felt the hot blush of her

embarrassment. She lowered her gaze, then, allowing a
saucy smile to curve her lips, replied, "So far."

Cody's fingers under her chin raised her head, making
her look up at him again. "I'm glad. I'd hate for you to go
home to Boston thinking you kissed a Wyoming toad, not
once, but at least four times."

"Do you suppose that you could quit talking about it
and just do it?"

And he did.

His lips moved over hers, gently at first, grazing her
mouth, teasing her senses. His tongue dipped and stroked,
seeking her reply, and she eagerly gave it to him.

Leaning into Cody's arms, she raised herself up on tiptoe, her arms moving around him, her fingers pressing into
his back. He embraced her, engulfed her, lifted her to
dizzying heights she never knew existed . . . and she let
him.

She pulled away from the kiss first, the bliss almost too
much to bear. Burying her face against his chest, Shaye
tried to catch her breath. It helped if she hung on to him . . .
tight.

In the corner of her mind that still fought for objectiv-
ity, she tried to reason. Would surrendering to the need
Cody woke in her be unethical? After all, Glenn Hubbard
was her client and Cody's ranch the object of her assignment. No. Glenn Hubbard was her father, too. What would
happen if she told Cody now? She shouldn't keep it from
him . . . he had a right to know. But when? Oh God, she
wanted to forget who she was, what she was, and this one
time—only this one time—follow her heart.

The argument escalated in her mind—her conscience
playing both plaintiff and defendant. No matter what happened tonight, she wouldn't stay in Dorland. She couldn't
stay. Her plans were set, her goals almost within her reach.

Perhaps it was cold and calculated, but she could only
afford one night with Cody. Just one night would be dan-

gerous, but the memories would be so precious. They'd be memories to take back to Boston with her, memories to keep her warm on those lonely, chilly Boston winter nights . . . memories for the rest of her life. Would that be so wrong? Or would she be taking something from Cody? Stealing? She couldn't risk giving anything of herself, so, yes, it would be taking.

I wouldn't be taking anything he wasn't freely offering. He knows I'm going back to Boston. And I'll have a special moment to keep tucked away in my heart . . . forever.

"Shaye?" He caressed the side of her face, pulling her away from her thoughts. He tipped her head up again until their eyes met and held. "We can step away from each other right now, ignore what I know we're both feeling. We can sit down and enjoy the supper Roscoe made for us. But you need to know . . . I don't think I can do that."

She didn't resist when he scooped her up and carried her to the blanket and gently laid her down. He followed, stretching out beside her. They stared at each other, and for a long moment he didn't touch her. He didn't have to. She was vividly aware of his body, the heat, and the undeniable need that being near him generated deep within her.

Her heart started racing as fast as a frenzied wind, and her mind spun as erratically as aspen leaves in the wind's path. No, now was not the time to tell him about Hubbard. But what she did have to say, she had to say it out loud so he knew . . . more important, so she knew. "I don't think I can do that, either."

Cody partially covered her body with his. Bracketing her head with his arms resting on the blanket, he lowered his head until his mouth possessed hers, and the kiss he ground upon her lips was charged with their combined hunger. His fingers moved through her hair, tilting her head first to one side, then the other, so that her mouth had to follow to meet and match the marauding demands of his.

Shaye moved against him, melding her body to his. She needed this. She craved the feel of his weight on her, the hard press of his body, and when he breathed her name, she surrendered to every whim and began to bring to life the fantasies she had been secretly entertaining for weeks.

Tugging at his shirt, she pulled it free of his belt. His skin, hot and smooth, burned against her palms as she slid her hands upward over his back, encountering inch after inch of work-hard muscles. She felt a ridge of flesh and then another; more scars. "And these?"

"Same pissed-off bull," Cody breathed in her ear, his words followed by the moist caress of his tongue.

Cody heard a small exclamation of excitement escape her lips, and once more he captured her mouth with his own. Slipping his arms around her, he drew her up against him, devouring her with his kiss, sending his tongue deep into her mouth. His reward was her eager response, the arch of her body, the shudder that ended in a sigh. He moved to his knees, pulling her with him until kneeling, they faced each other. Again their eyes locked, so much being said and understood in the silence between them.

He felt her fumble to open the buttons on his shirt and helped her, not caring when one and then another popped off. Tossing his shirt aside, he sharply inhaled as Shaye trailed both of her hands, side by side, down his throat, across his collarbone, and then separated them, widening their touch down over his chest. She stopped again, her fingers following the scar that ran from under his left arm and across his sternum.

"You're going to find a few more of those," he replied to her silent question. "Same bull—I lost, he won."

Giving a silent nod, she continued her exploration, her fingers tracing over his nipples, causing them to tighten. He involuntarily trembled, the sensation driving at breakneck speed through his body, hardening him with a degree of hunger he'd never thought possible.

His hands slid to her waist, and he popped the catch on her buckle. Pushing both ends of her belt aside, he opened the waistband on her jeans and began to slowly roll her T-shirt upward across her stomach to the swell of her breasts and over their peaks. Urging her to lift her arms, he pulled the shirt up over her head. In a moment the yellow top joined his blue shirt on the grass beside the blanket.

He drew a ragged breath. "Let me hear you say it. Tell me. Tell me you want me to touch you, to make love to you."

She replied with a sudden catch in her breath and a silent nod. It was all the answer he needed and everything he wanted. Her breath touched him in erratic, warm puffs, and her eyes, dark with desire, locked with his as he dipped his hand into her bra and scooped her breast from its lacy prison. He caressed the taut tip with his fingertips, moaning as Shaye closed her eyes and arched upward, pressing herself further into his hand.

With more luck than expertise, he unsnapped her bra with one hand, then lifted both breasts to his lips. He savored their firm weight, laving first one then the other, teasing with his tongue, sucking their beautifully hard, pebbled peaks into his mouth. He could taste her body lotion—peach—and knew he would never be able to eat a fuzzy, golden peach again without getting hard.

"Help me," she whispered, trying to open his buckle. "I want to . . . touch you."

Her words sent another blast of heat directly to his groin. It hurt him to move, but he pulled Shaye to her feet, grinning at the puzzled look on her face. He teased her lips with another quick kiss. "I want to feel you—bare skin on my bare skin." He rubbed his thumbs across her nipples, keeping them hard for his next kiss. "You might be able to get out of boots and jeans lying down, but I can't."

In the next few moments, boots came off, socks fell in a jumbled heap, belts and buckles clinked as they hit the ground, and jeans were tossed aside. In seconds they faced each other, their naked bodies hot and flushed with excitement.

He watched her gaze slide from his face to his chest, his stomach, and then lower. Pulling her closer, he took her hand and placed it against his stomach, then led her downward. He whispered in her ear, "I know you saw me in the shower the other day." He heard her gasp, felt her stiffen with embarrassment and try to pull away. "Shaye, no, don't . . . it's okay. I want you to know I was thinking of you. Wishing you were there under the water with me . . . wanting it to be your hand touching me."

He led her lower, following the arrow of dark hair from his naval down over his stomach. "Touch me . . . now." Placing his hand over hers, he wrapped her fingers around him, and together they rode the length of his erection.

"Come with me." He drew her back down to the blanket and, kneeling over her, pushed aside the plate of fried chicken, tipping over the bowl of sliced cucumbers and carrots. Her giggle began low in her throat and soon graduated to a full infectious laugh that he caught and joined.

"Am I about to become the picnic?" Shaye reached out, laying her hand on his thigh.

"Would you like to be?"

He saw her blush in the fading light of the day, the flickering flames of the votive candles adding to the glow on her cheeks. His gaze slowly swept over her. "Good Lord, Boston, but you're something special to look at."

Cody heard her draw in her breath as he lay down beside her. Propping himself up on his elbow, he cupped her breast and drew the raised crest into his mouth. She clutched him to her, her fingers raking through his long hair. Yes, this is what he wanted . . . whatever the cost.

He slid one leg between hers, his erection pulsing against her thigh, her skin feeling impossibly hot. "Shaye," he breathed, loving the sound of her name, loving the feel of it on his lips. "I want you . . . so much."

She took several deep breaths, then said in a rush, "Yes, please, yes."

He leaned over her and reached for his jeans. Fumbling in his pocket for a moment, he finally withdrew the foil packet.

"What is that?" Shaye sat up. "You . . . brought a condom with you?"

Cody heard the hard edge to her voice. Looking down, he saw the angry fire in her eyes. Oh, boy, this wasn't a good sign. "Yes . . . I thought—"

"Do you always carry condoms with you?"

"No."

"Why today?"

"Well, I thought—"

"This whole evening was premeditated, preplanned, wasn't it? You thought you'd get me up here and . . . and . . ." She growled like a she-bear and pushed him off the blanket. Grabbing her clothes, she ranted as she wriggled into her jeans, then tried to separate her socks from Cody's. She shot an angry glare in his direction. "Oh, I get it, you cowboys always just happen to have a few rubbers with you—just in case you find someone willing to play mattress rodeo buck and tickle with you for the night. Just like Boy Scouts . . . you're always prepared."

"Hey, now, wait a minute." Beginning to lose his temper, he forgot he was naked and stood. "That's not it at all." He took a step toward her, halted and frowned. What had she said? Mattress rodeo? Buck and tickle? "Where in the hell did you hear those expressions?"

"Maribeth. Maribeth told me all about what you cowboys call your . . . your . . . romantic liaisons. I bet I learned more from my little birds-and-bees talk with her than she did." She wrenched her T-shirt over her head and yanked it down over her naked breasts.

"I should have guessed." His laughter rolled, and he couldn't politely contain it. "My thirteen-year-old sister is a very reliable source in these matters." He sobered. "Shaye, tell me, in a calm, reasonable way—why my bringing protection is bugging you so damn much." Everything between them had certainly gone flat. "I thought you liberated women were glad when the man took the initiative." He reached out for her.

"No. Don't you dare touch me." She jumped away. "And how dare you laugh at me." She stalked away from the blanket, then rounded on him. "Did you think that you'd seduce me, and then I'd feel so badly about Hubbard going after your ranch that I'd figure out some way to stop him?"

Suddenly realizing he was the only one standing around buck naked, Cody snatched up his jeans. Turning them right side out, he hopped up and down on one leg, then the other, pulling them on, knowing how ridiculous he looked. Well, he'd found her comment just as ridiculous. "Is that what you really think this is about?"

"I don't know; suppose you tell me."

"I'll tell you this . . . that's pretty damned insulting. Isn't it enough that I've wanted to be with you like this since the day you walked into my life? I thought you'd be grateful that I respected you and thought enough about what we might have together to be . . . responsible."

"Grateful?" She stood before him, her hands firmly planted on her hips. "I'd be grateful if you took me back now. I want to go home."

She fisted her hands and moved them to her sides, and her breasts bobbed beneath the yellow T-shirt, their hard pointed tips clearly visible. Cody knew he shouldn't look, but God help him—he did, and he wasn't sorry. "Shaye, please, listen to me." He moved toward her, very carefully zipping his fly.

"No. Stay away from me." She pointed an admonishing

finger at him. "And for your information," her voice cracked, "I am not a liberated woman."

"What?"

"I'm not liberated. I do not sleep around."

"That's not what I meant."

She seemed to deflate and crumpled to the ground. Sitting with her knees drawn up against her chest and her arms wrapped around her legs, she looked every bit like a little lost waif. "I'm not a liberated woman," she quietly offered. "This isn't something I do all the time." She cast an accusatory glance at him. "Well, I don't. Hell, I've never done anything like this before. I've been with only one man in my life, and that was my husband."

He could see her tears as he hunkered down beside her, and he felt like a heel. "Shaye, sweetheart, I'm sorry. Maybe you're right. If falling asleep at night thinking about making love to you is preplanning, then yes, what almost happened tonight was preplanned." He gently pushed the hair out of her eyes. "I've wanted to make love to you from the moment you showed up at my front door with your ridiculous big black briefcase, professional attitude, and Hubbard's slick proposal." He caught one of her tears on the tip of his finger before it fell from her chin to her shirt. "Nothing between you and me has anything to do with Hubbard. It's just about you and me." He took her hand and, raising it to his lips, kissed her palm and folded her fingers over his kiss. "I would never intentionally do anything to hurt you or insult you. I brought the condom with me because I hoped, not because I planned."

Her voice was soft with pain when she spoke. "I've made a fool of myself, haven't I?" She gave him a small, sheepish smile, then looked away. "I made a terrible mistake when I married Michael, and I'm terrified of making another. For two years I lived with a man I thought I'd married for love, a man who in those two years had four affairs . . . that I know about." She glanced up at him and wiped another trickle of tears from her cheeks. "I made a promise to myself when he died that I would never let myself be hurt like that again. But do you know what is so ironic? I'm just as terrified of not taking another chance." She lightly touched his arm. "I'm sorry."

He helped her to her feet. "Come on, Boston, let's eat. It's a shame to let all of Roscoe's good cooking go to waste."

He led her back to the blanket, and the sight that awaited them made him groan for what might have been. Rumpled, with some of their clothes still scattered about, the blanket looked like a well-used love bed. And nestled in the middle, the foil condom packet glittered in the candlelight like an enticing little jewel.

Both of them stared at the blanket.

"Cody?" She reached for his hand, and he wrapped her fingers in his.

"Yeah?"

"How many did you bring?"

"How many what?"

"You know, foil packets."

For whatever difference it made, he answered. "Three."

"Are you usually that ambitious?"

What the hell did that mean? "No, I think it was just some wishful thinking."

"Are you still wishing? I am."

"What?" He quickly glanced down at her.

"I wish you'd show me."

"Show you what?"

"Show me what making love is all about."

"I don't understand."

She reached up and touched his bare chest, her index finger moving back and forth across his left nipple like a miniature metronome. She was driving him crazy . . . crazy with need. *Need, my ass, I'm so hot for this woman, I'm going to pop the seams on my pants any minute now.*

"Cody, I'm going to take off my clothes—well, actually, I'd like you to help me take them off. And then I'm going to lie down on the blanket, and if you don't lie down with me and make me feel again like you did before . . . I'm going to be very upset."

He placed his hand over his heart, stilling her finger. "The very last thing I want to do is upset you. The very first thing I want to do is make love to you . . . all night long." When he pulled her into his arms, a sigh escaped from the depths of his soul. She came willing, molding herself against him.

He kissed her, her tongue sliding against his in an exotic dance, and this time it was better than all the other times because this time they knew right where they were going, and they were going there together.

Shaye clung to him, and then without hesitation she slid her hands into the seat of his jeans and cupped his bare buttocks. Making a low, hungry sound, Cody shoved down his Wranglers, then kicked them aside. The next move was hers.

Shaye lowered her head to his chest and pressed her mouth against his skin, kissing randomly, nipping playfully, licking and sucking greedily. The more she tasted, the more she wanted. She'd never imagined any of this was what making love was all about.

"Are you planning on leaving all your clothes on?" he teased, lifting the hem of her T-shirt.

"Are you planning on leaving them on me?" she countered, coyly raising her arms.

"Not on your life." In one swift move he lifted the shirt over her head for the second time that evening and tossed it over his shoulder. "Now, let's equalize things." With a flip of his finger and a quick tug, her jeans puddled on the ground around her ankles. Before she could step clear of her pants, Cody lifted her up in his arms and carried her to the blanket. He held her as he dropped to his knees. He held her as he laid her down, and he continued to hold her as he settled himself between her legs.

Kissing her neck, he pressed his mouth to the bend where it sloped into her shoulder. Shaye's head fell back, giving him full access, and he felt the rapid throb of her pulse against his lips. He licked, his tongue sampling the sweet taste of her skin from her collarbone to the tip of her breast. He drew her budded nipple into his mouth and suckled, then licked further, down across her ribs to her belly and further still.

"Cody? I don't—"

"Shh." Despite her apprehension, he grasped her hips and lifted her to his mouth. He drove his tongue into her moist core, savoring the flavor of her desire. With the tip of his tongue he licked and caressed the hard nub of flesh at the apex, driving her closer and closer to the brink.

"Please, Cody . . ." Her words were nearly lost in a sob. She reached for his hand and pressed the foil packet into his palm. "Now . . . please."

He placed a kiss on her stomach. "I want you to help me."

Shaye hesitated for only a moment before she took the packet back from him and tore it open. She'd never felt so bold, so excited. She drew a tiny gasp as her fingers grazed the hot smooth tip of him, and together they rolled the condom down over his erection.

Her fingers encircled him and caressed his pulsing flesh.

"Easy." He stilled her hand and closed his eyes. "I want this to last . . . forever."

Kneeling between her thighs, he lightly rubbed himself against her. Then, for all the urgency they'd built between them, he gently stroked a finger through her cleft, opening her. "Shaye, look at me." Her eyes met his, and he slowly pushed into her, sinking deeper and deeper, his ragged sigh blending with hers.

She felt the glorious slide of his flesh, loved the feel of him inside her, filling her, becoming one with her. A sudden anxiety filled her as he withdrew and was quickly replaced with joy as he filled her again.

"Can you feel that?" He moved, pulsing deep inside her.

"Yes, my God, yes."

He began to move again, stretching and stroking her until she became oblivious to everything except him and where they were joined. She eagerly met each of his thrusts, reveling in the unbelievable sensations that were building inside her, layer over layer, heat over fervor. Lifting her leg, she wrapped it over his hip, drawing him into her, holding him. She tightened herself around him until she couldn't tell where he ended and where she began.

The bedlam in her body grew, encompassing her heart and soul, driving her senses wild. He drove into her again and again, and she matched his rhythm, giving as he took, taking all he gave.

Then she felt it again. A blossoming deep inside, a scalding heat sluicing through every nerve and cell, building higher and higher. And then it happened. She cried aloud as one exquisite explosion after another racked her body, the shocks and aftershocks going on . . . and on . . . and on.

Afraid she'd fall from the high peaks where she soared, Shaye clung to Cody until the tumultuous waves ebbed, until she felt him shudder, until she heard his breath rush from his lungs in a shattered gasp.

They lay entwined, riding the downward spiral together. The moments passed, the cadence of their breathing slowed, softened, until she could no longer contain her news.

"I've never . . . felt that . . . before," she whispered, against his chest.

Cody opened his eyes, his surprise clear. He gently touched her cheek. "Never? Never with . . ."

"Michael? No." She fought the rush of tears. "I didn't know how wonderful this could be."

Cody buried a kiss in her hair. "Believe me, I didn't know, either."

They drank the wine and filled themselves on Roscoe's fried chicken. When that was gone, they covered each other with sliced cucumbers and using carrot sticks drew silly pictures on each other with dill dip—then took turns enjoying the banquet. Before they packed away all evidence of their picnic and rolled everything up in the blanket for the trip back to the house, the remaining two foil packets were opened and thoroughly enjoyed.

By the time the horses were saddled, the moon was high and bright in the night sky, illuminating the grassy plain around them. They rode side by side, holding hands, sharing a kiss now and then. They passed a dozing herd of cattle, cut back across the rushing stream, watched a night owl catch its dinner, and were thankful Possum and Sophie behaved themselves as they headed home.

Shaye didn't know why, but the closer they got to the ranch house, the more tense and nervous she became. Reentering the real world meant she had to face the reality of what had happened, and she didn't know if she could do that. Every particle of her decision had crumbled. Once again she'd failed.

And then there was Maribeth and Roscoe. She didn't doubt for a moment that they would suspect what she and Cody had been doing. How could she face them? And how could she casually say good night to Cody and leave? *Thanks for the picnic, thanks for the hot sex, and see ya around.* Maybe she should take some liberated-woman lessons from Bunny Gibson. Now, there was a name she didn't want to think of, especially not tonight. She shot an anxious glance at Cody. He seemed so relaxed, so at ease with himself, while she was all tied up in knots.

"Don't you have a flashlight or a lantern?" She failed to keep the curt edge from her voice.

Cody shook his head. "What for?"

"So we can see where we're going. I can't see a thing."

"We don't have to worry about where we're going. Possum and Sophie know the way."

"You trust a horse?" Shaye tried to find a trail in the dark. "You trust these horses not to get us hopelessly lost?"

"Implicitly."

"How can you be so sure."

"Shaye, sweetheart, not only do horses have better night vision than we do, but if there's one place these two want to be, it's back in their stalls with a couple of scoops of grain and a soft bed."

"What if they're going to someone else's barn and not yours?" She heard his exasperated sigh.

"Honey, if you don't trust them, trust me. We're going in the right direction, and we're not going to be lost out here all night." He chuckled. "Now, if that's what's bothering you, are you just afraid we're going to have to spend the night out here, or are you afraid we're going to be out here all night and we're out of little foil packets?"

"Cody Butler, sometimes you're so . . . so infuriating."

"Yeah, but you love me," Cody teased.

Yeah, I do.

Chapter Twenty

From the foyer she could see that the light was still on in Hubbard's office.

"Shaye? Is that you?"

She didn't think for one moment that he was waiting up for her because she was late or because he'd been worried about her. He'd never cared what hours she kept, and he certainly wouldn't be starting now.

She stood in the doorway, finding her father at his desk. "Hi. You're working late."

He glanced up, his eyes sweeping over her before he dropped his attention back to the papers on his desk. "You know my motto—no success without hard work."

"Yes, I've heard it." She drove her hands into the pockets of her jeans and turned to leave.

"We're going to Laramie in the morning." Hubbard looked up from the work on his desk.

"We?"

"You're going with me."

"What for?" Shaye didn't want to get into a business discussion so late at night, especially not this night. She just wanted to slip into her bed and replay the whole wonderful evening with Cody in her mind. "You've been putting the deal for Systems Software together by yourself for weeks. Why do you need me with you now? Why isn't your corporate attorney going with you?"

"Prescott's in Europe . . . on some kind of damned vacation with his family."

She wished she could have told him that fathers, good fathers, went on vacations with their families, but the lecture would have come almost twenty-five years too late. Instead, she put on her professional demeanor and ignored the craving of the child deep within. "Hub, if there's any question about the paperwork, fax it to me. I'll be more than glad to check it out for you from here."

"You're going because they've had their attorney at the last two meetings and I want to even the odds a little." He slid his papers into a folder and then into his briefcase.

"If I'm going to be nothing more than window dressing, you could probably put a business suit on any one of your ranch hands and pass him off as your lawyer." Hubbard's quick glare told her he didn't find her suggestion humorous. "I just don't see the point of me going."

Hubbard closed his briefcase with a loud snap and rose from his desk. "Shaye, don't argue with me. Be ready at seven. I want to get out of here as early as possible." He hefted his briefcase off his desk. "Don't plan on getting back until late Tuesday evening, either. You'll need an overnight bag."

She sighed, wearily leaning back against the doorjamb. "Okay. Fine."

Hubbard stopped before he left the room. "I realize this is in addition to our original terms for the land deals. Don't worry, you'll be paid extra for your time." He switched off his office light and walked past Shaye, leaving her in the dark.

There's a metaphor here somewhere. She pushed away from the door frame. That's what it always came down to, though. Business. Rarely a fatherly hug, rarely a fatherly kiss. Business, always business. She'd once seen him caress the satiny black surface of his new Jaguar and wished she was the car. With a rueful shake of her head, Shaye turned and left Hubbard's dark office.

No matter how much she did for him, how much she accomplished, or how much she hungered for things to be different, her father would always be little more than an acquaintance. He would never be . . . a father. Why couldn't she concede that things would never change? Why did the grain of hope deep in her heart keep wanting to bloom?

She paused by the hall phone, picked up the receiver, then returned it to the cradle. It was too late to call Cody and tell him she wouldn't be able to make her next riding lesson, and it would probably be too early to call him in the morning before she left. She'd leave a note for Tess to call him.

Perhaps going to Laramie with Hub and missing her next few lessons with Cody was for the best. She needed time to work things through. She felt like a china plate teetering on the edge of the table. If she stood firm she wouldn't fall, but if she leaned too far over the edge, her life would smash into a thousand pieces. But standing firm meant not wavering from the blueprint she'd drawn for herself. How could she begin building her new life and have her own practice in Boston if she didn't start distancing herself, closing herself up again. A cynical laugh fled her lips. *I'm like the orchid that only blossoms once in its life and then never blooms again.*

With each step up the staircase her muscles twinged, and she smiled. Each ache reminded her of the trail ride, the picnic, and Cody. After closing her bedroom door, she slowly undressed for the third time that night, remembering every detail of the last time she'd taken off her clothes. She would never be the same; Cody Butler had touched her life and changed her forever.

It was hokey and straight out of a novel or a movie, but

she stood in front of the full-length mirror and tried to see if the change she felt inside showed on the outside.

She stared into her eyes, then touched her mouth. She found the tiny red love bites on her neck and on her shoulders. Her skin still had a rosy tint, and she discovered that her breasts—especially her nipples—were tender from Cody's loving. She slid her hand over her belly to the juncture between her legs. A tenderness lingered there, too. She wondered if she were to touch herself, could the explosions happen all over again.

So that incredible sensation was a climax. She hugged herself and laughed. *No, those absolutely incredible sensations were four climaxes.*

How was it possible that Cody Butler could open and fill her body with such fabulous excitement when all she had felt with Michael Frazier, her husband, was cold emptiness? The answer was so simple, so beautifully simple. Cody hadn't just used her for his own release and then discarded her. Cody had made love to her, with her, for her.

She cherished each and every ache and tenderness. If only they were tangible things that she could press between the pages of a diary like a rose—or an orchid—and keep the memory alive forever. *We'll always have Paris.* Bogart's dialogue from the movie classic *Casablanca* scrolled through her mind, bringing with it a disconsolate smile. *And I'll always have Medicine Creek.*

Moving away from the mirror, she slipped into her nightgown. After one last look at her reflection, she drew back the covers on her bed, turned out the light, and settled into her favorite niche on the mattress. She was asleep before the next ten ticks of the bedside clock had sounded.

Cody lay awake, staring at the ceiling. How did you hold a woman in your arms, make love to her, and then stand like an idiot while she drove away? He'd done it, but definitely not because he wanted to. He'd wanted to go after her, take her somewhere where they could hide themselves away and spend all night long in each other's arms. Instead, he'd seen her to her car and slouched in the driveway as she drove off.

The last thing he'd wanted to do was say good night to Shaye. The first thing he wanted to do when he saw her next was tell her he loved her, tell her he wanted her in his life.

Love? That part of the evening had definitely not been preplanned. The knowledge that his feelings for Shaye Frazier were a lot more than simple physical attraction had hit him like a flying brick. He confessed that's where they began, but that had all changed. What was there now was love—strong, deep, and solid love. No doubt about it.

Every moment of their evening together skimmed through his mind, every kiss, every caress. Her vulnerability had surprised him, and her tears had shaken and touched him. He had never suspected her pain or her fears. He prayed he could help her put them away forever, and he thanked God she had come back to his arms.

Cody closed his eyes, and the image of Shaye in the moonlight filled his mind and reached his senses. He grew hard just thinking about her and rolled over onto his belly, pressing himself against the mattress. *If this keeps up . . . ha, bad choice of words . . . I'll never get any rest.*

He gently pushed his thoughts of Shaye elsewhere, promising himself to come back to them in a moment or two. If he was going to have anything to offer her for a future together, he'd have to take care of first things first.

In the morning he'd check with the bank to make sure that di Prado's money had arrived and been deposited to his account. He'd add Roscoe's check, too. Next, he'd have to figure out what excuse he could give Roscoe and Maribeth for leaving town at the end of the week. If he planned to win any money in Cheyenne at the rodeo, he'd need to be gone the whole weekend.

Cody gave a short, cynical grunt. Wouldn't it be ironic if he drew the same damned black devil bull that had stomped the hell out of him in Lander a couple of years ago? The way his luck had been going for a while, it wouldn't surprise him at all.

The thought of the Brahma cured his problem, and Cody rolled over onto his back again. *I ought to be thinking positively, instead of beating myself up over what's in the past. It's about time I look to the future.* In about one week all of his trouble with the bank would be over. The loan would be paid off, Hubbard would be off his back, and Medicine Creek would be his again—free and clear.

He allowed his thoughts about Shaye and the moonlit picnic to return. He had to find a way to make her want to stay in Dorland . . . to make her want to stay with him. The image of her naked in the moonlight careened through his mind again and bounced off his libido.

Well, damnation. He breathed an exasperated sigh and rolled over onto his belly once again. Moments later he fell asleep.

"I didn't see 'em come back last night, but Roscoe said it was late, way after midnight." Maribeth cradled the cordless telephone between her shoulder and ear as she stirred the pot of spaghetti sauce on the stove. "If you ask me . . . mission accomplished." She giggled. "You can't tell me it takes that long to eat fried chicken."

The kitchen door opened and slammed shut, and Maribeth whirled around to see who had come in.

"Doggone it, Roscoe, you scared me to death. I almost dropped the phone in the spaghetti sauce." Turning back to the stove, she continued her conversation. "Julie, do you think we should back off?" She listened for a moment. "Me, too. Besides, I'm outta good ideas and

Cody's been acting really funny . . . like he's enjoying it all." She shot a sidelong glance at Roscoe. "He's gonna be comin' in soon for supper, so I gotta go. I've got KP duty tonight. I'll let you know if anything else happens. Bye."

Roscoe slapped his hat down on the table. "I can't get a blasted bit of information outta Cody." He plopped down in a chair at the table. "You'd think that after all the work he knew we went through getting them two together that he'd at least share a little." He stood, stomped over to the refrigerator, and opened the door. "Hey, you forgot to put the green peppers and onions in the sauce."

"I didn't forget. I left them out on purpose. I don't like that yucky stuff." She pointed the ladle at Roscoe. "If you want them in there, make your own pot."

"Well, Miss Congeniality," Roscoe grouched back, "you ain't the only one who eats supper in this house."

The kitchen door opened again, and Cody came in carrying the mail. "Something smells good."

"Don't you start up with me, too," Maribeth snorted.

"Geez, I give you a compliment on your cooking and you jump all over me."

"Cody Butler, you know darned well I can't cook, and you also know this spaghetti sauce is straight out of a jar. I didn't have a blasted thing to do with making it smell good."

"Before you make me cry, did I have any phone calls? Any messages?"

"I didn't take any," Roscoe offered, sniffling as he chopped up two large onions.

"No . . . Shaye didn't call," Maribeth replied with a cheeky grin. "But someone named Jess, or Bess . . . hmm . . . no, I think maybe it was Les . . . called and left a message on the machine. No, it couldn't have been Les, it was a woman . . . well, maybe if it was a Leslie. You don't know any Leslies, do you?"

Cody glanced up at his sister and blew an exasperated sigh. "Could it have been Tess?"

"Yeah. Could be. Tess." Maribeth shrugged and turned back to stirring the sauce.

"And?"

"Oh, the message . . . she, Tess, said to tell you that Shaye's outta town for a few days and won't be comin' over for her . . . riding lessons." The cheeky grin returned in a wider model.

"Tater, if your stupid grin gets any bigger, your teeth are going to fall out." He dropped the mail on the table and headed down the hall. "I'm going to take a shower."

Climbing the stairs, he felt an unpleasant weight settle over him. He hadn't expected the disappointment to hit so hard. A few days, two, three . . . how long until he saw her again?

Monday dragged by, and when Shaye's usual lesson time came, Cody closed himself in his office in the barn until it was almost midnight. On Tuesday morning he confirmed that di Prado's money had arrived. Even that news didn't ease his lousy disposition. By Tuesday afternoon he was driving everyone crazy with his foul mood and he knew it. Even Gene steered clear of him as they brought in a sampling of the cattle for Doc Campbell to examine when he arrived.

Standing alone by the quarantine pen, Cody watched the vet's truck kick up dust as it came down the lane. The three Newfoundlands rolled out from the shade of an old cottonwood next to the barn to greet the visitor as he pulled up and got out of his truck. The scent of medicines and disinfectants sent them hustling back to the safety of their naps.

"They're looking good, Cody." Doc Campbell meticulously scanned the cattle pen. "They're alert, eating, no more drool. Let's take a closer look."

Cody followed the vet into the pen and walked with

him as he moved through the herd, inspecting one steer after another. "Have you heard anything from the ag office yet?"

"No, not yet."

The vet shook his head. "I don't know what's going on. We should have had a report back from them by now. I don't know how you feel about it, but if those two ag officers were the state's best, we're in trouble."

They left the quarantine pen and stood beside Doc Campbell's truck.

"I've been at the state veterinarian conference in Laramie for the last couple of days. We discussed your situation in a few sessions." Doc Campbell reached into his truck, retrieved his bottle of water off the seat, and took a long drink. "Cody, no one else has reported any hoof-and-mouth in their areas. The only thing I can figure is that it came in with those steers you got from south Texas."

Cody shrugged. "Sounds reasonable, I guess, but I called Triple D. They haven't had anything show up, either. Their foreman promised to check around and see if there are any cases near the border or on the Mexico side." Cody leaned against the pickup. "Doc, those cattle were all shipped with current health papers. I don't understand any of this." He lifted his sunglasses. "What's the chance of them picking up something on the way . . . from a cattle hauler they may have been parked next to at a truck stop somewhere?"

Doc Campbell shrugged. "Possible, but not probable. It's a wild guess and maybe that's what we'll eventually have to look at. I just don't know."

Doc opened his truck door, then turned back to Cody. "By the way, I ran into your neighbor, Glenn Hubbard, while I was in Laramie." He shook his head. "I'm not one to gossip, I usually leave that up to Martha Tinsdale in the C.C.A. office, but if Hubbard's relationship with that lady lawyer of his is purely professional, I'll eat my boots."

Cody felt as though he'd been sucker punched and drenched in ice water. "What are you talking about?"

"I was at the concierge desk in the lobby of the hotel when they checked in. One key, one suite—under Hubbard's name." He took another mouthful from his water bottle. "He gives her the key, a hug and a kiss, sends her up to the room, and tells her he'll be up in a few minutes. Looked like a pretty cozy affair to me." Doc Campbell climbed into his truck. "Well, gotta go. I'll let you know if anything comes in from the state office."

Cody didn't know how long he stood in the middle of the barnyard after Doc Campbell's truck had disappeared up the road. He felt numb—sick to his stomach. Lifting his ballcap, he finger-raked his hair a couple of times and tried to shake the images from his mind that Doc's words had planted there.

Doc had to be mistaken. How well did he know Shaye? Hell, had he ever even met her? Hubbard wasn't married, he could have been meeting any woman . . . not Shaye. But when he'd called Hubbard's housekeeper, she'd told him they'd both gone to Laramie for a few days. It didn't take a lawyer to build the case. The lawyer was the case.

If his mood had been bad before, it now was pure acid. He tried to exercise di Prado's ponies and gave up when he found himself losing his temper over nothing. To the relief of every living being on Medicine Creek, he finally sequestered himself in his office until nightfall.

Sitting in the dark, Cody couldn't stop Doc Campbell's words from playing over and over and over in his mind. *Looked like a pretty cozy affair to me. Looked like a pretty cozy affair to me. Looked like a pretty cozy affair to me.*

Cody cranked the radio up, hoping a window-rattling

song by the Dixie Chicks would drown out Doc's words. The only thing that got drowned out was the Dixie Chicks as the three Newfoundlands howled along with the country tune.

At twelve-thirty he made his way up to the house. He'd missed supper and made a mess in the kitchen with spilled milk when he raided the refrigerator before he went up to bed. A hot shower didn't help him relax, and he tossed restlessly for one or two hours, pulling the sheets off the mattress and dumping the blankets on the floor. He finally gave up, grabbed his pillow, and settled in on the wicker settee on the porch for the rest of the night.

It was there Gene found him at eight in the morning, snoring, one leg hooked over the back of the settee.

"Phew, you look like a bad accident." Gene slouched in the chair across from the settee. "Thank God you had the decency to keep your shorts on."

Cody yawned, positive that two skunks had committed illicit deeds in his mouth while he'd slept. "What time is it?" He glanced at his watch. "Holy crap!" He swung his legs over the edge of the settee and drove his fingers through his hair, hoping to tame what felt like the worst case of bed head that he'd ever had.

He glanced up at Gene. "So what's up?"

"I don't think I'm going to make your day any better than yesterday. Hubbard's mustangs have broken through the fence again. They're up on the eastern rim." Rubbing his chin, Gene shot a sidelong glance at Cody. "Rafe said there's about thirty or forty feet of fence down, including the posts. What do you want us to do about 'em?"

Cody stood up, every ounce of anger from the last few days rising to the surface. "Take Rafe and two others and get those damn mangy bang-tails off my land." He strode to the front door and jerked it open. "I'm going to get me a piece of Hubbard's hide."

"I hope you're going to put your pants on first."

"Yeah, but I'll jerk Hubbard out of his."

"Cody, cool down before you do anything you'll be sorry for."

He rounded on Gene. "Believe me, pal, I'm already sorry."

Turning into Hubbard's lane, Cody floored the gas pedal, causing the truck to fishtail a little, his tires squealing on the black asphalt. He gave a disgusted grunt. Glenn Hubbard probably had the only paved ranch lane in the quad-county. If Hubbard had money enough to pave his road, he sure as hell had the money to hire some more ranch hands to keep his livestock in his own backyard. He was getting damned tired of Hubbard's livestock busting fences and mixing with his cattle.

Cody had no idea whether Glenn Hubbard was back from Laramie yet or not, and he really didn't care. He figured if he couldn't vent his anger on Hubbard, he'd be just as happy to corner the man's foreman. One way or the other, somebody would get the message to keep Hubbard livestock off of Butler land.

He drove his truck around the circular drive and parked at the side of Hubbard's grand house. Cutting the motor, he happened to glance to his left and felt his heart turn to stone.

The intimate exchange between the two people on the patio struck him as hard as if he'd been dealt a physical blow.

Cody watched Shaye, dressed in a bathrobe, step out of the house onto the patio, and into Glenn Hubbard's arms. He watched Hubbard hug her and kiss her lightly on the lips with a familiarity that defied any client-attorney relationship he could imagine. He watched Shaye smile, her adoration for Glenn Hubbard painfully obvious. And he watched her make a lie out of everything they'd shared on the blanket in the moonlight.

Doc Campbell's words twisted in his gut. *Looked like a pretty cozy affair to me.*

His laughter, dry and bitter, split the silence in his truck cab. With something akin to the worst physical pain he'd ever felt, Cody watched his hopes shatter.

Chapter Twenty-one

"Good morning, Butler. What brings you over so early?"

Glenn Hubbard removed his arm from around Shaye's shoulder and held out his hand, but Cody ignored it, his eyes riveted instead on the beautiful green-eyed brunette who had filled his dreams for the past month. His gaze slid from her sleep-tousled hair, down over her white terrycloth robe, to the tip of her bare toes. The cold betrayal that he felt in his heart filled his voice. "Mrs. Frazier, you *do* get around."

Clutching at the collar of her robe, Shaye pulled the edges together, covering the inches of bare skin at her throat. A puzzled frown creased her brow. Then Cody saw her expression change to shock and knew she'd realized what he was inferring.

She glanced at Hubbard and then back to Cody. "No, Cody. This isn't what you think. Hub is—"

"It obviously doesn't matter what I think," he interrupted.

"Of course it does. Please, let me explain."

She reached out to touch him. He stepped aside.

"I should have told you before—"

"Yeah," he replied, interrupting her again and forcing his shoulders to give a nonchalant shrug. "I guess you should have." He turned away, wishing he could encase everything he felt for her in a numbing solid block of ice. "Too bad you didn't."

He followed Hubbard to the table set with a cozy breakfast for two.

"Sit down, have some coffee and a scone," Hubbard offered, taking a seat and pointing to a basket of what looked like triangular biscuits on the table. "Shaye's gotten me hooked on them since she's been here."

"No. I didn't come for a neighborly visit."

"Suit yourself." Hubbard poured a stream of rich, delicious-smelling brew into his cup.

Cody's mouth watered. He hadn't had breakfast before he left Medicine Creek, and a cup of coffee sure would taste good, but he'd be damned if it would be Hubbard's coffee.

Glenn Hubbard looked up. "So what *did* you come for?"

Shaye moved closer and stood beside him, but Cody tried to ignore her and the ache that filled his chest. He could only deal with one thing at a time, and in truth, he wasn't sure he could ever deal with what Shaye had just dealt him. He hooked his thumb in the edge of his pocket and kept his eyes on Hubbard. "My men found about twenty, twenty-five head of your mustangs on my land this morning. It seems your horses also took down about forty feet of my fence."

"I'll get some of my hands up there right away and move them out." Hubbard took another sip from his cup. "I suppose I owe you for the line of fence, too."

"You suppose right. I'll make sure you get a bill. Don't bother sending your men up there, my crew are moving the horses back over now and are restringing the line. What I'd like from you, though, is some responsibility. This is the third time this has happened in the last three months. Don't let it happen again."

"These are wild horses, Butler. Not some pampered stable-bred polo darlings," Hubbard countered. "They don't have any respect for fences and property lines."

"Well, you'd damn well better teach them." Cody tried to keep a tight lid on his temper, but Hubbard was testing his limit. "I haven't defaulted on my loan yet, and from the looks of things that isn't going to happen. So until that unlikely event takes place and you hold the deed to Medicine Creek, keep your zoo at home."

He turned to leave and saw Shaye still standing in the middle of the patio, nervously fidgeting with the ties on her robe, her eyes wide with worry. While she watched, he grabbed a scone from the basket and took a bite. Making a big production out of eating the sweet, warm, buttery bread, that unfortunately tasted delicious, Cody fixed his gaze on her. He raised the half-eaten scone in salute. "You know, you were right. I never will forget my first taste." He glanced pointedly at Hubbard and then back at Shaye. "You two have a . . . wonderful day."

He wanted to run, to get away from her as fast as he could. He wanted to find something hard and unforgiving that he could drive his fist through so he could forget the pain in his chest for a moment. Instead, he forced himself to walk back to his truck in a deliberate stride. He heard her run after him, her bare feet making little slapping sounds as they fell on the flagstone walk. It took all of his resolve not to turn around and open his arms to her. He'd never thought of himself as a fool when it came to women, but all it took was one green-eyed Boston lawyer to prove him wrong.

"Cody, please, wait. I have to talk with you."

He didn't slow his pace. He didn't stop. He didn't turn around.

He felt her touch on his arm. He shrugged away. She touched him again.

"Please."

He stopped and turned. "What do you want, another . . . buck and tickle?" He looked over the top of her head at the wide expanse of manicured lawns, unable to make himself look directly at her. He shook his head. "Sorry, not interested. Remember? I don't share." He finally found the courage and looked down at her, finding pain in the green depths of her eyes. In self-defense he raised his brow in a cynical arch. "Obviously Hubbard does." He took a few more steps toward his truck, then stopped and turned to face her again. "I'm curious. Just how soon after we made . . . love did you climb back into Hubbard's bed?" Without waiting for her response, he left her standing alone on the walk, hoping he could make it to his truck before his strength failed him and he pulled her into his arms . . . loving her on any terms.

"Is that what you think? You think I'm having an . . . affair with Glenn Hubbard?"

He rounded on her, amazed to see how lost and small she looked, bundled barefoot in the terry robe. "Am I wrong?"

She began to laugh. Not the rich throaty laugh he loved, but a laugh that had an uncomfortable edge to it. "Yes. As a matter of fact, you're wrong . . . very wrong."

They stood beside his truck, staring at each other, sizing up each other.

"Fine, I'm listening. Dazzle me with your explanation," he insolently suggested, slouching against the front fender, his legs crossed at his ankles, his arms crossed over his chest. "If you can."

Shaye drove her hands into the pockets of her robe and dropped her gaze. "Cody, my mother and father had a very special marriage. My father loved my mother so much there was little room in his life for anyone else, including me." She quickly looked up, then lowered her gaze again. "When my mother died—"

"Is this going to take a long time? I've got work to do." Why had he said that? Why was he being so cruel? Three guesses and the first two heartaches didn't count.

She stopped and looked straight into his eyes, then continued as though he hadn't said a word. "When my mother died, I was eleven years old. I lost the only parent I ever really had. My father had never spent much time with me, and besides, he didn't know what to do with a child who looked so much like the love he'd just lost. In his . . . crippling grief, he decided it would be best if I went away to boarding school."

"Shaye, you've told me all of this before. I've got to go." He reached for the door handle, but before he could open the door, Shaye placed her hand over his.

"For the rest of my life, as I grew to look more and more like my mother, the more my father distanced himself. I did everything I thought I could to earn his love . . . everything short of plastic surgery. I excelled in school, went into law because I thought it would please him, I passed the bar exam the first time I sat for it, I married someone who I thought had the same ambition my father had, someone I thought my father would admire me for choosing. But I never measured up to his expectations." She paused for a moment and took a ragged breath. "Since I was eleven years old I have been trying to make my father proud of me, to earn his approval and his love."

"Shaye, that's all very . . . sad, but what's the point?" he muttered dryly.

"The point is I'm not having . . . an . . . affair with Glenn Hubbard."

She seemed to struggle for words.

"You still haven't said anything to convince me—"

"Cody, I'm not having an affair with Glenn Hubbard, because . . . Glenn Hubbard is my . . . father."

For the second time that morning, Cody felt as though he'd been punched in the gut. "Your what?"

"Hub is my father."

And the second wave of her betrayal hit him and engulfed him. It would almost have been easier for him to accept Shaye having an affair with Hubbard than what she'd just told him. "Am I the only one in Dorland who didn't know this juicy little tidbit?" He gritted the words out between clenched teeth. "You two must have had a great old time plotting behind my back."

"Cody, no." The sound of panic had returned to her voice once more. "That never happened. What kind of person do you think I am?"

"How would I know, Shaye *Hubbard* Frazier. Up until a moment ago I thought you were . . . somebody else."

"I'm so sorry. I know that I should have told you sooner, but I was afraid of . . . this." She wearily rubbed her brow, then pushed a strand of hair away from her eyes. "Hub and I decided not to tell anyone because we wanted to keep the land acquisition deals on a purely business level. He figured it would look unprofessional if folks knew I was his daughter. It all seems so pointless now." She lightly touched his arm. "Would it have made a difference with . . . us if you had known before we . . ." She trailed off into an inaudible whisper.

He'd never been given the opportunity to find out. How could he give her an answer that wouldn't have a razor's bite to it? "Probably." He shook his head. "I don't know."

In a voice filled with the sound of a child's insecurity and a woman's doubt, she asked her next question. "Does it make a difference now?"

A deep sigh fled his lungs. "Shaye, I'm sorry. Yes, it makes a difference. Maybe not the fact that he's your father as much as the deceit."

She gave a nearly undetectable nod. "I see." Her voice wavered. "I am sorry, too."

She squared her shoulders, and Cody could see her visibly gathering her composure. With a dignity that flew in the face of his censure of her, Shaye Frazier, with her head held high and as regally as her bare feet allowed, walked back to the house and out of his life.

The drive back to Medicine Creek seemed to take ten times longer than it should have, and once home, Cody wished it had taken another ten times longer to get there. The whole conversation with Shaye still burned in his brain, and he couldn't untangle any of the things he was feeling. All of his emotions reminded him of a mess of twisted ropes with no beginning or end in sight. Anger was snarled with regret, compassion with betrayal, resentment with heartache, and jumbled up with everything else was the pain of a love that had been deceived but wouldn't go away. It was just a whole lot easier to feel numb and tell himself that none of it mattered, that only Medicine Creek mattered . . . yesterday, today, and always.

He didn't want to talk with anyone but had too much to do to stay in his office for the rest of the day. In the early afternoon he carefully checked Possum over to make sure the gray gelding would be ready to go to Cheyenne. The horse needed his hooves trimmed and a new set of shoes. He'd ask Rafe to take care of it before he went home.

Cody waited until Gene and the rest of the men had finished work for the day before he went into the tack room and opened the old wooden trunk. He hadn't looked at the contents of the box for three years. Touching his bull rigging seemed to bring the pain back to his body. He lifted it out of the trunk, laid it over a saddle rack, and reached into the trunk again. The bareback bronc rigging was heavier, and the cinch clanked against the side of the wooden trunk as he lifted it free. Rosin from the handgrip of the bucking rig dusted the legs of his jeans and stuck to his hand. The feeling was both disquieting and familiar. Wiping the rosin off on a nearby saddle blanket, he laid the gear on top of the bull rig and reached back into the trunk, pulling out the dented metal rope can.

Everything looked exactly as it had the last time he'd seen it. It was almost as though only a day or two had passed since he'd last handled these things. Without dwelling too long on the memories his rodeo gear evoked, good and bad, Cody neatly rolled up the two riggings and stuffed them into a leather-trimmed duffel bag. Next, a couple of his best calf ropes and piggin strings went into the rope can, the lid difficult to close like it had always been.

Cody stood and surveyed the racks of saddles. Sentiment nudged him to take his father's roping saddle; common sense made him pick his own. Too much was at stake for him to switch saddles now.

Making sure that no one was around, Cody carried his saddle and rigging out to the two-horse trailer parked beside the barn. It was a starry night, just like the other night when Shaye . . . *No, don't go there . . . not now. You've got to stay focused and not let anything distract you.* His laugh was short and heavy with skepticism. *Yeah, and I'm the Queen of England.*

The two men worked together in the tawny early morning light, stepping around the three big Newfoundlands who jostled for their attention.

"You're really going to go through with this, aren't you?" Gene closed the door on the horse trailer, closing Possum inside. "I think you're insane, but you already know that."

Cody loaded the sack of horse feed and extra hay bales in the empty side of the trailer, closed the door, and faced Gene. "Yeah, well, you didn't come up with another plan." He laid his hand on his friend's shoulder. "Don't worry, it'll work out. I'm just sorry you won't be going with me."

Gene shrugged. "I can't miss my kid's soccer playoffs. You know how to reach me . . . if you need me."

"You mean when I get so wrecked that I need someone to come and bail me out of the hospital?" He laughed. "That isn't going to happen."

"Just so there's enough left of you so we can deliver di Prado's horses to him." Gene checked the trailer hitch, then looked up at Cody. "How does Shaye feel about you going?"

Gene's question had come out of the blue, surprising the hell out of him. "What's she got to do with anything?"

Gene raised his hand. "Hey, I just asked. I thought maybe you'd talked it over with her. Never mind."

"Fine." Damn, why did people keep mentioning her name as if it should mean anything to him? And why did the sound of her name keep hurting so much? Maribeth and Roscoe had asked about her last night, and he'd lied, making some lame excuse why she wasn't coming anymore for riding lessons. He wished someone would lie to him and tell him she never existed, tell him making love to her in the moonlight had never happened.

"So what'd you tell 'em?"

"What?"

"Yeah," Gene shot at him sarcastically. "You're really focused on this weekend, I can tell." He shook his head. "Man, you've got it bad."

"I haven't got anything," Cody argued. "Anything but a bank loan to pay off, a job to do to get it paid off, and a ranch to run."

"Okay, okay. I get it." Gene backed a step away. "So what'd you tell Maribeth and Roscoe?"

Cody tossed a second duffel bag with his clothes into the backseat of the truck. "I told them I was going to a cutting horse training clinic in Lander."

"And they bought it?"

He gave a repentant smile and lifted his shoulder in a nonchalant shrug. "So it seems."

Gene shook his head. "Be careful. I want you home in one piece."

Cody laughed. "Not *rich* and in one piece?"

The two friends stood staring at each other for a long moment, then Gene dragged Cody into a bear hug. "Go get 'em, cowboy."

The drive to Cheyenne left too much time for Cody to think about Shaye and what she'd told him. He'd never known rejection from his own family and had no idea, except from the pain he'd seen in her eyes, what it would be like. Kate and Jack Butler had loved each other to distraction, but there'd always been unlimited love left over for their children, their friends.

Why hadn't she told him about Hubbard before? Before what? Before the Fourth of July picnic? Before the Cowboy Ball? Or before they were making love up on the north plateau? Cody didn't know what made him angrier, the fact that she hadn't told him before all those times on her own or that she'd waited until she had to tell him because she'd been caught.

Maybe he should be angry at Maribeth or Julie or Roscoe for their meddling. He laughed, a harsh, cynical sound. No, there was no reason. They'd be upset to discover their little games really had nothing to do with him wanting to be with Shaye. So maybe he was angriest with himself because he'd allowed any of it to matter.

Even as he pulled into the outskirts of Cheyenne he could see the city was bustling with the annual hoopla over Frontier Days. The streets were full of tourists all decked out in their finest western clothes, the hotels were bulging at the seams, and a festive air had everybody in a happy mood.

Cody parked the truck by the entry office at the rodeo

grounds and picked up his stall assignment and back number. He wanted to get settled in, get Possum bedded down, and get some rest himself. Word traveled fast through the other cowboys that Cody Butler was on the grounds and was going to ride. A number of old friends just happened to stroll by while he was unloading Possum and his gear from the trailer. Cody had been looking forward to seeing everyone, and for a few minutes it felt good to be back and knee-deep in the buzz of excitement, but it didn't take long before Cody realized things weren't all they seemed to be.

"Hey, Butler, how the hell are you doing?" Buck Bodine said, giving Cody's hand a hearty shake. "Man, after Lander, we never thought we'd see you back. You riding pickup or arena crew?"

The question dug deep and hurt all the way. Cody pulled his bull rope out of the duffel bag and hung it on the side of the stall. "Nope, thought I'd give rough-stock another try."

"You're kidding, right?" Bodine's laughter cut through Cody like a serrated blade. "You always were a joker." He clapped Cody on the back. "Hey, the boys'll be glad to see you. The party king is back!"

"Not this trip, he isn't," Cody said, hanging his bareback rigging beside his bull rope. "I'm here to do business and go home. You guys are going to have to party on your own."

"That's too bad," Bodine offered, pointing down the barn aisle. "Look who showed up to help us party again this year."

Cody looked up as Bunny Gibson strolled into view.

"Hey, Cody." She rubbed her breasts against him as she took hold of his face with her scarlet-nailed hands and kissed him on the mouth.

She tried to slip her tongue between his lips, but Cody took hold of her shoulders and moved her away from him.

"Hi, Bunny. I suppose it would be polite to say I'm surprised to see you here."

"You're the surprise, Cody. I wasn't going to come to Cheyenne this year until I heard you were planning on riding again."

Cody quickly glanced up from moving his saddle. "Who told you I was riding?"

"You know my cousin Myra? She's working in the entry office this year and called me when your entry came in." She stepped closer. "I'm so proud of you."

She tried to hug him again, but he moved away and shot a glance up at Buck Bodine. "Look, if you two don't mind, I'd like to get some rest." Cody opened his sleeping bag in the corner of Possum's stall. "I've been on the road all day."

"Cody, I've got a room at the Holiday Inn. Wouldn't you rather get some . . . sleep in a nice, comfy bed?" Bunny dangled her room key. "I'd give you a nice long back rub, and then I'd help you get rid of all that tension." Bunny giggled and jiggled the key again.

It would have been easy, so easy, to take the key and everything else that came with it. There were no strings, no promises, and today there were no hopes, but red hair, brown eyes, and easy could never replace brunette, green, and . . . perfect. "No thanks, Bunny." He jerked his thumb at Possum. "That damned fool horse gets all nervous sleeping alone in a strange barn. I'm gonna have to hold his hoof all night long."

"Come on, baby." Bodine laughed. "Let the old man get his rest, he's gonna need it to even climb in the chutes." He slapped Bunny on the butt. "I'd sure like one of those back rubs."

"You would?" Bunny breathed. "Well, darling, why didn't you say so?" She shot a look at Cody over her shoulder. "Good luck, Cody. I'll be cheerin' for you, baby."

It had been a long time since he'd shared a stall with a

horse, and at first Cody thought it was Possum who was keeping him awake. He punched his pillow and turned over. Maybe he could sleep better on his right side. No such luck. Okay, maybe it was nerves. He hadn't rodeoed since his crash in Lander. This wasn't just climbing back on the bull after you'd fallen off, this was climbing back on with the weight of the world on your shoulders. If it was rodeo nerves, then why was it Shaye Frazier who kept popping into his head?

Damn her. Somehow she'd taken away his ability to eat and sleep and work in peace. She pushed into his every thought as though she owned him. Was her confession about Hubbard so impossible to take? Had he made the biggest mistake in his life walking away from her? He rolled onto his back and stared up at the butt end of the gray gelding. "You trying to tell me something, Possum?"

He hurt like hell. Every time he moved, he grunted, the pain shooting through him like a knife. Cody popped another couple of aspirin in his mouth and grimaced as he tried to swallow them dry. He'd finished the last of his Pepsi with his last two aspirins. Putting the small tin of pills in his pocket, his fingers touched the envelope with the check in it. His winnings. Another pain blasted through his shoulder, but he smiled. He hadn't come close to making top money, but the go-round money he had picked up would make up the difference he needed to pay off the bank. The check in his pocket was for fourteen thousand, four hundred and eighty dollars. Not bad for three days' work and all the pain in the world.

"Yahoo!" he shouted out the open pickup window. "Yippee!"

He turned the truck into the lane at Medicine Creek and couldn't stop the tears that filled his eyes when he saw the sign. *Medicine Creek Ranch, Champion Semmintal Beef and Quarter Horses. Founded by Jacob Butler—1854.*

He scrubbed his eyes with the back of his hand and drove down the lane, blasting the horn all the way. He turned the last curve in the land around the cottonwoods and expected to see Maribeth and Roscoe out front waiting for him. The front porch was empty and there wasn't a light on in the house. He slowed down but drove on down to the barns, pulling to a stop in front of the saddle horse barn. He'd unload Possum, feed him, and bed him down, check out the other stock, and then go up to the house and find out where everyone was.

With a final pat on the gray gelding's neck, Cody stepped out of the stall and hung the halter and lead rope on the hook on the door. He checked each horse in the saddle barn, then stepped out the back door and crossed the lot to the indoor arena where he housed the polo ponies di Prado had bought. Flipping on the light along the aisle of stalls, Cody opened the door to the little bay gelding's stall and stopped in his tracks.

In the middle of the stall, the bay stood splay-footed with strings of drool dripping from its mouth.

Cody raced from stall to stall, his panic rising with each sight that met him when he opened the stall doors. Four of the six polo ponies showed signs of hoof-and-mouth. Mouth lesions affected each, and in two the lesions had moved on to their tongues. "Son of a bitch," he hoarsely breathed, driving his fist into the wall. "Son of a bitch."

His steps heavy with defeat, Cody headed back to the saddle barn and switched the light on in his office. He dropped into his chair and, resting his elbows on his desk, cradled his head in his hands. He'd lost. He'd lost everything that every Butler gone before him had worked so hard to build.

He had every penny he needed to pay off the bank and a few thousand more, but Fate had obviously held back one more surprise for him. Raising his head, he noticed the blinking message light on his answering machine. He hit the button, heard the tape whir, and Doc Campbell's voice telling him to call as soon as he got in.

Picking up the phone, Cody punched in Doc Campbell's number. The veterinarian picked up in three rings. "Hi, Doc; I think I've got big trouble."

Thirty minutes later Cody knew everything he would ever need to know about vesicular stomatitis, a disease that mimicked hoof-and-mouth disease, but a disease that, unlike hoof-and-mouth, infected horses as well.

"You know, some things just kept nigglin' at me," Doc Campbell said. "According to all the literature, there hasn't been an outbreak of hoof-and-mouth in the U.S. since the early 1920s. The other thing that didn't make sense was the low number of steers you lost. Hoof-and-mouth would have killed a lot more." The vet paused, clearing his throat. "Cody, I'm sorry, son, I should have picked up on it being V.S., after the problems they had a few years ago in Colorado. I should have figured it was vesicular stomatitis first instead of hoof-and-mouth. My only consolation is that the feds didn't pick up on it right away, either."

"It's not your fault, Doc. I'd just like to know how it hit me, though."

"It's a virus like hoof-and-mouth. Some think it's spread by flies, but I've heard of cases showing up in the dead of winter . . . so who knows. After I got the report from the state office, I drove out to your place this afternoon and looked at your horses.

"Cody, there's no treatment for this except anti-inflammatory drugs. Maybe that's why we lost some of your cattle, we were going another route. I left some pain medication, butazoladine, to help them stay up on their feet and eat. We'll watch the rest of your horses and ride it through."

"I suppose the same federal regs apply, right?" Cody already knew the answer. He couldn't ship the horses to di Prado. Even if they all recovered, it would be at least twelve or fifteen weeks before they'd be cleared for shipment out of state. It didn't matter that the payment to the bank was due in two days. He'd have to send the Argentinean's money back.

After hanging up the phone, Cody stepped out into the night. He had some apologies to make to his family up on the knoll before he called Glenn Hubbard to congratulate him on becoming the new owner of Medicine Creek Ranch.

Chapter Twenty-two

"How about a drink?" Glenn Hubbard moved toward the credenza. "Vodka? Gin?"

Shaye shook her head. "No, I'm fine. Thanks."

"No, you're not. You look like hell." He poured some vodka into a glass for himself. "As a matter of fact, you've looked like hell and have been moping around since the morning Cody Butler came over and nailed me about my mustangs being on his property."

"Thanks, thanks a lot." Shaye touched her hair, tucking some loose strands from her ponytail back behind her ears. She turned to leave and made it to the door, where she stopped with her hand on the door frame. She looked back over her shoulder at her father. No, damn it, she wouldn't leave. Throughout her life she had dutifully left the room too many times. This time she was going to stay. This time she was going to deal with her wants and needs. She was going to undress them, dissect them, and lay them out on the table in front of Hub. Let him see what she had been hungry for all of her life. "Hub, we need to talk."

"Sure. I've got about an hour that I can spare. What do you want to talk about?" He set his drink down on the desk, sat back in his chair, and crossed his legs.

An hour. Shaye almost laughed out loud. She had been given an hour to bare her soul. To hell with that. "This may take longer than an hour. In fact, I may just make sure that it does."

To the startled expression on Hubbard's face, Shaye moved back across the room and sat down in the corner of the sofa. Curling her feet up under her, she began. The words came easily. They had been waiting a long time to be released. Throughout the next hour and twenty minutes she opened her heart to her father, telling him about her loneliness and the pain, telling him about the father she'd always loved and wanted, about the father she never had.

Throughout, Glenn Hubbard sat quietly, never interrupting, never taking his attention from his daughter. The sadness in his eyes gave Shaye the only evidence of the impact of her words. When she was finished, she sat quietly, her hands folded in her lap. It was now her father's turn.

"Shaye," Hubbard began, his voice breaking with emotion. "I had no idea. I had no idea at all." He rubbed his mouth as if trying to ingest what he'd just heard. "I am so very, very sorry." He left his chair and hunkered down beside her. "I never imagined that was how you felt." He hung his head for a moment and then, his thoughts gathered, continued. "I loved your mother so much, and you're right, it was a selfish and exclusionary love. I refused to share her with anyone . . . even you, our own child that was born out of that love." He bowed his head. "When Susanne . . . when your mother was dying, I couldn't bear the thought of spending my time with anyone but her, our time was so short. And then she was gone."

Hubbard moved up onto the sofa beside Shaye, rested his forearms on his knees, and hung his head. "I couldn't deal with her death, let alone the fact that your resemblance to her was a painful reminder of what I'd lost. It was a whole lot easier to immerse myself in work than . . .

be your father. Business became my wife—my surrogate family—and as I did with Susanne, I made it my whole life." He looked up and tentatively touched her cheek. "It's uncanny how much you look like her, sound like her, walk and laugh like her. Do you know that even your handwriting is similar to hers?" He took her hand. "Can you forgive me?"

Before Shaye could reply, he continued. "I can't change what has happened in the past, but I promise you . . . I will work hard to change the future . . . from now on things will be different."

As Shaye opened her mouth to answer, the telephone on Hubbard's desk rang, the sound shrill in the emotional-charged atmosphere of the room. Hubbard let the phone ring twice, fidgeting with each ring, before he rose and answered it. As he lifted the receiver, Shaye quietly left the room. *I never stopped being your daughter; too bad you chose not to be a father.* Nothing was going to change.

She sought the sanctuary of her bedroom. She felt as though a great weight had been lifted from her heart, and the odd thing was, for the first time in her life she didn't care if who she was or what she did pleased her father or not. She was free from the burden; his approval no longer mattered. Nothing had changed and yet everything was different.

Circling the room, she gathered a few of her belongings, a photo of her mother, her sweater from the back of a chair, her blue ballcap from the dresser, and put them together on her bed before she pulled her suitcase from the closet. She began emptying the dresser drawers and filling the suitcase. There was nothing to keep her in Hubbard's house a moment longer.

A knock on her door interrupted, and Shaye turned as her father came into the room. If he noticed the suitcase, he didn't say a word.

"I thought you'd want to know." He wearily rubbed the

back of his neck. "That was Cody on the phone. He's just agreed to my offer. Medicine Creek is mine."

"Oh, God. No!" Stunned, Shaye dropped the clothes she held and sat down on the edge of the bed, her fingers tightly gripping the duvet. "Why? Did he say why?" She ignored the sudden flow of tears that drenched her cheeks. "He sold the polo ponies. He had almost all the money . . . enough that I'm sure the bank would have stopped foreclosure. Why? I don't understand."

Hubbard sat beside her. "I don't know. He didn't say."

Shaye looked at her father expecting to see the expression of an elated winner on his face. Hub looked as stunned as she felt.

He finally noticed the suitcase. "What's this?"

"I'm sorry, Hub, I quit. You'll have to get Prescott to handle the paperwork. I won't close this deal for you."

Hubbard slowly rose to his feet. "I'm not surprised. I didn't think you would."

Cody's hand shook as he dropped the cordless telephone back into the charger. His gut gave a cruel twist, and he felt numb. Thank God Maribeth and Roscoe weren't here to see his final humiliation. He'd found their note by the phone when he'd come into the house. Maribeth was at Cissy Linderman's for a slumber party with some school friends, and Roscoe was in town for the evening, visiting a lady friend. A cynical laugh slid from Cody's lips. Who would have thought that one of the Bradshaw sisters, Emmaline, would become the love of Roscoe's life?

Cody slowly walked around the living room, his fingers trailing over his mother's bronzes, across the back of his father's favorite leather recliner, and along the edge of the mantel that had been part of Jacob Butler's original log cabin on Medicine Creek. He opened the étagère, removed one of his grandmother's beaded moccasins, and ran his fingers over the ridges of colorful beadwork. So many pairs of hands had created this home . . . and it only took one pair to destroy it.

Gently returning the moccasin to the shelf, he left the living room and walked through the rest of the house, going from room to room, touching one family heirloom after another, gazing at the faces in the photos, breathing in the essence of the Butler home. Everything Butler was now homeless, just like he was, just like Maribeth and Roscoe were. He prayed that he'd done the right thing; at least with Hubbard's money they could start over . . . somewhere.

He'd been adamant about keeping his best horses when he'd talked with Hubbard. Over the years he'd put together some of the best bloodlines in his breeding stock. Maybe he'd look for a small place, a hundred acres or so, and just focus on raising and training a few excellent show horses every year. There'd be room for Maribeth's llama, too. It was enough to make her give up her home; he'd make damned sure she kept as much as she could.

Going back downstairs, Cody allowed his hand to slide along the banister. Every Butler had touched this piece of wood before him. He was tempted to rip it out and take it wherever he went. Would Hubbard tear down the buildings? He didn't want to think about it. He didn't want to know. He intended to be long gone and far away before Hubbard's bulldozers arrived.

Cody took an opened bottle of Jack Daniel's from the kitchen cabinet and carried it out to the front porch. Sitting on the stoop, he placed the bottle next to him. Resting his forearms on his thighs, he dropped his head and closed his eyes. He'd told Hubbard he didn't care what happened to anything on the property, and he didn't, anything except the small cemetery up on the knoll. Hubbard had agreed, it would be protected.

Before he'd called Glenn Hubbard, he'd spent almost an hour on the knoll. Not waiting to saddle Possum, he'd ridden the gelding bareback, like his Cheyenne ancestors before him, with just the halter for a bridle. Once there, he'd slowly walked from grave to grave, made his apologies, then sat beneath the large oak near his parents' headstone, seeking the comfort only parents could give a son. The birthday flowers he'd brought his mother were now faded and brown . . . dead and gone.

The pain in Cody's rodeo-bruised body didn't half compare to the pain in his heart, and that was only a fraction of the pain in his soul. Gone. Now everything was gone.

Tipping his head back against the trunk of the tree, he had let go, no longer able to hold together, and finally allowed the tears to come. Somewhere, sometime in the midst of his anguish, he had felt a touch, a comfort sweet and gentle as it pressed against his heart. Like a loving embrace it had brought him an unexpected peace. Forgiveness.

As a parting gift, words, at first meaningless, slipped into his mind, and once there, Cody realized their truth, their gift. *Land is just land, it will never love you back.*

And now, sitting on the porch, he heard the sound once again. From the high western ridge the plaintive howl of a wolf joined the usual chorus of night creatures. Cody looked up and laughed; although the tone was bitter, it was honest. "Yeah, you win, you old *ho'nehe*. Come on in, the door's open."

He reached for the bottle. With no one home, getting drunk sounded like a marvelous idea. He couldn't think of anyone who'd blame him. After twisting the cap off, he cradled the square bottle in his hands and stared at the amber liquid it held. He put off taking a drink, almost savoring the moment before the first fiery swallow of liquor slid down his throat. What the hell was he waiting for?

Finding no answer that made a lick of sense, he raised the bottle to his lips, tipped his head back, and at that moment saw the headlights moving down the lane toward the house.

Cody lowered the bottle and watched the headlights disappear for a moment in the low dip in the road, reappear, then disappear again as the lane wound around the stand of cottonwoods and appear again for the last hundred yards to the house. The rich throaty sound of the Mercedes' engine identified his visitor.

He spun the cap back on the bottle—damn, not even time for a swallow—and set the bottle next to the porch rail. He didn't rise to greet her; as a matter of fact, he stayed on the porch stoop and waited for her to come to him.

And she did.

After sliding out from behind the steering wheel, Shaye closed the car door and stood leaning against the convertible. She didn't move; she just stared back at him. Long moments passed before either moved or before either spoke.

Finally Shaye pushed away from the car and slowly walked across the lawn to the porch. Her sandaled feet made a faint path in the dew-soaked grass. When she stopped at the bottom of the stairs, her eyes were even with Cody's.

"Did you come to gloat?" He didn't try to keep the bitterness from his voice. "Or did Hubbard send you over with some papers for me to sign before I could change my mind?" He leaned against the newel post. "If you want me to sign anything, I hope you brought the check."

"I'm sorry you'd think that's why I'm here."

"What else could be the reason?" He shrugged. "So tell me, why are you here?"

"I'm here because I . . ." She trailed off and blew her convertible-tousled hair out of her eyes. "I'm here because I thought you might need a friend."

He hadn't expected that. She'd blindsided him again,

but hell, he was getting used to that. But there was a wariness that still remained, a raw hurt that hadn't been healed. Her secrets had already burned him—twice—and he wasn't willing to get singed again. "And why do you think you would be that friend?"

"Maybe because I've seen both sides, yours and Hubbard's. And maybe because I'm standing here, wanting to be with you instead of celebrating with him."

"Aren't you afraid you're going to lose your big commission . . . your ticket back to fame and fortune in the big city?"

"I quit. I don't work for Hub anymore."

"What?" Cody pushed to his feet. "What did you do a fool thing like that for?" He wearily rubbed his temple. "Why did you throw it all away?"

"Cody, you have to have something before you can throw it away. I may have thought I wanted my own practice in Boston, a perfectly safe and planned life . . . but"—she shrugged—"it seems I really didn't."

"And Hubbard? What about what you want from him?"

She shrugged again and looked off eastward, as if she could see Hubbard's house in the night. "I finally realized I can't change my father. But the most important thing that I've discovered is that I don't need his approval or his affection to make me a whole, happy person." She looked back at Cody. "I finally had the courage to tell him how I've felt for all these years. It would be wonderful if things could be different between Hub and me, but it's not necessary. I don't need it anymore. I think my . . . emancipation was in the telling."

He took a step or two toward her, then stopped. Every grain of who he was, what he was, wanted to know what she did need. The question was asked before he could consciously stop it. "So what is it you do want?"

She took a couple of steps toward him, closing the distance that separated them even more. Her gaze never left his. "I want things that will be important for the rest of my life. I want things that really matter."

Still apprehensive, Cody backed away and threw himself back on the stoop, stretching his legs out in front of him. "Well, you're a little late. There's nothing here that I can give you that really matters." He gestured with a sweep of his arm. "It all belongs to your father now."

"Cody, what I want can't be bought or sold. It isn't tangible, not in the literal sense." She sat down on the stoop beside him and noticed the bottle of whiskey beside the porch rail. "Is that private stock, or do you share?"

Cody looked up at her. She may have been pointing to the bottle of Jack Daniel's, but the question seemed to be loaded with a much different meaning. What the hell, he'd take a chance. "I share only a few things." He grinned, picked up the bottle, twisted the cap off, and handed it to her. "You first."

She didn't hesitate but lifted the bottle to her lips, tipped back her head, closed her eyes, and took a deep pull. Cody heard the rapid flight of air before it left her throat in a gasp. He watched the shock hit her face and make her eyes water, and he grabbed the bottle out of her hands before it fell from her hand.

"Good stuff, eh?" He winked and took a drink himself.

"Yeah, great." Her voice was little more than a choked whisper.

"Do you need another, or was that enough liquid courage for you to tell me why you're really here?" He held the bottle out to her, and she grabbed it from him again.

"One more ought to do it." She didn't wipe the neck of the bottle but raised it to her lips and took another shot. She grimaced again, this time coughing against the burning liquor. She passed the bottle back.

He took the bottle from her, enjoyed another swallow,

recapped the bottle, and set it down on the porch. "Ready?"

"Yeah," she rasped.

"You're sure?"

She eyed the bottle, shivered, then nodded.

"Okay. Why are you here?"

She visibly squared her shoulders and, raising her chin a notch, looked him straight in the eyes. "Maybe *you* ought to take another big drink."

"Me?" Cody laughed. "Can't turn an offer like that down." He unscrewed the cap and took another hit.

"I'm here because I am in love with you."

He choked, her words hitting him like a Mack truck. He looked up to find a wonderful, infuriating smile on her face.

"I'm here because wherever you go, whatever you do, I want to go with you and be a part of your life."

God, he'd wanted to hear her say those words for weeks, but after the last time he'd seen her at Hubbard's, he hadn't dared to dream he would ever hear her say anything close to them.

Cody looked up just in time to see a shooting star streak across the midnight sky and made his wish.

"Are you sure?" He reached up and touched the side of her face. "Are you positive?" He felt her silent nod beneath his fingers, felt her move her head until her lips were against the palm of his hand.

"Yes, I'm positive." She kissed his hand, her breath warm against his skin.

It was amazing how fast some wishes could come true. He tilted her face up to him and covered her mouth with his kiss. God, how he'd missed her in those few short days. Shooting star or not, he made another wish, and only time, a lifetime, would see that one granted.

"Cody, why did you change your mind and sell out to Hubbard?"

As he told her about di Prado's horses getting sick and about having to return the money, Shaye held him close. When he told her about visiting the knoll, he felt her tears wet his shoulder.

He slid his hand around to cradle the back of her head and drew her to him. "Shaye, it's okay. I can leave. My . . . legacy isn't the land. It never has been. I understand that now. The Butler legacy is in the blood, it's the family, it's the love." He heard the words touch his heart once more: *Land is just land, it will never love you back.* He held her close, kissed her forehead, kissed her eyes, and tasted the liquid salt of her tears. "Shaye." He breathed her name against her lips and then kissed her mouth, claiming her with his lips, his tongue, his soul.

He pulled away and stood. "Come with me." He held his hand out to her. "I want you someplace soft and cozy, where I can love you all night long."

She reached up and slipped her hand into his. He led her into the house. They ran up the stairs to his room like a couple of enthusiastic kids. Tumbling onto his bed, they grappled with each other's clothes.

"I hate buttons," Cody grumbled.

"I loathe them, too." Shaye giggled, pulling at his shirt.

In moments the floor was littered with jeans and boots, T-shirts and sandals.

He pulled her down, pinning her beneath him. Holding her hands over her head, he dipped to capture one of her breasts in his mouth. As he drew the excited nipple into his mouth, Shaye arched up against him.

"No fair. I want to touch and nibble, too."

He released her hands and knelt between her thighs. "And just what would you like to touch . . . and nibble?"

"Everything."

And she did.

Breathless, she reached for him. "Love me now?" She drew him down to her, opening herself to him.

Cody reached for the bedside table drawer and then remembered. "I don't have any more . . . little foil packets."

"Do you think we really need them?"

He looked down and saw the woman he wanted to spend the rest of his life with, the woman he loved with all of his heart and soul. "Nope. I think it's time you learned how to ride . . . bareback."

Laughter, rich and naughty, filled the room as he filled her body, moving inside her, meeting her passion, giving himself to her completely. She met him, stroke for stroke, giving as she took. As his release simmered up inside him, he held her close, pushing himself deep into her. "I love you—God, I love you so much."

Together they built the divine friction that melded them together, drove them in an upward spiral, higher and higher, until they clung together on the electrifying peak where the universe exploded all around them, and all through them. Breathless, their bodies still joined, they clung to each other and rode the floating stars downward to reality.

Cody pressed his lips against her neck, tasting the salt and sweet flavor of her skin, feeling her racing pulse against his tongue. "Will you stay with me?"

"Wherever you are," she whispered, "wherever you go." Her lips trailed kisses along the point of his shoulder.

"Always?"

"Forever."

"I guess if you're not going back east, I can't call you Boston anymore. So what am I going to call you?"

"How about Sweetheart, or Honey, or Darling. Or how about Mrs. Cody Butler."

"Hey, I was going to ask you that next."

She nipped his shoulder. "Well, hurry up, cowboy. I'd like another . . . riding lesson."

•   •   •

The morning light broke through the window blinds, sending streaks of yellow sunlight across the floor and onto the bed.

Cody woke slowly, his senses telling him he wasn't alone. As he remembered the night before, a smile broke across his face. How could he have lost, but gained so much?

Shaye lay spooned against him, she the small spoon, he the large, and his bed was rumpled and disheveled with lovemaking. Oh, yeah, wishes definitely came true.

Shaye murmured, "Good morning."

"Good morning, yourself." The feel of her warm and willing against his body sent his senses reeling all over again. Would he ever get enough of this wonderful woman? Stupid question . . . no, never.

She stretched against him, catlike, and took a sniff of air. "Hmm, how sweet of you to get up and make coffee for us."

"What?" Cody jumped. "I didn't make coffee. What time is it?" He glanced at the bedside clock. "Damn, it's after ten. Roscoe and Maribeth are home." He placed a kiss on Shaye's neck. "We can either hide up here all day or go down and face the music."

"Don't you think we should let the Lonely Hearts Club know their schemes were a success?"

"They didn't have a damned thing to do with us—"

"Shh, I know." Shaye turned into his arms and placed a light kiss on his mouth, silencing him. "But let's just let them think it was all their idea . . . for a while."

In less than fifteen minutes they'd showered, dressed, and stood at the top of the stairs.

"Nervous?" He took her hand.

"No. Are you?"

He shook his head. "Shaye, you can still change your mind. I can distract them in the kitchen if you want to slip out the front door."

"What? And not get a morning cup of coffee? Not on your life, cowboy." She stepped into his arms and gazed up into his eyes. "Cody, I love you. There's no changing my mind."

Cody buried his hands in her hair and lowered his lips to hers. His kiss was tender and filled with every promise he could make. As she melted against him, Cody knew if he didn't pull away, he'd end up carrying her back to his room. "Shaye, come on." He took her hand and led her downstairs.

The scene that met them when they entered the kitchen left them both speechless.

"Well, well, look who finally woke up," Roscoe harrumphed. Getting up from the kitchen table, he poured them each a mug of coffee and set them on the table. "It's about time you two came down."

Maribeth added two more eggs to the mixing bowl, added a dollop of milk, and dumped the concoction of scrambled eggs into the skillet. "It's a good thing you two decided to come down. I was getting so hungry waiting for you, I was about to go pound on the door."

"Good morning, sweetheart." Glenn Hubbard stepped forward and kissed his daughter on the cheek. He held a small wrapped basket out to Roscoe. "These scones that Tess sent over are cold. I think we're going to have to pop them in the microwave before we eat."

"Hub?" Frowning, Shaye stepped into the kitchen. "What are you doing here?"

"I kind of invited myself to breakfast." He glanced up at the wall clock. "I didn't expect it to be a daylong . . . affair, if you two will pardon the word." He picked up his coffee and took a sip, then lifted his mug in salute. "Good morning, Cody."

Stunned by Hubbard's banter, Cody couldn't find his voice to respond.

"Bacon or sausage?" Maribeth asked, opening the refrigerator.

"Both," Roscoe answered, putting the basket of scones in the microwave. "I'm so hungry this morning I could eat a road-kill porcupine . . . quills and all."

Cody was having trouble accepting the ridiculous breakfast pitch-in taking place in his kitchen. All that was missing were the three Newfs. He could understand Hubbard showing up to get the deal closed for Medicine Creek, but that sure didn't explain his contribution to the breakfast menu. He wanted an explanation. "What's this all about, Hubbard?"

"I was just about to explain," Hubbard replied, refilling his coffee cup. "Okay, sit down everyone, I've got something I want to say to these two before we eat." Hubbard pointed to the empty chairs at the table.

"Oh, boy, here it comes," Maribeth whispered, scooping the eggs onto a platter. "Cody's in big trouble now."

"Be quiet," Roscoe hissed, pushing her into a chair. "Sit down and be quiet."

Hubbard paced across the kitchen a couple of times before coming to a stop in front of Cody. "I got a call from Doc Campbell this morning. We figure it was probably my herd of mustangs that carried that damned virus in here. Apparently a couple of head in Nevada showed up with vesicular stomatitis a week after I got my first shipment. No one bothered to let me know. Doc found out when he called them last night. He tried to call you, but you weren't answering your phone." He paused, looking at Shaye, then back at Cody. He grinned then continued. "Apparently this thing can skip and miss through a herd. Since none of my mustangs showed up with it, Doc figures my horses were carriers." He gave an embarrassed shrug. "Sort of like Typhoid Marys." Hubbard dropped into a chair across the table from Cody. "I'm damned sorry. I've caused you a lot of grief, the loss of some of your stock, a hefty vet bill, and extra payroll." He took a slow sip of coffee, then glanced back at Cody. "I also have to tell you . . . I've changed my mind." Hubbard sat back in his chair, a solemn expression on his face. "I don't want to buy Medicine Creek."

"What?" Cody couldn't believe his ears, but the hard twist in his gut told him he'd heard Hubbard's words correctly. Panic swept through him. He'd have nothing. The money he'd won at Cheyenne wouldn't keep them very long, wherever they lived. He began to rise from this chair. "You're backing out on our deal? You son of a—"

"Cody." Shaye took hold of his hand and pulled him back down beside her, her eyes never leaving her father. "If there's one thing I know about my father, it's that he doesn't back out of deals." She leaned over, kissed Cody on the cheek, and whispered in his ear, "Trust me, he's up to something." She turned to her father. "What's going on, Hub?"

"What's going on is this." He reached into his shirt pocket and withdrew a piece of paper. "Cody, this is a check for two hundred and seventy-five thousand dollars. I want to lease about a thousand acres of your northeast grass. This check will cover the first year's lease, the cost of your lost stock, and all the vet bills you owe Doc Campbell." He placed the check on the table. "I want you to be able to keep Medicine Creek. This will pay off your note at the bank."

Cody picked up the check and looked at it. He'd never seen one so large with his name on it. "Hubbard, this is too much. There's about fifty grand too much. Is this guilt money or charity?"

"Neither." Hubbard chuckled. "I'm leasing prime grassland. We'll have to move some fence, though. I'd even be willing to pay your men to help out. When you take all that I owe out of that figure"—he tapped the check with his finger—"that leaves about fifty-five thousand for a wedding present or the best honeymoon imaginable."

Cody laughed, putting his arm around Shaye. "Who says we're getting married?"

Hubbard stood, placing his hands on his hips, and leaned over Cody. "From the way I look at it, you've taken advantage of my daughter . . . kept her here all night long and ruined her good reputation. Rumors are flying and people are talking already." He shot a glance at Roscoe and Maribeth. "There are rumors, aren't there?"

"Oh, yes, sir," Maribeth agreed vigorously. "Lots and lots of rumors."

"I started some of 'em myself," Roscoe added, covering his whiskered grin with his hand.

Hubbard nodded, then glared down at Cody and jerked his thumb toward Maribeth and Roscoe. "See, rumors . . . just like I said." He paused, looking from Cody to Shaye, then back to Cody again. "I don't know much about these modern relationships, I'm just an old-fashioned father, so I'm not as lenient as some fathers might be with their daughters. If it takes a shotgun wedding to settle the matter, I say you're getting married." He pounded the top of the table with his fist. Then stood back and crossed his arms over his chest. "I'm a very wealthy man, Butler," Hubbard continued with a wide grin that broke into a hearty laugh. "I've got a lot of shotguns."

"No, Hubbard," Cody replied, lifting Shaye's hand to his lips and placing a kiss on her fingers. "I'm the wealthier man . . . I've got your daughter."

"Bingo!" Maribeth jumped up and cheered. "Now, let's eat!"